KILEY DUNBAR

Summer *at the* Highland Coral Beach

First published in the United Kingdom in 2020 by Hera

This edition published in the United Kingdom in 2022 by

Hera Books
Unit 9 (Canelo), 5th Floor
Cargo Works, 1–2 Hatfields
London, SE1 9PG
United Kingdom

A CIP catalogue record for this book is available from the British Library.

Print ISBN 978 1 80032 998 0
Ebook ISBN 978 1 912973 24 8

Look for more great books at www.herabooks.com

Printed and bound in Great Britain by Clays Ltd, Elcograf S.p.A.

1

Summer at the Highland Coral Beach

Kiley Dunbar is Scottish and lives in England with her husband, two kids and Amos the Bedlington Terrier. She writes around her work at a University in the North of England where she lectures in English Literature and creative writing. She is proud to be a member of the Romantic Novelists' Association and a graduate of their New Writers' Scheme.

Also by Kiley Dunbar

Christmas at Frozen Falls
The Borrow a Bookshop Holiday

Kelsey Anderson

One Summer's Night
One Winter's Night

Port Willow Bay

Summer at the Highland Coral Beach
Matchmaking at Port Willow

This book was written with all my love for my babies, Robin Valentine, and Iris Eden.

My heart's in the Highlands, my heart is not here,
My heart's in the Highlands, a-chasing the deer;
Chasing the wild-deer, and following the roe,
My heart's in the Highlands, wherever I go.

Robert Burns, 1789

Chapter One

January and the Big Fat Positive

Two pink lines. Beatrice was sure of it.

She took the test apart and held the little strip up to the light to make sure, and there they were, faint, barely there, but there all the same. What they call in the pregnancy and baby magazines a 'BFP': A Big Fat Positive.

At first, when she saw it, she had screamed, then had a cup of tea to calm down and immediately started to worry whether you're allowed tea when you're officially, incontrovertibly WITH CHILD.

The warmth of the knowledge spread through her and she found herself in front of the living room mirror peering at her face and wondering what the magazines were talking about when they said the first things you noticed in pregnancy were the sore boobs and the morning sickness. Beatrice felt great, better than great, and she looked to see if she was glowing yet, wondering when it would kick in.

She hadn't exactly glowed recently, and not at all during the recent few miserable months of doing not very much, other than eking out her redundancy pay, searching for work, and trying to chase away the feeling she was probably being a bother to her sister. Angela was in her own baby bubble, enjoying the last few weeks of her precious maternity leave with little Clara, and was, Beatrice worried, possibly too polite to tell her that the daily visits might be getting too much.

She wanted to let Angela and her partner, Victoria – Vic for short – know the good news first, but told herself she had best wait until Rich knew. He was, after all, the daddy.

She smiled to herself, wandering around the house that afternoon. Unable to settle to reading her book or to concentrate on job applications, she started clearing out a bottom drawer to pass the time and let her mind wander back to all those years ago when she and Rich were straight out of college and intent on double incomes and exotic travel and had spent years trying *not* to get pregnant. Then there had been that period after the wedding where they were constantly dodging everyone's questions about when they were going to start a family and she'd grown used to hearing the remarks about how she wasn't getting any younger – mainly from Rich's dad, to be fair. And Beatrice couldn't forget last year, the one leading up to her thirty-ninth birthday – the awful year in which she had lost not only her job but her lovely mum as well, a year she couldn't think about without her chest tightening and her breathing growing shallow and quick – when certain work colleagues, friends and Rich's dad had unanimously stopped enquiring about her plans for her uterus as though it were everyone in the world's business and started looking at her either sympathetically or like she was some sort of baby-avoiding witch. You guessed it, that last one was also Rich's dad.

'Well, aren't we going to surprise them all?' Beatrice said to herself as she cleared the drawer of clutter, making a charity shop pile and a recycling pile, trying not to glance at the clock and count down the minutes until Rich got home.

Only just back to work after the New Year, poor old Rich had another late meeting and another stressful, cramped commute on the eight o'clock train back from London where he worked in distribution rights for big screen movies, which sounded more glamorous than it actually was, to their two-bed new-build in the sprawling Warwick suburbs.

She couldn't account for the little prickle of nerves that buzzed up her spine at the thought of telling him tonight. He'd be made up. How lucky can one couple get? A baby on their third month of trying. That is, if you don't count that week in Madrid back in September when Beatrice forgot to pack her pills and they got a bit reckless after a night of rebujito cocktails and a touristy flamenco show that had ended in a drunken conga line through the beach restaurant's kitchens. They'd had to have the whole conversation on the plane home about how maybe it wouldn't be a disaster if they actually *had* made a holiday baby, and since they were both approaching forty it might be a case of 'now or never'.

There had been no holiday-cocktails baby after all, but its brief hypothetical existence had kick-started an intense few months of Really, Actually Trying, which, although she didn't admit it to anyone, was accompanied by a big sigh of relief at the end of what could only be described as an embarrassingly long dry spell.

In the quieter, lonelier moments during her days at home scouring the *Guardian* arts jobs pages and mailing out CVs to every arts organisation within commuting distance, she would get to thinking and could admit to herself that Madrid hadn't been the start of it at all.

Beatrice had known at least two summers ago that she had begun to change her mind about not being all that fussed about babies; around about the time she'd detected a slight hollow tone in her jokey, deflective answers to questions from those nosey enough to ask why she had been married for so long (eight years at that point, ten years now) and *still* didn't have kids.

Yes, she had first heard it two summers ago, the persistent little voice she'd tried to ignore for the sake of their careers and her busy, exciting working life, which had been nothing but fun and fulfilling and which she wouldn't change a thing about – apart from her recent redundancy, of course.

That was way back when her sister Angela and Vic had started the process of finding a donor service and embarking upon what turned out to be a long, expensive journey involving seven rounds of assisted intrauterine insemination, Angela's hopes for a growing family coinciding fatefully with their mum's cancer diagnosis.

Beatrice slid the empty drawer shut, flinching at the resounding bang it made.

'I'm not moping today. Here I am, *a whole day late* and with a BFP!' she announced to the empty house, gathering up a bundle of old payslips for the recycling bin.

Earlier that afternoon, she'd tried out an online due date calculator, which had told her that this baby would be making its appearance around the twentieth of September, just days after the big birthday she'd been dreading for months. But all that trepidation had melted away at the sight of those pink lines.

September would be beautiful this year, a time for long walks with a pram, lattes in hand. Rich would take paternity leave and they could plan a Welcome to the World party with cake and bubbly and look forward to introducing baby Clara, who'd be a wobbly toddler by then, to little baby Halliday.

September didn't seem very far off at all. There would be so much to do before then. Rich's Audi would need upgrading to a five-seater with room for a baby carrier, and she didn't fancy broaching the subject of converting his gym into a nursery quite yet but maybe in a few weeks she could plant the seed in his mind, get him mulling it over.

She wasted no time in getting straight online and ordering a *Your Pregnancy: Week by Week* book, remembering how her mum had given something similar to Angela when she was having Clara and how they had all pored over it together. Beatrice had the strongest recollection of the discovery that Clara was the size of a sesame seed at four weeks.

'A sesame seed. Imagine that!' Beatrice had said to her phone as she watched the book appear in her online shopping cart and she made the payment. She hadn't let herself think for too long about how her mum wasn't going to be around to look through this baby book with her, instead letting herself be distracted by the appealing buzz of shopping online for cute little things.

There was a whole bewildering world of baby accessorising opening up to her and it was all only a click away. She ordered a teensy tiny white baby hat and matching blanket with little clouds and embroidered rainbows all over. It was expensive but, she told herself, you're only newly pregnant once, and she wanted to celebrate.

That was what the empty drawer was for: squirrelling away sweet little things. Her body tingled at the idea of all the research she'd get to do and lovely long lists she'd get to draw up during her pregnancy. Beatrice was a long term devotee of list-making and had, in fact, already started drafting her first baby list. So far it included white newborn sleepsuits and those muslin cloth things Angela and Vic said they *had* to have hundreds of. God knows what for. It was still all a wonderful mystery and she couldn't wait to find out all about it.

'Oh come on! Is it only six thirty? Are you actually going backwards?' she accused the kitchen clock as she folded laundry, warm from the dryer. She'd grown used to talking to herself these last few months of job-seeking. Soon she'd have a bump to talk to and she'd feel less like a crazy, pyjama-wearing shut-in. Talking to a sesame seed whose existence she'd only just had confirmed felt a *little* peculiar but she resolved to keep giving it a go over the coming days until it felt more natural.

Rich would be all right, wouldn't he? Once he got over the surprise. She recalled reading that some men take a bit longer than women to adapt to the idea of being a parent. It's biology and the fact they don't have the whole BFP hormone spike and the sense of a tiny bundle of living cells bedding in for a long stay. They're less invested, at first. 'He'll be all right,' she said, glancing down to her stomach. 'I hope he will, anyway.'

Wondering if shaking hands were an early pregnancy symptom, she resolved to go and wait in the lounge and drink some water until she could research the whole tea thing properly. She carried the dismantled test with her, mentally rehearsing how she'd show it to Rich when he walked in the door, and hoping he'd had a good day at work and would be in the mood for surprises. She clasped the test to her chest.

'Maybe I do feel a bit sick, actually,' she told the little seed.

Chapter Two

Seven months later. The middle of nowhere.

'You may well think you've booked in for Gaelic lessons, but that's no' whit the computer's telling me.'

Beatrice let her shoulders slump and forced out a long breath through her nose, crumpling her lips to stop herself telling this flustering Scotsman exactly what she thought of his customer service.

'Warm Highland welcome guaranteed,' the online brochure had read. 'Sweet summer escape,' it said. So far, Beatrice's first and only experience of Scotland in her thirty-nine years on the planet had been disappointing, to say the least.

'But my name *is* on your booking system? Beatrice Halliday?'

'Aye. Nine nights, checking out on Monday the thirty-first of August, dinner, bed and breakfast, single room. Willow-weaving lessons included.'

The man was staring at the screen, his glasses reflecting its harsh blue light. The computer looked as old as the hills surrounding Port Willow, but it was still by far the most modern thing in the reception of The Princess and the Pea Inn.

'*Willow-weaving?*'

Beatrice pinched the bridge of her nose. It had been a long day, and now this. She found herself glaring down at the threadbare tartan carpet, sandy from the beach just across the road from the inn's heavy oak doors.

At least the website was accurate when it boasted that the inn was, 'Perfectly situated with idyllic sea views', not that Beatrice had paid much attention to the scenery as she dragged her wonky-wheeled suitcase down the narrow pavement from the train station in the spitting rain, passing by the gently curving row of squat sea-facing buildings that made up the entirety of Port Willow. She'd barely registered the little stone-walled primary school, the various holiday cottages in soft pastel colours, the post office-come-souvenir-shop, or the closed-up chippy, but at the back of her mind she'd thought the place was not at all promising.

All the while she'd been focusing instead on the bars on her phone and wishing she'd thrown an umbrella into her handbag before her hurried departure from Warwick at bleary-eyed far-too-early-o'clock this morning.

The road was lined on the pavement side with end to end parked cars and on the other side by a low sea wall with small gardens built into it here and there which jutted out over the beach, but the gathering grey clouds and increasingly heavy rain had meant Beatrice wasn't stopping to gaze at the blustery beach view. Plus, she'd had to have her wits about her. She'd nearly been swiped off her feet twice by cars' passenger doors springing suddenly open across her path as she finally gave up her GPS as a lost cause and upped her speed, head down, muttering all the while increasingly desperate, sweary threats to nobody in particular that The Princess and the Pea Inn had better be easy to find.

It was, as it happened, being the only pub in the village, slap bang in the middle of the little weather-beaten seaside strip. If she'd carried on walking past the inn door's stone pillars and covered porch she'd soon have come to the village hall, Patrick's fishmongers, the art gallery (Mr Garstang the watercolourist's front room which opened to visitors on Saturdays and every second Tuesday during the season), the little church of Magnus the Martyr, and the rambling, miraculously well stocked Port Willow general store where she could have had her pick of umbrellas, from beach parasol, to golfing, to Peppa Pig. But Beatrice felt she had seen enough. To her relief, she'd stumbled into the inn's reception just as the real downpour started and St Magnus' was tolling that it was three o'clock.

The inn doors had been propped open this morning to let the August sunlight in, and were now allowing heavy plashes of cold water to patter onto the doormat.

Beatrice had read that this inlet was warmed by the Gulf Stream and, as such, unseasonably temperate for Scotland, and it was, after all, August so she'd expected a bit of sunshine – or at least some blue in the sky.

Glancing past the flustering receptionist and around the dark interior she concluded that nothing about Scotland was as she'd hoped or expected.

Dry, cracked oak-panelled walls led off to a bar and dining room beyond the reception desk and to a creaking staircase leading up to the bedrooms, while a pair of cobwebbed antlers jutted out from the wall over the dour innkeeper's head, their points dangerously close to his scalp. The man was exceedingly tall, Beatrice noticed, even when hunched over his computer. If she could just get her hands on a hammer and a nail, she'd have those antlers raised and straightened in no time. And that panelling needed a good polish too. Things like that really bugged her.

'I dinnae ken what to tell ye. Perhaps a computer error's tae blame?' The man nervously bit his lower lip, betraying that he knew exactly what was to blame – himself – but he wasn't admitting it, not even for the sake of this poor bedraggled English woman, no matter how pale and short-tempered she looked.

As she let her suitcase drop to the floor, Beatrice's handbag slid down onto her forearm, its magnetic fastener pulling open. The corner of a soft blanket patterned with tiny clouds and embroidered with rainbows flopped out. She hastily stuffed it back out of view, securing the clip once more.

Taking a measured breath, she tucked a strand of her wavy brown hair, now windswept and threatening to frizz up, behind her ear. 'It doesn't really matter. Just… just let me into my room and we can sort out the lessons later. I just want my key.' Horrified, she realised she was close to tears and found herself angrily swallowing away the temptation to just let rip and sob in front of the stranger who was now rummaging painfully slowly in a Tupperware tub full of keys, inspecting each one in turn with slender, nervous fingers and every now and then looking up at Beatrice with cautious bewilderment.

Gene Fergusson had seen his fair share of single women arriving at the inn since his younger brother had set up the activity and crafting holidays part of the website back in the spring – in fact now it was the height of the summer season they were arriving in a steady stream, but none of them had turned up tearful, clenched-fisted and furious, like this one.

He'd checked in the new arrivals without (much) incident this morning, including the party of four wool spinners and dyers from Lancashire looking forward to a fortnight's B&B with tartan-making lessons at the mill nearby. They hadn't been pleased with the parking situation and demanded he set out traffic cones for them for the duration of their stay to ensure a reserved spot by the inn door. He'd pointed out he didn't possess any cones but thinking on his feet – and proud of it – he'd offered to put out the inn's hat stand and a fire extinguisher, and had received four frosty looks and bitter silence as a reward.

Then there had been those two brassy Geordies who'd made 'remarks' and been overly familiar with him, smirking as he found their keys. They were here for painting lessons with Mr Garstang in his little art gallery-slash-living room along the front.

And there had been a formidable band of posh ladies from Sussex in brand new matching lilac cagoules and blonde bobs, all set up for a week of silversmithing and stained glass workshopping in the next village. They had been quiet and observant as he checked them in. Too quiet for his liking. Their steady exchange of tuts, raised eyebrows and one or two busy dust-sweeping fingertips had told him exactly what they thought of The Princess and the Pea Inn. He'd let them carry their own bags upstairs, too afraid of what they might do when they saw their rooms to accompany them.

Beatrice could see the innkeeper's mind at work as he rummaged in the pot and she braced herself for more of his confused chatter.

'Kit... I mean *Doctor* Wake, the Gaelic teacher, hasn't arrived yet. The Gaelic lessons are new, you see? She's on her way, but isn't expecting to teach anything this week. She's planning on taking a week's holiday first, and eh…' The man gulped at the sight of Beatrice's stony expression. 'She, eh… she might no' mind starting work early, though. But I know your willow-weaving teacher'll be disappointed you're no' glad aboot taking their class…'

Beatrice's glassy stare was making his fumbling even worse and he couldn't seem to focus on the room numbers on the key fobs. All the while, she was wondering why the keys weren't hanging on the little numbered key board with the brass hooks. Fighting hard, she resisted the urge to snatch the box from his hands and hang each one neatly in its place.

The sound of the entire tub clattering onto the floor by the man's anxiously shuffling feet made Beatrice flinch, her nerves already tested by the long journey from Warwick to Port Willow, a journey she wasn't adequately prepared for, to say the least.

Had it really only been yesterday she'd made the booking? It seemed like days ago, but she still had the white wine hangover as evidence of the teary, alcohol-soaked afternoon that had led to the sudden rash decision to just get away, to be anywhere other than her silent, empty house.

She hadn't meant to do it, but that lunchtime glass of wine had been so cold and crisp in the airless English summer afternoon and so welcome after months without touching even a drop of alcohol. By the third glass she found she'd stopped crying and was suddenly swept up in one of the new fits of exuberant high spirits which she didn't seem to be able to keep a handle on and which were always mixed with agitation and restlessness like she'd never experienced before. To ward off the lingering threat that at any second she might descend into tears and despondency again, she'd put on some music for the first time in a very long time and let Harry Styles' velvety vocals and the wine whip up her mood into a higher pitch of off-key euphoria.

It hadn't felt good exactly, but being drunk and suddenly caught up in a new idea was definitely better than the profound depths of sadness that had held her fast for months now. She was going to get away, book an impromptu escape, just for her. Alone.

Watching the man scrabbling on the ground for the keys and bumping his head not once but twice on the same jutting antique leg of the inn's reception desk she felt the heaviness descending again, its sad weight pouring into the pit of her stomach and draining lead into her limbs. She'd made her escape, but now that she was here, she couldn't for the life of her understand why she'd wanted to come in the first place.

'Learn a new skill in a new place,' the website had enticed. 'Find a home far from home in the wild western Highlands,' it boasted.

All it had taken was three clicks of the mouse and the six hundred pounds of her redundancy money that she'd been saving for the buggy with detachable car seat and matching nappy bag, which she'd secretly had her heart set on since Christmas, flew out of her bank account and into the coffers of The Princess and the Pea Inn.

'*Ugh*, *idiot!*' she scolded under her breath at the hazy memory of it.

The resounding bump of skull against wood and a whimper rose up from beneath the desk, before the exasperated face of the lanky Scot appeared, red-cheeked and puffing.

'Begging yur pardon?'

'Oh, no, I didn't mean you, I was talking to myself... Look, never mind the key. I think I've made a mistake. I'll just head back to the station. Can you issue a refund and I'll get out of your...' Her eyes fell on the man's balding head and the thin, greasy, scraped-over strands barely covering the expanse of bare scalp. 'Hair,' she gulped. Biting her lip to stop herself wincing, she looked down at her suitcase, feeling, not for the first time today, utterly stupid.

'You cannae git a refund now yur here. And besides, that wiz the last train of the day.'

Beatrice's mouth fell open as the breath pressed out. Her lungs emptied and tightened as she berated herself.

What exactly had she been hoping to find here? Some sunshine? A sense of something fresh and exciting? A new Beatrice? Gaelic lessons, indeed. The wine and one too many lonely binge-watched series of *Outlander* must have ignited the sudden notion of running away to a remote part of Scotland where she could learn an ancient language and leave her old self behind.

Gaelic lessons in the Scottish Highlands? *Ridiculous*. She couldn't even get her online booking right. How the hell had she managed to check the box for willow-weaving, whatever that was? Stupid, utterly stupid. She was aware of the sound of her inhalation rushing in through parched lips, but the breaths that followed were too shallow and too fast to calm her.

'Ah, here we ur!'

Triumphantly, the man held out the key and straightened his spine to his full height, knocking the antlers on the wall so they now hung skewhiff and causing some of the cobwebs to detach and stick to the unbuttoned collar of his grubby grey shirt. Ignoring this and with a bright twinkle in his eyes that hinted he had more spark within him than Beatrice's first unfavourable impression suggested, he asked, wickedly, 'Do ye still want yur key? Or ur ye sleepin' under the jetty the night?'

The insolence of the words was softened by the music of his accent, but still, Beatrice was in no state for provocation. She was either going to give him a piece of her mind or she was going to cry.

Her thoughts raced. It wasn't too late to get a taxi back to civilisation. It would be expensive but she could be in Inverness in an hour or so, and from there she might be able to get a train South. She could be at Angela and Vic's around midnight if she left now. They'd let her crash there for a night or two until she was over whatever this restlessness was.

The man extended the key out towards her and gave it an optimistic little rattle.

'Now look here… *Mister.*' Apparently she was going to give him a piece of her mind. Her nerves thrilled at the sound of her voice, shaky but fierce, and the poor man looked instantly terrified. She realised she was pointing her finger at him, and since she had called someone 'Mister' for the first time in her life she decided she might as well find out where this was going.

'Look here,' she said again, steeling herself but feeling tears prickling her eyes anyway. 'I've been on *three* trains for eight hours today, and I've had nothing to eat but an extremely unappetising egg salad sandwich and a cup of tea hotter than the sun that scalded my lip…' She was now jabbing her finger at her mouth, hoping for sympathy. The man peered closely, utterly perplexed, and too afraid to tell her he couldn't see anything.

'… And now I'm in the middle of nowhere, and I'm knackered and grimy and fed up, and I haven't packed for rainy weather *at all*, and I just want to go home again, and I really, honestly don't give a toss about learning Gaelic or knitting bloody twigs together or…'

'Willow.'

'What?'

'It's… willow-weaving,' the man said blankly with a nervous blink.

She screwed her eyes tightly shut and let herself breathe. Shouting definitely hadn't made her feel better. She just felt unkind, brittle, bone-tired and shipwrecked miles from the life she once knew. She hardly ever lost her temper, so what was with shouting at someone she didn't know from Adam? Who even *was* she anymore? There was nothing else to do but apologise and make a run for it.

'*What's this*, Eugene?'

Beatrice's eyes flicked open and her stomach muscles flinched at the sound of the deep, terse Scottish voice from the doorway behind her.

The owner of the voice appeared by Beatrice's side. It was accompanied by narrowed eyes that told her he'd heard the whole thing and made her shrink with shame. He continued to talk. 'Are you checking in? Let me show you to your room. I'll thank you for those keys, Eugene.'

Beatrice looked between the two men, her curiosity sparked in spite of her frayed nerves by the similarities between them. 'There's *two* of you?' she said before she could stop herself. 'I mean, I mean… you're brothers?'

'Aye,' the newcomer said through tense, pale lips.

And yet how different the pair were. What one brother had sacrificed in breadth and beauty, making up for in sheer towering height, this younger one had clearly gained, and yet both men shared fine high-boned cheeks, eyes the colour of the sea in summer and square set jaws.

'I'm Atholl Fergusson, and this is Eugene. And you are?'

Thrown by the stiff formality of his words spoken in a clipped, heavily accented West Highland burr she could manage only a few words. '*Umm*, Beatrice, just Beatrice.'

Atholl Fergusson's mouth set again in a straight line. Unlike his unfortunate brother, Atholl evidently adjusted his Scottish diction for the benefit of his English guests and his features were framed with thick waves of darkest red hair that skimmed the collar of his muted red and brown checked shirt.

'Right then. Good,' he muttered under his voice as he whipped the key from Gene's hand and scooped up the suitcase. 'Follow me, Beatrice,' he said as he made briskly for the stairs.

'Actually, I wasn't sure if I was staying.' She watched him, still rooted to the spot, thinning tartan underfoot.

Atholl paused, one boot on the bottom step. For a moment she watched his back heave as he let out a sharp sigh. Turning back, he transferred his gaze from Beatrice's dark-circled, defiant eyes to Gene still clutching his pot of keys. He didn't even attempt to hide the second great huff of exasperation that stretched his broad chest.

'You'll have tae forgive my brother, it's been twenty years but he's yet to understand he works in the hospitality trade. Eugene, will ye please send up some tea and shortbread for our guest. I'll see she's settled in.'

With that Atholl directed a sharp nod at Beatrice, and made his way up the wide, creaking stairs.

She watched Atholl climb before glancing back at Gene, who was attempting to avoid any further interaction with her by banging at the side of the computer monitor with a soft fist as though it would somehow fix the bookings glitch.

Letting her eyes roll, she clutched at the handbag straps over her shoulder. What was the use in protesting? How long would it take for a taxi to get here from the nearest town anyway? Hours, maybe? And she was too tired to repeat again her plans for a retreat back to England. She really was stranded here until morning. And besides, the only innkeeper who seemed to have his wits about him enough to help her escape Port Willow had climbed the stairs and left her alone. And hadn't he totally disregarded everything she'd said about wanting to leave, anyway? That was plain rude.

In spite of everything, she found that most of her reservations about spending the night at The Princess and the Pea were temporarily outweighed by the thought of the tea and shortbread Atholl had mentioned. With a resigned shrug, she followed him up the stairs.

The door swung open and Atholl stood aside, letting her enter the low bedroom.

'Oh,' was all she could manage under the circumstances.

She took in the single bed, the small window framed with yellowing lace and a sense of the sea wall and the sand and shingle of low tide beyond, the small fireplace with its grate piled with dusty pinecones, the curious copper bath in the corner under the low eaves, and the painting of a mighty stag in muddy colours on the wall by the door.

'Is it no' to your liking?' Atholl asked, his eyes passing around the room, scanning for the invisible thing that displeased his English visitor.

'It's fine. I'm not staying long anyway.'

Atholl received this information in silence, a pinched line forming between his brows which Beatrice didn't see, preoccupied as she was wondering how she'd fit into the little bath without her knees touching her ears.

'You don't have anything a bit bigger, do you?'

'No. We're full. Not unless you want the princess room, but that'll cost ye double what you've already paid, and it doesn't get many takers these days.'

Money wasn't too much of an issue, yet. She didn't have much of anything else, but a little money she had. 'I'd like to see it,' she said, sending a prayer of gratitude to her mum who had, long ago, advised her to set up a secret bank account all of her own. During a whispered conversation in the kitchen at Beatrice and Rich's engagement party, she'd said, 'Remember, you mustn't tell anyone about it, least of all Richard. A woman should have enough money saved to buy her independence if she needs it.' The idea had seemed positively Victorian to Beatrice a decade ago but as the last of her redundancy money had run out she saw with crystal clarity what her mum had in mind.

Huddled there whispering over the party snacks while Rich blasted out a karaoke rendition of 'Poker Face' in the living room to much laughter from his work mates, it hadn't quite filtered through to her that a similarly secret bank account must have been the reason her mum had been able to get her and her baby sister out of the house and away to safety from the volatile, shouting father she could barely recall and had never wanted to know better.

If only she'd asked her mum more questions when she'd had the chance. What had it been like, packing bags and getting in that taxi to the refuge? Where had her father been that night? Exactly how much had she squirrelled away that she could afford the rent on their little house in Warwick which had become a happy childhood home, the only one she and Angela could remember? There was nobody left who could answer those questions.

The forced sigh that roused her from her thoughts told her Atholl found her bothersome, but she could put up with that if it meant getting a better room.

'If it's not too much trouble,' she added impetuously.

Atholl's neck stiffened and he hissed a breath through gritted teeth as he turned for the stairs.

She'd come all this way, seen the inside of three stuffy train station waiting rooms and cried in one revolting Pendolino lavatory; she wasn't going to sleep in a tiny cramped room after taking a tiny cramped bath if there was even the chance of something more luxurious. It was the least she deserved, and, given her impression of the inn so far, it would still be far less than she'd been led to expect from the inn's fancy website. She hadn't seen mention of any princess room on there either. It sounded far more suitable than the gloomy, wood-panelled cell her new red-headed acquaintance had just shown her.

She heard the creaking of the stairs beneath Atholl's feet and strained her ears to listen in to the exchange between the brothers as he reached the reception area below her.

'Where's the princess room key?'

This was followed by the sounds of rummaging in Tupperware once more.

'Another one no' like their room?' Gene asked softly.

'*Hmph!* This one's surely the worst of the lot. Just arrived and wanting to leave, afore she'd even *seen* her room. Aye, they're small rooms, but they're clean and they're warm. This isnae The Ritz. *Och*, for crying out loud, Eugene, can ye no' get these keys back up on their hooks? The inn's almost fully booked for the first time in years thanks to the crafters and, honest to God, what do you look like carrying on with yur wee tub o' keys in front of the guests?'

'Aye, aye, I'll sort it,' came the brother's dismissive, preoccupied reply in his feather light Highland brogue. 'Take it easy, brother. You've got guests coming in, isn't that whit ye wanted? Your idea's working.'

'It only works if they don't think we're some kind of joke. You have to take the inn more seriously now we're busy again, for my sake, as well as our guests. It is, after all, *your* inn. Is that… are those cobwebs on your shirt? For the love of—'

'Found it! The princess room,' Gene announced proudly.

Beatrice who had craned her head over the balustrade to better hear them found herself smiling at the strange set-up between the pair, and could only imagine the tensions that must run between them, daily testing this Atholl Fergusson's patience. No wonder he was so grouchy. She quickly rearranged her expression as Atholl bounded back up onto the landing before her.

'Right, shall we?' Leading the way along undulating floorboards that gave Beatrice a seasick feeling, Atholl pulled up at the ever so slightly crooked door frame with its brass plaque declaring this 'The Princess Room.'

As Beatrice followed him along the corridor she stopped to do a double take at its faded pictures and movie

22

posters lining the panelled walls and hanging squint on their hooks. Every one of them featured Gene Kelly.

Atholl caught her incredulous expression. 'They're, um, my mother's. She loves the musicals. I darenae take them down.' He grimaced awkwardly having made the confession.

Beatrice had no intention of pushing him for more details about this eccentric mother. All she wanted to do was flop down on a comfy bed and try not to think too hard about how exactly she'd wound up in this place.

Without another word, he let the door open and Beatrice passed through.

After everything she had been through in recent months, she'd thought nothing could ever surprise her again; shock her and shake her, make her nerves sing and snap with anxiety and tension, yes, but surely nothing could simply surprise or delight anymore? Nevertheless, the room took away her breath and made her eyes widen in wonder. '*Hah!* What's this?'

Atholl watched his guest through sharpened eyes, his arms folded as he leaned on the door frame. Beatrice stepped right up to the antique wooden bed with its tower of plump mattresses and quilts stacked one atop another, a confection of vintage lace and down, ponderously piled as high as the top of her head, and all canopied over with a flouncy awning suspended between the four intricately carved bedposts, the canopy almost touching the sloping, beamed ceiling itself.

'How on earth are you supposed to get into it?'

Saying nothing, Atholl unfolded an arm and pointed a finger to the end of the bed, indicating she should walk around. Sure enough, on the other side of the mattress mountain was a wooden ladder, its rungs twined with gold ribbon and white silk roses, the same decorations which held back the fairy-tale bed's four pale green chintzy curtains, tying them to the bedposts.

'It's incredible, but this can't be safe, surely? What if you forget you're up there, get up for a drink of water in the dark and fall to your death? There's no way I'd be able to sleep up there!'

'Your own wee room doesn't look quite so small now, I take it?' Atholl said, his eyes sly and glinting.

Beatrice felt a flush of irritation rise in her chest turning her cheeks red, a feeling which wouldn't have been quite so strong had she not found herself struck by the way he was rolling up his shirt sleeves to expose modestly muscled forearms, dark and freckled with the summer sun, and realising she had let her eyes linger there a second too long.

There was a hint of laughter in his eyes telling her that even if he hadn't picked up on her appraising glance – and she really hoped he hadn't – he *definitely* knew he'd aggravated her by being right about her preference for the other room after all.

Scanning the furnishings once more to avoid his smirking, she caught sight of the mustard-yellow chaise along the wall and the antique roll-top bath in the corner, at least twice as big as the sad little tub in the first room, and there were fluffy white towels on a stand beside it.

'I'll take it,' she heard herself saying, before immediately cursing her newly acquired petty streak. She wasn't going to show Atholl the sneaking shame that was threatening to burn her cheeks again, so she defiantly raised her face to his. 'I'll be going in the morning anyway. I'm sure I can survive *one* night.'

Not wanting Atholl to offer to bring her suitcase from the rejected room, she flounced back out into the corridor, making him press himself against the doorframe to let her past.

She didn't care if his face was set sternly or if he overheard her remarking to herself, 'What was I thinking, coming here?', but she caught his exasperated shrug of resignation as she trundled her case into the princess room. That shrug told her he thought it wise to leave the emotional Englishwoman to fizz and boil by herself.

But she wasn't done with him yet. She still had to risk asking the insistent question that had been worrying her since her arrival.

'Is there a phone I can use?' She held her mobile out for him to look at the greyed-out bars. 'There's no signal here. How do you manage?' It came out more curtly than she wanted, but it was too late now.

'Do you really need it? Can you no' live without checking Instagram for a few hours?'

Beatrice had no intention of telling him she wanted to ring her sister to let her know where she was and why she hadn't called round today.

'Do you even know what Instagram is?'

She'd only briefly flirted with Instagram herself when looking with Angela – who'd been scoffing and disinterested – at glamorous celebrity parents showing off over engineered and very expensive baby slings and carriers. If tested now, she'd have been unable to explain exactly how to use the app, but again this was something he didn't need to know. She never had settled on which carrier she'd like best, and it was irrelevant now.

Atholl was still huffing, pink-faced at her question. 'Well, no, but my point is, *this* is life here and now.'

He gestured to the low window by the landing, and she followed his gaze to the rain running in fast streaks down the pane. 'This is the holiday you've been looking forward to for months.'

Beatrice thought how he couldn't be more wrong on that score. The first she'd heard of Port Willow was around about glass number three yesterday. Atholl was still talking and his pale, freckled cheeks were still flushing a rather lovely, livid pink. 'You need to stop gazing into yur phones and start looking about you.'

'I get the impression you're not just referring to me here?'

'You, the other visitors, you're all the same.'

'That's a fine attitude to have when you run a hotel.' She felt her hands ball up tight, her chin jut out, and the angry agitation rising in another wave, bringing her close to tears yet again. She always hated how confrontation did that to her. No matter how convinced she was she was in the right, if she had to put up a fight there was always too much adrenalin and a shake in her voice and a loud heartbeat in her ears. Every time this made her even more cross until her only recourse was bursting into tears and accepting her defeat or retreating into silence, avoiding the fight altogether.

'This isn't *my* hotel, and I don't run it,' Atholl was insisting. 'At least, I'm no' supposed to be running it.' His own jaw was jutting now.

'Either way, can you afford to be rude to your guests like this? Hoteliery is a tough business to be in right now, you know?'

'*Ye don't say?*' Atholl snapped back before pulling his lips tightly closed and lowering his eyes for a brief moment, long enough for her to catch his frustration, not just with her, but with himself. He seemed to think for a moment before huffing, 'There's a pay phone in the bar corridor.'

Silence fell between them and Beatrice fortified herself not to utter the apology on her lips even though her legs were trembling and she was suddenly mortified to think how she must look, wishing more than ever that she could just slip invisibly away from everyone's prying eyes and hide out in peace.

Yet she held firm on her spot. Atholl had been rude and didn't deserve an apology, but from the way his blazing eyes lifted again to meet her own she knew she'd riled him too. She had been snarky and that wasn't like her at all, not usually anyway.

The old Beatrice Halliday would never behave like this, but then again, the old Beatrice hadn't been anywhere near as brittle and bitter and bashed about by life as this, and she would *never* have hightailed it to the Highlands without thinking through just exactly what she'd do when she got there. She didn't have a list, or a plan, or anything. She hadn't even told anyone she was leaving.

A creak on the stairs helped fracture the tension in the air. Gene Fergusson was at last making his way one slow step at a time, the teapot rattling on a tray as he climbed.

Atholl held Beatrice's gaze as though he was going to say something else, but when he at last opened his mouth, a loud call came out that startled her.

'*Echo!*'

He turned sharply and marched along the corridor before calling out again. Beatrice watched on as a shaggy black and white collie bounded up the stairs to meet him, his tail swinging wildly, knocking on the oak spindles.

As Atholl passed his brother, Beatrice heard him say, 'I'm getting away from this confounded inn for the rest of the day.'

The dog followed in his master's wake as Atholl crossed the threshold of the inn and strode into the cool of the summer rain. Beatrice wasn't aware that she was still staring at the space on the staircase that Atholl had occupied until Gene shuffled awkwardly past her into the room with the towering bed at its centre, the scent of freshly made shortbread piled high on a dish at last stealing her attention from the infuriating red-headed Scotsman.

Chapter Three

Telling Angela

'You're *where*? Look, Vic's home from work, we'll come and get you, just stay put.'

'I'm fine, honestly, Angela. And don't be daft. You can't bring baby Clara all this way in the car. Anyway, by the time you get here it'll be morning and the trains will be running again.'

'Well… if you're sure? Is it really so bad that you want to leave right away?'

'It's all right…' Beatrice stared at the framed picture above the payphone of a grinning, rain-soaked Gene Kelly swinging himself round a lamppost. 'It's just a bit… eccentric. I'll be OK for one night. Can I, *uh*, come over for dinner tomorrow? I'll pick up some nice bits from M&S on my way?'

'Of course you can, and you don't need to bring anything. But, Beatrice… *why* are you there? The last thing I heard you were planning on clearing out your spare room and suddenly you're in… where are you again?'

'Port Willow. Oh, I don't know, I just felt the need to get away. I do deserve a summer holiday, don't I?'

Beatrice knew her sister would also be thinking of the Greek island summer holiday that she and Rich had booked earlier that year, before so much had gone wrong between them. They'd have been there today, in fact, and she'd probably have been throwing on a nice dress right about now and getting ready for dinner after a long day at the beach. But Rich had said he couldn't face it, 'not with things the way they are', and Beatrice had made the decision to cancel the whole thing.

'But Scotland? Alone? And on a whim? Bea, why didn't you tell us? We could've planned it properly, come with you, maybe?' said Angela.

Beatrice shrugged, cradling the receiver to her ear and twiddling the curled cable. Angela knew the heart of her sister better than anyone. Hiding her sadness from Angela had been next to impossible, but Beatrice had done her best over the past few months. Angela couldn't have anticipated this desperate dash to the Highlands. Nobody could.

'Is this because of Mum?' Angela prodded.

'What?'

'Well… you ring me up out of the blue saying you've suddenly signed yourself up for Gaelic lessons in the Highlands, and I'm just wondering why? You know, you could have picked cookery lessons in Florence, or, I don't know, pottery painting in Delft?'

Beatrice couldn't help but snort a laugh.

'So… why Scotland? Are you there trying to reconnect with Mum or something? We always did promise her a trip to Scotland, an ancestry trail kind of thing. You remember, don't you? She always talked about wanting to rediscover her Scottish roots…'

A little hitch in Angela's voice halted the conversation and each sister knew the other was holding back the tears that persisted in sneaking up on them recently, taking away their breath and plunging them back into the horrible feelings of loss. Beatrice let her head hang, listening to the phone line crackling, the buzzing connection bridging the miles between them.

A Scottish adventure had been on their mum's bucket list, one of many things she never had the chance to experience. Their mother was born in Aberdeen but her parents had relocated to Warwickshire when she was a teenager. She always talked about her Scottish childhood with a fond, faraway look, and her recollections evoked an era that sounded somehow earlier than the nineteen-sixties when she'd lived there. Nostalgia did that, Beatrice supposed.

Their mother had described a time of neighbourliness, of safely playing kerby-ball – whatever that was – in the streets until late at night, and of not having much money but being happy. Despite their mother's fondness for the place, she'd never been back as an adult, but she had spoken in a soft hybrid accent for the rest of her life that evoked the Granite City she always referred to as home.

'It's not that,' Beatrice said, but thinking all the time that Angela might have a point, and realising that throughout her journey northward she'd been struck by little moments of recognition as she heard echoes of her mother's accent in the voices of the Scottish strangers she'd encountered.

Her eyes flicked open wide as it struck her that one of the *many* discomforting things about Atholl Fergusson had been this unconscious sense of recognition. She'd heard her mother's restrained Scottish brogue in his voice, a familiar reminder of lost home comforts in every sound he uttered. The thought shook her as she replayed his words.

'This is life here and now,' he'd said in his own particular way, a gravelly gruffness that carried passionate force behind it fading to soft breathlessness at the ends of sentences…

'Are you still there, Bea? Hello?'

'I'm still here.'

'You know, maybe a holiday isn't such a bad idea after all. Are you *sure* you want to leave in the morning?'

'What would I do with myself here?' Beatrice dismissed the idea of the willow-weaving lessons in an instant. 'I've never travelled on my own before and…'

'*Peep peep*, mind yersel',' came a jolly voice from behind Beatrice, and she pressed her body to the wall to let its owner past.

Beatrice watched the woman trundle by and couldn't help but smile at the sight of her. Obviously another employee of the inn, her thin grey hair was set in tight rollers around her head. She was wearing a white apron and wellies, with her sleeves rolled up revealing fleshy milk-white forearms, and she was pushing a wheelbarrow through the narrow hall from the bar room towards the kitchen with a great sack of frozen chips as cargo.

When the woman passed out of sight, Beatrice whispered, 'I don't think I belong here, Angela.'

A long beat passed between the sisters allowing Beatrice time to tell herself yet again that she didn't quite know *where* she belonged anymore. Attaching herself so closely to Angela and her little family had helped for a while, but she knew all along that they needed their own space.

'Bea…' Angela's voice was soft. 'We're worried about you. Wouldn't it be easier just talking about it a little bit? Easier than hiding away in your house? Easier than running away from yourself to Scotland?'

Beatrice heard the shaky breath down the line, Angela holding together her emotions for her big sister's sake.

'I'm fine, honestly. I'm getting better. Much better. Ah, would you look at the time. I'd better get myself tidied up for dinner.'

'Well, OK, but keep in touch?'

'I will. I'll text when I can get a signal on my way back tomorrow.'

'You know we can always clear out your spare room together at the weekend? How does that sound?'

Beatrice let the kindness pass unanswered, trying to force a smile into her voice. 'I love you, sis.'

'You too, Bea.'

Beatrice reached for the button on the receiver cradle and let the line die, knowing Angela wouldn't hang up first. Keeping the phone in her hand she let herself slide down the painted Artex onto the floor. She listened to the dial tone for a long time, crouching on the carpet, thinking of her sister's concern. *Talk about it.* Everyone wanted her to talk about it, but there were no words profound enough to give it all utterance.

And suddenly, out of nowhere as far as she could tell, there was Rich in her mind's eye, his face pale with the shock as she held the pregnancy test out for him to see.

Why now? Why would this particular painful memory want to intrude now? She found herself listless and tired, crumpled against the wall, letting it all play out before her.

In the end she hadn't been able to tell him the news on Big Fat Positive day. A strange kind of awkwardness and embarrassment that you shouldn't really feel with your own husband had crowded out the words when Rich got in from work that night. Suddenly she was suffused with worry that he'd think it had all happened too quickly.

With the reality of two pink lines staring them in the face and the hypothetical mini-Rich suddenly becoming fact, the idea of being a parent seemed a whole lot less cutesy and fun.

So she bottled it, keeping the news to herself for nearly a whole week, and, she had to admit, it was lovely. Nobody in the world knew about it except her and her sesame seed. She had found herself smiling dopily while they watched *Question Time* and Rich was swearing at the telly, amazed he couldn't guess something was up, but he didn't.

Had she been waiting for some other sign of the baby's existence, other than the test strips, before telling him? Some morning sickness maybe, which perversely she was looking forward to? During those secretive, happy days she'd jumped straight into planning; taking folic acid and knocking the caffeine on the head, and she rang the health centre and got a 'booking in' appointment straight away – all before telling Rich – and she'd been shocked to discover she'd have her first midwife appointment in less than three weeks, and found herself hoping for the same lovely midwife that Angela and Vic had.

In all it had taken five days to tell Rich, and she had really worked hard to set the scene with his favourite dinner (steaks, the nice onion rings she made from scratch, peppercorn sauce, Belgian beers, and the caramel profiteroles he loved). And yes, he did turn a little ashen on hearing the words and Beatrice had rushed to make him a sweet tea, which he didn't drink, now she came to think of it. He kept saying, '*Oh My God*' over and over, but he had smiled and hugged her, so that was a relief, and after that he was pretty quiet, just letting it all sink in.

'A sticking plaster baby.' That's what Rich's dad had called it when they found themselves unexpectedly faced with him a few nights later when he'd stumbled into the hallway, doused in vodka with the staggering walk that told them he'd been in the pub all day.

She remembered the hope on her husband's face as he blurted out that they were having a baby. She knew he was wishing for a fatherly reaction, an embrace maybe, some effusion of pride, anything. His mum, after all, had taken the news well, and she'd sobbed happy tears and promised that in the autumn she'd make the journey back from her sunny expat life in Portugal with her new husband, excited to meet the new arrival. But telling his dad was a different matter entirely.

True to form, the boozy bitterness had won out over any paternal sentiment he might have had hidden deep within him and he'd sneered and leered the words Beatrice would never forget. This man, the bad penny, the father who didn't have the compassion to even comprehend the pain he'd caused his son, had been perceptive and cruel enough to pinpoint the tenderest, most secret, hidden thing in their lives and he'd enjoyed making his observation. He had known their relationship had lost its spark long before she and Rich had even acknowledged it to themselves, and that irked Beatrice more than she had ever shown.

'You're having a sticking plaster baby to fix the mess you're in? I'm afraid it doesn't work like that, Rich, my boy.'

He'd been sent packing, but it was too late. As the door closed he'd slurred one last fatal blow, 'No child ever fixed a bad marriage, you know.'

The words had been like electricity, galvanising Rich into action, as his father's unkindness often did. Neither of them admitted it at the time – but it was becoming clear to Beatrice now as the low monotone of the payphone buzzed in her hand – Rich had been jolted out of his complacency, fully determining to be a good daddy in that instant, partly because he was a decent kind of man and partly to spite his father, to prove he wasn't like him.

There had been endless glasses of water brought and foot rubs and deep bubble baths drawn for her after that, and on one Friday afternoon, when Beatrice had opened the door to Rich after his long day at work, she'd been greeted by a giant yellow bunny with the word 'Baby' on its white tummy and Rich's smiling face peering out from behind it.

Later on, there had been red roses and a card with sweet words written inside. 'To the Mother of Our Baby on Valentine's Day.' The sesame seed had become an apple pip by then, and for a while everything was good and fruitful. Yet, the words that had spurred on Rich's attentiveness and spoiled their contentment were still out there and had etched themselves in their memories. Every time Rich kissed her stomach before he left for work in the morning she knew he was thinking of them too. 'A sticking plaster baby.' Beatrice hated Rich's father all the more because he'd been right.

She cursed the old man for this and for all the times he'd turned up asking for money, airing his opinions and making Rich feel torn and guilty. She had loved Rich all the more for his need of a dad – the same empty, conflicted need as her own. Neither of them had managed to salvage a father–child relationship from their messy childhoods, but they had found each other and they both understood what it was like to want a daddy not a deadbeat, and that could always be relied upon to bring them closer together. She sighed now, slumped beneath the payphone, bringing her chin to her chest, and she might have stayed like that if a door hadn't slammed somewhere on the ground floor of the inn.

Beatrice snapped out of the unwelcome visions from way back in the early spring, somehow more painfully vivid now that she had some distance on them. It dawned on her that her face was wet from crying and that the receiver in her hand was now sounding a high-pitched droning alarm as it demanded to be placed back in its cradle.

Echo, Atholl Fergusson's dog, ran past her, nosing its way in through the kitchen door. With a gasp she scurried along the corridor and up the inn's back stairs to her room where she could clamber up the ladder to her bed, bury her face in the pillows and cry out the bitterness.

There was no way she'd let Atholl, or indeed any of the occupants of The Princess and the Pea Inn, see her like this. Her pain and humiliation were her own secrets, and sharing them could never come to any good. If Rich's dad had taught her anything it was not to go looking for sympathy in case you're not met with any. Stoicism had worked out OK for her so far and she only had to stick this place out for another twelve hours or so and she'd be on her way again. For now, she'd take solace in the fact that nobody here knew her or her story and that suited her perfectly.

Chapter Four

Evening at the Inn

'It's blawin' a hoolie oot there!'

Beatrice registered the voice but resolved happily that it couldn't be directed towards her – she didn't know anyone in Port Willow, after all. That, and she had no idea what he'd said, so a reply was impossible anyway. Just in case, she shoved her nose deeper into her book, trying to look absorbed and unapproachable, hoping nobody in the inn's bar restaurant could tell she'd been staring at the same paragraph since she arrived and not taken in one word.

But the voice came again, soft and musical, like breath through a reed, and this time it was too close to ignore. 'Glad tae be indoors the night, eh?'

The man looked as gaunt and airy as his Highland accent sounded to Beatrice's ears. Easily eighty, with a green woollen beany pulled down over his head, his curling whiskers and fluffy grey sideburns framed bright, watery eyes which were rendered tiny and mole-like through the thick lenses of his specs. The rosiness in his cheeks and the way he held his hands behind his back as Beatrice looked up from her book told her this was no creepy barfly.

'I am. Does it always rain in Port Willow?' she said, lowering the book.

'Only recently, but we're in for a dry spell between the storms soon. English, are you?' The man had immediately adapted his speech for the Sassenach guest.

Beatrice nodded. 'I'm on holiday. Well I was, but I'm leaving on the morning train.'

The man seemed to be weighing up some words before pursing his lips and keeping them to himself.

'Are you a local?' she prompted, already sure of the answer. He looked perfectly at home among the dark wood panelling, the Highland landscapes in dull oils and the pewter tankards suspended on hooks above the bar. She would bet her life savings on one of those pint pots belonging to him.

'Born and bred,' he said. 'My father ran the harbour boats afore me, and now my laddie runs them. Mind ye take a trip around the headland before ye go, see the seals.'

She realised she'd quite like to go on a seal-spotting trip, if the rain were ever to stop, but sadly, there'd be no time for sightseeing before her hurried – and relieved – departure tomorrow morning. She didn't like to tell him this.

The man barely flinched at the sound of the Sussex silversmithing and stained glass crafters bursting through the door, shaking umbrellas, and exclaiming loudly about the 'typical' Highland weather.

'Are you one of these visitors that the brothers are so keen on bringing in from down South?' He indicated with a nod the women who had struggled out of their dripping lilac cagoules and were now loudly discussing ordering two, no three, bottles of pinot.

Beatrice searched the man's whiskery face for a hint of disapproval but detected none. As if to confirm this, he added, 'We need new life here in Port Willow. When I was a laddie there were three pubs down the front as well as the Kailyard Café, now there's only the Princess. The more folk visiting, the merrier, I say.'

At this the door opened again and in came a stream of young men in wellies and waterproofs, fresh from the afternoon tourist and fishing boats.

'All right, Da,' one of the men, a younger version of her interlocutor said as he walked by, patting his father on the shoulder.

The older man threw him a fatherly smile but had no intention of letting his conversation with the lonely-looking newcomer be interrupted. Over his shoulder, the crowd of sailors leaned against the bar waiting for it to open and scanned the room, surveying the new arrivals with interest.

'I was signed up for Gaelic lessons, but...' she tailed off with a shrug.

'Oh, aye? Not many in the village speak the Gaelic now. I know young Atholl has brought in a Gaelic tutor for the last of the summer, a lassie from the university, you'll like her very much, I'm sure.'

'Do you speak Gaelic...?' Beatrice paused as she prompted his name, since it looked like he was rooted to his spot and she was in for a long conversation.

'Seth. Seth McVie, and no, not I.'

Beatrice smiled and offered Seth her hand. 'I'm Beatrice, by the way. But I won't be taking any lessons at all now. There was some kind of mix up and it turned out I was signed up for willow-weaving and not Gaelic, apparently. Not sure what that's all about.'

'Ah! This port was famous for its willow growing and weaving. We sent our bonny baskets all over the world once upon a time. Those days are long gone, mind.'

'*Bar's open!*' called a Highland voice, and Beatrice didn't need to look across to know to whom it belonged. Something within her withered a little as she remembered her rudeness earlier.

'Does Atholl Fergusson run the bar?' Beatrice said in a low tone, as she shifted in her seat.

Seth's twinkling eyes crinkled into sunrays at the corners as a slow smile dawned. 'In recent months, yes. Since… well, I'm no one to blether other folks' business…' He paused to look around, giving Beatrice the impression he was *precisely* the type and she was about to get a nugget of Port Willow gossip.

Seth leaned a little closer, drawing a pipe from the pocket of his tweed jacket. 'You know the older, taller of the Fergusson lads, Eugene?'

Beatrice told him she certainly did.

'His missus upped and left. A midnight flitting, almost two years ago now. He woke up and she was gone, back to Canada where she came from. Now he won't do the evening dinner service because she always did it with him. Wonderful cooks they were, but he can't seem to face it without her, try as young Atholl might to encourage him.'

'Seth? Your usual?' Atholl called pointedly from the bar, his ears obviously ringing with his family's name.

Beatrice's elderly companion gave a chuckle and pursed his lips again as he slipped the pipe in his mouth. 'Aye, my usual please, Atholl. I'll just take a smoke outside. I'm sure the lassie Beattie would like a drink too.' With that, Seth looked meaningfully between Atholl and Beatrice and shuffled out the door.

Atholl appeared by Beatrice's side, a pad in his hand. 'I can take your food order too, if you've looked at the menu?'

Having had her mood lightened by Seth's jovial warmth, she was in no mood for Atholl's clipped efficiency and she determined to soften him. '*Beattie?*' she said with a smile. 'Is that to be my Highland name?'

'You'll no' be here long enough for nicknames,' Atholl replied, eyes fixed on the pad and pencil.

The wind left her sails again and she straightened her back to stop him seeing her shoulders slumping. After feeling so low for so long Seth had brightened her day, and here was Atholl Fergusson bringing the thunder clouds back.

'Have you seen the menu?' he asked again, softer this time, as if regretting his brusqueness, but Beatrice was so out of sorts she didn't hear the change in his tone.

'Yes, I've seen it,' she said, but snatched the folded card from the table and scanned it again, making him wait, just to spite him.

She had arrived early for dinner and found nobody in the bar, taking the only booth table in the place and settling herself in. Of course nobody was here, she'd thought. Customer service wasn't the brothers' strong suit. It came as no surprise that if the visitor information book in her room told her dinner was served from six until eight, the cranky Fergussons rigidly meant six and not a moment before.

'I'll have the fish and chips, and a ginger beer, please,' she said, when she couldn't hold him there any longer.

With that, Atholl was back behind the bar, scribbling on his pad. Beatrice tried to shrug off his rudeness, and justify her own, but was soon beset with the pained feeling that *she* was the cause of all his consternation this afternoon at check in. After all, when he'd appeared at the reception door he'd seemed, if not exactly *happy*, polite enough. But she had ruffled his feathers and now she wasn't welcome. And she was finding it hard to back down in the face of his terse manners. Why was she like this?

Maybe some food and a night's rest would set her back on track again. She was annoying herself now. All the more reason to get out of here as soon as possible and get back to – what? Normality wasn't an option anymore, but she could head back to Warwick and see what could be salvaged of her old life.

Beatrice tried to return to her book, making a show of turning the pages with unruffled grace but finding her gaze following a beautiful woman in a long floral dress and lace-up grungy boots who had just come in and been greeted with what for Atholl Fergusson probably passed as an effusive hug.

Suddenly she found her view blocked by the woman she'd seen earlier with the wheelbarrow. Her hair was now free of its curlers and the perm brushed out into soft grey waves. She placed Beatrice's drink before her.

'Sup up, dearie. Food's on its way too,' said the woman.

Thanking her, Beatrice wondered why she felt so stung that the grumpy, rude Atholl Fergusson hadn't carried her drink over from the bar himself. Had he purposely asked someone else so he could avoid having to talk to her?

'Eugene tells me you're here all by yourself, so if you need anything, be sure to shout on me. I'm Mrs Mair,' the woman was saying as she gave the booth table a wipe over. She leaned a little closer, her rosy-cheeked smile forcing her eyes into crescents. 'The Fergusson laddies do their best, but, you know... I'm always around if needed.'

'Umm, thanks, Mrs Mair,' Beatrice smiled back, awkwardly, and the woman shuffled away again, past the bar and through the door marked 'kitchen'.

Gene had told Mrs Mair she was travelling alone, had he? So she was already the subject of gossip at the inn? Great! The sooner she could make her departure tomorrow, the better. At least there were no wagging tongues and prying eyes when she was hiding under her duvet back in Warwickshire.

She threw another furtive glance towards Atholl and the pretty woman. Her hair was a brighter shade of red than his and hung in looser waves, and when Atholl talked with her at the bar, where she perched on a stool and spread open notebooks and a laptop, he leaned his chin on his hand and the room sang with their chatter.

Beatrice reached a hand to her own dull brown hair and ran her fingers through the ends. She had never been strikingly pretty, she found herself thinking. Not like that red-headed, pearly-skinned woman making Atholl smile.

Beatrice's maternal grandmother had once, long ago and without intending to hurt her, described her as 'pleasant-looking' and that had stuck in her head. Pleasant, plain, nothing too special. She'd probably looked her best around the time she met Richard. She was only twenty-eight then, and full of confidence and gusto from being happy and successful in her busy, exciting arts networking job. Her hair had been longer then too and she'd been a dress size smaller and she hadn't ever bothered with make-up other than a bit of mascara.

Richard had *seriously* fancied her back then when he was the proprietor of a cool, vintage cinema-mobile, all chrome, curves and black and white movies. There were fourteen leather seats inside Glenda – that's what the van was called – as well as a small screen and a popcorn machine. Glenda and Rich had done a roaring trade at festivals across the country.

As bold as brass, he'd told Beatrice he thought she was gorgeous the very first time they met at the Three Counties agricultural show where Glenda was showing *An American In Paris* back to back all weekend. Beatrice was manning the council arts stall and doing a bit of public relations, meet-the-locals stuff. After they got together he'd sold the company to a friend and moved into selling film rights, maybe not quite so exciting and itinerant, but certainly more dependable.

He'd sent her a huge bunch of roses at her office and asked her out three times before she said yes. She couldn't remember how she'd had the confidence to say no, especially when she'd thought Rich was fanciable and nice, but you could play games like that when you were young and there was all the time in the world.

Now, sitting under the bar room lights, she felt as though all the colour had somehow washed out of her and she knew she looked tired and every one of her thirty-nine years, eleven months – if not older.

She hadn't a clue she was being assessed admiringly by the group of farm workers who had recently arrived and were settled around two tables just across the room from her. They were smiling behind their pint glasses and nudging the youngest, handsomest one amongst them, telling him to get across the room and ask her for her name. But two of the crafting women *had* noticed them and, hoping to spare her a night of being chatted up by every lad in Port Willow, they'd made a beeline for Beatrice all alone at her booth.

'You can stop pretending to read now. Are you another one of us?' said a beautiful black woman wearing her hair in a halo of natural waves.

'One of us?' Beatrice echoed, a little dazed and realising the women might have caught her staring across the room at the handsome red-headed barman as he talked to the beautiful woman.

'A crafter?' said the other, a glamorous platinum-blonde woman, all Fake Bake tan over white skin and with phenomenal lashes.

Both women, Beatrice realised, had rich and rounded Newcastle accents.

'Oh, yes I suppose I am. Are you willow-weaving?'

'No, we're painting,' replied the blonde, who Beatrice guessed was the eldest of the two, though both looked as though they were in their thirties. 'Thought it would make a change from us painting faces and tinting hair all the time,' she added.

'You're beauticians?'

The blonde got in first with a reply. 'Aye, this is our staff outing and our summer holiday combined. We're partners in our spa in Gateshead, Bobby Dazzlers?' She said this as though Beatrice might have heard of it. 'As if we don't get enough of each other at work.'

The other woman reached out a hand graced with silver rings and long, fiercely pointed, coral-pink finger-nails. 'I'm Jillian, by the way; and she's Cheryl.'

'Beatrice. Good to meet you. I'm not really a crafter though. I'm signed up for willow-weaving lessons but, between you and me, I'm not exactly keen. In fact, I'm thinking about heading home again tomorrow.'

'And do what? Regret you've missed your holiday?' said Jillian, reaching for the menu, and Beatrice realised with some relief — followed by a hot wave of anxiety — that she wouldn't be dining alone after all.

If she was going to be making small talk with these women over dinner she'd have to be on her best behaviour and try to act normally. And just *how* did she do that, again?

Her new dinner companions were examining her, she knew, trying to work out why on earth she was here. She had no intention of telling them. The only good thing about this mad dash to the Highlands was the anonymity it offered. Nobody knew her and that made things so much easier. Beatrice changed the subject.

'Did you get in today too? Done any sightseeing yet?'

'This morning,' Cheryl replied, and Beatrice wondered if she saw disappointment cross her face at her evasiveness. 'We've been walking all day. A bit too long a walk!' Cheryl reached under the table to rub her foot.

'And we got soaked,' Jillian added. 'But the scenery around here is stunning. Breath-taking, you might say.'

That was when Beatrice realised Jillian was looking over at Atholl behind the bar and smirking while Cheryl nudged her in the ribs to shut her up. So they *had* seen her staring at Atholl.

The beauticians' laughter drew Atholl's eyes to their booth. The look of confusion and ire on his stern face as he broke off from his conversation with the pretty woman made Beatrice stifle a laugh too and the women huddled their heads closer together.

'Hold on a minute!' An idea suddenly struck Beatrice, lighting a fire behind her eyes. 'I *knew* I recognised you both.'

Cheryl and Jillian exchanged satisfied smiles.

'You were on the telly, weren't you? That fly on the wall salon show? Ooh, what was it called... *Geordie Shorn!*'

'Eee, I'm surprised you remember that, it was a while ago now. We were a lot younger then.' Jillian touched the spot behind her ear and raised her eyes with comedic fake modesty.

Beatrice grinned back. She didn't want to admit she'd seen just the one episode on one of the more obscure channels and that had been only a few weeks ago during yet another sleepless night when she'd had little more than channel-surfing and Walnut Whips to get her through the lonely hours until sunrise.

Relieved she now had a topic to grill them about, Beatrice asked all about the salon and what it was like being a local celebrity and the talk flowed. Mrs Mair reappeared to take the women's orders and soon all three were sipping ginger beer and the atmosphere in the restaurant warmed considerably, in spite of the rain falling outside.

The easy chatter and smiling made-up faces of her new friends reminded her just how much she had been starved of company recently. Her hands shook a little with the novelty of spending time with other women, a sensation that felt like stress and elation all at once. The strange excitement made her worry she was being too effusive and the women might think her a little odd, and her nerves loosened her tongue and made her unguarded.

The food arrived just as Beatrice was in full flow commenting on the state of the nicotine-stained bar ceiling. 'How long is it since the smoking ban? A decade? Longer than that? Are these landlords just lazy, or hopeless, or what? Give me *an hour, a paint roller, and a tray of white emulsion and I'd have it sparkling.*'

Atholl Fergusson settled the plate in front of her with a pointedly steely silence which sent her sinking into the padded bench. After he'd left, she explained how she had got off on altogether the wrong foot with Atholl and now she couldn't seem to stop annoying him.

'He looks like the broody type, love. I wouldn't worry,' Cheryl soothed.

The three looked down at their steaming plates simultaneously. 'Oh,' exclaimed Jillian, prodding the food with her fork. 'Eee, I knew it was pub grub, but I was expecting something a bit...'

'Fancier?' Beatrice said, looking at the sad oven chips and slim piece of battered cod, obviously the frozen variety and not the bubbly-battered fresh from the sea type that Scotland was supposedly famous for. The shrivelled peas, limp lettuce and dry lemon wedge did little to make the meal more appetising. 'Oh well, dig in,' Beatrice said with a shrug. 'It might taste better than it looks, and I don't want to complain, again.'

As the women ate, without much enthusiasm, Beatrice filled them in on what Seth had told her about poor heartbroken Gene and his runaway wife, the one-time resident gourmet, immediately feeling guilty for sharing gossiped details of someone's private life, but anything was better than talking about herself.

Seth had by now settled himself at the bar and was chatting with the beautiful woman with the laptop. Atholl was topping up her coffee mug. So he *can* be friendly, Beatrice thought. Maybe he reserved the smiles for his favourite customers.

Beatrice tried to focus on her dinner companions and her uninspiring meal again, but she couldn't help getting distracted when Atholl's face broke into a broad grin as he greeted the bar room's newest occupant.

A man in a white coat and hat had struggled inside carrying a polystyrene tray of ice liberally topped with coral-pink crustaceans and gleaming steely blue and pearl white shells. Beatrice caught the smell of the sea as the man followed Atholl into the kitchen and she heard Atholl calling Gene's name.

'If I'd known they were expecting a delivery of fresh seafood, I'd have held off ordering,' Cheryl said, following Beatrice's gaze.

'Something tells me that's not on the menu,' Jillian added, pointing at the blackboard above the booth emblazoned with the chalky words, 'No Specials Today', which she read aloud.

Seth, who seemed to have supernaturally good hearing, caught the exchange and after checking that Atholl and Mrs Mair were in the kitchens, called over the heads of the other diners. 'Nor any other day, either, more's the pity. Not so long ago the Princess was legendary along this coast for its Cullen Skink and its mussels in garlic cream. Legendary!' He lowered his voice to add, 'Us locals know to order Mrs Mair's homemade Scotch broth followed by the shortbread wi' a wee nip for pudding.'

The men sitting around the bar all agreed in a rumble of *ayes* and *he's no' wrong*s and Beatrice realised every one of them had a bowl of broth in front of them. Seth bit the stem of his pipe to punctuate his point and lowered himself from the stool, readying himself for another rainy smoke outdoors.

The pretty woman at the bar beside him raised her head from her paperwork and looked as though she were about to speak when sudden cries from the back room stalled everyone in their tracks.

'I willnae have you interfering in my business, Atholl. You cannae fix *everything* ye ken!' Gene loped into the bar room swinging a waxed jacket over his shoulders. 'I'm sorry you've had a wasted journey, Patrick.' This was addressed to the bemused fishmonger who followed behind him, still carrying his box, with Atholl at his heels. 'We won't be taking in any seafood when there's naebody to cook it!' The bar door swung as Gene slipped out into the street.

Suddenly everyone in the restaurant became utterly absorbed in draining their drinks as Atholl surveyed the room through narrowed eyes – everyone excepting the table of Sussex crafters who all loudly clucked their disapproval at the disruption to their evening.

The pretty red-head stood up as though she were going to make after Gene, but decided against it, and sat down again.

Beatrice watched on as Atholl collected himself and apologised to the fishmonger, helping him out the door with his catch. 'He'll come round one of these days, just not today,' Atholl said, his voice thin and weary.

The altercation had stripped away all the atmosphere in the restaurant and Beatrice found herself gathering her book and saying goodbye to Cheryl and Jillian. Seth was still outside with his pipe, she supposed, and Atholl was clattering glasses behind the bar with his back turned to the room. The woman at the bar smiled a quiet goodnight too as Beatrice padded away.

She wouldn't be seeing any of them again, what did it matter if she headed to bed early, or if these near strangers thought her oddly antisocial? She wasn't here to make friends. She was only an accidental holidaymaker and tomorrow's departure would put that right again, and yet it had been good to talk and laugh and remember that the world was, if nothing else, interesting.

Chapter Five

Three a.m., up in the air

Even though she was aware it was only a dream and that it would hurt all the more when she awoke, Beatrice refused to allow her waking consciousness to rouse her fully.

She let herself luxuriate in the lovely delusion a little longer, running her hands over her great round belly, spreading her fingers over the warm bump, solid and soft at the same time, muscle spread thin, flesh taut like a drum, and inside, the vital warmth of the little curled thing, heartbeat resounding, sharing blood through paper-thin skin.

But it didn't last. Beatrice felt the dream slipping away, the night encroaching, and the heavy realisation that her hands were clamped across her flat stomach.

She hadn't dreamt like this before and cursed her brain for conjuring up such realistic feelings of fullness and contentment. She reached for Richard on his side of the bed and finding nobody there, curled reflexively onto her side, already crying, and slowly becoming aware of where she was.

The darkness in the room was cut through with silver moonlight below her. *Below* her? Springing up in bed, her head met with the velvety material of the canopy that hung between her and the ceiling. Of course, it was all coming back to her, how she'd fought with the red-haired innkeeper so she could sleep here, just to spite his smiling eyes. Just to spite herself.

Swiping at her tears with her pyjama sleeve she cursed the new irate, awkward streak she'd been lumbered with lately; it was apparently not something she could do anything about. It seemed bound to her like a suit of armour, and yet it offered little in the way of protection and she seemed only to wound herself when she lashed out from under it.

She'd worn the armour ever since the night Rich had left her. Late coming home from work, he'd eventually called to say he'd checked into a hotel and that he was sorry, he couldn't do this any longer and that she had to face her feelings and get help. He'd cried uncontrollably and sounded truly unhappy. Beatrice had found, after begging and bargaining until all her pride was gone, that he was resolute in spite of the tears.

She peered over the side of the bed only to be hit by the full realisation that she was up in the air, in the dead of night, in the middle of nowhere, curiously precarious.

She'd been so tired as she'd hauled herself up the creaking ladder into bed after dinner and all the effort of being cheerful and chatty that she had forgotten to draw the curtains in the low windows. Now the moonlight was spilling across the dark, polished floorboards.

What a ridiculous room. Why would anyone choose to sleep here? Unless they were trying to spite a smirking, eagle-eyed Scotsman who found *her* ridiculous. She wouldn't admit to herself that the bed was comfortable and warm like a nest, or that the moonlight carried with it the rippling effect of the water in the bay beyond her window and spread a kind of shimmering, silver magic over everything it touched in the princess room. No, she wouldn't let herself be charmed by the outlandish room she'd insisted on taking just to rile and punish haughty Atholl Fergusson.

Atholl must have some kind of sixth sense which meant he could see her armour. He had instinctively detected her prickliness and for some reason he wanted to tease and test it, to feel out its boundaries. Not fair, and not kind, thought Beatrice with a sniff. Well, she resolved, she'd made her towering bed and she'd just have to lie in it a bit longer. She'd be out of here soon.

Over by the door stood her suitcase. There were chocolate biscuits in there if she dared risk the perilous descent to get them.

'As if I haven't had enough of men interfering and cajoling. Face your feelings,' she harrumphed as she made her way down the ladder slowly in the half light. 'Face my bloody feelings. I'm going to *eat* my feelings, thank you very much, Richard Halliday.'

Huffing a deep sigh as she padded across the floor and unzipped her carefully repacked case, her mind drifted back and forth between the ache of being forced to think about Richard's sudden, uncharacteristic abandonment of their ten-year marriage and the wave of irritation that thinking about Atholl Fergusson's antagonism brought on.

She pulled the biscuits from the suitcase, taking them over to the moonlit window before sitting cross-legged on the floor and tearing the packaging open. It was far easier to think of Atholl than Richard, so she did, and her annoyance grew. She absently snapped a biscuit in two and took an angry bite.

Seriously, who would think a Princess and the Pea themed room was a good idea? It was a stupid story anyway. The spoiled prince of a faraway kingdom had his pick of beautiful women, but his family were so worried none of them were suitably genteel enough for him, they devised a test to see just how much discomfort one woman could put up with. The queen (because there was always a meddling parent, wasn't there?) put a pea under the prospective princess's piled mattresses. Presumably it was one of those big, dry, wrinkly ones that English grannies used to keep in jars and never eat and not a fresh one or it would have been a flat green splat by morning. When the poor woman awoke she was stiff, bruised and unhappy, far from home, knowing something just wasn't right, but unsure exactly what. The princess's universe was thrown off kilter by something as tiny as a pea and that was all the proof the stupid prince needed that she was the woman for him.

Beatrice sighed, watching the waves from her window which were now right up against the sea wall, thinking how her own world had been turned on its head by a thing as tiny as a pea, only her Happy Ever After wouldn't be waiting for her when the morning came.

In fact, nothing happy remained in her life, apart from Angela, Vic and her little niece, and thank goodness for them. She'd have been lost without them when it happened back in March. Her eyes drifted out to the dark horizon as the memories dragged her back to the spring.

Everything had been fine that morning. Rich had gone to work and Beatrice got on with her usual morning routine, only slower because she had been so sleepy lately. She had searched the arts jobs pages, even though she knew that at twelve weeks pregnant her chances of being offered a job at any point that year – maybe even for a year and a half – were practically non-existent.

In the afternoon Rich had picked her up and they'd gone to the hospital. Already this felt like a familiar routine, since they'd visited for an unscheduled ultrasound weeks before when Beatrice had seen a spot of red when she went to the loo and her heart had sunk. But all had been well. The sonographer had showed them a jump-jiving heart and they'd heard a thin beat over the hospital noises and collapsed into each other's arms in relief. The sonographer printed out the scan image for them to keep, a little white peanut wriggling in the dark, and Rich had handed over his mobile and asked the sonographer to take a picture of them, Beatrice's gelled-up belly on show and all.

Beatrice loved the picture, loved how it captured Rich's toothy smile and bright, wide eyes, his arm clasped around her shoulder as she lay on crinkly paper on the big trolley, and there by her side the sonogram monitor with their peanut frozen in that moment, Beatrice's eyes fixed upon it.

The nurse had told her to take it easy and let them know if there was any more blood, which there hadn't been, and so the routine twelve-week scan had rolled around; the day they'd find out if they were having a boy or a girl. Richard whistled all the while he was driving.

They had been disappointed to find it was a different sonographer this time, less smiling and, they suspected, less likely to help them pose for a picture with Beatrice's small bump on show. Rich had chattered and joked and said something about a daughter wrapping him around her little finger, but Beatrice couldn't quite hear over a sudden cacophony of panic and dizziness that she didn't like to mention to anyone.

Looking back, Beatrice realised she had known what was coming, but the blankness on the screen and the silence where there should have been a heartbeat still hit her like a bomb blast. The sonographer had cried too.

The next day after the horror of the anaesthetic and the awful, empty awakening with the cannula in her hand and her heart cut open, she cried into the hospital pillow, gripping it until the joints in her fingers ached. She heard the doctor tell her in cool tones that 'it' hadn't grown for a week or so and there was no way she could have known, and that he was very sorry, and Beatrice had curled up on her side again while the other women in the ward watched her from their beds and she screamed out for her mum. One of the nurses pulled a blanket over her and rubbed her back and offered in a kind voice to phone her mum for her, and Beatrice couldn't even breathe through the heaving sobs to let her know that her mum was gone too.

Staring out at the rain hitting the motorway tarmac on the way home she told Rich she thought maybe she could remember the moment, a week or two before when she'd been lying on the sofa napping and felt the strangest sensation of movement and a sudden, gentle falling away, but then there had been nothing and she had put it down to her imagination or the possibility that she had felt the first kick.

Rich held the wheel tightly as she told him that the whole horrible hospital procedure now felt somehow like a theft, and that if she could, she would have parcelled up all their hopes and dreams and love in crisp brown paper like the precious bundle it was and kept it close forever. But they had left the hospital with nothing.

After that she had stopped talking about it, and Rich, his face grave and set like a white mask that Beatrice couldn't bear to look at, had let her, and she hadn't uttered a word about their little lost son ever since. In fact, she had found there was very little else to say about anything. Their little sticking plaster was torn away leaving them untethered, slowly drifting apart again.

Now Beatrice made her way back up the ladder in the dawning light, drawing the bed curtains closed around her and letting herself sink into the pile of mattresses where she wept silently until sleep came again.

Outside in the bay and on the hazy horizon, the fishermen cast nets and pots over the sides of bobbing boats. The sea had settled into its gentle summer flux once more and Port Willow awakened to a calm morning after the storms.

Chapter Six

Directions to the Coral Beach

'Excuse me, what's this?' Beatrice asked, suspiciously eyeing the speckled brown discs.

She'd emerged from the princess room tired-eyed and yawning and surprised herself by making it to the breakfast room with ten minutes to spare before service ended for the morning. The unfortunate Gene Fergusson, wearing chefs' whites, big floppy hat and all, had just set her plate before her on the white linen tablecloth.

'*That* is the full Scottish. Whit ye ordered.'

He'd presented her plate with a little flourish of the white cloth in his free hand. How different to the ineffectual, flustering man she'd met yesterday. He was clearly in his element making breakfasts. Presumably his runaway wife hadn't been responsible for the morning food service with him, or doubtless he'd be unable to look at a frying pan ever again.

Beatrice worried momentarily she was about to spoil his composure. 'No, I mean these things?' She nudged the unidentified food items with her fork, separating them from the crisp onion hash and curiously square slices of sausage on her plate.

'That's yur haggis.'

'Oh! Right.'

'Something wrong?'

'Nope! Nothing wrong. I love a bit of haggis at...' she peered at her watch, 'five past eight in the morning.'

Gene chose to be happy with this reply and strolled back to the kitchen, whistling.

The breakfast room windows opened onto the inn's back garden enclosed by a low stone wall where red crocosmia heads bobbed in the light breeze, scattering the last of the night's raindrops.

Beatrice gazed out at the dewy, bright morning. She had never been one for breakfast. Even when she'd left home at seven o'clock every morning to get to the Arts Hub across the country in Oxford she had only needed a coffee or three to get her through until lunch but today the plateful in front of her looked so delicious – excepting the haggis – she determined to make a valiant effort with the streaky bacon and buttery field mushrooms.

Gene was back again, pouring her coffee and setting down a rack of hot granary toast, which she set upon immediately with the salty Scottish butter.

'I'm not normally a breakfast person,' she remarked to the retreating cook between mouthfuls, but he didn't seem to hear her, so she looked around at the other diners, all preparing to leave for a day of crafting and summer sightseeing, but there was no sign of Cheryl and Jillian. Beatrice registered a little pang of disappointment before dismissing it as silly. She was, after all, leaving in a few moments. They'd likely never think of her again.

Swirling her spoon in the cup she ran through the journey she would be embarking on today, a reverse of the humid, cramped, seemingly never-ending trek of yesterday beneath grey English clouds and Scotland's rain-soaked rails.

A splash of coffee spilled in her saucer and the question arose again in her mind, the inevitable, awful question she had been putting off answering for weeks. What exactly was she going to do now?

Slicing into a juicy grilled tomato, rich with the heady scent of the summer greenhouse, she tried to think of the future but found it impossible to picture. There seemed to be very few options open to her. Instead a series of 'if onlys' queued up to darken her mood. If only she had a job to go home to. If only she hadn't hired Helen Smethwick. If only she'd listened to Rich's warning that her small area of expertise in the arts sector – the place where creativity met with community and charity – was desperately under pressure and would soon collapse in on itself with the weight of underfunding and corporate greed. But she had pressed on, telling him the Arts Hub was her home and she couldn't imagine working anywhere else.

She sighed, making a start on the delicious triangles of golden fried bread, so greasy and so satisfying as she mopped up the runny yolks of the fried eggs.

She'd thrived on the work. Every week day, and plenty of Saturdays too, for the last nineteen years, there she'd been, at her desk, delegating tasks, calling the meetings, running the joint.

It had started as a graduate job, and it had all felt so easy, walking straight out of uni and into a junior role. Her first task had been helping an alms houses charity write a funding bid so they could run a local food festival in their grounds. Her bosses had been so pleased when she actually won the money and the festival had gone ahead she had been promoted by the end of the year and had bought her first car to celebrate; a second hand, shiny red Fiat, her pride and joy.

Success had come easily, at first. Then, after a couple of years and an ever increasing workload, there was a sudden restructure and she found herself at the head of the organisation: manager of the Oxfordshire Arts Hub, bringing communities and arts practitioners together to put on cool, worthy and creative community events.

Looking back, the Hub had been visionary, inclusive, and wonderful. Back then, the lottery money and the government initiatives felt never-ending and Beatrice had revelled in her team's successes. They had been a happy bunch. Barely a weekend went by when they weren't photographed grinning for the local papers opening fetes, helping out at coconut shies and coffee mornings, or dressed up in swanky clothes for community theatre premieres or down at the mall for the opening of artisan pop-up shops – all very much unpaid extras they did for the love of it. They'd supported countless projects, social enterprises and start-ups and Beatrice had managed the whole show, calm and competent, thriving on the buzzing energy of the creative networks around her. It had been great for a long time – until it suddenly wasn't.

The last thing she'd done in her role was hire Helen Smethwick, her new assistant with HR responsibilities. Her arrival was long overdue; they'd been running on a skeleton staff and goodwill for years. Beatrice hadn't realised Helen was married to the new head honcho at the council and he had new ideas for money-saving strategies which Helen had every intention of helping him see through, advising him from the inside on what – or *who* – could go.

Six weeks after Helen's arrival the council announced the cuts. The Hub was to lose half its office space and all senior staff were invited to apply for voluntary redundancy. The trouble was, Beatrice was the oldest and longest serving person there. When the cuts came in, her nineteen years of dedication and hard work were rewarded with a long tussle to keep her job, a month's notice and a four grand payoff last September.

Helen Smethwick had Beatrice's job now and as far as she could tell from the social media campaigns it was business as usual, only money was tighter and funding harder to come by than ever before. Nothing about it felt fair, but at least the younger staff, people she considered friends, even if their texts were now few and far between, had been protected. That had been some comfort to Beatrice.

Beatrice wasn't aware she was gulping her coffee and devouring her plateful at an unusually fast pace for her. She was licking her lips and buttering another slice of toast and wolfing the smoky, salty bacon and the herby, savoury sausages, loving every bite, but in her heart she was back at the house she had shared with Rich for so long. She was thinking about the recent endless afternoons at home when there were no job interviews and no emails, no matter how many times she clicked 'refresh', and there wasn't much to do but potter around the house. All her friends were at work at the Hub and they were unlikely to call during the day – at least none of them had yet. So she'd read anything and everything until it was time to cook Rich's dinner.

It was during these lonely afternoons she wished she had a dog. Dog owners were never stuck for something to do. But Rich was afraid of dogs. He always said he was allergic to them but she knew he was terrified of even the tiniest Chihuahua. She thought for a second that even though she was at The Princess and the Pea Inn in the back of bloody beyond and the Wi-Fi was atrocious, she might have another coffee and try scrolling through slowly buffering pictures of abandoned puppies on the Warwick shelter's website, something that had become a daily habit back at home lately, but she gave up the idea when she saw the greyed-out bars on her phone.

Every one of those poor mutts had a story sadder than the next. It was the old ones she felt sorriest for, those that were greying and leggy with lumpy hips and slow saunters; the kind of big old dog that still ate its way through a fortune in food and was ancient enough to rack up the vet's bills. Nobody wanted a dog like that, except maybe Beatrice.

She was sighing and setting down her cutlery on her plate when Gene appeared again.

'Are you finished there?'

She looked down at her plate, surprised to find that, yes, she was finished, and every tasty morsel was gone, apart from the haggis which Gene was peering at with a forlorn expression which Beatrice chose to ignore.

'Yes, thanks. Do you know when the first train leaves this morning?'

Beatrice didn't have high hopes for an early start; the station had one platform and one rail which carried the single carriage train along the cliffs and off to Fort William, where she'd no doubt have another long wait for a train to Glasgow or Edinburgh before finally finding a train to Warwickshire.

'You don't like haggis, then?'

'Well, no, but everything else was delicious, thank you.'

Gene swooped away to the kitchen with the plate, calling for Echo, who presumably was going to be the recipient of the rejected haggis.

'Oh come off it, you can't be put out by someone not fancying a mouthful of unidentifiable brown offal first thing in the morning,' she muttered, hearing the sound of a plate being scraped.

She glanced around. The breakfast room had emptied at some point, Beatrice wasn't sure when. Had she been lost in thought again? That happened a lot recently too, and she didn't like it.

'Eugene? Mr Fergusson? You didn't answer me about the trains?' Beatrice called out, peering at the swinging kitchen door. No reply came, but Echo bounded into the room and pushed his way into the kitchen for his treat.

'Well, that's not very hygienic, is it? Dogs in the hotel kitchen,' she muttered again as she stood and reached for the handle of her suitcase.

'You wanted to know when the train leaves this morning?' came a deep voice from the breakfast room doorway. Beatrice cursed her stomach for flipping at the sound. This wasn't dopey Gene, but Atholl.

Taking a deep breath, she found she was bracing herself for the sight of him. And it was just as well she had. There he stood, hair towel-dried and fresh from the shower, the deep red of his curls even darker now, his skin pale and cheeks ruddy, and wearing a thin bottle green jersey over a checked brown shirt and soft-looking summer cords with the chunky tan boots she'd seen him in yesterday.

'That's right,' she raised her jaw as she answered him, meeting his blue eyes without flinching. In spite of his smiling eyes, his pale pink lips were set straight. *He really is so vexing*, thought Beatrice.

'It doesnae.'

'I'm sorry, what?'

'It *doesn't* leave this morning, or any other time today. It's Sunday.'

Gene suddenly swung through the kitchen door and greeted his brother with a firm pat on his arm before setting about clearing the other tables.

'*And?*' said Beatrice.

It was Gene who answered her. 'My mother used to say if God wanted folk to gad aboot on the Lord's day he'd never have allowed Sunday matinee movies on the telly.'

Beatrice swallowed, letting her eyelids close, ignoring this little insight into the Fergusson matriarch who sounded as barking as Gene and as irritating as Atholl. 'So I'm stuck here?'

'Train at nine the morra,' Gene added matter-of-factly, whipping the white linen cloths from the cleared tables.

Beatrice looked down at her repacked suitcase by her side. She'd made up her mind to go and now she was thwarted. She didn't know what felt worse: the sense of being trapped in an empty home in Warwick, fretting and fed up, longing for an escape of any kind, or being stuck here after a failed attempt at escape with the Highland cast of *Fawlty Towers*.

'Is it your room that's bothering ye?' Atholl pitched in calmly, now leaning on the doorframe with Echo sitting obediently at his feet. 'I've already asked Mrs Mair if she'll give it a thorough going over today since ye were so displeased wi' the inn. And besides, you've got yur willow-weaving classes startin' the day. You'll no' want to miss them.'

'No, no, I already said, what with the mix up and everything, I'd really rather not do any class at all. I wasn't even *that* keen on the Gaelic lessons, if I'm honest, and willow-weaving seems…'

'Whit?' Atholl probed, sharply.

Too quiet, she thought. Willow-weaving seemed too quiet and too still, and she didn't want time for introspection. What she wanted was to blast all thoughts out of her head. Perhaps that was why she'd booked this wretched trip in the first place. Learning Gaelic in a classroom full of beginners might have been lively and challenging and all those long vowels, rolled r's and 'lochs' with guttural, curling '*och*' sounds would have filled her mouth and her head and chased away some of the fidgeting, unsettled feelings she couldn't seem to switch off these days. But willow-weaving? Faffing about with bits of twig didn't sound engrossing or diverting at all.

'I'll just stay here in the village today, if that's all right? Give the class a miss.'

'Well there's no shops open,' said Atholl. 'And Reverend Park's kirk service isnae 'til ten, so you'll have a quiet day ahead. Besides yur teacher will be waiting for you, and there's no phone at the But n' Ben school to ring them.'

'Surely they won't mind one absentee?' Beatrice found herself brushing invisible toast crumbs from her navy palazzo trousers and striped Breton top. She'd dressed for comfort and for a long train journey home, wondering all the while what she'd find when she got there.

Atholl watched her, his eyes narrowing and the bright light in them dying. 'It's only yourself that's booked in. It's a one to one class and they'll be waiting for ye. If you don't get walking now, you'll be late.'

'That's ridiculous. No phones?'

'No signal, even if there was a phone. The But 'n' Ben's a fair way doon the headland.'

Beatrice steeled herself with a deep breath. 'Why must everything be so complicated here? I suppose I'll just have to walk doon, I mean, walk *down*! I'll cancel the classes and ask the teacher for my refund, throw myself on their mercy! I think mine is a pretty reasonable request, don't you?' She flashed Atholl a wry smile which he didn't return. 'Just point me in the right direction, please. Can I leave my case here? I'll be back within the hour and I'll have some tea in my room or something.'

Atholl shrugged his shoulders. 'Eugene, can you give Beatrice directions to the But 'n' Ben, please? She'll want to see the headland and the top of Rother Path on the way.'

Gene met his brother's eyes before shrugging and walking Beatrice through the inn to the door. When they were outside and breathing clean, salty sea air, Gene raised a bony finger and pointed Beatrice's way along the street.

Everything looked so different this morning – blue instead of grey in the sky, sandy dust drying on the road instead of the petrichor of yesterday's rain, and tourists exploring the freshly exposed shore as the tide retreated.

'You'll walk all the way along the front, past the chippy and up by the school, follow the pavement and keep climbing the hill 'til you're out of breath. Stop at the stile in the fence and climb over intae the field. Follow the clearing through the corn 'til you come to the muddy path.'

'How do you know it'll be muddy?'

Gene snorted his amusement and carried on. 'Keep to the edge o' the path all the way doon tae the rocks, then ye need to get on your hands and knees and climb doon until ye see the coral. The But 'n' Ben's up above it.'

'The coral?'

'The coral beach?' He threw her an uncomplimentary look. 'It's famous, I'm sure of it. Cannae mistake it, it's like nae other along this stretch o' coast. But mind tae keep tae the rocks.'

Beatrice was shaking her head, astonished. 'OK.' She'd never heard such odd directions.

'If ye get lost, call for Echo; he'll come and find ye.'

'Echo?'

'The inn dug?'

'I know who he is. Is he the fourth emergency service round here, then?'

'He's got better hearing than any man and he'll come runnin'.'

With that Gene swooped back inside the inn, leaving Beatrice free to laugh. For the first time in a long time, she *really* laughed and the convulsive motion loosened her knotted shoulders. This was it. It was happening. She had known her laughter would come back to her one day. She laughed all the way along the road by the sea wall, glancing at stranded boats on the sand and as she walked on past rows of parked cars and the tiny picturesque terraced cottages, she couldn't stop. Gradually, she felt her throat tighten and her eyes stinging. She was laughing, at last, but crying with relief and sadness at the same time.

How could a woman get herself into such a state? All alone in a strange village with tears on her cheeks, laughing like the gulls on the lampposts while shattering deep sobs forced their way through her throat. She reached for the little red post box on the sea wall to steady herself. A few breaths and she'd be fine, she reassured herself. She'd grown used to giving herself comfort. And besides, she had come this far.

On Friday hadn't she been stuck at home, guzzling wine in her pyjamas? She'd planned a solo trip and actually undertaken it, not bottling it at the train station, but really, actually making her way to another country. And here she was about to ask for her money back from a teacher she'd never even met. Money she'd rather put to better use doing something else, but what exactly that might be, she didn't know. Yes, this was really something. A sneaking sense of pride warmed her. Even if she was doing her damnedest to get away from this peculiar place, she had at least started out on an adventure, and she'd let herself think about some really difficult things, and she'd interacted with a bunch of strangers, and she'd laughed too. Yes, that was something.

'You'll be fine, Bea,' she said aloud, checking with a glance behind her that nobody was in earshot.

Somehow, out here under the morning sun and thinning watery clouds she believed it a little better than she had at home in Warwick.

Walking on along the street, wiping her tears with a tissue and blowing her nose, she passed the few closed-up shops and the shuttered ice-cream kiosk. The church bells rang behind her but she didn't turn around.

'Keep climbing the hill 'til you're out of breath,' Gene Fergusson had said. And so she faced the steep pavement ahead, took one long stride, then another, and another, her eyes fixed dead ahead and the sun on her face.

Chapter Seven

The Coral Beach

The path was indeed muddy, but she had come this far in the increasingly close morning air and her black pumps were now horribly mucky. Beatrice hadn't bargained on the midges that clustered above the mud as she walked, crablike, along the thin grassy verge that lined the path. They stuck to her lip balm and made her head itch, but after a few moments of sideways walking she came to the top of the hill and reached the rocks Gene had mentioned and suddenly the midges cleared.

Down below her over the rocky outcrop gleamed the slightest hint of sunlight on turquoise blue sea. How on earth could a craft school exist down at the bottom of this boulder-strewn route? It was barely a path at all, just a slight clearing through the gorse, grass and jutting lichen-speckled rock that led down towards the sound of gentle waves.

Gene was right, she had to use her hands and knees, as well as her bottom and feet, to lower herself down some of the steeper rock steps. Butterflies and moths rose up from the long grass at the sides of the trail. Eventually, after she felt she'd climbed downhill at least ten metres, she found the view opening out before her, and the sight made her pause. She might well be running late for class but this view asked to be stared at from the very conveniently placed rocky platform, flat like a table top. She sat for a moment.

A deserted beach of pure white, scattered with golden seaweed and shaped like a crescent moon lay inside a bay of sun-bleached rocks down below her. The water that lapped the shore was shallow and a wonderful tropical blue. She had never seen such an enticing bay and she'd swum in the Mediterranean umpteen times with Rich. On the low headland up above the little white beach were steeply sloping meadows with, at one corner, a wild-looking garden with colourful flowers. Inside the garden's low stone walls stood a little whitewashed cottage with a silvery thatched roof. She knew it must be the But and Ben. There were no other buildings nearby to confuse it with. There were no signs of life though, and the cottage's low door was closed.

Beatrice was loathe to leave her spot on the rock with its gentle sea breeze, and she was hot after the long scramble, so she stretched her legs out in front of her, staring at the bay and the grey mountains enclosing it in a broken circle. The gap between the band of mountains far in the distance opened up into an endless stretch of calm blue sea. The impression that the whole vista gave her was of being held in the palm of a hand.

In and out went the waves and in and out flowed Beatrice's breath.

'I've got time for a paddle,' she told herself, deciding to clamber over the last few feet of rocks and down onto the beach, where she kicked her shoes off and immediately regretted it.

'*Oww!*'

The white coral shards that made up the beach were razor-like in their sharpness. She picked her way gingerly to the water's edge, letting the cool water soothe her skin. 'In for a penny,' she told herself as she rolled her trouser legs up into shorts so she could have a proper dip.

The quiet exhilaration of the cold water on her skin was broken by the buzz from her phone. 'No way? *A signal!*'

Warmth flooded her chest. It would be Angela checking on her. She could snap pictures of the beautiful bay and of her feet under clear, cool water and maybe her sister would be convinced that she was doing all right at last. It wouldn't be totally accurate, but it would, at least, be comforting for her. She peered at the screen, but the message wasn't from Angela at all. It was from Rich.

> The house is sold, exchanging in a fortnight so you'll get your half soon. You'll need to clear your things, sorry. Hope you're OK. You're not answering your phone. I'm sending a van to collect my gym stuff on Tuesday. I gave them my key in case you're busy. Hope it's not too upsetting for you, love Richard x

She'd known this was coming; the house had been on the market since soon after Rich left, his idea, wanting to help her 'move on' quickly, but nothing could have prepared her for the shock of it happening so suddenly.

The tingling cold started at her scalp and spread its strange grip down over her face and shoulders. Was she going to faint? She wasn't holding her phone any longer but couldn't say for sure where it was. Looking around, she tried to stay upright as she staggered out the water, the coral cutting into her feet with each unsteady step.

The drumming of her heartbeat in her ears and the awful spinning seemed suddenly to pause when she found herself faced with a pair of round, frightened eyes fixed upon her.

There on the shoreline stood a tiny calf, frozen to its spot, red in colour and as beautiful and doe-eyed as a cartoon animal. The calf shook its tagged ears but stood stock still.

Shaking her head to clear it, Beatrice focused on the pretty creature. 'How on earth did you get down here?'

She scanned the hills above the But and Ben, spotting what looked like a feeding trough in the corner of a hoof-trodden meadow and no one around to help her fix this. How was she going to return this baby to its enclosure? She looked the calf over. Even if it was only small, it was still an actual real life cow, stocky and probably weighing as much as she did herself. Looking around for a stick she wondered if she could drive it back up onto the hill behind the cottages. How hard could it be?

Her eye settled upon a long stalk of sea kelp. '*Ouch, ouch, Oww.*' The coral cut at her soles as she made her way towards it. Once it was in her hand, she pulled her shoes back onto her wet and aching feet and realised the kelp was floppy and probably not up to the job of steering the beast away from the dangerous water.

When would the tide come in? She had no idea, but judging from the pattern of seaweed on the highest reaches of the coral beach the water would come in right up to the rocks.

'Can cows even swim?' she asked the calf.

It blinked.

'All right then. Come on.' She motioned using her flopping kelp for the calf to turn back along the beach towards a path that seemed to lead up to the But and Ben. But the baby wouldn't budge. So she tucked the kelp under her arm and clapped her hands, softly at first, and then, getting no reaction, more loudly.

'*Yah!*' she called, feeling every inch the cow wrangler, when suddenly the movement began. The baby startled and dashed past her in the direction Beatrice had clambered down the rocks.

'No, no, wrong way, little one!'

Beatrice watched in horrified confusion as the calf bounded and slipped its way up through the rocks. What the hell was she supposed to do now? Call the RSPCA and report a rock-climbing cow? There was nothing for it but to follow the animal, all thoughts of Rich's message, her lost phone, and of the teacher waiting for her in the cottage school forgotten.

That's when she heard the great howling cry behind her, accompanied by snorting and the crunching clip-clop of kicked and scuffed coral and pebbles under hooves.

'*Oh, shit.*'

A great horned bull was making its way towards her in pursuit of the calf, and following behind him, crossing the beach at an alarming pace, were at least twenty heifers of different sizes and colours and even more calves behind them, all heading directly for her.

'A stampede! I've caused a bloody cattle stampede!'

The runaway calf that started this whole thing was nowhere to be seen, but only as she glanced around looking for it did she notice for the first time that between the boulders on the path that she herself had scrambled down moments ago there were hoof prints squashed into the mud and grass. The animals must pass this way often.

The bull keened a deep sound, calling the others on. Beatrice was trapped between the panicked herd, the rocks and the sea, and her heart was beginning to pound wildly.

Another ridiculous situation to get herself into. How did she do it?

The cows at the back of the group had split away and were trying to overtake the rest by splashing through the water to get to the front, cutting off Beatrice's escape route into the deeper water. There was one thing for it: she'd have to climb and she knew she had only a fraction of a second to get onto the steep rocks and out of the way of the heavy bodies which were now bumping into one another, jostling and shoving as they funnelled through the narrow gap that the calf had gone through.

Hauling herself from the knee-deep water onto a rock as though she were pulling herself from a swimming pool she managed to avoid the heavy clatter of the bull's feet, and as she flattened herself against the sheer rock face, he passed by, his wide haunch bumping her stomach as it squeezed through the gap in the rocks, knocking her breathless for a moment during which she watched the heifers stumble past two at a time, knowing that if one should slip it would push her from her perch on the rock.

The sound of their snorted breathing and distressed calling was startlingly loud. The calves at the back of the group struggled up the incline, and their wild-eyed mothers listened for their returning calls.

Beatrice's hand shook as she held the ridiculously limp sea kelp stalk above her head, ready to slap the behind of any cow that attempted to turn, stamp on her feet, or invade her little safe space. But something else had joined the fray, something sleek and black. It was moving between the herd, coming between her and the animals.

'*Echo*,' she whispered, afraid of startling the animals more, and the dog bounded up onto the rock and sat upright by her feet facing the cattle, his presence making them swerve a little away from her rocky perch, giving her room to breathe.

The reassurance that flooded her body as she slowly reached her free hand down to touch his warm head was like a shot of anaesthetic calming the stress cortisone and adrenalin coursing through her. 'Good boy, Echo,' she whispered again. The dog quickly licked her wrist before turning back to his task of keeping the crazy English lady safe.

Out of the cacophony of her heart's pounding and the herd's hollering, a man's voice rose commandingly loud, '*Geet up! Go oan!*'

As the last of the animals passed by her shaking body, she saw him standing on the coral. Atholl Fergusson.

Steeling herself not to cry with relief that the moment was over even though her shredded nerves willed her to sob, she wouldn't let *him* see her weakness. Anyway, he was shouting, red-faced and angry.

'What the hell do you think you're doing?'

'What am I doing? How was I supposed to know there'd be a herd of mad cows roaming the beach? They don't put that in the bloody brochures! *Come to the beautiful west Highland coast, get eaten by midges and crushed to death by free roaming cattle!*'

'This is their route between pastures on the hills. It's more their beach than any human's.'

'Well that's ridiculous!' Beatrice was stuck for words now, regretting having shouted yet again. She wasn't accustomed to angry exchanges and confrontation, in fact she'd do anything she could to avoid them usually, but this situation was very unusual indeed.

Her chest heaved as she became aware he was surveying her.

'Good God, would you look at the state of ye.'

Only then did she realise her trouser legs were still unevenly rolled up from paddling and her knees were grazed and bleeding from her hasty scramble onto the rocks, and she was becoming aware of the salt water sting searing through her wounds. It occurred to her that she was still holding the flaccid sea kelp, her only defence against twenty wild cattle on a seaside rampage. She threw it to her feet in disgust and embarrassment, her cheeks burning.

'I'll have tae lift ye down. May I?' He raised his arms, hands outstretched the way her mother had reached for her as a child when she needed rescuing from the top of the climbing frame in the park having been over ambitious and ended up stuck at the top and panic-stricken.

'I can manage, thank you.' Her reply came out louder and shakier than she would have wished, and she lowered herself onto her bottom and shuffled down over the edge of the rock, coming to stand in front of Atholl, ignoring the sea water filling her shoes again, a feeling of defiance flooding her.

'Come up to the cottage, you'll need tae be cleaned and bandaged.'

'I'm fine. You can go on your way,' she said, unconvincingly, as a trickle of blood made its way down her shin.

Atholl raised a challenging eyebrow. 'It'll take one minute. Besides, it's time for yur lesson anyway.'

She eyed the cottage wearily, and heaved a ragged sigh. There would most likely be a kettle in there and she could do with a cup of strong tea after what she'd just experienced. Her hands and her balance, she realised, were still unsteady. 'All right then.'

Atholl led the way over the coral, walking a few paces in front but occasionally turning his head back. Echo ran off along the beach and disappeared into the gorse. Atholl didn't seem to mind so she concluded he was a Littlest Hobo kind of dog, off having adventures and saving damsels in distress all day long with little supervision from his master.

The path leading up from the beach to the But and Ben was lined with sea holly, frothy camomile and a cloud of buzzing bees and hornets. The grasshoppers halted their clicking as Beatrice followed Atholl through the garden gate and in the low door of the cottage, surprised to see him walk straight inside without knocking.

'Is this the classroom?' she asked, casting her eye around the squat room, taking in the thatch and rafters only a foot or so above her head. There were a few rustic-looking cabinets, an unlit fireplace under a wide chimney, a long table with benches on either side, and very little else. 'Where's the teacher?'

Atholl stopped rummaging in the first aid kit to deliver a look that asked whether she was concussed as well as grazed. '*I* am the teacher. Surely you figured that out?'

The memory of Atholl scolding Beatrice this morning, telling her to hurry to class burned in her brain. He'd enjoyed withholding that little bit of information, payback for her criticising the inn and not wanting to take his willow-weaving classes or eat his brother's haggis, she supposed. Her anger would have burned all the harder had she not been exhausted from the stampede. She could have been killed, and all for his own sick satisfaction. She glowered at him in silence.

'May I?' Atholl came to kneel on the bare earth floor at her feet, raising his hand to her knee but not making contact.

'I can do it myself.'

'No, you drink this, to stop the shaking.' He pressed a small glass into her hand and the vapours coming off the peaty spirits told her this was whisky. She hated whisky but was surprised to find herself sipping as she watched Atholl wiping away the blood with clean hospital gauze.

'You haven't dipped that in whisky too, have you?'

'And waste my fifteen-year-old Dalmore?'

Her flesh stung as he did his work, as did her pride, and she found she was glad she'd made the effort to shave her legs and that Atholl was so absorbed in fixing plasters he didn't see her wincing and shuddering as the alcohol burned her throat.

'There, you'll live,' he said with a note of finality and a backwards step that made her dimly aware of how much she'd liked him so close to her, working in his quiet, capable, economical manner, his fingertips skimming over her skin every now and then. Close up, she'd noticed the dark freckles over his cheekbones and the deep red brown of his lashes, and she'd become aware for the first time of how well the dark green jumper and brown checks he wore complemented the ruddy chestnut of his hair.

'I'd better be going now then,' she said, collecting herself, trying to remember that she was angry with him.

'If ye wish. Start again tomorrow morning?'

Exasperated, she let her mouth gape and her eyes widen. 'Tomorrow? I'll be on my way back to Warwick tomorrow. In fact, that's what I came down to talk *to the teacher* about,' she said, pointedly. 'I wanted to ask about getting my money back. I don't want to fiddle about with sticks and twigs in this place, especially if I have to risk life and limb just to get to the classroom!'

She reached for the table top to steady herself under his unreadable gaze. Was he really angry with her after what had just happened? He looked paler than he did before and seemed to be biting hard upon the inside of his cheek, making his jaw work and flex and his lips bloom into an unconscious pout.

She reached her fingertips to her temples and rubbed away the headache that was coming. Was it the whisky bringing on the drowsiness, or was she going into shock, or was it the scent of warm lavender drifting in through the opened window, strong and dry?

'That "fiddling about with sticks and twigs" is my attempt at starting a willow-weaving business of my own.' He crumpled the wrappers from her sticking plasters into a soft fist before stuffing his hands into his trouser pockets and turning away from her, seemingly surveying the whitewashed wall.

Beatrice blinked at him in the dim light and he kept talking, low and slow.

'You've come all this way just to insult my inn rooms, fluster my brother and ask for your money back? You've barely seen the place.'

'What's there to see? Rain, midges, mad cattle charges. I just want to go...' She almost said 'home', but the word didn't come.

'Well, there's no refunds to be had. Go if you wish, but I've a bedroom and a classroom empty for more than a week now.'

Beatrice stood, feeling the big square dressings on both her kneecaps crinkle and pinch as her legs straightened. *Again* with the feeling ridiculous. Leaving her barely touched whisky on the table, she made for the door. 'I thought I needed a change of scene. I was wrong, OK?' It's something else I need, she thought, but what, she had no idea.

'Well you'll never find out what it is you're after if you keep running from pillar to post.' There was consternation written across his face.

Her neck stiffened. Could this guy read her mind, and what was it to him, anyway?

'You don't know the first thing about me,' she snapped, riled that he'd pinned her so accurately.

'I know you wanted to come here at *some* point. And maybe it's no' what ye expected, but if you let yourself enjoy it, ye might find you'd like to stay out your holiday wi' us, and ye might learn a few things too.'

'The last thing I need is another smart-mouthed man telling me what I need.' She fumbled with the latch on the low door and made sure not to bump her head on the frame as she flounced out.

Pulling the door closed behind her, she faced the wide circle of blue in the bay and inhaled the fresh, warm, salty air. But the buoying feelings of decisiveness, authority and self-righteousness she'd expected to come, didn't arrive. Instead, she felt a shrinking smallness, and then shame.

Why was she behaving like this? Who *was* she?

Inside the cottage, Atholl watched the door slam, shaking his head and instinctively raising Beatrice's glass to his lips, draining it dry and holding back the urge to throw the glass into the fire grate and watch it shatter.

As Beatrice slunk down the cottage garden path, defeated and embarrassed, she spotted a painted wooden sign to her left pointing along a wide, dry path between two grassy meadows alive with butterflies. 'To Port Willow' it read. She cursed Atholl Fergusson and the wicked sense of revenge that had made him urge his docile brother to send her down the rocky road, and she found herself cursing his handsome face and his haughty, straight-talking manner too.

How dare he antagonise her like this? When she'd been through so much recently? When she was so fragile and so alone? But, of course, he couldn't know. She had never told anyone about her lovely mother, her lost job and her precious baby boy. Sorrow had piled upon sorrow for months now and it all weighed invisibly on her shoulders, but she had no intention – or indeed any means – of starting to talk about it all now.

Walking at a pace along the path her heart thumped as she remembered what a fool she'd made of herself on the beach. 'Stick to the rocks,' Gene had told her. He must have known about the cows and even though his brother wanted him to send her on a fool's rock climb, Gene didn't want her flattened under-hoof. These Fergusson brothers would be the death of her. How she hated them and their ridiculous inn.

A sleek brown hare shot across the path a few paces ahead of her. Breaking her stride she tried to follow it with her eyes but found it was already hidden in the long meadow grass dotted here and there with bobbing blue cornflowers.

The moment allowed her a chance to stop and breathe.

Glancing back to the But and Ben behind her, she considered walking back in there and letting Atholl know how reckless he'd been, how dangerous his stupid ploy was, but instead of picturing herself spitting fire at a repentant Atholl Fergusson, she saw him kneeling at her feet cleaning up her grazed legs and was struck by the memory of his gentle touch. Her cheeks burned as she turned back for Port Willow, shouting into the still, warm air. 'Everything about this stupid Scottish trip was a mistake!'

The church spire of St Magnus' came into view in the distance, an easy walk now along the gently sloping meadow path. She set off once more planning to hide away all day and take the first train home tomorrow. Nobody need ever know about how she booked a spontaneous getaway to the Scottish Highlands at a moment's notice, just so she could escape the resounding emptiness of her life. One more day here and she'd be home to watch the men load the van with Rich's gym equipment, and to pack her own belongings into boxes, readying herself to hand over keys to her house's new occupants, and then – what? She had no idea.

Chapter Eight

A Lion and a Unicorn

'You down there, are you all right or am I calling the coastguard?'

Even through the fog of tears and the headache that crying her heart out always brought on, Beatrice registered how the harshness of the woman's words were softened by the trilling Highland accent.

'You're not dead, are you? I've no mind to be hauling a body up the sea wall today, I've got my fish supper to eat.'

Beatrice craned her neck and looked directly above her. Red hair tumbled over the Port Willow bay sea wall like Rapunzel, and a broad, kind smile greeted her. The sun shone behind the woman's head in a halo. It was the woman from the bar last night, the one Atholl had been so friendly with. Beatrice shielded her eyes and cleared her throat. 'I'll be all right, thanks. I'm fine.'

'Righty-o.' The woman pulled her head back over the wall and disappeared from view.

'Oh! She really has left.' Beatrice might have imagined that when someone happened upon a strange woman blubbing over an abandoned lobster pot against a sea wall at low tide they'd be a bit more insistent about helping out.

She wiped the tears away with her sleeves and pressed the heel of her hands into her tired eyes. Maybe if she sat still long enough the headache would eventually clear and she could drag herself off this beach and into the inn behind her where she could sleep away the rest of the day in peace.

The approaching footsteps over sand and shingle and someone coming to a stop a few feet away told her she'd have to pull herself together sooner than that.

'Here, I didn't know if you were a tea or a coffee girl, so I got one of each.'

The redhead had walked along the sea wall and down the steps to her rescue after all. Before Beatrice could say anything her companion was sitting beside her, mirroring Beatrice's position by resting her back against the wall.

'There's a coffee shop here?' Beatrice asked in surprise, reaching for a cup. 'I'm most definitely a coffee girl, if you don't mind. Thank you.'

The takeaway cup was handed over and Beatrice took a long, appreciative drink.

'There's a café in the back of the general store along the front. Haven't you been in yet?'

'Not yet,' she said with a sniff and knowing she wouldn't set foot in the place in the future either. 'This is just what I needed.'

'Nothing like a cuppa,' the woman smiled sagely, crossing her long legs at her ankle boots and looking out to sea.

There was kindness in that, Beatrice thought. When someone's been ugly-crying and has the blotchy red face and snotty nose to show for it, the nicest thing to do is sit close and avert your eyes.

'I'm Kitty,' the woman said to the blue sky.

'I'm Beatrice. I don't normally do this sort of thing.' Beatrice ran through the number of times she'd found herself doing *exactly* this sort of thing in recent months; crying in the supermarket aisles, in the queue at the bus stop, and that time she'd worried the dental hygienist by sobbing in the waiting room for no discernible reason.

'Everybody needs a good weep sometimes,' Kitty soothed. She let Beatrice drink her coffee and the pair watched a boat bobbing at the entrance to the bay as a young man threw a fishing line from its prow.

'Hungry?' Kitty asked.

'Famished, actually.' How strange, Beatrice thought, after Gene's big breakfast this morning. 'It must be the sea air.'

'Good, because I've got these and there's no way I'll manage them by myself.' Kitty unwrapped the paper parcel and the smell of fish and hot vinegar swirled around them.

'Now *that* is what I call fish and chips.' Beatrice turned to her companion with a smile. 'Thanks, I might just try one or two bites.'

Kitty nodded contentedly and they made a start on their impromptu meal, listening to the gulls spreading the word there were potential fish supper scraps to be had.

'You'll be lucky,' Kitty called to the largest and boldest gull, who was side-eying their lunch a little way off down the sand, making Beatrice laugh.

'I won't pry,' Kitty said eventually, after licking salt from her fingers. 'But I'm a very good listener if you have a sorry tale to tell.'

Something in her quiet warmth told Beatrice that Kitty would also be good at keeping her tale to herself, but there was no way she would blurt it all out, not to a stranger, and especially not when her spirits were reviving under the noon sun and blue sky.

'I'm OK, honestly. Just had a bit of a morning.'

'*Och*, tell me about it. I'm supposed to be starting my Gaelic lessons next week but that daft Eugene Fergusson has messed up the bookings and I've no one to teach.'

'Ah!' Beatrice's eyes widened as she turned to face her companion. 'You're the Gaelic tutor. *I* was one of your students. Now I'm a willow weaver, apparently. Well, I was… I'm leaving tomorrow.' The words didn't carry much conviction as the sea breeze took them away.

Beatrice felt rooted to her peaceful spot at the foot of the sea wall and the view of Port Willow bay seemed to be opening itself out before her for the first time as the sun at its zenith made the landscape shine. Low rugged hills, white cottages, a great grey-walled castle on the shore opposite and a Lion Rampant flag flying from its turrets presented themselves to her.

To top it all off a thin, watery rainbow stretched across the sky. It hadn't been there a moment before, Beatrice could have sworn. The brightly painted, colourful boats bobbing out on the water reflected the sunlight and cast their own glittering, broken rainbows through the water. For a moment, Beatrice let herself imagine the effect was nothing to do with science and refraction and more to do with magic.

'I hadn't realised how pretty it was here.'

'Sometimes you need to sit still and just look,' Kitty said, sipping her tea, scanning her eyes lazily along the horizon.

'So what will you do now you've no students?' Beatrice said, breaking off a satisfyingly large chunk of flaky white fish in crisp, bubbled batter.

'It'll work itself out, I'm sure. I had a week's holidaying planned first, just relaxing in Port Willow, and Atholl's brought me in until the end of September and I'm sure he'll sort some students out for me, so I'm not going anywhere and I have plenty of uni work to be getting on with in the meantime.'

'Seth mentioned you worked at a university.'

'Ah, yes, the all-seeing Seth.' Kitty spoke through bites of their lunch. 'I saw him grilling you last night. He doesn't miss much. I run the Gaelic programme at a uni about thirty miles north of here. It's a lovely job and I have my summer free to do things like this.'

'Sounds ideal.'

'I think so.' Kitty's eyes swept along the bay. 'This beats any gap year beach in Thailand or summer holiday job in a library, or whatnot.'

They'd come to the bottom of the chip wrapper already and between them had greedily hoovered up most of the batter. Kitty threw a scrap to the patient gull who rewarded her with a loud caw before snatching its prize and flying off along to the jetty at the far end of the beach.

'I tell you what would go down well as a pudding,' Kitty's eyes glinted. 'A gin and tonic.'

'Well, I don't know about Gaelic, but *now* you are speaking my language, Kitty.'

'Come on then.' She helped haul Beatrice up from the sand.

'Let's see if Eugene Fergusson can still pour a good mixer.'

'Let's. Do you think he'll let me use the inn computer? I need to let my sister know I'm not going back to Warwickshire today after all, but I've lost my mobile with her new number in it.'

'I'm sure he'll no' mind.'

'Kitty? Thank you… I really needed to see a friendly face today.'

'My pleasure.' Kitty smiled warmly. 'Umm, Beatrice?'

'Uh-huh?'

'Is your bum as wet as mine?'

She reached a hand behind her and grimaced. 'The sand *was* quite damp, wasn't it?'

Their laughter resounded across the bay, and when Beatrice stumbled over the top step onto the road Kitty caught her arm and held it fast all the way to the door of The Princess and the Pea Inn.

–

'Did the bar look like this last night?' Beatrice said, glancing around. Had there been sparkling white fairy lights strung in taut, neat lines along the bar shelves causing the glassware and whisky bottles to glimmer? And the table tops now gleamed with heady scented beeswax. Weren't they sticky and dull yesterday? And…

'Gene? You're looking smart!' Beatrice couldn't help grinning at the sheepish look on his face as he swept a cloth inside the pint glasses.

'It was those Geordie women, wasn't it? The hairdressers. Practically ambushed me, they did. After breakfast. Something about not being able to forgive themselves and calling me a follicle criminal, which I didnae much appreciate. Anyway, they did this to me.' He ran a hand over his shorn head.

'I like it,' Kitty said immediately, before ordering two GlenWyvis Highland gins with full fat tonic and orange peel, which Gene efficiently set about preparing.

'You look ten years younger now,' Beatrice chipped in, and she meant it. 'And has the bar had a bit of a makeover too?'

'It needed a going over, I think,' Gene replied, looking round the room with a little spark of pride in his eyes. Beatrice wondered if he was standing even taller than he had this morning; he seemed to tower over the bar.

'Atholl will be pleased,' said Kitty.

Beatrice caught Gene's eyes flicker briefly towards her own, and she was glad to see the look of shame.

'That reminds me, I've a bone to pick with you, Eugene Fergusson.'

'There's no need. Atholl came storming in here an hour ago looking for ye, said you hurt yourself on the rocks. I'm sorry, I didnae mean you any harm directing you over Rother Path. It is a braw walk and safe, usually. I think it was just his wee joke, really. Are you all right now?'

After the dulling effects of her torrent of tears, the fresh air and summer warmth and her deliciously satisfying feast of salty, yummy fat and carbs there was no fight left in her.

'You're both lucky I didn't get flattened, but I am all right. Echo saved me, just like you said, though I never called for him. He found me.'

Gene was shaking his head. 'Atholl sent him ahead. He'd watched the whole thing happening from the But n' Ben window and he set the mutt running, knowing his own feet wouldn't carry him as fast. But my brother reached you all right, in the end, I hear?'

'That's right.' Beatrice fought the colour rising in her cheeks, hoping she was still blotchy and pink enough from the morning's excitement and tearfulness to mask her blushes.

'On the house.' Gene set two tall glasses on the bar, breaking the buzz of tension in the air, and reminding Beatrice she had a favour to ask.

'Gene, do you mind if I use the inn computer, just for a second?' she asked.

'Go right ahead, the reception machine is on.'

'No password or anything?'

'Eh, no. Should there be?' He shrugged as though the suggestion were an odd one.

'OK, back in a sec. Thanks, Gene.' Beatrice hopped off the stool, taking her drink with her.

The reception was empty – no sign of any guests, or Atholl, thank goodness. So he'd come looking for her, had he? She wondered if the warmth in her chest was caused by the first few sips of gin or the knowledge that he'd wanted to see her, no doubt to apologise.

Her thoughts were interrupted by the need to concentrate on remembering her Facebook password. Angela was far more likely to log in to her social media accounts than she was to check emails during her cosy days at home with baby Clara. She thought hard, searching her memory and taking the opportunity to straighten the antlers hanging on the wall behind her. 'That's better. Right, password, password…' It had been many months since she'd had to log in but after two failed attempts she struck upon the right one. 'Ah, there, I'm in,' she told the empty room.

And there on the screen was her profile picture, posted back in the spring and unchanged since that happy, relief-filled day when she'd had the early scan and all had been well. There was Rich, grinning and proud, holding the sonographer's wand, and Beatrice, her stomach bare and glistening from the gel, caught gazing at the moving image on the screen.

'Oh, no.' Beatrice felt the blood draining from her face and clicked frantically at the little cross in the corner of the pane, trying to close the page but finding the screen frozen. 'The damn thing's crashed! Does nothing work in this bloody place?'

'Very little,' came a soft voice from the door. ''Ow do?' said Seth, making his way for the bar room. 'That thing's always on the blink, best to shut it down and try again later, that's what Atholl always does.'

'Good idea.' She powered down the machine, and listened to its noisy fan and clicking hard drive die away into silence. She was suddenly aware of the gulls cawing from the bay outside.

'Come on, lassie. I see ye have a drink, let's get settled at the bar.'

With one last dismayed glance at the blank monitor, Beatrice lifted her glass and followed Seth. Just before they passed into the room where Gene and Kitty were deep in conversation, Beatrice reached for Seth's arm, stopping him in his tracks, and she lowered her voice when she spoke.

'Seth, does Kitty know Atholl and Gene, then? From before the Gaelic lessons thing, I mean?' Beatrice asked.

'Atholl and Kitty have been friends for years. She first holidayed here with her family way back in the eighties and that's how they met. They'd fly their kites together on the beach.'

They both glanced towards Gene who was wiping the bar down and nodding as Kitty spoke animatedly to him. Seth's eyes sparkled and he led Beatrice into the room.

'My usual please, Eugene. Beatrice here was just asking me if you two played together as children.'

'Oh, well… I was just wondering…' Beatrice flustered, throwing Seth a wide-eyed glare. What was he playing at?

'Och, no, it was Atholl that Kitty always played with. I was older than the pair of them,' Gene replied, seemingly unfazed by Beatrice's curiosity and the fact she'd been asking about what kind of relationships the three of them had.

'Too cool to play with his wee brother and his pals,' Kitty teased.

'There's nine years between me and Atholl,' Gene explained.

'We always thought you'd marry young Atholl.' Seth perched on the stool he'd sat at the night before, his neck craning so he could see past Beatrice and direct his remark at Kitty, a mischievous whiskery smile making his eyes shine.

Beatrice heard Kitty laugh and witnessed the muscles flex in Gene's freshly shaved jaw, almost imperceptible, but there all the same.

'Och, no, Seth.' Kitty let her glass settle on the bar as she wiped her mouth with a napkin. 'It was never Atholl I had my eye on back then.' This was addressed straight at Gene with a challenging grin before she returned her attention to her glass, the ice cubes chinking.

Now Beatrice understood what he was up to. Seth chuckled and sipped his dram, and a slow pink blush spread across Gene's neck. Beatrice caught sight of it just before he snatched at Seth's money and turned his back on them all to stab at the cash register's buttons, long enough for a flash of inspiration to hit her.

She glanced at Kitty for the briefest moment and saw the dimples form in her cheeks and her lips pursing in a sly smile confirming her suspicions; she had liked Gene once upon a time, and there was still some lingering affection there, if she wasn't much mistaken.

'You're not married or seeing anyone, are you, Kitty?' said Beatrice, trying to sound as natural as possible, not helped by the little chuckle from Seth by her side.

'Free as a bird,' Kitty smiled, her straw still between her teeth.

Gene suddenly slunk away into the back room, telling Seth to ring the bell if anyone wanted serving, and Beatrice and Seth exchanged cautionary glances, but Kitty didn't seem to mind their questions.

'The bar certainly looks smarter, doesn't it?' Kitty said to Seth.

'Eugene must have taken a long look at himself this last day or two since you arrived back in town, Kitty Wake,' Seth replied.

Beatrice's head snapped round at this. 'Your name's never kittiwake, is it? Like the bird?' She was delighted.

'It's Catriona, the Gaelic version of Katherine, but my parents shortened it to Kitty, our surname being Wake. And it stuck, and I like it.'

'It suits you,' Beatrice beamed, her glass almost empty now.

'I think so.'

'Do you know what I think? I think Gene might have taken a shine to you in the years since he was an indifferent young man, Kitty Wake,' Beatrice blurted, suddenly transported to a time when teenage hormones rampaged and high school matchmaking and gossip could set her up for days.

The rush that accompanied this regression was like the same sudden exuberance that follows teenage woes.

Beatrice briefly wondered when the hormonal roller-coaster effect of her recent grief and sadness would wear off. It occurred to her it might be here to stay and she delved back into the bottom of her gin glass to slake away the notion.

'Not likely. He had his chances back in the day,' said Kitty.

'But he was such an obtuse laddie,' Seth added knowingly. 'He'd run a mile if ever a bonny lassie told him she liked him.'

'Were there many?' Beatrice tried to imagine a younger Gene shrugging off the attentions of queues of Highland lassies. Somehow she couldn't quite picture it.

Kitty shrugged and drained her glass.

'And he married someone else?' Beatrice pushed. The idea that this sullen Scot could have his pick of *two* women; one a stunning university-educated language expert and the other a culinary genius, struck Beatrice as outlandish, but this was Port Willow after all, maybe miracles happened here as well as magic in the skies.

'He was different back then. He was brighter… happier. He never knew I liked him, I'm sure, and I was only seventeen or maybe eighteen when I gave up having a crush on the daft beggar. He would never even have looked at me, anyway, what with the age difference. I was just a kid. Then he married his Canadian girl and soon after, I stopped coming to the village for summer holidays – too busy doing my doctorate by then.'

'The brothers were the most eligible laddies in the village then, you know?' said Seth, packing his pipe with tobacco and getting ready to leave, adding with a chuckle, 'Asides from yours truly, of course.'

'You've got a son, didn't you say, Seth? Did you marry?' Beatrice asked, enjoying his company and hoping to delay his departure.

'I did.' Seth settled on the stool once more. 'Mary and I were married fifty-four years altogether. And I've missed her every day these last nine years she's been gone.'

'Oh, Seth, I'm sorry.'

'Don't be, lass. I was one of the lucky ones. Most of the lads in the village never married, or they went off down south or off around the world and Lord knows what happened to them, but they never returned to Port Willow so I imagine they found partners elsewhere. We've always had a problem of too many laddies and not enough lassies in this place. There's no' enough here to keep our smart, bonny lassies at home.' Seth nodded his head to show he really was leaving, hopped off the stool and turned for the door. 'Yes, I was one of the lucky lads,' he said again with a smile as he left, letting the door swing closed behind him.

'I remember Seth when I was wee,' Kitty said, leaning her head conspiratorially towards Beatrice, though there was nobody in the bar to overhear her. 'He and his wife didn't get on, and she moved to the other side of the island once their son was at the high school. And every day he'd ride his bicycle over to visit her, and on Fridays he'd take a posy of flowers to her. They got on like a house on fire once they'd separated. It was quite the love affair, apparently.'

'And they never moved back in together?'

'And risk spoiling their romance? Goodness, no.'

'Wow, that's unusual. But what about you? Didn't you meet anyone special?'

'There were a few all right lads, but I haven't met anyone special recently,' Kitty conceded. 'Most academic men aren't ideal husband material, you see; always working late into the night, never taking their summer holidays even though they've earned them, chasing promotion and preferment, *pfft*! No thank you. And they seem to be the only chaps I get thrown together with in my line of work. The rest have been farmers and fishermen away from dawn till dusk. I have a theory that nice, available Highland blokes who *aren't* out grafting twenty-four seven are like *Brigadoon*; one rises from the mists every one hundred years.' Kitty laughed.

'I know a bit about busy men,' Beatrice said, but in a tone that told Kitty she couldn't bring herself to say more. Thoughts of Rich swiped the breath from Beatrice's lungs and she felt suddenly tired. Rich always worked so hard, doubly so since Beatrice lost her job. He liked the idea of breadwinning for her. All that work and long hours away from home must have taken their toll somewhere along the line, but she couldn't pinpoint exactly when. Perhaps it had been slowly eroding their joint lives, eating away at their intimacy and their happiness day by day and they'd both been too busy to notice.

Kitty spoke first, calmly steering the conversation back to safer ground. 'So, are you resolved to stay a little longer then? Maybe you'll get as proficient as Atholl at the weaving if you give it a try?'

Kitty was pointing an elegant finger up above the bar and Beatrice followed its line.

'What on earth is that? Atholl didn't make that, did he?'

Kitty simply nodded.

In the dark space above the optics hung a wild-looking, chestnut-brown Lion Rampant and a white unicorn; twin symbols of Scottish sovereignty. Beatrice screwed up her eyes to make out the details. How could long willow whips become these light, airy, magical sculptures? Their delicate feet seemed to tread the very air they were suspended in; their broad, hollow haunches formed of nothing but tightly interwoven supple branches spoke convincingly of movement and musculature; their wild dark eyes, elegantly poised heads and pricked ears conveyed pride, stoicism and dignity.

'*Wow!* So Atholl's *an artist*?' Beatrice couldn't draw her eyes away from the sculpture.

'One of the best, I imagine.'

A vague impression returned to Beatrice; it was becoming clearer now. Back at the But and Ben there had been baskets made of willow on the long table, and curved horns of plenty upon the walls filled with dried flowers and sculpted fruits, and many other curious objects which Beatrice had been too flustered, and perhaps too bloody-minded and stressed out, to see clearly.

'Oh no.' A memory hit her hard. 'I think I insulted him. I said... I called his work "messing about with sticks" or something. I don't remember my exact words, but I know I was dismissive and rude. And that's not all he's heard me saying. No wonder he's sick of the sight of me.'

Other memories crowded in now, painful in their fresh clarity. She'd criticised the inn rooms that he and his brother must be proud of, even if they were a bit dated and dusty, and she'd taken one look at the place and said she was leaving, *and* she'd turned her nose up at the food last night – though, she felt she really did have a point there. Either way, the Fergussons had been hospitable in their own way and she'd wanted to run a mile. 'Talk about getting off on the wrong foot!'

Covering her face with her hands and cringing did nothing to take away the embarrassment. It was the same mortification that seemed to accompany her everywhere she went at the moment and in the rare moments she was free from its restraints, she seemed to resort to taking big, bold swipes at the people around her, and especially at Atholl Fergusson. Beatrice looked through her fingers at Atholl's willow sculpture again and groaned.

'I have a feeling he'll forgive you,' said Kitty, in a low whisper. 'But don't let him get away with being a miserable ass, either. It takes two to willow weave, remember.' Kitty was hopping down from the bar stool.

Before Beatrice knew what was happening, she felt the sea breeze from the open door behind her and Kitty was pressing a quick peck to her cheek. 'I'll be here most days if you need anything,' she said in a low voice, and then she was gone.

Beatrice turned on her barstool only to see Kitty passing a steely-faced Atholl who seemed to be frozen to the spot on the bar room doormat, his cheeks ruddy from the building summer heat.

She turned swiftly back to face the bar and pressed her elbows into it, holding her face with her hands. Why was her breathing failing her, she wondered? Her chest tightened with the sound of his heavy steps approaching. He didn't pass through the raised bar hatch, much to her surprise, but settled himself on the stool previously occupied by Seth, pushing aside the empty whisky glass with the back of his wrist, bared now he'd removed his jumper and rolled up his shirt sleeves.

Looking at her own glass, wishing it were filled again and offering her something to do with her hands, she felt Atholl's eyes assessing her.

He cleared his throat in a low growl and when he spoke, his voice was gentler than she'd heard before. 'I thought you might have called a taxi and left.'

'Are there any taxis to be had on a Sunday in Port Willow?'

'Good point,' he said with a nod, before reaching his arm over the bar and running his hand along the shelf beneath, coming up with a clean glass.

Gene must have filled a jug with water and lemon and left it by the beer taps and Beatrice watched as his younger brother deftly filled his glass and lifted the jug to her own, his brows lifting to ask her assent. She nodded, and he poured. Silence filled the bar and they both drank.

'I've, uh, I've come to apologise for shouting back there at the beach. You were frightened and I could have been… gentler. And I shouldn't have sent you over the rocks. I don't know why I did that, but I never expected you to meet with the cattle…'

'I know. I haven't exactly been an easy guest either. I don't *mean* to be rude and awkward. That seems to be my default setting at the moment.'

A sharp, wry laugh shook Atholl's shoulders. 'I might be guilty of something similar myself.' He drank quickly from the glass, and Beatrice nodded with a smile, her eyes cast down, muttering an apology which Atholl waved away.

'My question to you, Beatrice, is what do we do about this? Can I make amends? Will you stay if we try to make you happier?'

'Don't be nice to me,' she blurted out. Her lips quavered without her permission and she wondered if she was going to cry. Biting her bottom lip, she looked down at her glass.

With a look of sudden recollection he reached into his shirt pocket, retrieved her phone and placed it on the bar. 'Echo brought me this. It's quite sandy and I suspect it's had a drink o' water.'

'I must have dropped it when the cows started running at me.' She was relieved at the shift in focus and pursued it. 'Am I the first visitor to cause a stampede?'

The light flashed in her irises and Atholl must have caught it because he broke into a smile too. 'That I know of, aye. That's the most excitement seen at the coral beach since a U-boat ran aground there in the forties.'

Beatrice scanned his face. The crinkles at the corners of his eyes and the crackle in his voice were all she needed to push her over into laughter too. She shook back her by now very messy hair and laughed in unrestrained relief.

'I imagine I was quite a sight.'

'You can say that again. I feared for a moment that the beasts would disperse and I'd find they'd crushed the life from ye, but I knew Echo was in amongst them and he'd no' let that happen.'

'Where is he now?'

Atholl tipped his wrist, looking at his watch. 'Well, it's after two, so he'll be down at the chippy waiting for his lunch.'

'Really?'

'Like clockwork. Jim Tosh will gie him the leftovers before he closes up. Echo's a wandering dug but he'll no' go far from the high street at lunch times, never knowing if he'll miss a bit o' battered haggis or a sausage.'

The pair smiled at one another, warmth and sleepiness spreading through Beatrice.

'So, what do you say? Will you let us make it up to you? Stay a day more?' he said.

The idea did hold some appeal now Beatrice had seen the broad sky over the bay and tasted the clean salty air and the sweet gin. Atholl was leaning a little closer now, a note of entreaty in his voice. 'And if you can put up with me, I would verra much like to give you that willow-weaving lesson and we could hae some lunch at the same time... should you like it?'

'Well... all right, then. I will stay one more day. Just promise you won't try to feed me any of that battered haggis from the chippy. It might be all right for Echo, but...'

'Hey, don't knock it 'til you've tried it,' Atholl said with a smile.

Chapter Nine

Monday: A Morning's Willow-weaving

Atholl guided Beatrice through the willow field that backed on to the But and Ben above the coral beach. The morning sun was already high in the clear blue sky and Beatrice was glad she'd chosen to wear her long black sundress, factor thirty and dark shades, and even more glad Atholl was in dark cords that looked as though they'd been softened by washing a thousand times and a t-shirt that perfectly showed off his biceps speckled with light freckles.

Echo darted in and out of the long rows of willow and Beatrice told herself it was the dog's excited tail-wagging that was distracting her and not the way the sun struck Atholl's blue eyes and fine cheekbones. Atholl was describing the work that went into the care of the willow. She tried to concentrate.

'I cut them back to the ground every year and these tall, supple branches grow straight up to the sky. Fourteen feet is what I'm aiming for, perfect for basketry, and there's three different varieties growing here for a choice of colour and strength.'

'I didn't know people *farmed* willow. They look so strange in the landscape... so unexpected?'

'Folk have been weaving willows for their dwellings for thousands of years. Everywhere in the world has its own version of it; grass, leaves, or branches. People have always weaved natural materials to make the basic things they need for survival, be it clothing or shelter. Once upon a time, and not so long ago neither, every community in the British Isles would have its own wee parcel o' land for willow cultivation, but that way of life is over now.'

Beatrice wanted to tell him she liked the way his eyes were shining with enthusiasm but felt she couldn't, so instead she smiled and let him talk as they wandered through the maze of willow.

'When growing is done with a bit o' care, you'll feel a connection to the landscape around you. Dinnae laugh when I tell you, but I cannae help feeling that when we break with the old traditions we lose our instinctive connection to nature, and I'd like to fix that a bit.'

'I'm not laughing. That sounds perfect to me.'

They made their way through the willow coppice to the back door of the But and Ben. Atholl reached for the key hidden under a white seashell on the windowsill.

In long, propped up boxes along the cottage wall stood tall bundles of straight willow rods which Beatrice couldn't help running her fingers over as Atholl tried the key and let the door swing open. The bundles were neatly sorted by variety, length and thickness, and each tied with a willow whip in a twisted knot around their middle. The stems reflected the sunlight in hues from copper to golden green.

'I cut those in January, they've been drying for baskets all this time. I have more willow than I can keep up with. That's what gave me the idea to bring in makers, like yourself. I've been supplying paying visitors to the tartan mill, the silversmith, the glassworks and the art gallery for weeks now. It's certainly increased our custom at the inn all of a sudden, and the crafters are enjoying learning something new but it seemed right to start having folk up here too, to learn how to work the willow. You, uh, were my first booking.'

'Oh! And I said I didn't want to take the lessons after all. You must have been so disappointed.' Beatrice smiled awkwardly and was relieved to hear Atholl's wry laugh. She looked around at the neat coppices behind the cottage. 'I'm sorry about that. I'm not much of a crafter, remember.'

'No. I suspect you're more of an escapee.' Atholl threw a quick glance to check she wasn't offended by his arrow-like accuracy. He was right; she'd washed ashore here with no plan other than getting away from home, and from herself. Unwilling to acknowledge the truth of Atholl's observation she looked around, taking in the blooming roses, tall thistles and the long metal tank and smaller stone trough that ran along the back wall of the cottage beneath its low windows. Both troughs were full to the brim with water.

'Don't tell me the cows come round here too?' Beatrice said, looking around nervously for any sign of marauding cattle.

'Uh? Oh, no.' Atholl laughed. 'No, those are for soaking the willows. If you want to make baskets with your store of cut whips you need to soak it until it's mellow and soft again like freshly cut willow. Here, sit by the door in the shade.' Atholl spread a blanket over a rustic wooden chair by a rambling rose that had taken over the wall and much of the cottage's low roof. 'I'll away in and get the tools if you'll unpack the picnic?'

Heading inside the cottage, he left Beatrice to rummage in the basket and draw out a tall jar of honey with suspended golden blobs inside. Beatrice peered at them and grimaced. More weird Highland food. What could it be this time? She was relieved to find a flask of strong milky coffee, and ham and pickle sandwiches on fresh buttered doorstop bread.

Nothing about the meal was elegant or dainty, in fact it was like Atholl himself: rugged, hearty and wholesome. He reappeared just as this thought was running through Beatrice's mind.

Atholl placed the wooden toolbox upon the bench and unpacked the strange-looking items; pins, pliers, secateurs, a medieval-looking wheel for punching holes in leather and a series of long metal spikes the use of which Beatrice couldn't fathom.

'Are we going to be performing surgery? On an elephant?'

'You'll see. It's all fairly straightforward once you get the hang of it.'

'And these?' she said, indicating the jar of honey.

'*Hah!* Those are honey buns; heather honey buns, to be precise. My mother's recipe. Those things inside are cakes. You make them fresh then preserve them in honey, perfect with cream on a sunny day like today.'

Rugged, hearty, wholesome *and* sweet, Beatrice thought, though if it showed on her face Atholl seemed unaware. He was busying himself by pulling up a low stool to sit on, a hewn section of a tree's trunk that someone – Beatrice guessed it was Atholl – had varnished so it gleamed in the sun.

'Mother's heather honey buns have become one of Gene's specialities. Well they *were*. I had to beg him to make them for us this morning.' Atholl cocked an eyebrow and looked up at her through the curls falling over his forehead. 'Do you *approve*?'

Beatrice let out a laugh at the boldness of his question and the mischievous smile on his face as he risked asking it.

She watched him work, tipping her head a little to one side. He had brought a tall bundle of soft willows from the cottage and laid them over his thighs, and was pulling at the stripped willow strap that bound them together.

'Right, can you pour out the coffee, and we'll get started? We can eat as we weave. I always work better with food to hand.'

Beatrice found the two mugs and they both watched the steam from the flask as it moved on the warm air. Beatrice inhaled the rich coffee aroma appreciatively.

'So, what would you like to make?' Atholl asked.

'What's easy?'

'Nothing.'

'Oh, OK, what's *easiest*? Give me the dummies' guide to willow-weaving.'

'How about a simple decorative wreath?'

Perhaps Atholl Fergusson didn't notice the fraction of a second where Beatrice processed the association between wreaths and mourning. It had passed with the tiniest pinch at the sides of her eyes and the widening of her pupils. Just another of the many million instances where her everyday life was shot through with sad little reminders of her losses, each one passing unvoiced. And yet he was watching her with an attentiveness she wasn't used to and it made her lower her eyes to his hands as she tried to concentrate on the lesson.

'Go on then,' he urged. 'Take your first willow.'

Beatrice surveyed the bundle he held out to her, at a loss which to choose. Was any one better than the other? Her inexperienced eye couldn't tell.

'Don't be shy. You must choose with decision. Grasp the one that's right. And once you've chosen, stick to your choice. If you want to build a fluent, strong piece you need to be bold.' Atholl was offering a smile in the calm, steady way Beatrice was coming to recognise as peculiarly his own – at least she had never seen another like it.

'Fluent?'

'Aye. You want to make a piece that talks to you, and you talk with it. Working together with the willow to make something… intentional.'

Beatrice didn't feel intentional when she grabbed at the first willow that seemed to stand out to her. 'Will this do?'

He placed the bundle by his feet. 'You tell me.'

'Well that's an infuriating answer.'

Atholl laughed again but soon let his attention settle on the single willow he had in his hand. 'Each willow has a natural curvature of its own. See?' He held the branch between pinched fingertip and thumb extended at his arm's length in the air, letting its soft green body bend gently as he ran a fingertip along its middle down to where it touched the ground. 'This inner arc is called its belly, and this…' He switched his stroke to the outer curve, running the back of his hand along it in a smooth sweep. 'This curve is called its back.'

Tracing the slow stroke of his rough-skinned hand somehow triggered a message from Beatrice's eyes to her own belly, and a burst of something – adrenaline or endorphins – surged through her bloodstream. She recognised the heady, desirous feeling from a time long ago, pre-pregnancy, pre-Richard even, and found she was grasping her willow, pressing her nails into her palms to chase the feeling away.

Far away, it seemed, Atholl was still softly talking and his hands were working, bending the willow before seizing more and setting to work on intertwining them with the first as the wreath took shape. Beatrice found her own hands responding as she mirrored his movements and worked the willow, her mind flitting to the wonderful unicorn and lion sculptures she had seen the day before above the bar.

'What do you do with your finished pieces? Is there demand for willow sculptures?'

'It's never occurred to me to sell them. I mean, a few visitors have asked for prices and I have done one or two commissions for private gardens in recent years but your average shopper down South will buy things like this from fancy online shops with their warehouses in China, not from a one-man maker in the Highlands. It's all upside-down to my mind.' Atholl's eyes remained fixed on his work.

'Do you have an online store?'

'Well, no. I've wanted to set one up for a while but helping Gene with the inn takes all my time. What I'd really like is a real shop here by my wee bit o' land and workshop, and, uh...' His eyes were alive in the afternoon sun as he stopped to check his enthusiasm before continuing more slowly. 'I'd like to run a true school here to teach other folk the craft, and no' just one-to-ones either, but whole classes full.'

'That sounds easy enough. You've got the willows growing, you've got the classroom, all it needs is a bit of renovation and you could have a proper shop, and a little kitchen too for refreshments, and you could update the inn's website to include a storefront for your willow products.' Beatrice swallowed, considering her next words, before going on. 'You know, I could help you apply for funding for some Crafts Council or Heritage Fund money to get it off the ground, and it would be easy to connect you up to guilds across the country, maybe form some partnerships, and we could link it all up to the inn's website. You said yourself the crafting holidays have taken off, so you could reach people all over the world, and I bet you could get featured in some lifestyle mags and on travel blogs. The Boden catalogue sometimes features real artisan blokes as models these days – total hunks they are – and it does little stories about their craft products; you could be in one of them easily, and it wouldn't be long before you could entice some reviewers here, and... *what?*' She paused. 'Why are you looking at me like that?'

Atholl was grinning. 'Enjoying yourself?'

'What? It's what I do. Well, it's what I *did*. I used to run an arts network.' A feeling she hadn't had for a long time was kicking in, a kind of intellectual muscle memory made up of her competence, expertise and enthusiasm. 'I was good at it,' she said with a decisive nod, but letting her eyes drop to her wreath.

'I can tell.'

She heard his quick intake of breath that told her he was about to ask questions and she felt her shoulders stiffen. Maybe he noticed, because instead of probing he exhaled and reached for the sandwiches. 'Hungry?'

They ate in silence, working at their wreaths in between delicious savoury bites, accompanied by the shushing sounds of the waves on the coral beach behind the cottage. A heron watched them unseen from one of the ancient Scots pines at the far end of the coppice marking the boundary between the land that enclosed the But and Ben and the rolling fields beyond that stretched inland all the way to the foothills in an uninterrupted patchwork of green and yellow.

As the sun reached its summit in the cloudless blue sky, Beatrice felt her focus return. Concentration and diversion settled upon her, things she missed most from her old life. Her hands seemed to find the rhythm of the task.

The willow in her grasp glowed like copper in the intense summer light. She felt, rather than thought, how she and the man beside her were recreating a scene that could have played out here by the door of the But and Ben at any time in the last three centuries. Finding she was smiling, she looked up at Atholl, and there he was, deep in concentration, his brows smooth with relaxation, absorbed and intense.

'You're happy,' she heard herself saying.

'Aye.' His voice cracked as he spoke. He cleared his throat. 'I don't get enough time to do this, but it's where I'm happiest. Are you enjoying it too?'

Beatrice nodded. Atholl hefted the bundle of willow across his thighs again, his tongue loosened and eloquent with the focus of his work. 'There's no machines can do what we're doing now. See how this whip is shorter, and that, thinner? And here the buds were spaced wide apart but on this one they were close together? You make allowances for each individual willow; you incorporate it differently depending on its strengths.'

Beatrice peered at the willows as he spread them in his hands.

'No, there's no machine can do this,' he repeated.

'So you resist the modern world, one willow sculpture at a time.'

He laughed, a hearty rattle at his throat. 'You could say that.'

'Damn the man!'

'Aye, damn him.'

They both laughed this time and Beatrice felt herself swept along in his enthusiasm. Atholl was soon weaving again, cutting short some splayed ends of willows so they stuck out from his wreath like the flames on a Catherine wheel.

'It really is beautiful,' she said. 'No matter how modern and mechanised the world gets or how uniform production methods make things, people will always want beautifully crafted, unique things that connect them to nature and remind them they're human.'

'Aye,' he stopped to observe her at work for a moment, his lips parted and eyes narrowing. 'Exactly that.'

'How did you learn to do this?' Beatrice asked.

He took his time answering, rotating the wreath between his thighs and cutting the decorative edges of the willows to the desired lengths.

'There was a willow grower lived at the But n' Ben, Hector his name is, and I was apprenticed to him when I left school. I was with him a good few years but I never got the chance to involve myself in the business properly. We lost our father for a long time to dementia – bloody awful thing it is – and then when he passed away we found my mother didn't want to run the inn on her own anymore and the inn passed to Gene. For a time, my two younger sisters helped us out and we did well enough, but when Mum moved back to Skye my sisters went with her, and they're married now and living with their partners over the water, so Gene and I have been running the inn alone, and well… you see how that's worked out. I lease the But n' Ben and the willow fields from Hector – he retired across to Fort William. I expect when he passes away I'll be turned out and the school sold.'

'Not unless you buy it,' Beatrice cut in.

'Ach, I've often thought of it, but how can I? I have Gene to babysit and the inn to manage now he's given up the cooking and can't work the computer systems to save himself. Christ, some days I think he's given up on being a human being altogether. Having the occasional guest, like yourself, here at the workshop is, realistically, all I can see myself managing in the future.'

'Well, bring in a chef. Let Gene continue with the breakfasts and have the new person do the dinners. Easy!'

'And break Gene's heart even more? I expect Seth's filled you in on my brother's marriage? And you must have heard Gene on Saturday night when he stormed out of the restaurant. He thinks his wife's coming back one day and they'll carry on where they left off.'

'Will they though? Is she honestly coming back after all this time?'

Atholl's chest swelled with a deep breath. He didn't speak but Beatrice had the bit between her teeth and wasn't about to give up now.

'I could help you write a business plan if it's a bank loan that's needed. It wouldn't take me long. That way you could make your old teacher an offer? He might not accept it, but what's there to lose? Other than this place, which you obviously love.'

Silence again. Beatrice didn't push him, instead letting him think. Eventually he spoke. 'No. Gene is right. I can't fix everything. This is a knot only time will untie.'

'You're not even going to try?'

'You don't understand, Beatrice. I spend my life fixing things. Fixing up the inn, trying to attract new business, protecting Gene from harm, mainly from himself, and it's *maddening* that I can't fix this situation, infuriating, in fact. But I can't.' The hint of terseness in Atholl's voice told her to stop. 'But, uh… I *am* grateful to you for the offer. It's the first of its kind. But I manage alone.'

Beatrice didn't dare risk a return to the stroppiness and tension of their first encounters, so she nodded and let silence fall between them.

Working the willow was beginning to hurt her thumbs so she placed the wreath on the ground beside her and reached into the basket for the spoons and white china dishes Atholl had packed that morning.

Atholl eyed her every now and again over his own wreath, substantial and intricate, so unlike her own smaller, looser efforts, as she unscrewed the lid on the tall jar of honey and attempted to fish out the little buns with a spoon.

The first came out streaming with honey, and the sweetness filled the air as she settled it in the bowl and poured cream over it. This one she passed to Atholl, before repeating the process.

Atholl seemed glad to stop working, even lifting his stool and shifting it over to the door so he could sit in the shade by Beatrice's side to eat. The buns – sticky Madeira cakes – were, Beatrice noticed, in the shape of fat little hearts.

She took her first bite. '*Mmm*, you must tell Gene these are delicious, and thank him for me. I could attack this whole jarful given a big enough spoon and some alone time.'

She was relieved to see Atholl smiling again, a drop of honey and cream at the edge of his lips. She realised with a jolt of horror that part of her wanted to watch him lick it away but she knew she couldn't without being all too obvious and, she told herself, this was meant to be a forty somethings' crafting holiday, not some X-rated *Love Island* rendezvous, so she had better just calm the heck down. She forced her gaze out over the fields behind the willows instead.

'What's that sorry-looking field over there? That's not willow, is it?' she said with some relief at having found a change of topic.

Atholl followed her line of sight. 'Ah, that would be Lana's field. Her lavender.'

Beatrice cocked her head in confusion and shovelled another bite of sweet sticky honey bun into her mouth.

'Lana is Gene's wife. He planted the lavender for her as a wedding present.'

Beatrice processed this nugget of information. Eugene Fergusson's heartbroken brooding made more sense now, being a counterbalance to his romantic gestures and deep love for this Lana, the runaway.

'She loved it. The plan was, she'd get the field established and she could use the lavender in her baking, and what wasn't used for the restaurant would go in the still for turning to oil, and that she would sell.'

'The still?'

'Aye, a great copper monstrosity Gene bought her. It's still in its boxes in the storeroom at the inn; they never got round to putting it together before she left.'

'What went wrong? If you don't mind me asking?'

'Wrong? I don't know. Other than her not loving him enough to stay.'

Beatrice nodded and pressed her lips together. She knew a little about that. Rich's text appeared again before her eyes and she thought of the van that would be arriving at their house tomorrow to take away the last of his things.

'She went back to Canada – that's where Lana was from originally – and Gene has been moping ever since. He's only really good for the breakfast service since Lana was always out tending the lavender field in the mornings and he doesn't associate morning service with her. Anyway, lavender seems a lot of work compared to willow. I daren't touch the stuff for fear of offending him and now the whole field's gone to weeds. The lavender bushes themselves are leggier than Echo and as dry as bone. I'd take a torch to them if they weren't so near my willows. I even considered hiring a cultivator to rip them all out and start willows in there... but I daren't say that to Gene.'

He placed down his empty bowl and set to work cutting a leather hanging strap for his wreath. Beatrice's mind was working as deftly as Atholl's hands.

'Maybe you've been going about it the wrong way?'

Atholl tilted his head, but kept his eyes on his work.

'You're looking for new solutions when you say you like old-fashioned ways best?'

'Go on.'

'Reconnect people with nature, you said?'

Atholl looked up, eyes blank and wondering.

'We need to encourage Mother Nature to intervene.'

'I'm no' sure I'm understanding ye.'

'*Nature*, Atholl. Let's set nature to work. I have a feeling Gene just needs a little encouragement to love again and then nature will take care of the rest.'

The penny dropped and Atholl's mouth quirked. 'Push him together with Kitty Wake, you mean? You hadnae struck me as the romantic type.'

'*Gently* push them together, yes. And what do you mean? I'm the *original* romantic! At least, I've always been good at matchmaking. It was me who introduced my sister to her partner Victoria, actually.' She laughed and placed her own bowl down. 'Oh, God, that reminds me, Angela's expecting me back in Warwick tonight, and I still haven't told her I've stayed on another day to do some willow-weaving. She'll be glad I'm staying longer, I think.'

'And are *you* glad?'

'I am. This was nice. Thank you. So… just out of interest… how *did* I strike you?'

Atholl inhaled through gritted teeth, considering his answer before breaking into a broad grin. 'Well… more of the… torn-faced type, what with all your mumpin' and carrying on.'

'You cheeky devil! Well it takes one grumpy sort to know another, thank you very much. You can hardly talk.'

'Fair enough. You might have me there.' A smile accompanied this concession.

'So, it turns out I am quite the willow weaver,' she grinned, holding up her efforts for his approval.

'That's no' bad for a beginner. Another two or three years and you'll be quite proficient.'

'Two or three hours might be my limit. You have to be honest with yourself about where your strengths lie, but I did enjoy myself, thanks Atholl.'

'My pleasure. So, tell me, then. What's this plan you have for my poor brother and Mother Nature?'

It hadn't taken long to devise, only as long as the walk back to Port Willow where the pair went their separate ways, looking for accomplices; Atholl to Patrick's fish-mongers and Beatrice to find Cheryl and Jillian.

Chapter Ten

Up on the Roof

'*Beatrice!*'

'*Jesus Christ!*'

Beatrice flattened herself against the wall on her way back to the princess room at the sound of her name hissed in the darkness. It was so late she hadn't thought anyone would be up, but there she was, Kitty Wake, outside in the moonlight on what appeared to be a flat roof above the inn's front porch peering through the open window onto the landing just beyond Beatrice's room door.

'Oops, did I scare ye?' she hissed again.

Beatrice's hand hovered on the door handle. Could she make her excuses, say she was really sleepy and nip inside? That would look even stranger than her creeping around the inn corridors late at night. Kitty was the last person Beatrice wanted to bump into this evening because she knew lying wasn't her strong suit and Kitty would surely suspect something shifty was going on.

'Come on out and see this moon.' Kitty circled her hand, beckoning her through the window and putting her in mind of Cathy calling to Heathcliff. Beatrice knew she'd have to pop outside for the sake of politeness if nothing else. The clamber over the ledge and into the night air was inelegant to say the least, but Kitty reached for her arm and helped steady her.

'Are we supposed to be out here?' Beatrice asked warily, cautiously testing the strength of the roof with a few taps of her feet.

'We used to sit out here all the time when we were wee – me and Atholl and the other holidaymaker kids. We had a contest going to see who could drop their lolly stick onto passers-by's heads without them noticing. I was the champion, of course.' Kitty threw Beatrice a proud wink. 'The trick was to choose someone with a nice big eighties perm and aim straight for the hairsprayed high bit on the crown. Worked a treat.'

'I'll stay back here, I think,' said Beatrice, perching on the windowsill. 'I've had enough adventures on this holiday; I don't want to add falling through a roof to my list of catastrophes.'

'I'm heading to bed soon, I just wanted to catch a bit of moonlight. *What?* Don't look at me like that. Folk pay a fortune to fly to Greece and Italy to soak up the sun, what's wrong with absorbing a few moon rays in the Scottish Highlands?'

'Something tells me you're a bit of a hippy at heart, Kitty Wake.'

'I like the simple things in life.'

Beatrice took a breath through gritted teeth and hoped her hunch was right and that included Eugene Fergusson.

'Are you OK, Beatrice? Are you still feeling out of sorts?'

'Oh, no. I'm fine, honestly. In fact, I heard some good news tonight. My sister rang the inn looking for me. Poor Mrs Mair had to come to my room to wake me up. Vic proposed to Angela last night – Angela's my sister – and they've already set a date for the wedding so we had lots to talk about. November the sixteenth, would you believe?'

'Not long then.'

'I know.' Beatrice looked down at the three beermats hastily snatched from the bar, now carefully bullet pointed in biro with wedding planning ideas and notes. 'Anyway, we were chatting for an hour and got carried away making to do lists. I didn't realise the time and now I'm chilly from standing in the bar corridor for so long. That payphone seems to be the only way of getting a line out of this place.'

'You might be right there. I don't bother with my mobile while I'm here, no point. And you know what? It's bliss. Besides, if someone really wanted you, they'd reach you one way or another, as your sister's call proves perfectly.'

Beatrice nodded with a smile that she hoped hid all thoughts of Rich that had come gatecrashing into conversation, yet again. He hadn't tried very hard to reach her since he walked out on her. She supposed he had nothing more to say.

Kitty tilted her head to one side as though quietly considering Beatrice, making her worry she might be hoping to find out the secret of why Beatrice was here and why she'd wanted to leave Port Willow again so soon after arriving, or why she'd been sobbing on the sand yesterday like a washed up, melancholic mermaid.

Beatrice found herself rambling to distract Kitty. 'Me, Angela and her fiancée are really close. This is the longest I've gone without seeing their baby, Clara. She's teething – Clara, not my sister. I could hear her screaming in the background, poor thing. I think they're all fed up at the moment, not enough sleep, too many tears. All that pain for a thing as tiny as a milk tooth.'

'It's funny how you don't remember any of it, isn't it?' said Kitty. 'Probably for the best. I don't really know much about babies, mind, and I'm glad I chose to go into teaching adults and not kids. Grown-ups are far easier, less prone to tantrums too.' Kitty cocked her head. 'Mind you, I've been to a fair few staff meetings at my uni…' She gritted her teeth and sucked in air.

'I can imagine.'

'They must be missing you too, your sister and her family?'

'I think so. But they think it's a good thing I decided to take a holiday, if a little surprised I didn't tell them. I got a bit of a telling off the other day when I called, but it's fine. They look out for me. And I try to help them out any way I can. I babysit a lot.'

'See, I wouldn't have a clue what to do there. I imagine it's different if they're your own; you'd learn how to do all the nappies and feeds and things, but someone else's bairns? That's a whole other story.'

'It's definitely tiring. It's non-stop too. I forget how much I like my own space to think and watch TV and have a wine or two. And there's no medals dished out at the end of a long day's child-caring either!'

'*Hah!*' Kitty laughed. 'You'd think there would be. I feel sorry for mums; they get a raw deal.'

Beatrice was annoyed to find she was thinking of Helen Smethwick from work; her nemesis, and a self-crowned supermum.

The memories of the day back in early March when she'd called in unexpectedly to the Arts Hub to let the girls know her Big Fat Positive news came flooding back. She felt all over again the awkwardness and instant regret of turning up in her jeans and trainers when they were all absorbed with their daily rituals that had, apparently, gone on just fine without her since her redundancy. She hadn't actually met up with any of them since her leaving do back in September and she realised why as soon as she walked in the door. In spite of the hugs, it turned out nobody wanted to be reminded of their poor redundant colleague and their own occupational survivors' guilt.

Helen Smethwick had been there, and she looked at the early scan picture for a long time, smiling and offering her congratulations, but Beatrice knew what she was thinking; that she'd got knocked up now because she had nothing else to do with her life.

Helen had joked about Beatrice taking drastic action to avoid getting another job, and as always Beatrice just wanted to smack her, because Helen knew exactly how many jobs she had tried to get since September since she had handled all the reference requests. 'Eight interviews?' she said *sotto voce* while she poured Beatrice's decaf. 'But no actual job offers then?' she added, without even trying to hide the fact she was incandescent with delight. At least, that was how Beatrice had read the mood in the strangely subdued office that she had once thought of as her second home.

Aside from Helen, Vic and Angela were the only mums she knew who were her age. She *had* known plenty, once upon a time. The girlfriends she'd met at uni had all sprogged up about a decade ago and disappeared without trace one by one into their baby bubbles. She often wished that she'd made more effort with them, tried to be more helpful, asked them out more, but they'd all been so busy with washable nappies and baby music classes they'd gradually lost contact. And there was a point where the effort all felt a bit one-sided and it was just too late to reconnect.

She missed them still, it occurred to her, standing there on the moonlit rooftop in Port Willow under Kitty's calm, smiling gaze. It hadn't occurred to her how lonely and isolated she had let herself become over the years. She might have stood a chance of getting back into contact with her uni friends if she'd had a baby way back then. They'd have had all that stuff in common and could have discussed breast pumps and Kegel exercises over coffee and breastfeeding.

'Penny for them?' Kitty said.

'Oh, just… um, thinking of some of the mums I know.' Helen Smethwick's sour, pouting face appeared again and the words coming out of her mouth were something Beatrice had heard her say at Hub nights out or thrown into snarky conversations around the water cooler. 'You don't know true love until you're a mum.'

'Well, that's bullshit,' Kitty's voice crackled.

Beatrice gasped and snapped her eyes to Kitty's. 'Did I say that out loud? Sorry! It's just something one of my ex-colleagues used to say. And, yeah, it really annoyed me too.'

'Supermum, was she?'

'*Hmm*, you could say that. She looked down on me because I didn't have kids. I never really understood that.'

'Wee bit of jealousy on her part, maybe?'

'I hadn't thought of it like that.'

Beatrice let her memory work and found herself thinking of Helen's Instagram-perfect family and the effort it must have taken to maintain that flawless, problem-free front. She'd say things like, 'When I'm at work I know my kids think of me as a role model, and when I'm at home I know they get my undivided attention. Because it's so important to make happy memories isn't it? Well, you wouldn't know, Beatrice, but the greatest privilege of my life is making the kids' dreams come true and devoting myself to their happiness.'

'Helen was forever wheeling out the Mary Poppins act, and even when I was *really* tempted, I never once said what I wanted to,' said Beatrice.

'Which was?'

'Which was… is that why you stay at your sister-in-law's every second weekend and drink yourself into oblivion on Smirnoff Ice? Or is that why I heard you crying in the work toilets the other day after the school phoned yet again about Jeremiah picking fights in the playground and you swore like a navvy at him when you finally got to talk to him on his mobile?' Beatrice smiled wickedly at Kitty. 'Best to hold your tongue in those situations, I find. And Helen's crowing might have hurt more if I hadn't caught those glimpses of how far from perfect her family life was, like everyone else's. But why pretend it isn't? There are no awards for grinning and bearing it. Oh, well,' Beatrice said with a shrug. 'You never wanted kids, Kitty?'

'Nope. Everyone tells me I'll change my mind, like they dinnae see how offensive that is. I'm happy as I am with my work and my friends and my family. I've heard it all, though. *But you're nearly forty! You'll regret it one day if you leave it too late!* I've actually had people say that to me, can you believe it?'

'Yes, I can, unfortunately.' Beatrice remembered how much those comments had hurt, and how they all suddenly stopped after she lost her baby, only to be replaced by awkward silence on the topic.

Kitty spoke again. 'All I'm missing is my man to go on adventures with… or just to sit with, like this, and I'll be sorted. But he hasnae exactly been forthcoming so far, so…'

'You'll just wait.'

'Aye.' Kitty turned her face to the pale moon. 'I'll wait.'

Beatrice stood to go, and when Kitty noticed her leaving she too stood up and pulled her in for a hug. 'Sweet dreams,' she said, giving her a gentle squeeze across her back.

'You too.'

Beatrice swung one leg back through the low window into the corridor while Kitty settled herself down again, cross-legged under the night sky.

'*Umm*, Kitty?' she said, tentatively, remembering again the plans she and Atholl had worked out so carefully that afternoon. 'If I ever annoy you by acting like a pushy know-it-all, I'm sorry. OK?'

Kitty squinted her eyes and laughed. 'Unlikely, but all right. I forgive you in advance for any and all misdemeanours. How's that?'

'OK. Just remember you said that? OK? Night then.'

Kitty smiled placidly before turning her face away again, closing her eyes and losing herself in the sounds of the waves lapping against the sea wall.

Chapter Eleven

Matchmaking

In August, the evening tides bring the water right up to the sea wall submerging the wide, curving, stony sands of Port Willow beach but by morning the shore is revealed again, the moored boats are stranded once more, the bay is scattered with shells, sea glass, and the occasional frilled pink jellyfish, and the oystercatchers and red shanks gather to stealthily pick the shore clean.

The locals live by these rhythms set by the sea. The men bring home the early catch against the receding tide and the work of sorting it into iced boxes on the jetty begins long before the milk float trundles its way silently along the row of pastel-painted cottages in hues of pale lemon, salmon pink and baby blue.

The postmistress on her bicycle is next on her rounds, followed by teenage twins delivering the morning papers with earbuds firmly wedged in, shoulders hunched and eyes cast down as though unaware of how beautiful their surroundings are.

Beatrice observed it all with her morning coffee from her people-watching vantage point; her bedroom windows on the first floor of The Princess and the Pea Inn. She had woken up early, on this, her third morning at the inn, not long after sunrise, to see it all.

Clattering sounds from the kitchen below told her Gene had started his breakfast preparations and the smell of sausages and bacon began drifting upstairs tempting her appetite – which she was astonished to find was growing by the day.

Rich would be pleased if he knew. 'You can't live off coffee and chocolate biscuits forever,' she'd heard him remark many times over the early summer months before he suddenly extricated himself from their shared life and all of her messy emotions and what she was slowly coming to realise had been erratic behaviour.

She thought for a moment that if her phone ever dried out and sparked into life again she could send him a picture of herself grinning over her breakfast plate, haggis slices and all, before dismissing the notion as ridiculous. They hadn't spoken for at least a month; she very much doubted he'd want to receive a daft selfie out of the blue. He'd think she was still crazy.

Beatrice swallowed down the bitter thoughts, wondering why she was being besieged by these horrible, intrusive memories so often since her arrival in Port Willow.

Last night on the phone Angela had said again how this whole spontaneous holiday might be a good thing for Beatrice and had urged her to stay on in Scotland until the end of her booking, even though Beatrice protested she still hadn't fully made up her mind what to do. 'You need a bit of head space to think things through,' Angela had said, and Beatrice had uttered the same reply she always did. She didn't want to think things through. She didn't want to remember.

What she wanted was to be busy. Looking out at the scenes of village life below her window brought back a small kind of contentedness she hadn't felt in a while, and she was surprised she could find a little solace seeing the bustling lives of these strangers.

Beatrice pulled the lacy curtains aside once more and leaned towards the glass. Soon the tourists would be up and about. Their cars, burdened with bike racks, lined Port Willow's waterfront end to end. Last night she'd watched their attempts at parking and turning around on the single lane road between the cottages and the sea wall. There was often no room for turning at the top of the village and many cars had to reverse the length of the street, repeatedly aborting their efforts when met with a car coming the other way. The manoeuvring was a logistical wonder and a source of fascination for her, less so for the tutting locals who had the good sense to leave their vehicles at the station carpark.

Sipping her coffee, she tried to imagine the village in a time before cars, when it was a quiet bay of fishermen's cottages and families, willow weavers and – Atholl had told her – artists of all kinds who came for the light and the Highland vistas.

Beatrice couldn't quite understand how she hadn't appreciated the views on Saturday. Her memories of arriving by train were hazy at best. But she was feeling the fog that had clouded her thinking for the last few months lifting a little each day here, and she was actually looking forward to the day ahead. She had a job to do. She had a plan. And best of all, she had a co-conspirator in Atholl.

He too had emerged out of the mists, coming into increasingly sharper focus as her time in Port Willow progressed and she smiled over her memories of his quiet presence and calm direction yesterday as they weaved rustic willow wreaths over their sweet, sunny picnic.

He had been as enthusiastic about the matchmaking scheme as she was, if a little less convinced of its chances of success. She wouldn't let his reservations worry her. If anything, she wanted to prove to Atholl that a little love *could* fix up his brother and she wanted to prove to herself that love could follow on from heartbreak at least once.

Dressing for breakfast in cropped jeans and a loose white cotton top, she wondered at how hungry she was – and how excited she was for her day ahead – telling herself it had nothing to do with Atholl and all to do with the spot of matchmaking she'd devised, and if she didn't hurry she wouldn't get it all sorted out before this evening.

—

Atholl had told Beatrice that Kitty was staying in one of the back bedrooms at the inn and she had shoved the note under her door where she was sure it would be seen. It read:

> *Dear Kitty,*
>
> *I meant to say last night that I want to thank you properly for rescuing me from the beach on Sunday and for knowing when a woman needs chips and gin. It was lovely talking with you and I'd really like a chance to repay your kindness. Are you free tonight? Come to the jetty and wear something fancy, or don't, if that sounds weird, but be prepared for a lovely evening!*
>
> *Lots of Love,*
> *Beatrice x*

Beatrice had shovelled copious amounts of bacon and toast into her mouth and even managed half a slice of the fried haggis before telling herself it was an acquired taste and she'd brave it again tomorrow morning. As she gulped her coffee she heard, but couldn't see, Atholl, his musical voice drifting through from the inn's kitchens.

'Have ye a minute, Gene?'

The lull in the kitchen clattering told her Gene was listening.

'There's an inn guest arriving tonight by boat. They mentioned they'd need help with their luggage. Can ye meet them from the jetty at eight, please? I'll be doing the evening meals or else I'd do it myself.'

Beatrice picked up the grunt of what she hoped was agreement over the sizzling sound of fresh bacon hitting a hot pan.

'And can you wear something smart.'

'Smart? Is it the queen comin'?'

'Well she's long overdue a visit, is she no'?' Atholl replied good-naturedly and, to Beatrice's ears, evasively. 'They sounded well-to-do on the phone and they're expecting a welcome so please put your suit on? Like Dad used to in the old days when some of the guests arrived by water.'

But Gene said nothing. Had he agreed? She knew she'd have to wait until later to find out because she'd spotted Atholl leaving the inn through the back door and passing the breakfast room window. The fluttering sensation in her stomach surprised her. Had she wanted him to look in at her and smile? Well, he hadn't. She heard him out on the street calling for Echo and the sound of obedient, scurrying feet pattering down the stairs above her, the two of them heading off to complete the next task on Beatrice's list.

'Morning, Bea, pet!' Cheryl and Jillian pulled up chairs at Beatrice's table in a cloud of hairspray and perfume and leaned in conspiratorially.

She'd been caught staring after Atholl Fergusson again, thought Beatrice, but the women were too focused on the task at hand to tease her.

'We've everything we need, now are you sure about this?' Jillian asked, her gold hoop earrings swinging as she whispered, throwing a glance at the kitchen door.

'I *think* Gene has taken the bait,' Beatrice replied in a low voice.

'Well, he's had that messy mop fixed so we may as well do the whole shebang!' Cheryl said, excitement crackling her voice.

'So, it's manicure, facial, manscaping those brows and taming that chest wig that's escaping his shirt?' Beatrice whispered.

Cheryl laughed. 'Eee, I thought it was going to jump out and run up someone's trouser leg when I first caught sight of that fuzz.'

'It is a bit Burt Reynolds,' Beatrice laughed, before biting her lip when she was met by the blank looks of the two younger women. 'Never mind, before your time. Just make sure he's got his collar done up and he's looking presentable and don't, whatever you do, let on that he's actually going on a date. He'll run a mile.'

Jillian nodded sharply like a private taking orders, thoroughly enjoying the secret mission. 'Yes ma'am. Eight o'clock?'

'Eight o'clock. And I'll pay you later, when I get some cash.' Beatrice wondered where on earth the nearest cash machine might be. In her haste to catch the train on Saturday she hadn't thought to stock up on real money and now that she was beginning to run out she didn't fancy catching the train to Lochalsh to get some more.

'Divn't be daft. We're doing this as a favour for that poor Gaelic teacher. She looks so lonely sitting at that bar staring at her laptop all hours of the day,' Cheryl replied.

'Let's hope it works,' whispered Jillian, just as Gene emerged from the kitchen to take the newcomers' orders.

'So, you're, um, you're staying then?' Cheryl asked, a little too loudly and self-consciously.

'Maybe for a day or two longer,' Beatrice nodded.

She pretended not to see the amused glances between the two women. Beatrice gulped the last of her coffee, looked at her watch and made her excuses to leave. There was still so much to do and the wonderful feeling of being useful again made her almost lightheaded. Even if it didn't work, she had to try. Kitty had been so kind to her, and Gene's heartache resonated so deeply with her own sense of abandonment and loss. At that moment all her focus was concentrated on bringing the pair together. The resultant excitement felt like a shot of anaesthetic temporarily numbing her own pain.

Chapter Twelve

Surprising Gene

The sun was setting over the bay as Beatrice made her way along the seafront, coming to a stop beside the smart holiday cottages that had once upon a time been the schoolmaster's house and salting lofts.

Scanning the street she caught sight of a few holiday-makers returning from sunny seal-spotting daytrips or a long day's hiking in the hills on the other side of the bay.

After a few moments, Seth cycled past with his wrapped fish supper in the basket on the front of his bike. Beatrice watched him pass silently and he gave her a knowing wink. She heard the brakes squeak as he came up alongside the pavement at the entrance to the jetty, and stepped off his bike, rummaging in his pocket for a large key which he worked in the lock of a rusty fuse box beneath the signs advertising his family's boat trips and informing visitors of the high and low tide times. The waves were gently lapping towards the sea wall. Soon the sand would be covered again and the jetty bounded by water. Seth looked around at Beatrice, flashed a quick thumbs-up and turned another key inside the box.

It had been a hot hour's work stringing the glass bulbs along the jetty with Seth that afternoon, never sure if they would be spotted by a curious Kitty or Gene. As the lights blazed into life now, shining in the mellow early evening light, Beatrice was fully satisfied their efforts had been worth it. Clapping her hands gleefully, she beamed her gratitude at Seth as he locked the box and cycled off to eat his supper at home, a smile of satisfaction curling beneath his grey whiskers.

Surprised to find her heart was pounding, she scanned the street again and checked her watch. Five to eight. She took a deep breath and leaned back against the cool stone of the cottage wall behind her.

That was when she felt the hand grasping her own. Stifling a gasp, she turned and found Atholl Fergusson standing in the half light in the narrow passageway between the cottages and holding a finger to his pursing lips, his eyes smiling. She looked down at his hand enclosing her fingers, and Atholl, suddenly ruffled, released her.

The panicked look in his eyes told her of his sudden regret and embarrassment at touching her, and the realisation that she minded him letting her go burned in her chest and made her blush. It felt all the worse to hear him stumbling over his words in his haste to move on from the moment's awkwardness.

'I'm sorry, I uh… I'm sorry. She's on her way down now, in a bonny red dress, no less.'

Overlooking his apology in the hope he could be spared further embarrassment, she tried to squeeze some hope and excitement into her voice. 'And Gene?'

'No, he's just opted for a suit.'

'We're in so much trouble if they aren't up for this.'

'Hey, did my brother help send you into the path of careering cattle or didn't he?'

'Good point. I shouldn't be helping either of you!' She watched him smile at her remark. 'Have you got the wine?'

Atholl produced the bottle from the bag by his feet. 'Vintage champagne to sweeten him up.'

'It's not Gene I'm worrying about now. Oh God, here she is.'

Kitty Wake drifted along the seafront in a sixties-inspired dress, her red hair tied up in a smooth ponytail and bouncing as she walked. 'Beautiful,' said Beatrice to no one in particular.

'I'll be off then,' Atholl whispered, withdrawing into the shade once more.

'You're not staying to help?'

'I've the starters to bring. And no, Gene'll take it better if he thinks it's just you scheming, at first, at least.'

And with an emphatic thumbs-up and a mouthed, 'You'll be fine,' he was gone.

Beatrice smoothed down the white linen apron she was wearing and stepped out into the street to meet her new friend. At least, she hoped they'd still be friends after this.

—

'What do you reckon?' Atholl whispered.

'I feel a bit weird watching. We should go in.'

'And miss your handiwork? Naw,' he replied. 'Besides, I've brought us these.' He offered up two steaming bowls of Cullen Skink.

Beatrice had been lying, her chin resting on her hands, on the flat roof above the inn porch. She'd only meant to pop outside for a second, just to check on the surprised daters from a distance and unseen, but the night was so warm and the stars so bright she'd stayed to breathe in the clean, salty air mixed with delicious seafood scents. Atholl, now finished helping with the evening service, had sneaked out too, and was settling himself down beside her.

'How ever did you get Patrick to agree to come in and cook tonight – especially after Gene sent him away so unceremoniously the other night?' Beatrice wondered aloud, stirring the dish and inhaling the mouth-wateringly savoury steam, all hot garlic and salty stock, fresh parsley, lobster, smoked haddock and cream.

'In return for a daily delivery of seafood fresh from his boats, of course. He's a braw cook and understands what to do with the day's catch, as all good fishmongers do. And he's known us both since we were bairns so he didn't mind giving us a lesson.'

'Will the inn *really* be serving seafood dinners again? What about Gene and all his objections?'

'We'll see. For now Mrs Mair has learned the Cullen Skink recipe by helping Patrick in the kitchen, and she insists she's a decent cook, given the chance. And if her Scotch broth and shortbread's anything to go by, maybe she *could* go some way towards replacing Lana in the kitchen.'

'You mean if you supply her with something other than industrial quantities of oven chips?'

Atholl had a faraway look in his eyes. 'And if Gene cannae be tempted back into the kitchen by the taste upon his lips tonight, I'll have to look further afield for a new head cook. I'll have done my best for Gene and it'll be time. It'd be a shame, though. This Cullen Skink is braw but nothing compared to Gene's cooking.'

Beatrice followed his gaze across the road at the scene on the jetty, attracted there by the light sounds of Kitty's laughter carrying on the evening breeze.

They could just make out that Kitty's bare shoulders were now draped in Gene's suit jacket, and even though they'd finished their cranachan and coffee at least half an hour ago they were still sitting drinking the last of the champagne as the moon rose in the heavens above them. Beatrice took all this as a good sign. They'd actually pulled it off.

They'd taken it well, the surprise, Beatrice told Atholl as she took her first ever taste of Cullen Skink.

'*Mmm*, this really is delicious, Atholl.' She threw a chef's kiss and a wink towards him and he laughed heartily.

'So it turns out I didn't need to use any of our pre-prepared arguments on Gene, after all. There was a milli-second where I thought he was going to turn on his heel and run off like he did on Saturday night when you ambushed him with Patrick and his box of seafood.' Beatrice was laughing too between savoury mouthfuls. 'I even put on my trainers this evening in case I had to bolt along the road after him. But he took one look at Kitty standing there all wide-eyed and stunned into silence, and he patted down his suit, ran his hand over his head, all flustered and red but then he crooked his arm and said, "If you've nae objection, will you come to dinner wi' me, Kitty Wake."'

Atholl laughed at Beatrice's impression of his brother.

'Good for him. He brushes up well, does he no'?'

'He really does.'

Beatrice didn't like to say she had been almost as surprised as Kitty to see Eugene Fergusson looking fresh-faced after his makeover by the Bobby Dazzler duo, who had revelled in their mission. He had a hint of movie star glamour about him now in his dad's baggy-legged vintage demob suit and a crisp white shirt. His skin had been bright and dewy, and his eyes dazzlingly blue behind his contact lenses.

Kitty had smiled and blushed down towards her feet and Beatrice had simply watched it happen: the way Gene's eyes danced over Kitty's red dress and how his shoulders had melted and his chest swelled with the deep intake of breath as he realised what was happening – he was being set up on his first date in years.

'You were right, Beatrice,' said Atholl. 'They look like a very fine couple together.'

Beatrice smiled, thinking of the way she'd followed them to the linen draped, candle-lit table at the end of the jetty and how Gene had stooped his back and leant a little awkwardly to the side so Kitty could comfortably hold his forearm. There was a hint in the way they moved together that spoke of something shared, something that just fitted.

'Gene even pulled Kitty's chair out for her to sit down,' Beatrice said, still watching the couple, thinking dreamily of the sweet old-fashioned gesture and how Kitty had smoothed her retro petticoated skirts beneath her as she sat down, all the while looking up into her date's shyly bowed face, her eyes reflecting the golden glow of the lights strung along the walkway.

They hadn't spoken during the stroll along the jetty or as Beatrice uncorked and poured the cold champagne but Kitty had masked a grin when Beatrice threw her a wink over Gene's shoulder and she'd left them to their date, assuring them Atholl would be out in a jiffy with the inn's new seafood specialities and Gene had remarked gruffly,

'I knew my wee brother would hae something to do with this,' and he and Kitty had broken into harmonious laughter together.

Beatrice tore her eyes from the couple and instead considered Atholl eating absorbedly in his white t-shirt, jeans and apron. His hair had formed in tight curls around his forehead from the steam of the kitchen.

The heat of the Cullen Skink warmed her against the little chill in the air, a sign that August was slowly passing and the cooler, shorter days were on their way. 'Delicious,' she said again with a smile, but in that moment her heart felt suddenly dull again after the excitement of the day and the slow realisation that her task was completed. She had nothing else to occupy her now, other than thoughts of returning to Warwickshire.

'Beatrice?' Atholl's voice came to her as though through a wall. 'Are you all right?'

'I'm just tired; it's been a long day.'

'That it has. You did well today.'

'*We* did. And Cheryl and Jillian, Seth and Patrick, and Mrs Mair. Talk about a team effort.'

'You have a knack for bringing people together, Beatrice.'

She smiled, saying nothing and wondering what she would do now. They'd fixed up Kitty and Gene – any further meddling in their love affair would be babying Gene to an unfair degree, wouldn't it? And she'd taken her weaving lesson – Atholl surely wouldn't want her hanging around the workshop any longer – and she really ought to try to fix her own life back at home. Yet the idea of stepping onto the platform at Warwick station lined her stomach with lead.

She was pulled out of these thoughts by the sound of Atholl clearing his throat. When she looked at him her heart sank even further.

'Beatrice, I, *uh*… I don't want to upset you but…'

'Oh no, what?' She knew her skin was blanching, just as Atholl's was flushing.

'Beatrice… I needed the computer in the reception this morning and, *uh*… when it powered up there was a Facebook page frozen open on the screen…' His Adam's apple bobbed as his words tailed away.

'Oh.' She felt herself shrink. Had he seen her profile picture with Rich at the hospital? He must have, why else would he be mentioning it now, and why so awkwardly? It would certainly explain the recent softening in his attitude. Hadn't he been kinder to her today? Hadn't he touched her hand earlier on the waterfront when they were waiting for Gene and Kitty to arrive, and hadn't he immediately regretted it and snatched his hand away like she was a damaged thing, something he had to be extra careful with?

She hadn't liked Atholl being brusque with her, but this? This wasn't what she wanted at all. Even if her first few encounters with the Fergussons had been tough, she had at least found relief in being with people who didn't know for sure why she was a total mess and who didn't look at her with sympathy in their eyes – but that was exactly what Atholl was doing right now. Except, there was something else mixed in with his searching gaze, not just sympathy, but curiosity and caution too. Had he seen the relationship status on her profile, which most definitely still said *Married to Richard Halliday*?

What must he be thinking? Did he think she might be married with a child and a husband somewhere out there in the world missing her? Maybe he'd guessed she'd been dumped and was hiding from the breakup? Or maybe he'd grasped at the truth of what had happened – that she was grieving for a lost child and a marriage that was all over bar the shouting? But he couldn't know about her losing her mum too, or about the redundancy, and she was glad of that. She looked down, wanting to disappear from under that gaze.

'Beatrice...' Atholl was shifting closer.

'I was just trying to contact my sister... stupid computer crashed...'

'You can talk to me... if you like?'

Beatrice looked up from her bowl to find Atholl's eyes level with her own, entreating her to talk. 'You helped me with my problems,' he was saying. 'I hate to call Gene a problem, but you know what I mean. Will you not let me help you?'

'How can you help me?'

'Your sadness. I can listen, I can help...'

'You can fix me?'

'No, that's not what I'm saying, but...'

Beatrice began to stand, handing him her bowl which he took, his eyes wide and mouth open.

'What I've got, you can't fix, Atholl.'

He drew his neck back and Beatrice saw the concern in his eyes.

'Look, I'm fine. I'm just tired.'

Atholl was on his feet now, his hand running nervously through his curls. 'Don't go yet.'

Beatrice was already stooping to pass through the low window from the flat roof back onto the carpeted corridor that led to her room. He didn't follow after her but she heard him bidding her a fraught goodnight.

As she turned to close the bedroom door, she caught a glimpse of him leaning taut muscled arms on the window frame, his skin pale as pearl in the moonlight, wearing an expression of exasperation and alarm that made her shudder. It was a look she had seen on Rich's face many times in the weeks before he left her and she had tried so hard to ignore its significance then. She never wanted to see that look again.

Chapter Thirteen

Baby-making

Leaning against the closed door as if to barricade it shut, Beatrice clutched a palm to the pounding in her chest as the memories flooded back, along with the heavy, burning lump right at her core.

She'd felt it before, but tonight its presence was more pressing than ever and she at last understood what it was. It was words.

Words swallowed down, stuck inside, and never spoken aloud.

The feelings had been too large to express and the lump was compounded by her pain at the loss of her lovely mum – a woman who had barely lived her life at all when she got sick. Her mum had escaped a horrible man, whisking her children away from him to a safer place when they were just babies and worked all her life to provide for them, then just as her life was looking a little easier and there were weddings and grandbabies and travel on the horizon, the diagnosis had come and swept away all her plans for a bright future with her thriving family made up exclusively of women and a little baby girl who she adored so much.

That was when the words first started to get trapped, thought Beatrice, still leaning heavily against the door. Then Helen Smethwick had rocked up and turned her loose from the job that had anchored her for nearly two decades, the only occupation she'd known and the source of so much of her pride and confidence.

The ache of this had lain on top of her grief for her dying mum, layering it over like sediment, thick striations of shame, powerlessness, and bitter anger piling up.

Then there had been the loss of her baby and the great blow it had dealt her marriage, and Rich's dad with his coldly confident, 'I'm sure it's for the best,' and 'There must have been something wrong with it.'

Wrong?

Beatrice turned the key in the lock before racing up the ladder and onto the towering princess bed, burying her face in the pillow so she could scream the word. '*Wrong!* I just wanted my baby breathing in my arms, no matter what.'

Clasping her hand to her mouth, she let herself cry into the soft down, knowing no one could hear.

At the time, although she hadn't been able to fully process why she had kept the words inside and she was unable to anticipate the disastrous consequences of bottling up her most painful feelings, she had made a decision. She decided to channel the hurt that she *felt* into something that she could *do*.

She couldn't be nothing but grief and loss and failure. Instead she would do what she did best – make a plan and put it into action. She would do research, write a list, consult the experts, and she would find out how to fast-track herself and Rich back to happiness. She was going to get pregnant again and quick.

Beatrice groaned to think of it and the emotions buried deep within her shifted. 'Again with the clarity,' she murmured into the pillow before rolling onto her side. She could see it all.

She had awakened one morning in May feeling oddly brighter; the first day of her second proper period since the miscarriage – day one of a new cycle. Her head buzzed with the hope and excitement of it all. Potentially, she could get pregnant that month. Even though she knew they could have gone for it the previous month, and she'd been dying to, what with Rich steering clear and looking so sad, she had held off mentioning it. Talk about willpower.

But now she was ready – or that's what she'd told herself. She'd started taking her folic acid again, inspired by the online baby forums about mums who got pregnant in the months after losing a baby and how they got to full term and a take-home baby. Rainbow babies, she had learned they were called – babies made after miscarriage.

She'd discovered there were certain foods that could aid conception – Brazil nuts and pineapple cores – and she had gorged on them in secret and Rich hadn't thought to ask why she was carrying four pineapples back from the shops in her backpack.

She'd confessed her action plan to Angela and Vic one night over dinner at their place while Clara slept on Vic's chest and Vic tried not to dribble rogan josh over her slumbering daughter. Beatrice told them all about how she'd surprised Rich with the idea, now a fully formed, bullet-pointed action plan.

'So, I made Rich his favourite dinner last night and told him about how we could start trying again any day now – in fact I'll most likely be fertile in about two weeks, but he was horrified. He said he wasn't sure he wanted to try again, and I burst into tears over the profiteroles and asked why, and he said he didn't think he could go through it all again, if the worst should happen. And I ended up shouting, "*You* can't go through it? *You* can't?" and storming out, and the whole time he was looking at me like I was nuts. A bit like you are now, Angela, come to think of it!'

And Angela had replied, 'Of course I don't think you're nuts; you're grieving. It's only natural you'd want to try again.'

'I get it,' Vic had chipped in. 'When we were trying for Clara, in between all those failed rounds of assisted insemination, we were the same. It was a huge rollercoaster of hope then despair then hope again. I understand the desperation. I really do.' Vic looked down at Clara and the word *desperation* rang in Beatrice's ears over the sound of Angela snapping a poppadum and squirming in her chair.

'I'm not desperate.' Beatrice had looked between her sister and Vic. 'You think I'm desperate?'

'That's not what she's saying, is it?' said Angela. 'We just know those feelings, and they're a lot to deal with, that's all. They can overwhelm you if you're not careful. Consume you, even.'

Beatrice saw the wary glance Vic threw Angela. They'd spoken about her before, clearly. What was this? An intervention?

'Well, if you've been there, you'll understand why I want to do this quickly and efficiently.'

'This is Mother Nature you're talking about. You can't rush these things. Even with the best fertility doctors our money could buy, it took us so long to get Clara.'

Three pairs of eyes fell upon the sleeping child and Beatrice sighed.

'So where is Rich now?' Vic asked.

'At the pub. *Apparently* I'm obsessed with getting pregnant again. It was all my talk about ways of increasing cervical mucus to aid conception that did it.'

Vic let her fork settle on her plate with a queasy look on her face. Beatrice didn't let that put her off.

'But he did ask what was with all the pineapples and really he needn't be so flaming squeamish. He turned so grey I thought he was having an aneurysm. I can't help thinking of Charlotte on *Sex and the City* when she's in couples' therapy with Trey, her drippy, mummy's boy husband. You know, Kyle MacLachlan? Yum!'

Angela shrugged.

'Never mind. Anyway, Charlotte taunts Trey for being sex-shy and shouts about how at all costs she *mustn't scare the penis*!'

Angela and Vic screamed with laughter at this, making Clara wriggle and squeak but she didn't awaken.

'Aren't you glad you didn't have to scare any penises to conceive Clara?' Beatrice had blurted, before seeing the look of shock on their faces and immediately feeling guilty because the memory of all those injections, blood tests and scary procedures Angela had had to endure – as well as all the expense and the waiting – must still be so fresh for them both. 'I'm sorry! What I'm saying is, I know you had a really hard time of it and I know I'm not the only one who's struggled, but you three just go to show that with the right planning and a lot of effort you can get your take-home baby in the end. And that's what I want.'

'OK, we get it, just please give yourself some time too, OK?'

'Ange, the last thing I have is time. I'm thirty-nine, this might be my last chance.'

The couple had smiled with crumpled, closed tight lips, a little shadow of defeat and resignation in their eyes.

'I don't want to upset you, but… you're a bit… jumpy today, a bit… hyper,' Angela said, looking down at her food, trying to sound unthreatening.

'I'm fine, honestly. Totally fine,' Beatrice said with a wave of her hand. 'Anyway,' she continued, determined to make them relax again. 'Tomorrow I'm bulk buying milk chocolate-covered Brazils because the plain ones are awful. Who cares if Rich raises an eyebrow or two at them? Obsessed, indeed! I'm *organised*, that's what.'

Lying on the towering mattresses, Beatrice finally accepted that Angela, Vic and Rich – especially Rich – might well have had a point. But at the time, the action-planning really had given her something to feel hopeful about.

She recalled the days following the miscarriage which she'd spent wandering round town in trainers and sweats, or on long walks along the canal, out to the supermarket and the big Boots, anything but sitting still and alone with her thoughts.

She had felt better when moving. It was a salve for the restlessness that wouldn't leave her in peace.

Then she had struck upon the idea of asking Angela if she could push Clara in her buggy one day so that she had some company and looked less weird ranging about town on her own.

Walking with Clara had been a revelation. She just slept in her buggy or sucked on rice cakes, looking about her, and they'd gone miles together – all the way to the castle on one occasion. She remembered the grave look on Angela's face when she'd taken Clara back home that afternoon, turning her over to Vic for a feed, when she'd said, 'It was nice. People stop and talk to Clara and to me. They think I'm her mummy.'

And the walking had helped when the letter arrived from the hospital letting her know the date of her six-month scan, still weeks away, and she'd torn it into pieces wondering how the system could have let that happen and telling the empty house that she had thought she couldn't feel any worse, but it turned out she could. Rich was at work and missed the whole thing and when he came home that evening the scraps of paper were in the bin outside and they went unmentioned forevermore.

She'd gone in secret to the GP too and heard there was no explanation for the miscarriage, none that they could ever know of. The GP told her he wouldn't be prepared to investigate further unless she'd had a few. Beatrice had experienced a dizzying wave of nausea at that.

'A few?' she'd replied. 'How are you meant to endure this more than once? God, those poor women. I hadn't really thought that this could happen again. And all those poor daddies.'

In those first few desperate weeks she had felt sadder when she thought of Rich than when she thought about what she herself had lost. She had truly felt sorry for him. And she couldn't fix it.

Normally, if there was a problem, she could swing into action and come up with some solutions. Like when Vic and Angela had needed help finding a donor service and paying for a few rounds of their assisted inseminations. Her talent for organising stuff – as well as half her savings – had come in really handy then. But her efficiency and organisation hadn't been enough to help her in her own time of crisis.

All the temperature charting and ovulation prediction kits and the mad bicycling of her legs above her head after sex, and all those bitter, chewy pineapple cores and Brazil nuts – none of it had helped her. Rich had taken his broken heart and left.

She had scared him away and proved his vicious, boozy old dad right. No baby ever fixed a struggling marriage. And no myopic striving to conceive when she and Rich should have been grieving had fixed it either.

Beatrice felt the sleepiness come over her. The inn was silent and warm and she became aware of the waves shushing against the sea wall over the road. A small sense of peacefulness reached her. Was this it? Had she had a breakthrough? All by herself? *Hah!*

Yes, she had been right after all, hadn't she? You didn't have to spill your heart out to get some clarity on your feelings. Vic, Angela, Rich – and Atholl Fergusson – had all been wrong!

Atholl Fergusson may well have thought he could see through all of her silence and withholding and he may well have wanted to encourage her to talk, and so fix her, but that wasn't going to happen. She would never tell him or anyone else the humiliating story of how she drove her husband away by turning a cooling marriage, which may even have been salvageable at one point, into an uncomfortably fraught place that Rich couldn't bear any longer.

It's better to leave Port Willow now, she told herself. Let Atholl think of her as cold and sad and then forget about her altogether, even at the risk that her sadness might be compounded by leaving this lovely, eccentric place before she'd had the chance to get to know it properly and just when she was beginning to connect with new people and enjoy herself.

Yes, she'd get out of here in the morning, taking her scraps of fresh insight with her, along with the heavy lump of words within her chest.

Chapter Fourteen

An Invitation

Beatrice had been standing over her open suitcase for at least five minutes, frozen to the spot. She knew that if she was going to make the morning train she'd have to leave now.

Could she sneak out and along the front without being seen? Everyone would be up and about by now. The aroma of bacon and toast was wafting in through the open window and the calm music of receding waves gently churning pebbles accompanied her thoughts. Could she really leave without saying goodbye, especially to Kitty, and more especially, to Atholl?

The gentle tap at her door that turned to insistent knocking sent her shoulders flying up to her ears as she looked accusingly at its source.

'Beatrice? Are you in there? Beatrice?'

She held her breath, registering the concern in Atholl's voice, before exhaling with a sharp blow. She opened the door only to witness his eyes crease as he spotted the gaping suitcase on the floor behind her.

'I came to apologise for prying...' he began.

'No, don't. *I'm* sorry. I didn't mean to snap at you. It's just I came here to get away from... everything, and I'm not ready to talk about it. I can't see how I ever will be. OK?'

Atholl's gaze passed over the suitcase again before scanning over her body and flicking back up to her eyes. Could he tell she'd dressed comfortably for the train journey back down south, in her jeans and white trainers and a thin navy jumper? If he *could* tell, he wasn't going to let that stop him talking.

'I, *umm*, I've come to issue an invitation, actually. To Skye, with me, if you'd like? I guessed you might have had your fill o' weaving and Kitty told me the other day you hadnae pressed her for any Gaelic lessons so... I have one of Seth's boats for the day... and a picnic.'

She caught Atholl's look of hope and then embarrassment. Now he was taking an interest in the door jamb, absentmindedly fingering the hinges. She couldn't help smiling, even though it was accompanied by a creeping sense of defeat.

'You want to spend the day with me?'

'Aye, why would I no'?'

Despite everything within her telling her to retreat and that it was time to leave, she found herself agreeing to go. Skye sounded intriguing and she could avoid talking about herself for a few hours if it meant going to one of the places that her mum had always wanted to see but never had the chance, and, of course, it would be nice to spend a little more time in the presence of Atholl Fergusson with all his kindness and those blue eyes she never seemed to tire of seeing.

'Really?' When he smiled back, his lips pursed closed over his teeth and his cheeks flushed.

'You did say I should see more of the place and everyone else seems to think I should stay and have a proper holiday. One more day can't hurt?' This came out as a genuine question but she doubted Atholl could understand her reservations.

'Well, then. I'll see to the last of the arrangements and meet ye by the jetty after you've had your breakfast. Come prepared for all weathers,' he said, turning to go.

'Actually, I'll follow you down.' Beatrice grabbed her keys and made after Atholl. 'Have you spoken with Gene since last night? How did it go?' she asked as they reached the turn in the staircase, the kitchen sounds and the low murmur of the diners' chatter growing louder… and was that someone singing?

'See for yourself,' Atholl threw her another smile as he turned for the back door of the inn, pointing Beatrice's way into the breakfast room before disappearing out of sight into the morning sunshine, Echo joining him with delighted bounds.

Sure enough, a woman with a beautiful voice was quietly singing and mixed in with her sweet melody was a low, booming hum. Beatrice sneaked a peek in the kitchen door and there, side by side in matching white aprons, were Kitty and Gene.

'*Green grow the rushes-o.*' Kitty trilled, as Gene scraped butter over a triangle of toast before offering it to Kitty who smilingly took a bite before he too bit into it, all the while gazing at each other's faces.

So, thought Beatrice, Atholl isn't the only Fergusson brother whose pale cheeks are prone to flushing pink.

Two other crafters, older ladies who Beatrice recognised as some of the wool dyers who had also arrived on Saturday and who were taking lessons at the tartan mill in the next village, bustled past tutting and shaking their heads as they left. Their table was still pristinely set with fresh linen, their cutlery untouched and napkins still folded. Had they been served at all? Their grumbling as they left told her Gene hadn't even emerged from the kitchen to take their orders.

'If you're hoping for breakfast, you'll be lucky,' a voice piped up from the corner of the breakfast room. Turning round, Beatrice was delighted to see Cheryl and Jillian sitting with empty, sauce-streaked plates in front of them. 'We've been waiting for more toast and coffee for twenty minutes but those two love birds are still working their way through the entire Robert Burns songbook,' said Cheryl.

'So, it worked then!' Beatrice was already pulling up a chair at their table.

'According to Seth, Gene walked Kitty through the bar last night, taking a bottle of bubbly from the fridge before disappearing to her room, so draw your own conclusions about that,' said Jillian, not even bothering to whisper; there was no way they'd hear her over the singing.

'Amazing what a difference a makeover and a bit of encouragement can make,' Beatrice grinned, giving Jillian's hand an excited squeeze. 'I think we've done well there.'

'I'd say so,' she smiled back. 'I'll be expecting an invite to their wedding at this rate. We'd better get going anyway, we're moving on from oils to watercolours today, and we've got no chance of getting another brew here, have we?'

The singers had fallen markedly quiet all of a sudden. Cheryl leaned backwards on her chair and peered around the kitchen door before adding, knowingly, 'Now *that* kind of behaviour is definitely *not* going to get your sausages cooked.'

The three women tiptoed from the breakfast room together, only stopping to silently close the kitchen door on the couple who were wrapped in each other's arms, Kitty raised up on her tiptoes, kissing Eugene tenderly while the haggis slices burned in the pan.

Chapter Fifteen

The Skye Boat

It didn't matter that Beatrice was hungry, in fact she was glad to give the fried food a miss this morning as she realised her stomach was churning not because it was empty but because it was full of nerves – even though she most definitely *wasn't* going on a date.

No. Categorically this wasn't a date. On dates, you have to talk about yourself and answer awkward questions and she had no intention of doing that. This was just two people celebrating a bit of successful matchmaking with some sightseeing and tomorrow she was going back to Warwickshire to help Angela and Vic with their wedding plans and to see what her house looked like now the removal men had been and done Rich's dirty work.

She was going to Skye with Atholl to be nice and to prove she wasn't a moody cow, and maybe also because he was pleasant to be with. But that was all.

Back in her room she grabbed her bag, stuffed in her umbrella, sun lotion and shades, before stopping in front of her mirror to smooth her hair and brush on some mascara. Then, thinking again, she rushed back to the bathroom to brush her teeth for a second time that morning and slick on pale lipstick and dab perfume at her wrists.

Holding onto the sink she fixed a hard stare in the mirror. 'Get a grip, Bea. He's just another person who's taken pity on you. This is nothing more than a day's sightseeing on Skye, never mind it's with Atholl.' The words faltered and she shook her head in exasperation.

Was this how she was going to greet Atholl outside the inn, red-faced and flustered? 'Ridiculous!' She gripped her bag and headed downstairs. Ready or not, she'd agreed to go and no amount of awkwardness and inconvenient tummy butterflies was going to hold her back now.

–

He was waiting by the jetty, just as he'd said, a wicker picnic basket by his walking-booted feet. He was in black outdoorsy trousers and the same brown and orange checked shirt she'd seen him in the first time they'd met. Today it was worn open over a grey t-shirt like some Celtic model in a Barbour advert.

Echo sat obediently by his master's side on the board-walk, watching her and panting wide-mouthed as though he were smiling at her.

She gave herself another quick assessing glance down her body as she approached them along the sea wall, glad she'd worn her trainers thinking how muddy the walking in Skye might be, less glad they were white.

Coming to a stop in front of Atholl and Echo she found she was grinning but having trouble looking Atholl in the eyes. Why was she the one feeling this new kind of awkwardness when Atholl looked somehow cool and self-contained? As she was searching for her sunglasses in her bag, a good distraction from her awkwardness, she spotted the boat, already loaded with Atholl's jacket and woollen blankets.

'We're rowing? I thought when you said we had one of Seth's boats we'd be in something with an engine!'

'You'll see more if we're cutting through the water in silence.' Atholl stepped one foot into the little rustic-looking boat and steadied it enough for Echo to jump in and crawl the length of the hull beneath the two wooden benches before curling up in the stern ready for a snooze at sea.

Atholl's hand was reaching out for her own. Was he thinking she was going to make her excuses and run?

She didn't remember stepping into the bobbing craft, but she was sure the sensation of Atholl's strong hand clasping her own was indelibly imprinted on her nervous system.

He passed her the picnic basket which she stowed under the little bench she'd perched on and she watched as Atholl stepped into the boat, making it rock. Beatrice was relieved to catch a glimpse of a warmer Atholl when he laughed and grimaced all at once, finding his balance, deftly slipping the rope and pushing the boat off from the jetty.

'There's only one set of oars, Atholl, that doesn't seem very fair.'

He'd already grasped them and was adjusting them in the handles. 'You enjoy the journey. I don't mind rowing.'

And so she settled on the bench as best she could, holding the sides of the rocking boat until Atholl had it turned and facing out towards the mouth of the bay. When he made the first stroke she just happened to be making a remark about the blue skies and wondering if the weather would hold but found herself stopping mid-sentence, dry-mouthed and staring at the muscles moving in his forearms and at the broad expanse of his chest as the oars met the deep resistance of the water, his shoulders and biceps straining against the soft, washed-out fabric of his shirt.

'It's set to be warm all day,' he replied.

He was smiling. Had he noticed? How embarrassing. She vowed to be more sensible and turned her head to watch the gulls swooping over the water and the little fishing boats crisscrossing the harbour mouth. By the time the silence was beginning to feel crushing they were nearing the open water. Atholl steered them close to the rocks but the waves grew choppier.

She wanted to simply listen to the slap of water on the prow and the sounds of the gentle wind that was lifting her hair but felt she couldn't. She wittered something about wishing she had a camera to photograph the scene and Atholl greeted her chatter with silence, his eyes occasionally passing over her face before quickly flitting to where the oars met the water.

Eventually, when she spoke again, Atholl talked over her. His voice was unusually quiet and she could just make out something along the lines of, 'On the subject of bonny views, you, *uh*…' But her own overlapping words erased the sounds.

'Go ahead, you first,' he insisted, with what looked like relief.

'I was going to say, Gene seems happy.'

'That he does. And he's given me his word he'll help with the evening food service again.'

'No way!'

'No' bad, eh? Aye, he said Patrick and Mrs Mair did a good job wi' the seafood last night but if *he'd* made it he'd have served it wi' samphire and no' green beans, and he'd have gone easier on the garlic, and I said, well, there's only one way to see wha's recipes are better, and that was it, hook and line.'

'Amazing! So it all worked?'

'We'll see. Anyway, he's rustled up some bannock cakes for you, so you must be in his good books.'

'It certainly looked like all was forgiven when I saw him and Kitty kissing in the kitchen this morning.'

Atholl smiled and pulled another long stroke at the oars, his thighs tensing and his feet planted firm and wide.

'What were you going to say?' Beatrice asked.

'*Umm*, I forget.'

She filled the silence that followed. 'Bannocks, you say? What's a bannock?'

'A bit like a wee scone. They're good for breakfast.'

'No heart-shaped honey buns today then?' Beatrice remarked, finding she wanted to provoke him again. He was being altogether too serious and gentle, and a part of her missed his sparky wickedness. Kindness is all very well but not if it's provoked by sympathy. She wanted him to be nice to her for other, harder to admit, reasons. The boat fell silent again until the rocks at the harbour mouth came into closer view.

'Look! Seals!' Beatrice exclaimed. 'Actual seals.'

Atholl suppressed a delighted laugh at her surprise and let the oars settle, dripping in their holders.

The great rock jutting from the water was populated with seals of many colours and sizes basking in the sun, some raising their tails and their whiskers to the sky, others slumped sleepily, eyeing them as they drifted past. Even Echo raised his head to look.

'Good boy, Echo. You sit still, leave them be,' Atholl murmured under his breath.

The rest of their journey took them around a rocky promontory, the rowing visibly harder. Atholl leaned back into his exertions, pulling hard, filling his lungs then blowing through puffed cheeks and pursed lips. Beatrice sneaked surreptitious looks every so often, not knowing which was the more attractive view: Atholl's freckled porcelain skin, flushing cheeks and blue eyes narrowed fiercely with the work of steering their vessel, sweat beading at his hairline and turning his loose red waves into glistening tight curls; or the emerging views of the impressive new bridge they were passing under and the smart pleasure boats and ferries crossing the steely blue strait with the great green wild peaks of the Isle of Skye before them.

She found herself closing her eyes, listening not to the gentle waves and the cutting splash of the oars but zoning in on the increasingly deep breathing of her captain.

The crossing seemed to last only moments but after Atholl had steered the boat to ground on a pebbly bay that led to a private garden and a small carpark beyond, he took a long time to slake his thirst, drinking from a bottle of water from the picnic basket. Beatrice refused to indulge her longing to watch him so she simply imagined his moving throat and his head thrown back as he drank with one foot on the boat, the other onshore, asking herself all the while what exactly had gotten into her today.

'*Echo!*'

The whoops and screams of approaching children made her turn her head. 'Uncle Atholl, can we keep Echo here for the day again?' the littlest of a gang of five or six ecstatic kids cried.

'Go on then, but no jumping off the quayside with him this time; he's an old dug now.' Atholl registered Beatrice's surprise. 'Some of these are my cousin's bairns, and this is her garden. Most of my family are from the isle originally and live here now, Mum included. I moor here when I visit. This lot are happier to see Echo than they are to see me!'

Echo, his tail wagging, ears pricked up in delight, ran off with the children along the little beach.

'That's the last we'll see of him until we return. He'd rather help them eat their lunch and chase skimming stones than come with us,' Atholl said with a shrug.

Again, he was offering her his outstretched hand, again she held her breath at the all too brief sensation of his strength as he helped her onto dry land.

Together they dragged the boat up the beach until it rested on grass. That's when Beatrice made out the faded word on its side.

'*Mary?* Isn't that Seth's wife's name? You said this was his boat?'

'It is. All of Seth's boats are called *Mary*, you'll notice. But he's too old to row it, and it's no good for tourist trips anymore. So, any of the Port Willow residents can borrow it when they like.'

'*Hmm*,' Beatrice contemplated this as they walked through the garden and past great mallow bushes, the pink blooms alive with hornets and bees, the picnic basket swinging between them, each holding a side of the handle and Beatrice aware she wasn't pulling her weight in its carrying. She thought of what Kitty had told her of Seth's unusual love story. 'They lived apart for most of their marriage, didn't they?'

'That's right. They made it work.'

'I'm not sure I get it. Why stay together if you can't stand actually living together?'

'There's a lid for every pot and that's the way those two fitted.' Atholl shrugged as though this made perfect sense, and Beatrice found herself beginning to think it did.

They stepped off the mossy lawn onto a tarmacked driveway with a ramshackle garage by the roadside. Beatrice found herself looking up at the towering trees lining the road.

Atholl observed her for a moment before turning his own eyes to the treetops. 'Do ye see that nest up there at the top of yonder tree?'

It took her a moment to follow the line of his gaze and focus on the wide platform of twigs precariously built into the uppermost crook of a spindly, ancient pine.

'You cannae see from here but there's a female osprey on that nest. Were we to stand here all day you'd see her mate flying to her, bringing food for her and their chick.'

'I wish we *could* stay here all day then!'

'Ospreys are bonny creatures and special in so many ways – and rare too, only two hunder pairs of them in the Highlands. Ospreys mate for life, ye ken? But they spend half the year away from their mate too.'

'They do?'

Atholl's eyes flitted briefly to hers.

'They spend the winter apart, someplace warmer than Skye where the cold is something frightening. But they come back to their home every spring, they repair their nest together and they raise their young.'

'And then they separate again?'

'Aye, every autumn they part, knowing they'll find each other when the warmth returns to Scotland again. If they survive their migrations, that is.'

'That must be quite a reunion,' Beatrice smiled.

'I imagine it must be.'

'Are you saying that's what Seth and Mary were like? A pair of ospreys?'

'Aye, and all true lovers too. The longest winter and the greatest of journeys made all alone couldnae keep them apart forever. Not if they're true pairs.'

The look Atholl threw her at this was unreadable. Was he asking about her? If she was paired for life too and if this was a temporary migration? Why on earth would that interest him? No, he was talking about Seth, of course. She had, after all, asked about his curious relationship with Mary. But Beatrice couldn't help thinking of Rich and their own pairing. She'd never thought they'd be separated by hundreds of miles like this. She could never have imagined even a year or two ago that they'd not have spoken for weeks. She didn't even know his address now, and their shared nest had only yesterday been emptied of the last of his possessions by the removal men who'd have let themselves inside using the key Rich no longer had a use for. Rich still had no idea where she was. Maybe she should have tried to reach him to let him know?

'We're so remote out here on Skye, aren't we?' she said at last, her eyes still fixed on the nest.

'That we are. What makes ye say that now?'

Beatrice looked around at the beach behind her and the great mountains in the distance.

'Oh… I don't know. I just feel very far from Warwickshire all of a sudden.'

'You'll be home soon enough,' Atholl said, holding his voice level in contrast to the distinct shakiness of Beatrice's own.

'I suppose so. It's hard to remember what home feels like in a landscape like this. It's like nothing I've ever seen before.'

Atholl's lips curved and he laughed with a satisfied sniff. 'You're right, there's no other place like this on earth. I hope you'll be happy today, Beatrice.' As he spoke, something up above the road caught his eye and Beatrice found herself wishing he hadn't snapped his attention away from her quite so abruptly. 'And there he is, *look*!' Atholl's voice turned to an excited whisper. Beatrice froze as she caught the briefest glimpse of white and brown wings flashing against the blue summer sky. The osprey had come to an elegant stop upon the nest and disappeared from sight.

'I saw it!' she gasped.

Atholl's gaze met her own and they shared a satisfied smile.

'Is Skye full of surprises? We've only just arrived and I've seen an osprey.'

'You'd better believe it. This isle is alive with wonders.'

Beatrice grinned again and for a moment she couldn't seem to tear her eyes from his.

'*Umm*, anyway...' Atholl raised his free hand to rake his fingers through his hair before reaching into his pocket for a key. 'This is our transport for today.' He led the way around to the side of the garage and came to a stop beside a curious old car.

'Is this yours? I think I recognise this kind of car. My grandad had one when I was tiny. I definitely remember this bit.' She reached out to touch the deep green paint and the wooden struts that formed the boxy sides. 'I remember it looking like a Tudor house on wheels.'

'Morris Traveller; it's a design classic.'

'Are you a classic car lover? A petrol head?'

'*Eh*, no. This is the car we all share when we come to island. It belonged to some cousin or other once upon a time, and it's always parked here, or somewhere on the island, depending on who's got it. I asked Elsie if we could have it today.'

'Elsie?'

'My eldest cousin. She owns the house there. Some of those bairns were hers. God knows who the others belonged to.'

'Shouldn't we call in to see her? We can't just take the car and leave?'

Atholl considered this for a split second before dismissing it with a decisive frown. 'Naw, I dinnae think that's a good idea. We'd never get our day on the island. My family have a way of monopolising your time, and believe me, they'd be all over you. We can call in on the way home tonight.' He unlocked the passenger door and swung it open.

'Hop in!'

—

Beatrice gripped the seat and squinted at Atholl's determined expression as the gears screeched.

'Are we going to make it?'

The hill was the steepest she'd ever scaled in a car. A queue of tourist traffic was forming behind them. Beatrice glanced out the back window and winced to see increasingly dark exhaust fumes billowing behind them. 'We're losing speed, Atholl. Are we going to come to a stop? Will we roll backwards?' She tried to quell the rising alarm in her chest by concentrating on Atholl's features, which were set in firm concentration.

'Rusty's no failed me yet and he won't today,' he said, his jaw clenched around the words. 'But if you know who the patron saint of old bangers is, it might be a good time to start praying to them.'

She noticed the crinkle at the corners of his eyes. He wasn't afraid in the least, and so she told herself this probably meant she shouldn't be either.

'Come on, Rusty! You can do it!' she cried out the window into the summer air, which was growing cooler with every second of their climb.

Atholl looked across at her, a grin forming. 'That's the spirit! Come on, Rusty, old pal! We believe in you.'

The cars behind beeped their horns and the pair burst into triumphant cheers as Rusty reached the brow of the hill and they picked up speed. 'He's no' so good at the inclines but he can fly down the valleys like a rally car.'

But Beatrice was too distracted to reply. Spreading out ahead of her as far as she could see were enormous mountains, skies higher and wider than any she'd ever gazed up at, glinting sunlight hitting a thousand scintillating tarns and lochs as small and dazzling as sequins from this distance, and something utterly unexpected that took away her breath.

'Is… is that snow?' She pointed a finger to the highest peak ahead of them before realising that all the mountains were capped with sparkling white where they soared into cloudless blue.

Atholl gazed out the windscreen with a look of pride and awe. 'You're in the heavens up here, Beatrice. With the very angels themselves.'

'You have a way of making everything sound like poetry,' she said. Beatrice curled her feet beneath her on the seat and turned to lean her elbows on the window ledge, the fresh air blowing her hair back over her shoulders as she scanned the mountaintops for a glimpse of her own angel. Were such things possible up here on this curious island? For a second, she had believed so. 'It's beautiful here,' she said quietly. Deep down, she knew these weren't really the words queueing up behind her lips. What she'd really wanted to do was tell him about her baby, but she swallowed down the impulse, wondering where it had come from. She'd have to be extra careful on this strange island if its unfamiliarity and magic were going to provoke feelings like that. She tightened her fists as a reminder not to say too much and risk spoiling everything about their sunny daytrip.

–

The walking was hard going. Beatrice was torn between taking in the stunning scenery, and scanning the uneven peaty and puddled ground for the great gaps and trenches that seemed to exist only to trip the unwary tourist.

It had been a struggle finding a free parking space at the side of the curving mountain road, and when they had finally pulled to a stop, Beatrice had laughed at the sight of Atholl lifting two bricks from under the tartan travelling rug in the back and wedging them behind the wheels like aeroplane chocks.

'Not confident about Rusty's brakes then?'

'I wouldnae say I had absolute faith in them, no.'

Picnic basket in hand, Atholl pointed in the direction they were to walk: upwards, along the pebble-strewn and pitted road. Beatrice glanced behind at the great stream of visitors all walking downhill from their parked cars and along a boggy path between two steep slopes. The visitors had wellies and walking gear on, many had ordinance survey maps hung around their necks in waterproof covers and she was sure she caught a glimpse of the Sussex crafting ladies in their cagoules yomping alongside a burn, gripping their single ski poles. The sight made her think of the summer cardigan she'd stuffed into her bag, suddenly feeling drastically underprepared for the hike Atholl was taking her on.

'Everyone's going the other way though, Atholl?'

'Precisely,' he nodded sagely. 'Let's take the road less travelled.'

Gaining altitude all the time and walking at a steady pace, they followed the road until the long line of parked cars was far behind them and they found themselves in a low cloudy patch where all the island's midges seemed to have congregated. The change in temperature left Beatrice's skin cold, dew-spotted and clammy. She flapped her hands ineffectually at the little biting insects in the air as Atholl led the way with a look of calm determination.

At the brow of the hill, the road took a sharp turn to the right and Atholl explained this was where they left it.

After marching for a few hundred yards across ferns and heathers, they passed down out of the mist again, leaving the midges behind, and Beatrice smiled at the sight of hazy sunbeams breaking through the mists.

'That lot back there were heading for the fairy pools,' Atholl said, once they'd both caught their breath after the ascent. 'It'll be heaving out at the pools today.'

'Fairy pools?'

'Have you no' heard of them? Most folk coming to this part of the world come specially to see them.'

'Ah! Well I didn't exactly do much research into the area before I booked my trip; it was a bit of an impulse decision.'

Atholl cast a glance that told her he'd thought as much but he wasn't going to pry, and Beatrice was grateful.

'What the day-trippers don't know is that if you cross over the brae and up the pass between these hills there are more fairy pools; they're just a little harder to get to.'

'It looks like quite a hike, Atholl,' said Beatrice between breaths, still finding the walk tiring.

'It'll be worth it. Did you bring your swimming things?'

'I didn't know I was supposed to.'

Atholl smiled wickedly but kept his eyes on the boggy ground while Beatrice's imagination ran through every possible scenario of what an afternoon of costume-less fairy pool swimming with Atholl might look like. She hoped he was teasing her and that meant he wasn't going to rein in the kinder, more humorous parts of his tendency to provoke her. She was used to people walking on eggshells around her back home and even if Atholl had abandoned the scowling, arm folding and exasperated huffing since they'd got to know each other better, she still hoped he wasn't going to put on his kid gloves to handle her.

Soon they came to a deep burn cutting across the moor and running surprisingly fast with bronze water. Beatrice scanned its length for a passing place.

'It's run off from the rains we've had, but don't worry, I'm a local boy.' Atholl was already stalking off alongside the burn, stopping at a great rock jutting out amongst the heathers. Passing behind it, he reappeared after a second carrying a long plank over his shoulder and proceeded to set it down over the water.

'A bridge?'

'*Uh-huh*,' he nodded, and she walked over, not attempting to hide her surprise at Atholl's resourcefulness.

Following after her with the picnic basket, he left the plank in place.

'I spent my childhood playing out here. My granny's house was just over that pass there.' He pointed into the distance, but Beatrice couldn't make out any buildings at all. 'Now it's my mother's. She lives there with my sister Sheila and her man Teàrlach and their bairn, Archibald. He's only a month old.'

'Archibald? That's quite a name for a little baby.'

Atholl was smiling and talking about his little nephew, but Beatrice could feel the pull of her own thoughts dragging her attention away from him. Abigail. Natalie. Rosie. These had been her favourite baby girl names, and she'd written them neatly inside the jacket of her copy of *Your Pregnancy: Week by Week* back in the winter months. Gabriel, Charlie and Ruben were inscribed there too. They had never settled on a name for their son, but had they been afforded the luck and luxury of nine months to decide, Archie could well have ended up as one of the top picks, and Richard would have been a nice middle name, after his daddy. She found herself wondering if Rich had dreamed of a son bearing his Christian name as well as his surname. She'd never know now.

Although they were walking downhill the terrain was pitted and ridged and Beatrice's thigh muscles began to ache. The burning woke her from her reverie again. Atholl had been talking all this time, but about what she didn't know.

'Can I?' he was saying, while jutting an elbow out to her. 'You're wearying.'

She slipped her hand into the crook of his arm. Weary? Yes, that was the word for how she'd felt these last few weeks. Weary. But somehow walking steadily in silence with Atholl, matching his long strides step for step, was bringing her back to herself, and when they at last reached a narrow valley and she heard the rush of many little waterfalls cascading into deep pools arranged down the valley in tiers, she began to smile again.

'The fairy pools?' she cried.

'Aye.'

The scene held her transfixed for a moment. She understood how these pools had got their name. The waters were clearer even than those at the coral beach but instead of a tropical turquoise their depths shone with a silver glimmer. Tiny waterboatmen rowed across their bright surfaces, winged insects flitted between the minuscule wild sweetpeas that bloomed yellow like Highland butter and grew everywhere around their banks. The pointed spires of purple bee orchids flowered a little further off in the longer grass alongside tough little thistles and clovers. A damp, mossy, sweet smell rose from the soft earth which was everywhere dotted with rabbit holes, grassy tuffets and exposed grey stones.

Beatrice could well imagine that the Skye fairies were watching her from their magical little hideouts as Atholl asked her where she wanted to sit and she picked out a dryish-looking spot on a grassy bank under a cluster of scrubby bushes right by a flowing shallow rivulet filling one of the wider pools. Atholl spread the blanket on the ground and joined her on it. When she leaned over and dipped her fingertips into the inviting water, she found it was freezing cold and snatched her hand back with a yelp.

'Changed your mind about swimming, Atholl?'

'Possibly.'

She laughed with relief and took her time looking around at the clustered mountains surrounding them in the near distance at every point of the compass, dwarfing them in the landscape.

'I feel tiny in scenery like this,' she said at last.

'It's always good to get a bit o' perspective. This is where I'd come to think… and to get away from my family.'

'What are they like?'

'They're fine. They're loud. A wee bit intense. It could be a bit much sometimes living on top of one another at the inn. I was glad tae get away every day on my willow apprenticeship. Mum and Dad kept Granny's cottage here on Skye even while they ran the inn. They had a lot of staff so we could sometimes get away to the island, and Gene did a lot at the inn back then too. When everyone moved back to Skye somehow I ended up staying on permanently at the inn wi' my brother.'

'Didn't you ever want to leave, move in with someone, maybe?'

Atholl took a while answering, focusing on unscrewing the lid of a thermos and pouring out steaming coffee into two plastic mugs. 'I *was* ready to leave at one point, but alone. I never met a lassie who'd want to take on me and my family.' He laughed.

'You almost moved out? But what happened?'

'My old willow teacher had planning permission to add a mezzanine loft to one end of the But n' Ben for a bedroom and to put a partition wall and kitchen into the downstairs, and between us we planned the building project. When he retired I was ready to do it, had the quotes from Davy McTavish the builder and everything, and it wasnae all that expensive either. I'd been looking forward to living and working there, but then Lana left

Gene… and what with looking after him and the inn… well, you've seen it for yourself.'

'Oh.' Beatrice sipped the coffee contemplatively. 'There really wasn't ever anyone you wanted to move in with?'

Atholl peeled the lid from a box full of flat little cakes. 'Bannock?' He held the box out to her, and a delicious floury, sweet smell circulated in the clean, warm air. 'For someone who keeps herself to herself, you like to go delving into other folk's business, don't you?'

This, she was grateful to see, was said with a wink. But Beatrice took the warning, and a bannock, and instead of pushing him further, she watched the water flowing past, glittering in the sunlight.

Atholl spoke eventually. 'I've had girlfriends in the past, if that's what you want to know, but none of them ever wanted to settle in Skye or in Port Willow. They went off to colleges or jobs in the South, and there was a fair amount of competition for the lassies who stayed.' Another wink as he bit at the bannock. 'And none of them ever fancied me anyway.'

Unlikely, thought Beatrice.

'They all liked Gene back before he married.'

Beatrice decided to keep her thoughts about that to herself too. Yes, he'd scrubbed up nicely for his date with Kitty and he had some of the same handsome features as Atholl but he was so rangy and thin and just nothing like as solid and handsome as his younger brother. Could Lana breaking Gene's heart have transformed him physically as well as emotionally? Beatrice kept her eyes on Atholl's moving mouth as she polished off her bannock.

'There *was* someone serious, well I thought we were getting serious,' he said. 'Maggie arrived as a holidaymaker

178

taking a long let in the loft rental above Mr Shirlaw's general store. She'd come into the inn every now and again and we'd get chatting at the bar, then she started coming in for dinner most nights. Anyway…' Atholl blew a deep breath through puffed cheeks and ran an index fingertip over his hairline pushing back a curl. 'I thought we'd talked about every subject under the sun and we knew each other pretty well. She'd, *uh*, stay the night too and didnae seem to mind me spending evenings in the kitchens or pulling pints. But, then one day, out of the blue, her husband arrived in the village.'

'Her husband?'

'Aye. He was news to me as well. She even had the nerve tae introduce us. He worked away on the rigs most of the year, apparently, and she'd spend her summer holidays alone. He'd gotten leave and decided to join her on her trip as a surprise. I don't know, maybe I was the first fellow she cheated on her man with. Who knows? But he took one look at me and the shock must have been written all over my face. Aye, and the guilt too. Even though I'd cuckolded him without knowing, he twigged what we'd been up to in an instant. I got a black eye for my devotion and Maggie packed her bags and left with him, back to wherever they came from. I never really understood what the appeal was for her. I suppose I was nothing but a Highland fling.'

'You wished it was more?'

'Maybe at first, but that was cured by the sight of a fist flying at my nose attached to a very angry husband.' He bit into the bannock with a wry smile.

She understood. He was making light of this affair but it must have caused him pain at the time, and embarrassment too. He must have been thanking his lucky stars when this

Maggie arrived in Port Willow, seeming to be single and available, wanting to warm his bed. How many times had Beatrice been reminded of the scarcity of women here in the village since her own arrival? Seth had told her it was a decades-long imbalance.

'Poor you,' she said. 'That's rubbish, I'm sorry. Was there nobody else after Maggie?'

'Not a one. Not with Gene to mother and...' His words faltered at the sight of Beatrice's eyes narrowing as she peered into the distance over his shoulder.

'It can't be?' she said in lowered tones. Somehow, thinking of Eugene Fergusson had conjured up a powerful image of him emerging from over the brow of the hill and marching towards them.

Then she heard the voices.

A quick glance at Atholl who hadn't turned around to see the apparition told her he could hear them too.

'*Aww*, for the love of...' He flicked the half eaten bannock back into the box and drew a knee up to his chest. 'He's behind me, isn't he?'

'Yep. And he's not alone.'

Down the hill danced at least six redheaded children with Echo bounding and scurrying between them. Gene's shaved head towered above them all. On one arm he grasped a smiling Kitty, and on the other an elderly, white-haired woman.

Atholl kept his back to the invaders. 'He's told the whole family we're here, hasn't he.' It wasn't a question, but Beatrice nodded in response.

He had time to offer her a wary look before murmuring a deep, 'I'm sorry, Beatrice. I wanted you to have peace and quiet today...' before the marauders joined them.

'Well, if it isn't another courtin' couple hiding in the heathers,' the frail white-haired woman called out.

Atholl rose to greet her with a straight-lipped smile before offering her a kiss on her cheek, flushed red from her walk.

'I suppose this is your doing?' Atholl said to his brother as Eugene offered an outstretched hand which he shook – warmly, Beatrice noticed. Those two may bicker but there was love beneath it all.

'Mrs Mair's in charge at the inn. You can't sneak Beatrice to the island without telling yur family,' Gene said, highly amused, before adding with a provoking innocence, 'Why would you no' want her to meet our mother?'

Kitty threw herself down on the rug beside Beatrice and whispered near her ear. 'Sorry about all this. Gene had rung round the family before I knew what was happening, so I joined in for damage limitation.'

'It's fine, honestly.' Beatrice waved Kitty's remark away, but Kitty drew closer to her.

'They're harmless, just a bit batty. I've known them since I was a bairn.'

The children were already stripping out of their clothes and making for the pools, not seeming to mind the cold water and screaming and splashing one another in delight. Beatrice shielded the bannocks from the flying water and shifted over on the rug to allow Atholl's mother to sit down.

'Well, dear. You're the Beatrice I have to thank for making my laddie smile again,' she said.

Beatrice watched Gene lowering himself onto his own picnic blanket spread on the bank and holding out an arm for Kitty to slide in beneath, which she did, leaving Beatrice alone on the rug beside Atholl's mum.

'I was only too glad to help Eugene and Kitty out,' Beatrice remarked, watching the new lovers snuggling up together.

'I wasnae talking about Gene,' the old woman said with a sly smile and a glance towards Atholl who was standing up watching the children and Echo bounding in the water and pretending not to hear. 'And here he is gallivanting on Skye! I thought he was wedded to that inn. So tell me, Beatrice, are you enjoying your stay?'

'I am, thank you. Port Willow is beautiful.'

'*Mm-hmm*,' the woman agreed, nodding contemplatively and looking at Beatrice through large spectacles which were perched near the end of her nose. Beatrice entertained the idea that Mrs Fergusson had flesh as smooth and pale as unbaked pastry before dismissing the thought as unkind.

'And why are you here alone, dearie?'

'*Mother!*' Atholl was paying attention now.

'It's awfy unusual for a young lassie to travel alone, even here in the Highlands where they're safe.'

Beatrice simply nodded and hoped the moment would pass, but she found Kitty, Gene and Mrs Fergusson were *all* watching her and waiting for an answer.

'Well, *um*, I, *um*...'

Suddenly a mewing sound drew everyone's attention away at once. It was the cry of a baby carried to them on the breeze. A young woman in a long blue sundress was approaching with a baby tied to her chest inside a colourful shawl.

Beatrice's shoulders slumped in relief and she sighed as the weight of everyone's scrutiny lifted, everyone's except

Atholl's – he was watching her through narrowed, penetrating eyes. Beatrice feared what he might have seen in her moment of surprise at hearing the cries and masked her face in a delighted smile.

'Sheila, you got my message,' Mrs Fergusson called to her, and Beatrice realised this was Atholl's sister and the famous baby Archibald.

Soon everyone was properly introduced and huddled round eating the bannocks. Sheila produced a bundle of something sweet and beige wrapped in foil that looked like fudge but was crumbly and firm.

'Scottish tablet,' Atholl's sister said with a smile as Beatrice bit into her first piece.

It was delicious but as the sweetness hit her she winced and immediately imagined her teeth dissolving. 'Goodness!' She swallowed the melting goop. 'How is it made?'

'A whole bag of sugar, large can o' condensed milk, wee scrape o' vanilla and a splash of whole milk. Then you boil it up until it looks like a raging furnace in the pan.'

Beatrice laughed, before Sheila censured her with a dramatic frown. 'You may laugh but it's no' for the faint-hearted. You only know the stuff's ready when the bubbles have risen to the top o' the pan, your eyebrows are singed clean awf and you truly fear for your life. Then you turn off the heat and stir it 'til it's calmed itself and pour it into a tray to set. I've known folk lose fingers making the stuff. Melted, they were!' Sheila concluded her recipe with a wicked grin and a wink thrown to the children who had gathered behind Beatrice waiting for the bundle of tablet to make its way round to them. Her voice and mannerisms were so like Atholl's it was uncanny.

They were alike in other ways too, Beatrice observed. Beautiful red hair, a hint of wickedness in their temperaments, but kind with it; both were pale with dark patches of freckles under their eyes and a summer tan that seemed only to linger around their hairlines, cheekbones and the bridges of their fine noses, and she had the same blue eyes like Isle of Skye fairy pools reflecting the heavens.

'I'm wondering how old ye are, Beatrice?' Mrs Fergusson said between bites of tablet.

Kitty immediately began loudly remarking about there not being a cloud in the sky and how she and Gene had seen a black grouse dancing for his mate on their way from her car, and Beatrice detected Kitty's subtle dig at the oblivious Gene's ribs, which he mistook entirely.

'Are you wanting to go for a walk, Kitty?' he asked.

Beatrice watched helplessly as Kitty shrugged a silent apology and she and Gene wandered off towards the pools.

'Grouse? Was she talking about grouse, Beatrice? So are ye Kitty's age? How old can that lassie be now, Sheila? Isn't Kitty Wake approachin' forty?'

Sheila, in a move which Beatrice would remember from that day onwards as the most generous act any stranger had ever performed for her, deftly handed baby Archibald to her mother with a quietly spoken, 'He's wanting his granny, poor thing.'

And with that Mrs Fergusson was struck into adoring silence, cooing to the sleeping boy.

'I saw a braw patch of wild flowers beyond the Gowk Heid Rock, Atholl,' Sheila added triumphantly, before helping herself to a bannock and Atholl's coffee cup.

'Aye, good idea.' Atholl frowned drolly as he helped Beatrice to her feet, and within moments they were walking again.

'I have to apologise for Mum, she'll no' be happy 'til you've given her your life story and shown her your passport and driving licence. Oh, and whit's your blood type?'

'Don't apologise, I thought she was lots of fun,' Beatrice said, stretching the truth more than a little. 'She seems harmless enough, looking out for her children.' That part was true, there was no malice, only nosiness in Mrs Fergusson.

'I really am sorry. I thought we'd get a wee bit of time to ourselves today and enjoy the island. Can we at least try to reclaim a part of our day out?' said Atholl, as they approached a rock apparently dropped into the landscape from above, standing on end and taller than Atholl.

As he passed behind the rock out of view of the clan at the fairy pools in the near distance he produced the bundle of tablet and offered Beatrice another piece. 'A bit of sleight of hand. Sheila will think Gene has it; he's a devil for tablet.'

The rock was warm when Beatrice leaned her back against it and took another piece of the sweet stuff.

'So,' Atholl began. 'I won't be asking your age or why you're here, unlike *some* people, but there must be something you can share with me? I know next to nothing about you and you've met almost all my family now and you *are* living in my home, are you no'?'

'Temporarily, yes,' she smiled. 'OK, I'm Beatrice Halliday, but you already know that. I'll be forty pretty soon, and that's… all right, I guess. I recently lost my job, and pretty soon I'll be put out of my house too, so technically I should be at home looking for a new place.' She felt her fists tighten as she gave away the information, skirting dangerously close to the secrets she'd promised herself never to reveal.

Atholl received the information without any outward sign of surprise or sympathy but he did move closer beside her so he too could lean on the rock. He crossed one ankle over the other, leaning his head back casually before seeming not to know what to do with his arms and standing up straight again, all of which made Beatrice smile. For the first time it struck her that his self-consciousness could be a sign that he might be beginning to like her a little. She tried to pack that thought away, alarmed and hopeful in equal measure.

Knowing she'd have to talk again to stave off the awkwardness, she pressed on. 'What else…? I like arty stuff. I'm trying to get back into community enterprise work, bringing people together and creating things: performances, clubs, that sort of thing. My work's always been about community cohesion. And… I like dogs, don't have one though, and I have a baby niece called Clara who I adore. And… that's me,' she shrugged.

'OK,' Atholl said in a dry tone, clearly unsatisfied.

'And I like dating shows,' Beatrice blurted in desperation. 'I like a glass of wine with a cheesy dating programme where there are cameras right up in the faces of a couple going on an awkward dinner date.' She laughed lightly. 'I like when it all goes perfectly, and they leave the date together at the end, and over the credits it says, "Katie spent the evening with Craig in the Soho nightclubs. Since then, they've been on a date to London Zoo and are planning a weekend away in Margate"; that sort of thing.'

'Oh aye?'

'Yep. Love them.'

'Like you loved sending Kitty on a date with Gene?'

'I suppose so.'

'I thought he was hard work *before*, he'll be even more hopeless now he's falling head over heels for Kitty. I'll never get away from that inn now. And it was pretty bad timing to have your matchmaking coincide with the Port Willow ceilidh. I mean, it's good he's promised to start cooking again in the evenings and now he'll have someone to birl at the dance but the moonbeams in his eyes'll make it difficult for him to make the Cullen Skink and run the bar these coming days.'

Beatrice laughed again. '*My* matchmaking? You thought it was a brilliant idea. "A stroke of genius," you said.'

'Maybe I hadnae thought it through properly or considered its impact on me getting my workshop up and runnin'. It seems even less likely now. I don't know what's worse, Gene heartbroken or Gene in love.'

Beatrice's laughter ended with a sudden realisation. 'Hold on. Did you say there's going to be a ceilidh?'

'Aye, it's almost Harvest Home.'

'Nope, none the wiser.' Beatrice squinted.

'It's the end of the harvest and the start of the ceilidhs. We host it. Long ago, every pub and hostelry in the area held its own dance, and the farm workers would celebrate the end of their toilin' and the fisherfolk would celebrate the start of the autumn tides, but it's a small affair now, almost forgotten, apart from at The Princess. My mother loves the ceilidh so I do it for her, really.'

'I've never been to a ceilidh before, it sounds good.'

'Och, it is, but it's no' been the same without Gene.'

'He doesn't turn up for it?'

'In recent years he's taken to his bed at the ceilidh. In the run up he'll help organise it a wee bit, but I host the night by myself.'

'He takes to his bed?'

'You see, he and Lana married at Harvest Home. Their wedding reception *was* the ceilidh – a braw night that was. Seth got carried away on the elderflower wine and danced himself right off the end o' the jetty. Aye, it was some night! But Gene can't stomach it now. Maybe things'll be different now he's found Kitty.'

'I hope so too. I just knew they were right for each other.'

'But how did you know she liked him still?'

Beatrice turned her face to meet Atholl's and realised they'd somehow, perhaps unconsciously, shifted closer as they'd talked. 'It was obvious from the first moment I saw them together. Had you really no idea?'

'None at all. It was obvious? How?'

'Oh, I don't know; the way her eyes lit up when she saw him, and she was putting her hand on her neck, like this.' Beatrice raised her fingertips to her throat, lightly touching her skin. Atholl's eyes followed them.

'And that means something?'

'God, yes! Have you never seen *Love Island*? It's an unconscious sign that you like someone, touching your own skin somewhere you'd like to be kissed.'

Atholl's throat moved and Beatrice was aware of him balling his fists where they hung down by his sides. 'Made you self-conscious, have I?' she laughed.

'I didn't know you were a master body language reader.' He laughed too. 'What else is there?'

Beatrice thought for a second, keeping her eyes on Atholl's. 'Well, there's wetting your lips.'

'Is that so?'

'And you might unconsciously mirror the person you like, copying their gestures or even their accent, that sort of thing.'

'I'd never heard of such a thing.'

'Or you might find yourself instinctively touching them, putting a hand on their arm for a second or something, sort of showing them you'd like to touch them… properly.'

'Like this?' Atholl seemed to surprise himself by raising his hand, slowly bringing it into the lightest contact with Beatrice's, his fingertips grazing her skin before quickly dropping away again.

'Yes,' she faltered. 'That's exactly the sort of thing. That would send a strong message.'

'Beatrice?'

'*Hmm?*'

They were face to face now, Atholl leaning his head against the rock so they were the same height.

'What will you do now? Are you staying out the rest of your holiday wi' us? I… I wish ye would.' He let his fingertips settle against the back of her hand once more before slipping them inside her curled palm and clasping her hand in his. 'You're due to check out on Monday morning after the ceilidh, and that's only five sleeps away. Will you not stay for the dance?'

This wasn't a time for thinking, for weighing the pull of her responsibilities and her real life back at home with her newfound delight in her impromptu holiday. There was a handsome man asking her to stay near him and ever so slowly leaning his head towards hers and his shining blue eyes were softly closing.

Beatrice's words seemed to catch in her throat but they made their way out. 'I'll stay. Of course I'll stay.' She let her own eyes close and leaned into the solidity of his shoulder, their lips only inches from meeting. Already her breath was hitching and her nerves jolting, sending hot tingling electricity racing to the nape of her neck and the base of her spine. She knew this was a kiss she would feel all the way down.

'*Uncle Atholl!* Echo's up to his oxters in mud! Uncle Atholl!'

'For the love of God!' Atholl let his lips brush past hers with a frustrated cry and for the briefest second he pressed his face onto her shoulder, a scrape of lip and tooth grazing her neck as he did so and sending every cell in her body haywire, but he was withdrawing already and watching the children descend upon their hideout behind the rock, screaming in delight as a dripping, muddy Echo caught up to them, wagging his tail at the sight of his master before proceeding to shake mud from his shaggy coat and sending filthy splashes over everything around him. The children screeched once more before running away to wash off in the pools.

Atholl, his face spotted with mud, reached out a hand towards the shell-shocked Beatrice's hair and attempted to pick away the splashes of grime.

'Don't...' Beatrice began, making Atholl step back again instantly.

He opened his mouth to speak, eyes wide with guilt, but she didn't let him talk.

'I was going to say, don't you dare apologise again.' Beatrice reached her pinched fingers to the tip of her tongue and removed a drop of muck with a grimace. '*Pfft!* Yuck! And I was going to say, I'm having a perfect day, even if I have been bitten half to death by midges, grilled by your mum and caked in mud by your dog, *and* I'll have the shakes for a week after that tablet sugar high.'

Atholl laughed with relief. 'I'll have you write that in the inn's visitors' book before you leave us. Come on, Sheila'll have some baby wipes can take care of this mud.'

With that he led her back to the little party, walking a pace ahead and leaving Beatrice's nerves buzzing like the swooning bees drunk on nectar from the blushing purple clovers at the pool sides.

The rest of their afternoon passed in a blur of gathering wild flowers – delicate ling heather, forget-me-nots and white campion – or searching for pretty rocks in the pools with the children. They all ate bannocks and oatcakes with cheese and Mrs Fergusson's greenhouse tomatoes. Someone produced a bottle of Highland mead that tasted of honey and summer which they swigged with handfuls of mellow raspberries. The children filled Kilner jars with brown bearded fish from the burn that they caught with their cupped hands, a trick uncle Eugene showed them.

On a few fleeting occasions throughout the afternoon Beatrice was struck by just how much she was being treated as though she was part of something very special: a family. Everyone made sure to fill her in on the decades old in-jokes that circulated amongst them, and she was beginning to think she'd heard the name of every islander and member of the Fergusson clan and had discovered all their ailments, love stories, recipes and secrets.

Mrs Fergusson reminisced about her late husband and how she'd fallen in love with him on a Harvest Home dance floor oh so many summers ago, and how he'd been a dead ringer for Gene Kelly, only with red hair and freckles and at least two feet taller, but in all other regards they were near-identical, and Atholl had smiled and peeled apples for the children never letting on he'd heard this story a hundred times before.

By five o'clock there was a chill in the air and a dampness settling upon the ground that told them the party was almost over. Mrs Fergusson, rocking baby Archibald, saw Atholl and Beatrice gathering their things ready to leave and remarked innocently that Beatrice hadn't yet held the baby and that if Kitty Wake had managed it earlier without running for the hills then so could Beatrice.

Perhaps everyone mistook Beatrice's reluctance as nerves and unfamiliarity with babies. She had, after all, held Clara in her arms, rocked and danced her on more occasions than she could count, but the prospect of cradling the newborn boy, still curled like the new fronds of a fern and so small in his white sleepsuit, cotton hat and powder blue woollen blanket, was a different matter entirely.

Kitty, who had been leaning dreamily against Gene and humming a soft tune, was suddenly looking at Beatrice with pinched, quizzical eyes. Mrs Fergusson asked if she'd never held a baby before as she threw a wink at Atholl that made Beatrice's insides churn and her fists clench in her trouser pockets.

There was nothing else for it but to sit down again and let the soft, warm and surprisingly heavy bundle that was the sleeping Archibald mould himself onto her lap. She spread her fingers out around his small, rounded body with her arms crossed under him for support.

No thoughts whatsoever articulated themselves as Beatrice absorbed the baby boy's weight. She was no longer aware of the people smiling at her or of Atholl occasionally glancing at her, expressionless, as he packed away the picnic basket. She stared hard at the delicate pattern on his blue blanket, then at the fleshy pink sweetness of his moving mouth as he dreamt of drinking his mother's milk.

'Was there ever a finer wee boy in all the world?' Mrs Fergusson was saying, and Beatrice heard her thoughts churning in reply.

There was. There was…

She wasn't sure which had started first, Kitty's soft singing or her own instinctive, slow rocking of the slumbering child, but after a few moments she became highly aware of both.

Kitty's sweet voice lifted and she smiled as she sang the beautiful melody.

Had we never lov'd sae kindly,
Had we never lov'd sae blindly,
Never met – or never parted,
We had ne'er been broken-hearted.
Fare-thee-weel, thou first and fairest!
Fare-thee-weel, thou best and dearest!
Thine be ilka joy and treasure,
Peace, Enjoyment, Love and Pleasure.
Ae fond kiss, and then we sever!
Ae fareweel alas, for ever!
Deep in heart-wrung tears I'll pledge thee,
Warring sighs and groans I'll wage thee.

The sound was drowned out by another, louder commotion in Beatrice's ears. It took her a moment to realise it was her own heartbeat resounding and her escalating breathing rushing in and out. Her hands shook beneath the bundle in her arms and the edges of her vison seemed to dim away into blurry darkness shot through with sudden starbursts of light which she tried to blink away but only grew more vivid.

Somehow, Beatrice wasn't sure how, Sheila had baby Archibald in her arms again and the first whines of his crying were ringing out between the valleys. Beatrice knew she was apologising repeatedly to anyone who would listen as the hills distorted into swirls of green and purple. She couldn't think and she could hardly breathe but she was aware of her feet pounding on the ground as she ran and the awful, exaggerated echoing sound of their impact hurting her deep inside her brain.

She knew what was happening even though she couldn't articulate it at that moment. It had happened before, after the first time she'd seen her mum hooked up to the dripping red chemo bag with the cannula in her arm. It hadn't happened right there in the ward but days later beneath the harsh strip lights of the supermarket aisle, and then again many times after that in quiet queues at the bank and the library and again waiting for Rich to get home one night when all the trains were cancelled because of summer flooding on the line, and each time the panic attack had taken her by surprise, stolen her breath, and always managed to convince her she wasn't going to survive it this time.

And yet she was still running, her hand clasped to her stomach, hardly seeing where she was going, all the way back up the brae towards the river, hoping she was heading in the right direction to meet Atholl's makeshift bridge over the water, barely able to ask herself what she was meant to do when she reached the road.

The fall, when it happened, sent her tumbling headlong into the heathers and damp earth, her fingertips sinking into mud up to her knuckles as her ankle stung and smarted. The jolt helped her focus and she gasped some deep breaths. Running away, again, was the only thing she could think of doing.

'I have to get away from this place,' she told herself in a panting, wild-eyed whisper. 'Go where people won't know I'm broken, and I won't be tested and questioned…'

She glanced back angrily at the offending rock that had tripped her only to see Atholl tearing up the brae towards her.

When he reached her, he instantly threw his jacket over her shoulders and spread his hands out across her back, drawing her close to him.

'Beatrice, what on earth's the matter? Can you no' tell me? Please, say the words and let go o' the burden that's hurtin' ye.'

The long breath caught as she filled her lungs with air, thinking it would act as a stopper. Instead it burst from her chest again and with it came all the trapped words spilling out along with violent, unrelenting tears coming in contracting waves that cramped her stomach.

'I've made a mistake. I can't do this… any of it.' She shook her head frantically.

Atholl didn't let her go, but loosened his grip so she had room to breathe in great gulping gasps between words.

'It doesn't matter how remote I am, how far from my own life, I can't seem to recover. I'm lost, Atholl. I don't know who I am or what I'm doing. I've no job, and no home, and I don't even have my mum to tell all this to anymore, and… and I keep looking everywhere for something I just can't get back… and I…' These last words were forced from her with a pained cry that ended in deep convulsing sobs.

Atholl's eyes flooded but he didn't speak.

'… and I can't fill the great, gaping hole in my heart for my baby.'

Clasping her chest, she howled her heartache out. The wild flowers she'd gathered earlier, and which Atholl had been holding for her as they made ready to leave the picnic and which he'd carried during his sprint across the hill in pursuit of her, tumbled to the ground at their feet.

In an instant Atholl's arms were tight around her again as he sat on the rough ground, pulling her onto his lap. Letting her weight sink onto him, Atholl rocked her as she screamed into the crook of his arm, bent double with pain until eventually it passed and her tears stopped and the sky turned pink in the sun's slow descent towards the horizon. All the while Atholl stroked her hair, cradling her like his own child, letting his silent tears fall and dry upon his face.

Without speaking he supported her all the way back to the car where she sat stupefied into silence even as they passed back down the steep winding roads in the fading light.

He handed her into the boat and she sat shivering under his jacket in the prow as Atholl rowed her back into the calm haven of Port Willow. On her lap she clasped the posy of wild flowers that Atholl had once again gathered up and returned to her.

As they rounded the rocky promontory of the harbour and saw the semi-circle of gleaming lights of Port Willow along the bay she found herself speaking quietly over the soft dip of the oars in the water. Atholl strained to pick up her words.

'I didn't get any documentation or anything. You know you should get something to keep… sometimes I wonder if it's even recorded in my medical notes, but someone was alive and then they died, so their life should have been marked somehow.'

The moonlight glittered in the gentle waves as they cut through the water and Atholl listened intently. Beatrice's eyes glazed as she thought back to the spring and saw herself. The memory made her wince.

'I was just sitting for days on end in a pastel-coloured spare bedroom with a baby blanket and a few scraps of unworn baby clothes and nothing else to show for their little life.'

'I understand. You wish there was something special you could do to remember your child,' Atholl said at last, making her eyes snap to his.

'That's it exactly. But what? What are you supposed to do?'

'There must be something.'

'There's nothing.' Beatrice let her eyes fall from his face. She knew what she'd see there; pity and sadness, yes, but awkwardness and discomfort too. Nobody likes talking about these things, she'd learned, and so she hadn't talked about them.

'I'd better get you home. You're exhausted.' Atholl fell into silence.

Beatrice shifted her gaze to the lapping waves over the boat's low hull, hugging her arms around her body to stave off the evening chill. She didn't speak again.

-

At the door of the inn, Atholl took her hand. 'Gene will be back by now if Kitty took him by the Skye Bridge in her car. Tell him to make you a hot toddy.'

'You're not coming in?'

'Not yet.' Atholl shook his head, his skin pale as ice in the moonlight and he left her to find her own way inside.

Chapter Sixteen

Atholl's Gift

'Angela? You there? Pick up? I know it's late. You must be putting Clara to bed. Listen, I've had a hot toddy or two – God, whisky's disgusting, isn't it? – I thought you'd want to know that I told someone about the baby. Not just someone. Atholl.

'He's the landlord here, well, he isn't really the landlord as such; his brother is. Anyway. I said it all out loud. Mum. The house. My job. Everything. Come to think of it, I'm not sure I mentioned Rich? It's all a bit blurry to be honest. At any rate, it hurt. And now I feel like it's all happened all over again, except I'm in a B&B in the Scottish Highlands and I can't stop crying and I've nothing but a Drambuie coffee for comfort. God, I miss you and Clara, and Vic too.

'Gene looked at me like I was a ghost haunting his inn when I walked back in tonight. Oh, Gene's Atholl's brother. He barely said a word, other than offering to get his girlfriend up and send her in to see me, but I couldn't do that, not after the show I made of myself with his family today. Without doubt they'll all think I'm crazy too. *Ugh!* Angela, I was out of control. I talked about it, though. But it didn't help, and this feeling, this empty ache, isn't going anywhere, and I'm all out of options now.

'Run? Don't run? Go home? Find a new home? They're all the same. It hurts regardless.

'And now Atholl's run off into the night. I saw him sprinting along the seafront, going God knows where, desperate to get away from the lunatic English woman who was rude to his poor mother, cried all over his shirt and frightened the living daylights out of little baby Archibald.

'I know none of this makes sense. I'll have to fill you in on the embarrassing details when I get back, but *ugh*, clan Fergusson think I'm a baby-crazed lunatic, just like Rich did.

'Oh, whatever! I'm annoying myself now. What does it all matter? I'm downing this dreadful drink and climbing up to bed… but I can't see myself getting to sleep. I've got the old restlessness creeping in again.

'I knew talking about it wouldn't help. I could kick myself!

'Angela? Angela, are you there? Is this thing even recording? Look, don't worry about me. I'll see you tomorrow. I'm sorry I'm venting at you. I'm fine. Honestly. I'm fine.'

–

'Beatrice, are you asleep?' Atholl whispered at the door.

He held his breath, listening to the sound of the ladder creaking as she climbed down then bare feet padding across the floor and finally the key turning in the lock.

He was met by the sight of Beatrice wrapping her dressing gown around herself and knotting it, then reaching into a pocket for a tissue.

'Atholl. Listen, I'm sorry I scared you off, I know it's a lot…'

'*Shh shh*, it's all right,' he hushed her gently. 'What you said about not being able to say goodbye properly, of having nothing special to do to mark your baby's wee life. You set me thinking. I've been up at the But n' Ben…'

He produced a parcel from under his arm and unwrapped the brown paper tied with string that protected it. 'I thought maybe, if you want, you could make use of this wee thing?' He handed her the intricately weaved hollow bassinette shaped curiously like a Russian doll or an ancient Egyptian sarcophagus with a round hole where the face would be.

'I made it myself of the spring's youngest willow back in March when it was still green with life.'

'It's lovely. What is it?'

'It was for a talk Seth was giving about old Highland customs. It's a swaddling basket. You'd wrap the baby in cloths and bands, tucking them up tight so they could sleep, and then they'd be placed inside the basket and worn over the parent's back while they worked in the fields or at the fishes.'

'It's beautiful. It's tiny, though. Too small for a newborn.'

'It was only a model, to show what the real thing would be like.'

She turned it over in her hands, her eyes misting, and she looked up at him, hesitatingly, still unsure of what he intended her to do with the pretty object.

'There's another Highland custom, an ancient one, going back to the earliest folk on the land,' he said softly.

Beatrice listened.

'When a loved one passed they would say their good-byes and swaddle them too like a bairn and they'd place them in the water, letting the tides carry them home.'

Beatrice took his meaning and she bobbed her head as the silent tears came again.

After a long moment he spoke. 'Do you want to do it now? There's a braw moon lighting the harbour.'

'All right.'

Those were the last words they said to each other that night as Beatrice, the mother of a loved son, threaded the Highland posy of forget-me-nots, heather and white campion into the loose basket work, weaving each flower in amongst the shoots from the sappy willows as Atholl watched on.

When her work was done she left the inn, crossing the dark road and leaning over the sea wall. Atholl stayed by the inn porch, close enough to see her kiss the little bundle before lowering the empty bassinette onto the surface of the gentle waters. He couldn't hear the prayer on her lips but he whispered a solemn 'Amen'.

Neither could tell how long it took for the horizon to claim the floating focus of so much of her grief but by sunrise it was gone and Beatrice was asleep soundly in her bed.

Chapter Seventeen

Holidaying Alone

When Beatrice awoke it was late morning. She'd been dimly aware of the heavy downpour outside and its pattering and splashing had lulled her into a deeper slumber. The sound that roused her was Atholl Fergusson's voice bidding farewell to the guests who were checking out down in the reception. Breakfast must be over by now.

When she slipped downstairs half an hour later on the hunt for coffee and any leftover bacon that might be going spare in the kitchens she was hit by the warm air coming through the inn doors and a smile from Atholl, not cautious or careful, just glad. The reception was empty now, apart from Echo asleep at Atholl's feet behind the desk; he must have come back with Kitty and Gene last night.

'Good morning. You slept.' Not a question, and delivered with a satisfied stretch of Atholl's lips at the corners.

'I actually did, a proper sleep.' She thought of the state she'd been in last night when she called her sister and how Atholl's kindness and clever ideas had helped settle all that regret and sadness. 'I feel ready for anything today.'

'So… I guess you've had enough of willow-weaving then? You don't fancy attempting a bit of basketry or making a figure?'

'Umm…'

'That's OK,' he said quickly. 'Kitty's around somewhere if you'd like to have a go at the Gaelic lessons? I mean, they *are* the reason you're here.'

Beatrice smiled. Only she knew that they really, *really* weren't the reason why. She screwed up her nose a little and shook her head rapidly. 'Mmm, I don't really fancy lessons at all, sorry.'

'You're, *eh*, no' leaving are ye?'

'I know I really should be leaving. There's so much that needs to be done back home.'

'Oh, of course.' He took a step backwards that only Beatrice registered; it looked so unconscious for Atholl. His expression seemed to settle back into the unreadable formality of their first acquaintance.

'Last night I thought I would go back, but then you appeared with the bassinette and… I feel differently today.'

There was softness in his voice when he spoke. 'Well, do you just want to stay close to the village today and rest? You had a tough day yesterday. I can arrange a deckchair on the prom garden for you? Send over some tea?'

In spite of his thoughtful words, Beatrice felt she could see him shrinking by the second, somehow growing smaller, retreating into himself once more. And yet, here he was, still trying to fix her, thinking of what she might like and wanting to accommodate it.

'You must be sick of me by now. Is she staying? Is she going? Why's she crying?'

Both of them managed to laugh. She looked out the inn door towards the little strips of garden that interrupted the sea wall at intervals all along the front. She had wondered about who owned them. Nobody ever seemed to use them. Each was enclosed with a low fence and little painted gates. The one opposite the inn was populated with squat, weathered palm trees and, curiously, vegetable beds sparsely planted with onions, garlic and nasturtium flowers.

'Is that Gene and Lana's little garden out there?' she asked.

'Aye, it was.' He turned his lips down at the sides and cocked his head as though impressed she'd made this connection. 'It's the inn's kitchen garden and very much *not* my territory. There's not much in it now. But it's a braw place to sit and watch a sunset. The gardens are the only place the villagers keep just for themselves, a place where visitors don't go, and there's not many spots like that around Port Willow, I can tell you. You'd be welcome to sit there all day, if you'd like?'

Beatrice imagined herself with a blanket and a book watching harbour life and the tourist boats going by. As much as it appealed to her, her mind was already ranging elsewhere.

'Maybe this afternoon, thanks Atholl. Right now there's something I really want to do, have to do, in fact.'

'Can I ask what it is?'

'Of course you can, Atholl.' Why was he being so formal again, after everything that had happened yesterday? She found she couldn't look at him when she spoke.

'I'm going to stay another day at least… and I just need to be alone… to walk and to try to really think about some stuff. Something I've not let myself do for months. I'll need a map if you have one?'

He produced the concertinaed booklet from behind the reception desk in an instant. 'One map. And just in case, I'll make you a packed lunch, aye?'

'Aye,' she echoed. 'Thank you, Atholl.'

–

There wasn't a sound up on the hills behind the village other than the occasional buzzing wasp and a soundtrack of bird song. Without looking at the map Beatrice had followed the main road that led out of Port Willow and after a short while there were no houses to be seen, just a wiggly up and downy pot-holed single lane road with boggy marshes and heathers on either side and, a little further off, the edges of sparse forests.

The walk was exhilarating. The air was fresher than any she had ever breathed, pine-scented, with a ghost of vanilla from the gorse scattered here and there amongst the grey rocks and flowering in big yellow clouds as far as her eye could see.

'Well this beats walking up and down Warwick high street or round the Royal Priors, hands down,' she told the blue sky.

After a while she left the road, following the arrow painted onto a roadside rock that said *Wester Ross National Scenic Area. No fires.*

She was wandering along a narrow path between the heathers when she heard a scurrying sound behind her. She'd read about adders, Scotland's only poisonous snakes and how they basked in the sun, shedding their skins in the summertime. She froze to the spot, casting a wary eye around her trainers, looking for moving caramel and chocolate scales like the ones she'd seen on the information board way back at the beginning of her walk.

Nothing seemed to be slithering nearby so she walked on, placing her feet a little more gingerly than before and wishing she'd worn long trousers and not her black sundress and the baggy beige cardigan with the big pockets that Rich always said looked like knitted oatmeal but which she loved anyway. She had nothing on her face but sun lotion, and it had made her face shiny and her sunglasses slide down her nose.

Maybe Atholl had thought she'd looked odd this morning too, given that she had completed her outfit with her white trainers. She really hadn't done her most coordinated packing for her Highland dash, there simply hadn't been time.

But he hadn't looked at her like he thought she looked scruffy. In fact, when she thought back to when she came down into the reception this morning, she wondered if she'd seen a little flash of wanting in Atholl's eyes. Had she imagined it?

She looked down at the bag in her hand and the picnic he had packed for her. Something inside smelled wonderful, like freshly baked bread. Why was Atholl so nice to her? She reached inside one of the paper bags and found two rosy apples and as she polished one against her cardigan sleeve, she felt something that made her blood run cold, something wet and warm nudging her ankle.

Her scream sent a flock of tiny birds scattering from the heathers as she spun round, the white heat of panic making her momentarily dizzy. Could she take on an adder all by herself? Or was it a wild cat, or a boar, or a Lion Rampant?

'Oh it's you.'

Echo promptly sat on his bottom and wagged his tail wildly.

'Have you been following me all this time?'

Echo panted, obviously very pleased with himself. As she leaned down to pat his head he took the opportunity to stick his nose into the picnic bag.

'Oh, I see. You're not here to keep me company, you can smell the picnic too. Well, all right then, come on. Let's find somewhere to sit down.'

Echo bounded past her along the path before heading off towards the forest's edge.

'Don't go too far, I'm not Bear Grylls you know,' she called after him, and to her surprise, the dog turned to wait for her.

After striding along the treeline through the longer heather and shrubby, sharp bushy plants Beatrice didn't recognise at all, they came to a cluster of rocks. 'Perfect,' she announced and they settled themselves and unpacked Atholl's picnic which turned out to be a slice of a satisfyingly sharp-tasting lemon drizzle cake and a big flat floury breakfast roll somewhat overfilled with cold bacon, square sausage and, of course, haggis.

'Delicious,' she said to Echo who grudged her every bite until she relented and started passing him torn off hunks of food which he wolfed down.

They watched a hawk of some kind – Beatrice thought for a second how she wished Atholl was there to identify it – circling and hovering before swooping down into the heathers hunting for its own lunch.

Apart from the occasional car crunching along the road a good three hundred yards away they were completely alone.

'So tell me, Echo. Your master? What's he like to live with, eh?' There was a flask of hot coffee at the bottom of the bag which she unscrewed. 'He seems kind and caring, right? If a bit gruff at first?'

Echo stared out at the grey mountains beneath the broad sky, sniffing for rabbits.

'It must be nice living here, you lucky boy. I didn't like the Highlands at first, mind you, your boss was so grumpy and rude then. And so was I, I suppose.' Echo, full of food and giving up on the rabbits, turned towards her and lay his head over her knee. 'Aww, thanks boy. See, I'm not grumpy now, am I? Or badly behaved. Being here seems to have helped me get out of some old habits I'd got stuck with. I was sad, you see, for a long time.' She placed a hand on the dog's warm skull and he closed his eyes contentedly, rolled onto his side and let his head shift onto her lap. 'But I've managed to process some of those feelings a bit and it was your boss that did it… he helped me say goodbye to some difficult things, and he got me talking. And now look at me, talking to you like a weirdo.'

She smiled at the sound of Echo grunting as she shifted a little, trying to make herself comfy on the rock.

'The trouble with talking about your feelings is you just keep finding more feelings underneath, even messier ones. Like suddenly wishing I could phone my husband.'

Echo sleepily raised a bushy black eyebrow and glanced up at her before drifting off to sleep.

'*You're* surprised? Tell me about it. I didn't think Rich and I had anything more to say to each other, but now…' Beatrice sighed and drained the little coffee cup before refilling it, trying to remember when the feeling had first appeared. She had been dimly aware of the need last night and had awakened this morning with it pressing upon her again. Watching that bassinette floating away from her made her realise how much she wished Rich had been there to say goodbye too. Somehow the farewell felt one-sided and only partial – and a little wrong – without her baby's other parent there.

'But he's not around, Echo. Got his own place now, which is kind of sad, isn't it?' She absently stroked the silky fluff that ran along Echo's floppy ears, half thinking how white it was, half lost in thoughts of Rich and how their house had been cold and empty for a long time even before Rich moved out. Familiarity had replaced passion long ago, and yet losing that familiar, comforting presence had been devastating. 'I hadn't really thought about it 'til now… too mixed up with losing Mum, and my job – a job I was so good at and honestly it was my reason for existing for nearly twenty years – and then of course, there was the baby. But you know, Echo, my whole way of life was yanked out from under me, and Rich did a runner right when I was at my lowest point. That's hardly fair, is it? I mean, I know I was hard work at the end, but it still stings.'

Something unexpected bubbled up in her blood and for once it wasn't accompanied by guilt or grief. She was just straight-up, honest to God, angry.

'The bastard!'

Echo suddenly sat up, alert, scanning the landscape and sniffing the air, his ears pricked up into points.

'It's all right, Echo. We're on our own. Come on, snuggle up again.'

He didn't need much convincing and after a few ear scratches from Beatrice he curled into a ball against her thigh, but kept his eyes open this time.

'Didn't mean to scare you, sorry little mate.' Beatrice examined her feelings and they felt clearer than ever before. Yes, she was angry but the brittle bitterness had left her.

'Even if he is a bastard for leaving, I still wish I could reach him and tell him about the bassinette… and talk about the baby a little. I told your master about him, but it's Rich I should really be talking to about him. But I don't even know where he is.'

She missed her husband, plain and simple, but the feeling of being abandoned, of being unwanted didn't ache quite so much as she expected.

She circled her hand through the thick fur of Echo's neck. Where had it come from, this new lightness that was soothing her pain and had allowed her to laugh again, to admire beautiful views, to chat and gossip with new friends at the inn, and to very nearly *almost* kiss another man? A man who wasn't her husband but a handsome, broad, rugged red-haired Scotsman. Was Atholl the source of this new lightness? She didn't have to probe her feelings too deeply to know that, in part, he was.

'*Pfft!* But what's he like, eh? Your boss. I'm not the only one changing, am I? He almost killed me on those rocks at the coral beach. You know, you were there. And he did nothing but antagonise me… and patch up my knees, and give me a nice room to stay in… and try to teach me new things like willow-weaving… and Highland customs that can really help a girl out of a fix…' She let out a long breath and her shoulders fell. 'And he introduced me to his family when I was all alone, whisked me off to Skye… Maybe he isn't softening, maybe he was soft all along and it was me that was as hard as nails.'

But he did seem to be giving way even more, she thought. Was it seeing his brother on the brink of finding love and independence that did it? Was it getting degree by degree closer to running his willow workshops as a business that was making him happier? Or was there more to it?

'You don't think your old man might… like me… a little bit, do you, Echo? He *definitely* leaned into that kiss, didn't he? Before you turned up all covered in river crap and spoiled it, thanks very much.'

She replayed the moment yesterday and was convinced their lips had almost touched. And she'd seen his Adam's apple bob as he'd swallowed hard when she was talking about the signs of attraction. Thinking back she could have sworn the conversation was having an effect on the very air between them, charging it with a low electric buzz. Yes, he really had leaned in for a kiss. She couldn't have imagined all of that? And his respectful tenderness last night? The way he'd kept his distance, waiting by the inn door until she had said her goodbyes.

'There's only one way to know what he thinks about me for sure, Echo. I need to tell him I like him, right?'

But the simplicity of the idea and the flush of enthusiasm and adrenalin it brought on within her suddenly waned at the thought of Rich and the life she'd run away from. The whole mess was still back home in Warwickshire waiting for her.

She flicked the last drops of coffee from the cup and screwed it back onto the Thermos. 'I'm supposed to be leaving soon… so what would be the point? I really *should* be getting back tomorrow if I can. There's so much to do at home. I've got to move out of my own house, you see, as well as working up the courage and the energy I'll need to sort things out with Rich. And there's Angela and Vic's wedding plans to put into action, and I'd love a cuddle from little Clara…' This thought alone cheered her. 'Yeah,

I'm going home soon and, honestly, I hardly know Atholl Fergusson, right? And I don't want to make a fool of myself with him if he isn't interested in me, and anyway, I am still technically married to Rich.' She worried her bottom lip and readjusted her sunglasses. 'Where's Angela when I need her? She'd tell me to chill out and enjoy my holiday. Put yourself first, she'd say, and don't get all worked up over nothing.'

She nodded to herself sagely. 'OK. Today's for me. This holiday's for me. Calm down, Bea.'

She reached into the bag she'd carried all the way from Mr Shirlaw's general stores since she'd called in for midge repellent and sun lotion this morning. There had been a rack of second hand books by the door and two bright, inviting covers had stood out to her.

One was a slim romance novel, and for fifty pence it had become hers. Mr Shirlaw had called out to his wife back in the stock room that she'd never guess what, he'd sold it after all these years. She'd come out to see who its new owner was and they'd chatted about the weather and her walking route and they'd tried to wheedle some gossip about Kitty and Gene, and it had felt easy and friendly – like she was one of the locals and not some fly-by-night who couldn't stop prevaricating about whether she even wanted to stick around for the full duration of her holiday in Port Willow. But her mind was made up now. Yes, she'd stay a little longer and try to relax and enjoy the new lightness in her chest and in her mind where there had been nothing but cloudy heaviness for so long.

She fingered the book's spine and its dog-eared pages before finding she could think of nothing she'd rather do than sit still and devour the whole thing, and so that was what she did.

The story was about young love and there was no marriage or baby talk and nothing really bad happened so nothing felt too close to home for comfort. It was like a lovely, absorbing dream, light as air.

And she sat there for hours, occasionally stopping to pour water into her cupped hands for Echo to drink, and got sunburn on her nose and midges in her hair in spite of the citronella oil and the factor thirty, and it was wonderful.

As she walked back to the inn that evening with the sky turning a cool pink before her as the sun sank, she told Echo, who trotted along happily beside her, that she could do this.

'I can be on my own. It's not so bad after all. See, Echo, it's easy!'

As soon as they reached the waterfront Echo caught the smell of fish and chips and ran off, leaving Beatrice to amble slowly back to the inn, swinging the picnic leftovers, litter and her new books in their bags, letting them bump against her calves. She was smiling to herself, her shoulders loose and her body at ease. Yes, she thought, I can do this.

The note she found taped to her door after she climbed the stairs ready for a long bath and a longer sleep, the absolute cherry on top of her perfect summer's day, confirmed for her that she had new friends and that they wanted her to stay and be happy. She clasped the note in her hands as she let the door shut behind her, grinning as she re-read it.

The Harvest Home ceilidh planning committee convenes tomorrow at ten a.m. sharp in the bar

room. *We'll be needing our chief organiser there,*
so dinnae miss it! Atholl asked for you specially
(wink wink!)
  Night night, Kitty
  X

Chapter Eighteen

Best Laid Plans

'*Somebody* made quite an impression at Skye, I see.'

Beatrice was learning that Kitty whispering was as loud as anyone else talking normally but since they were alone in the bar room she didn't mind.

'Oh no, with Atholl's mum, you mean? I'm mortified I ran off like that, she must be wonder—'

'Not Mrs Fergusson, no. Atholl himself! He was loiterin' round the inn yesterday like a lost thing. I saw him casting an eye along the high street umpteen times watchin' for you coming back.'

'He was probably worried about Echo. He followed me on my walk… *What?* Why are you waggling your eyebrows at me?'

'You're no' the only one that can matchmake, you know.'

'Oh Kitty, no! Stop grinning like that. No, don't do anything.' No amount of hand waving and panic was going to stop whatever Kitty was planning, she could tell. 'Please just leave it…'

'All set?' Atholl's voice was bright and cheerful from the doorway. Both women turned to watch him come in like schoolgirls caught talking about a teacher.

Beatrice swallowed, shame-faced, before it struck her that Atholl wasn't in his usual checked Barbour shirts and cords, instead he wore a navy and white thinly striped top with a widely slashed neckline that showed a tantalising glimpse of pale collar bone. The cotton stretched perfectly over his biceps and shoulders reminding Beatrice with a jolt of how good it had felt to be held against them, so warm and hard and broad, that afternoon on Skye.

Kitty was distinctly giggling. There was nothing Beatrice could do but sit straight in her chair and inspect her hands.

'Everything all right?' he asked warily as he pulled up the chair next to Kitty.

'Actually, Atholl, I'm keeping that seat for your brother,' Kitty said solemnly.

'Oh, right-o.' Atholl shifted his long body into the chair directly across the small bar table from Beatrice.

Kitty looked back and forth between them, pleased with herself and tipping her head none too subtly at Atholl to say something.

Atholl cleared his throat, drawing his chair in and shuffling some papers in his hands, until at last he looked up. 'Mornin', Beattie. Good walk yesterday?'

'*Beattie!*' Kitty spluttered with a laugh that she couldn't hold in and promptly got up and left the table.

'Where are you away to?' Atholl asked her.

'I'll bring us some coffee. You cannae have a meeting without coffee, Atholl.' As Kitty left the room, and consumed with the wicked spirit of revenge, she threw a wink over Atholl's back towards Beatrice.

'You dinnae mind me calling you Beattie just now? I dinnae ken why I did that.'

Beatrice was surprised to find she didn't mind it one bit, even though it was a name she'd have associated with her great granny's generation. 'I like it. Seth gave it to me, my Highland nickname.'

'That's right, he did.'

Beatrice could have sworn that a look of blushing shame crossed Atholl's face as they both remembered the way they'd sniped at one another less than a week ago and how he'd chided her for the fact she wouldn't be sticking around long enough for nicknames.

Realising they were both still looking at each other and nobody was saying anything, Beatrice rushed out some words. '*Umm*, so, yeah… I had a perfect day yesterday. Thanks for the picnic. We both loved it. Echo and I, that is.'

'I wondered where the wee menace had got to.'

'My dog in shining armour. I think he was protecting me from adders.'

'I hate to burst yur bubble but he'd have run a mile had he seen one. Hates 'em.'

She found she was still watching him and it was hard to draw her eyes away from his pale curling lips. Had he looked this good before she spent her day alone thinking about his kindness and how she'd caused him nothing but trouble since she arrived?

'Well, there were no snakes, thankfully, and it was actually really, *really*, peaceful out there. I don't think I could have got a day like that anywhere else in the world but here in the Highlands.'

'I'm glad tae hear that. I missed you though.' Atholl blurted the words before inhaling a breath that stopped his lips and widened his eyes.

'Coffee's up!' called Kitty as she bustled in with a tray and Gene, still dressed in his chef's whites, loping placidly behind her.

Beatrice, a little put off by the interruption and wanting to hear more about all the missing her that Atholl had been doing, eyed Kitty's tray as it was set down, noticing eight tumblers amongst the steaming mugs. 'Whisky? I'll stick to coffee thanks.'

'The whisky's no' for us,' said Atholl. 'You'll see,' he added wryly.

Beatrice shrugged, amused. 'O-kay.'

She passed Atholl his mug, turning the handle to face him before reaching for her own, not noticing the little lift in his brows at that gesture.

Aware that he was watching her as she took her first sip, it was just possible she exaggerated the long '*mmm*' as she lowered the mug again and rubbed her shoulders into the chair contentedly. 'Nice coffee, thanks Kitty.'

Kitty smirked knowingly as she settled beside Gene, her hand sliding over his thigh as she pulled her chair closer to his.

For a moment all eyes fell on Gene who had the look of a lottery winner upon his face. Beatrice was aware of Atholl bobbing his head and smiling to himself at the sight of the new couple. She wondered if he too could feel the charge in the air that they were creating and a part of her wished she could mirror Kitty by reaching across the table and laying a hand upon Atholl, but of course, she couldn't. That would be totally inappropriate. They were just friends, after all, and if she wanted more she'd have to tentatively find out whether he really was interested in her. And just how did she go about doing that again? Asking him suddenly seemed impossible.

'Go ahead, Bea, call the meeting…' Kitty prompted.

'Me?'

'We all ken you're *quite* the organiser.' This was delivered with a salacious twist of her lips.

'And we're glad o' it,' Gene piped up, pressing his hand on top of Kitty's against his thigh, making Kitty turn her eyes back to his and they both seemed to get lost in their shared gaze.

A little flustered, and a tiny bit jealous, Beatrice shifted in her chair so she wouldn't have to watch Eugene and Kitty's flirting. '*Ahum*,' she cleared her throat, suddenly nervous. 'OK… *um*, this is the Harvest Home ceilidh planning committee. I *have* actually made a few notes.' She drew out the list she'd hastily scribbled last night. 'First… music?'

'I've had the Garleton band booked in since last year,' said Atholl. 'I'm picking up one of the lads from Fort William on Saturday morning and the rest are coming in their van with their instruments in the afternoon.'

'Oh, OK, good.' Beatrice made a note. 'Food?'

'That'll be me.' Gene raised a bony finger. 'It'll be shortbread and sandwiches. And Mrs Mair's gonnae bake ten loaves o' her famous black bun this afternoon.'

'Perfect.' Beatrice ticked at her list, aware that Atholl was watching her over his coffee cup. 'And drinks?'

'I'm no' too late, am I?' Seth had let himself in the pub door and was pulling off his bicycle clips.

Beatrice watched him shuffle in, his eyes bright behind his spectacles, and still wearing his green woollen beanie even though the sun was streaming in through the bar windows.

'Is that for me?' Seth asked, lifting a whisky and sipping it before anyone could answer.

Atholl met Beatrice's eye and smiled meaningfully. She grinned back.

'What are we talking about?' Seth asked, squeezing in beside Atholl, forcing him to shift around the table a little. Beatrice jolted at the sensation of Atholl's booted foot coming to rest up against her own, bare, foot. She had slipped off her black summer pumps under the table at the start of the meeting. Instead of moving away now, she crossed her ankles, letting her bare arches softly press against Atholl's boots. Their eyes met in sudden heavy silence.

Kitty was talking to Seth, saying something about making Gene's Highland punch recipe but Beatrice couldn't hear a thing.

Atholl's eyes, suddenly heavy-lidded, followed Beatrice's hand as she raised it to her ear and nervously lifted a strand of hair, tucking it behind. She hoped the long silver earring she'd exposed was shining against her throat, drawing his eye all the more, and yet, all the while, she was beginning to wish he'd tear his eyes away before she lost her cool and melted onto the floor.

'Bea. *Bea?* Earth to Chairperson Bea,' Kitty called through the heat haze.

'*Oh!* Yes, where were we? Right...' Beatrice tried to concentrate on the notes in her hand, but dammit, if Atholl wasn't hitching up the sleeves on his Breton top and his wrists were just right there flexing in front of her...

'New clothes, brother?' Gene interjected, suddenly alert to Atholl's new look.

'Oh, *uh*, aye.'

'Boden, is it?' Kitty didn't even try to hide her delight.

'*Eh*… well, yes,' he flustered. 'Beattie mentioned she liked them and I needed some new things, so… Can we no' get on wi' this meeting!'

Beatrice sat upright again, feeling Gene and Kitty's leery smirks burning her cheeks. Shifting her feet away from Atholl's she was struck almost breathless to find him stretching his legs beneath the table searching for her once more and gently slipping a boot between her feet.

'So… other entertainment!' Beatrice said in an unexpectedly pitchy voice, intently consulting her list, peering at the words through exaggeratedly narrowed eyes. She *would* concentrate. Meetings were her thing. She was good at this. Then again, she was normally sitting across the table from Helen Smethwick or nice but dim Ben, the twenty-year-old Hub intern who was forever bored and fiddling with his phone, making everyone wonder how he'd got the job until it came out that he was Helen's nephew. Beatrice was definitely not used to working opposite distractingly handsome Scotsmen with all the muscles and the rough-skinned, crafty hands and the tight red curls and long auburn lashes…

Seth was looking expectantly at her. 'I said I'll be reciting my poetry. You'll be wantin' to write that doon.' He nodded at Beatrice's notepaper.

'Jist make sure it's something tasteful,' Atholl warned. 'Like Robert Burns, and no' that filthy limerick about the young lady from Ecclefechan that you did last year.'

Seth wasn't exactly convincing when he promised he would keep it clean. Then Atholl had surprised everyone by announcing he'd play his fiddle. Beatrice had noted this down too, her eyebrows raised and wondering if there was no end to his talents.

Before long the other whisky glasses had been claimed. First, by Mr Shirlaw from the stores who dropped round the first prize for the raffle, a fine fishing rod.

'It's for charity,' Atholl told Beatrice, watching her scribbling her notes. 'For the lifeboats.'

In came Patrick the fishmonger, and Davy McTavish the builder, followed by Tam from the chippy, all asking if the inn still needed their spare chairs and tables to line the road outside with and each one was rewarded with a dram from the tray.

Just as Eugene was explaining that there would be so many people coming to the ceilidh that the drinkers would spill out onto the streets to find seats, and so the roadside would be decorated with bunting strung from each window and streetlight, the silversmith dropped by with a thin twisted ring in a pretty box, and the owner of the tartan mill called in with a kilt pin to raffle, both of the visitors effusively praising Atholl for supplying the sudden boost to their businesses with his clever crafting holidays idea. Atholl met their warm embraces and slapped their shoulders and handed out the tumblers and not a man refused.

Finally Mr Garstang called by, offering a skilfully made watercolour of Port Willow harbour as a prize. Beatrice grabbed the opportunity to ask how Jillian and Cheryl were getting on with their lessons.

'Aye, they were making guid progress at first, before they got hold o' the notion that I needed a… what did they call it?'

'A makeover, by any chance?' said Gene.

'Aye, that's the one. Said I was a secret silver fox, whatever that is, and now look at me.' He swept his very arty black beret off his head to reveal choppy cropped locks, definitely the handiwork of the Bobby Dazzler girls. 'They've paintings they wanted to donate to the raffle too, but they're no' quite finished them yet. Anyway, I'd best be making tracks, we're doing thermal mud masks this afternoon. Oh, and Beatrice? That's you, isn't it?'

She nodded.

'They told me to mention they'd come to your room before the ceilidh to do your hair and make-up.'

At this, Mrs Mair, who had been pottering at the bar, announced that she had a dress and dancing shoes for Beatrice to wear. They had been her daughter's but since she was in South Africa now, she wouldn't mind her borrowing them.

Delightedly, Beatrice noted all this down, and everyone raised their drinks to toast a very successful meeting. Soon she was asking if anyone had any other business and getting ready to draw the meeting to a close.

Gene interrupted her closing remarks. 'Whit aboot the caller?'

'The what?' said Beatrice.

'A caller tells everyone on the dancefloor what to do next… for the uninitiated,' Kitty added. 'And the ceilidh band are supplying their own.'

'For the Sassenachs like me, you mean?' said Beatrice. '*Ooh*, there's an idea!' All eyes were upon her as she spoke animatedly. 'If you had a dance teacher, your guests could do their craft lessons during the day then there could be lessons here in the bar after dinner in the run up to future ceilidhs.'

'She's got a point, Gene,' said Kitty. 'There could be lessons in the summer before Harvest Home and at Christmas leading up to Hogmanay.'

Gene thought deeply. 'There was a dance teacher staying here for a while, a Scottish wummin. Do you mind her, Atholl? I forget where she was from. She'd ken the steps. What was her name? Maggie something, was it? You must mind her...'

A heavy thump resounded from under the table somewhere in the direction of Kitty's boot and Eugene's shin.

'Oh, sorry, Atholl,' he said hurriedly, before clearing the empty cups back onto the tray.

In the sudden air of awkwardness Beatrice realised he had been talking about Maggie, the married woman who'd neglected to mention her husband and, who had at best, embarrassed Atholl, and at worse, broken his heart. She didn't dare glance up at him to see how he'd taken this reminder of how he'd unwittingly played the other man in this Maggie's marriage, but she saw his knuckles blanching white and heard the glasses rattling on the tray as he took it from his brother. And so the meeting ended, the committee left the bar and Beatrice went back to her room more than a little disappointed that Atholl hadn't glanced over at her as she walked past the sink where he rinsed the glasses in silence.

Chapter Nineteen

A Package Arrives

'*Special Delivery!*' Atholl called from behind the princess room door half an hour later, and his voice was so warm Beatrice felt sure he must have recovered from the shock of everyone hearing Eugene talk about Maggie whatever-her-name-was at the meeting.

When she opened the door, Atholl was smiling and holding out two postal packages. 'Well, I know what's in this one, Beattie, because I took the liberty of ordering it for you,' he was saying, handing her the plastic-wrapped box.

She didn't know what was more astonishing; the fact that he'd bought her some kind of gift or that he was now, apparently, intent upon always calling her Beattie. Both made her smile.

'Thank you,' she said. 'I, *um*, do actually know what that other package is.'

'You do?' Atholl handed it over too.

'I popped in to the café in Mr Shirlaw's shop yesterday to use one of their computers. I wanted to contact my sister and tell her I was OK, and I ended up buying something online, had it sent here, next day delivery. I'm amazed it's made it to be honest. I hope you don't mind?'

'Not at all, this is your home while you're here, Beattie.' He'd said it again, soft and lyrical in his deep Highland burr.

'Come in for a sec, if you've time? Are you going out?' she prompted.

'Only to dig out the bunting from the inn's store room. I hope Gene didn't chuck it in there all in a tangle last year.'

He stepped inside and let the door close as Beatrice excitedly tore open the result of her online shopping spree. It had been so long since she'd seen a high street shop – the Port Willow general store may have everything needed for village life, but it was lacking in the fast fashion department – the temptation to treat herself had been too much to resist.

'It's this!' She held the bikini against herself, smiling a little awkwardly. It was skimpier than she remembered it looking online.

When she glanced up, Atholl was smiling too, with the familiar closed lips drawn a little to one side to hide his sudden bashfulness. She'd seen that smile a few times and each time it melted her a little more. His eyes were shining in spite of the flush on his pale cheeks.

'Very nice. But if you're planning on wearing that to the ceilidh I'm afraid to say you've got our Highland customs all wrong. It'll be more of a kilts and tartan sashes kind of thing.' His eyes crinkled at the sides.

'Have you got swimming things, Atholl?'

'Of course.'

'Well then… will you take me to the coral beach later today, once the water's warmed up a little with the sun.'

Atholl only nodded, his eyes fixed on the bikini she crumpled in her hands.

'That's not all I wanted to ask you, actually.'

He swallowed before replying. 'It isn't?'

'No. You see, that day on Skye you gave me something I couldn't have imagined for myself – a way of beginning to say goodbye.'

His fingers twitched by his side as though he were going to reach for her, but he didn't. Instead they both smiled, acknowledging the huge burden that had been alleviated, if only a little, by the simple ceremony they had created together two days ago.

'Now I can give you something back,' she went on. 'A way to your own fresh start.'

'I'm listening.'

'Wait there.' She turned to rummage in the bag she'd carried on her walk yesterday, the romantic novel falling onto the floor at her feet. He stooped to return it to her and when he stood again, found her holding out a larger book with a big, hopeful grin on her face.

'I spotted this at the store yesterday and I read it last night.'

She held it out for the perplexed Atholl to look at.

'A book about evergreen herbs? I'm not with ye.'

'You will be soon. Are there spades up at the But and Ben? Can we go there first before our swim?'

In their hurry to snip the tags from her bikini, pack sun lotion and beach towels and make sandwiches to take with them, the other package Atholl had brought for Beatrice lay forgotten upon her dressing table.

Chapter Twenty

The Summer Earth

The sun was already high in the sky when they reached the But and Ben and the air was alive with lazily buzzing insects and the chatter of unseen sparrows hiding from the fierce heat.

Atholl leaned on the two spades watching Beatrice walking up and down the rows in the middle of Lana's lavender field. The gardening book was tucked under her arm, open at a particular page illustrated with photographs in blues and green.

'So you see, it's an old remedy for reviving neglected lavender that can't otherwise be salvaged by pruning,' she said.

'Digging it all up?'

'Yup.'

'And burying it?'

'Well, not completely buried, you have to leave the newest growth peeping out of the soil.'

Atholl contemplated the task.

'There must be at least two hundred lavender bushes here; it'll be back-breaking work digging trenches deep enough to submerge all those. Do you know anything about gardening?'

'I've a little herb garden back home. Well, it's more of a container by the back door, but I've kept some rosemary and mint alive for years now. And I've worked on a community walled garden project back in Warwick. I helped plant the potatoes!'

Atholl didn't look as impressed as she'd hoped.

'Look, the book says there's *a chance* they'll regrow, and you'll have a new visitor attraction for your crafting guests, and it'll be a lovely asset for the workshop and café. Your visitors can look out at the sea of blue lavender as they drink their tea with heather honey buns, and you can set up that lavender oil distilling thingy that you talked about *and* you can even teach lavender oil distillation and sell it in your own shop! Can you picture it, Atholl?'

This last part was delivered on tiptoe and with an animated stretch of her arms as she scanned the field around her, already able to envision the revived lavender on a bright spring day, as opposed to the tired rows of leggy, brittle, grey-stemmed bushes with the sparsest of flower heads drooping in the scorching heat and choked with dandelions that she could see now.

Atholl looked from her bright eyes to the ground. 'And this gardening expert in your book, do they say how long it'll take for them to fully recover?'

'Well…' she hesitated. 'There's no guarantee they will recover. The roots might never settle and the plants could rot away entirely.'

'*Whit?*'

'But, it *could* work! And the book says these things take as long as they take. What do you think? It's worth the risk to save them, right? And if it doesn't work, you can do as you said and rip them out and plant more willows.'

Atholl was nodding again with a contemplative frown. 'But by then you'll be long gone and I'll be in a braw mess sorting out your bright ideas by myself.' A beat passed between them. Beatrice swallowed. 'Are you wanting to help me with this digging?' he added.

'Of course. Two spades, remember?'

'Well then, I'll get the kettle on, we might manage a whole row by dinner time.'

To give Atholl his due, he didn't blanch at Beatrice's excited cries accompanied by an exuberant handclap and some kind of rain dance amongst the dying shrubs.

'Anything to keep you happy. And *busy*,' he shouted over his shoulder as he approached the workshop door.

The close and building heat of a late summer's day made the work hard going but the pair kept their spades to the ground and their backs bent. Atholl dug his willow knife into the soil to release the most stubborn roots as each lavender came up one at a time. Beatrice filled the watering can from the trough by the door and damped down the plants' roots while Atholl backfilled the newly dug, deeper trenches with his homemade compost from the heap behind the willows. It wasn't long before they were sinking the first rescued lavender into its planting hole and Atholl firmed it into the fresh earth with his boot.

'So, umm, did you speak to your mum, or your sister yet? About me running off like that?' Beatrice asked between trips to the water trough with the metal can.

'It's no' their business. And you don't need to explain yourself to anyone.'

'Really? You don't think I should ring them?'

'No. I do not. They liked you, and that's enough for family, isn't it?'

'Oh.'

Beatrice found herself thinking of Rich's dad. He'd have demanded to know what was wrong with her and she'd have ended up humiliated by his questions and put in her place by his callous, casual remarks. She could hear him now braying about their lost baby and how she really shouldn't be trying again so soon because nobody knew 'what was wrong with Beatrice yet' and she'd risk losing another child if she recklessly forged ahead with her plan to get pregnant again. Rich had asked him to leave, yet again, and there had been another blazing row on the doorstep. How had they lived with his toxicity for so long, she wondered? How must Rich be managing alone with it now? Had he told his dad where he'd gone or was he making a clean break? She thought of all those years watching Rich eaten up with worry about his father's dependence on alcohol and all that energy expended hoping for his father's approval, only to be disappointed time and again. Many times he'd seen Beatrice take the brunt of his father's casual misogyny and cruelty but he'd always open the door to him whenever he stumbled up their driveway, which told her Rich would probably still be in contact with his dad now. Her heart ached a little and she hoped he'd made an especial effort to talk to, or even visit, his nice, dependable mum in Portugal this summer, the only uncomplicated, loving family member he had left.

But here was Atholl Fergusson with his – she was realising – laid back attitude to family affairs, happily digging at the ground, the topic already forgotten, seemingly secure in the knowledge his loved ones wouldn't mind Beatrice's eccentricities one bit.

'What about Kitty and Gene, do they know... about me?'

Atholl's look told her that of course they didn't. It was her news to tell if she ever wanted to.

So they dug on, the branches scratching their skin and the acrid, sappy perfume of lavender roots rising in the now humid, salty air. The thrum of distant combine harvesters and the call of the gulls watching the moored fishing boats being hosed down over the hill at Port Willow jetty accompanied their work.

'You know, Beattie...' Atholl began slowly, weighing his words. 'Mum would understand. My mother's first baby, my big sister – Ida was her name – was lost when she was only a few days old. My mother was only young at the time and she and Dad grieved sore for her. When it came to the time Ida would have gone to school my mother wanted to do something for her, so she decided to make an inn bedroom into a fairy-tale room, so other wee lassies could sleep there and imagine themselves a princess, turning her grief into someone else's joy. Gene was born shortly after that, then myself, then Sheila and Kelly came along. We all held sleepovers in that room with our pals when we were wee. And for a long time, that was the inn's most popular room with the visitors; we were famous for it. But that was a long time ago. It's old hat now, I suppose.'

'I like your mum's imagination, and that she had a way of turning some of her sadness into something else. She must have been pretty resourceful.'

'She's no' one to sit still. She's a do-er, like somebody else I know.'

Beatrice shrugged and laughed. 'Who can you mean?'

Atholl laughed too before turning contemplative. 'So, you said that digging these lavenders could help me somehow?'

She prepared herself for the task of convincing him. 'Well, they were Gene's ex-wife's, right?'

'They're no' divorced. As far as everyone's concerned they're still married.'

'OK, they were his wife's. He's been stuck in the past waiting for her to come home, but now we've successfully got him cooking again and he and Kitty seem to be getting on well…'

Atholl joined in. 'And he even came to the ceilidh planning meeting this morning which is more interest than he's taken in Harvest Home since Lana left, so aye, I'm with you so far, but what's your point?'

'I thought we could help him move on if we gave this field a new lease of life. If instead of watching it turn into a desolate bit of weedy scrubland, he could see it flourish from a fresh start too. Maybe maintaining the field was Lana's job at first, but now that responsibility might weigh on Gene and he can't face it.' She indicated the field with her hand. 'It's become a rotting relic, a reminder of better times. And you know those tasks that you know you *should* tackle, but you just can't face? Maybe it's one of those.'

A niggling, invasive thought arose as she spoke, bringing back thoughts of Richard and all their unfinished business, but she pressed on, shaking the anxious feelings away, trying to convince Atholl.

'If we can encourage him out here to take care of the field he planted in the first place, it might make him happy – relieved even – and he can move on. We just need to get it freshened up so he can take over, so it isn't too overwhelming a task for him.'

'And so helping *me* in a roundabout way because he'll be one step closer to recovering from Lana leaving him, you mean?'

'Exactly! *And* because it's nice to help him, of course. He's so close to standing on his own two feet again; soon you'll be able to tell him you're leaving the inn in his capable hands and you're setting up a proper willow crafting business here, with a proper visitors' centre and a busy workshop, and everything you told me you dreamed of.'

'You've got it all figured out, then.'

'He needs one last gentle shove in the right direction, and *voilà*, everybody's happy!'

'A shame you'll no' be here to see it.'

Beatrice dug her spade into the ground just as Atholl stopped digging and surveyed the landscape.

After a moment's heavy silence, Atholl said, 'The season's changing, can you feel it?'

Beatrice wondered if he'd been thinking of September coming and how she'd be checking out on the last day of August, the day after the ceilidh, and now only three days away. 'Don't say it's nearly autumn, I can't bear it. The long dark days. I'm dreading them. I want it to stay summer forever.' She suppressed a shudder and tried to focus on Atholl's voice.

'The harvests are nearly in across the county and the nights are drawing in. The ceilidh's come round fast this year. My only hope is that Gene can stomach it.'

'I hope so; it seems a shame to hide away from life.'

Atholl cocked an eyebrow, throwing Beatrice a level look, amused but not unkind.

'Oh, all right! I know I can't talk, running away to the Highlands and everything, but he *must* be recovering by now. It's been a long time.'

'What did your horticulturalist say about the lavender?' He nodded towards the book, now cast aside on the chair by the cottage door. 'These things take as long as they take.'

There was nothing she could do but smile and absorb the sentiment and they worked on in silence. Beatrice's clothes clung to her and she could feel the sweat and grime on her neck beneath her hair. She was glad they'd be swimming soon. Eventually she called out, 'I'm getting tired now.'

'You've done well. That's two rows of lavender replanted and one meeting chaired and it's only two o'clock,' Atholl replied.

She smiled and wiped her hair back off her face. 'I've enjoyed having a place to be and things to do. It's been a good distraction from everything.'

'There's no' many women would spend their summer holidays helping out a family o' strangers.'

Beatrice smiled at the word. They had been strangers but now they were beginning to feel like family. 'I've enjoyed it.' It struck her that she meant it. She had found moments of calm and quiet and belonging, things she thought she could never recover.

'Any excuse to make a list, eh?' He laughed and she pitched a gardening glove at him, and they both called it a day and headed down to the coral beach to cool off.

Chapter Twenty-One

Undercurrents at the Coral Beach

It wasn't until Beatrice was barefoot on the shards of coral and attempting to wiggle into her bikini while keeping the towel wrapped around her that she fully realised what she'd let herself in for. It would have been considerably easier if Atholl *wasn't* standing by the water's edge undressing and piling his clothes on a rock.

It was the ideal afternoon for swimming, the kind of late August day that promises building heat and clear blue skies until nightfall.

The perfect crescent of white coral reflected the glaring sunlight, making Beatrice squint and wish she'd remembered her sunglasses. The turquoise water lapped gently at the sharply rising rocks that enclosed the little beach and everything appeared sun-bleached and subtropical.

Beatrice scanned the shore for signs of other humans – or worse, crazed cattle – before she struggled into the bikini top, glad to see she and Atholl had the bay all to themselves. Not even Echo had followed them on their trip out to the But and Ben and down onto the serenely quiet beach.

'Are you no' ready? Can I turn round yet?' Atholl called from the water's edge as he peeled his stripy top off.

'N… not yet,' she cried, still holding the towel around herself despite being safely clad in her bikini. She wanted just a second longer to take in the view of Atholl Fergusson, his hair gleaming in the sunlight in messy copper coils as he lay his discarded top on the rocks and worked at the buckle on his belt, causing the muscles between his shoulder blades and down his back to flex and move.

Taking a moment to give herself a stern talking to about trying to be sensible and *not* stare in slack-jawed wonder at Atholl, she tightened the towel around her and made her way to his side, taking a sudden great interest in the coral shards under her feet while Atholl finished undressing and stood before her in black swimming shorts, gazing out to the hazy blue horizon.

'So, *um*… ready?' she managed. 'It's not going to be cold, is it?'

Atholl's blue eyes met hers. 'Define cold.'

Beatrice laughed and hesitantly dipped a toe into the water. 'Hah! *That* is cold.'

'There's nothing for it but to wade in, then go for the dive, get it over with quick.' Atholl was looking out at the water again. 'But you'll need to lose the towel.'

Glancing down her body, she wished with all her might she'd bought the tasteful – well, OK, boring – one piece she'd seen online as it would have covered her up a bit more. Atholl's eyes were fixed firmly on the clear water dead ahead so she quickly removed the towel and threw it onto the rock.

'Do it together?' she said, feeling the warm air on her belly and thighs and a sense of surprise that she wasn't as mortified as she'd thought she would be a moment ago.

Atholl's hand slipping around hers stilled her breath and she stumbled taking her first steps into the shallow water.

'You all right?' Atholl asked, his eyes briefly flitting to Beatrice's.

'This coral's so sharp, it really hurts your feet.'

'I know. You get used to that too. I swam here a lot as a bairn and I don't remember it bothering me.'

Beatrice tried to admire the beautiful bay she'd dreamt of swimming in since she saw it from the top of Rother Path on the first day of her trip but her nerves were screaming from the pain on the soles of her feet, the cool water – now up to her knees – and the warm reassurance of Atholl's hand still enclosing hers, squeezing her fingers gently and steadying her in response to every stumbling step she took.

'It's not really coral, you know?' he said.

This sharpened her mind. 'It's not?'

'No, it's bashed up ancient algae.'

'Oh.'

'No' as romantic as coral, is it?'

Beatrice shook her head and laughed. 'It's still pretty,' she said, but the words were taken by an involuntary squeal as the water reached her belly. '*Sheez!* It's cold, s'cold, s'cold!'

Her free hand flapped in the air as though she could lift herself above the water and she gritted her teeth. Atholl laughed heartily, grimacing too, as the water wrapped around his waist.

'It'll pass, just hold on,' he said, turning to face her, letting go of her hand and instead clasping her forearms in his palms. 'You all right?' he asked, still baring his teeth with every gentle wave that lapped around his taut stomach. 'It really is freezin'. Yur mad tae want tae swim.'

'Why did you say yes, then?' she said, shivering but forgetting her shyness and grinning, and all the time aware of the broad expanse of Atholl's pale chest just a touch away should she dare let her hands do what they wanted. Keep your eyes on his, she told herself.

'Because you wanted to swim, of course. And you're on holiday and it's a beautiful day so you *should* swim,' he said with a shrug, his hands still wrapped gently around her arms. 'We should just go for it,' he said, feet rooted to the spot. 'Dive under the water, I mean,' he added quickly with another laugh, but neither of them showed any intention of breaking their connection to plunge beneath the cool, clear water.

Beatrice glanced down at where he touched her skin. 'I've got goosebumps,' she said, and in an instant Atholl responded, running his hands up and down the length of her arms to warm her and letting his eyes, at last, fall across her neck and linger over her body. She definitely wasn't imagining it this time.

Saying nothing, she let him look.

Knowing they'd have to speak eventually, Beatrice found herself weakly mumbling something about never having bathed in British waters before but Atholl spoke over her.

'No, you go,' she urged.

'I was saying how bonny you look today.'

'Oh.'

'Which you do. Very.'

Warmth, nothing but warmth, flooded her chest. Things like this didn't happen to her. Handsome, strapping Scotsmen with Highland accents like flowing water over rocks didn't whisk her away to swim in secluded summer bays, or gaze into her eyes like they were drowning in them, and they certainly didn't compliment her on her looks.

'You're allowed to just say thank you,' he laughed.

She released the breath she'd been unwittingly holding and laughed too in spite of herself. 'OK, thank you.'

'Can't have you squirmin' and turnin' blue over every compliment you're given.'

'I'm not really used to compliments.'

In the silence that followed, Atholl kept his hands moving over her arms, circling the tops of her shoulders too, his touch growing lighter, his eyes following the movement over her skin, letting his hands tangle in her hair as they converged at the nape of her neck. He cradled her face, his fingertips grazing the soft skin between her ears and hairline, his thumbs straying in slow sweeps across her cheekbones.

All the time Beatrice's breathing seemed to quicken and their bodies moved closer together, swayed by the gentle flux of the currents around them.

Her eyes had closed by the time she pressed herself against his bare chest and her nerves thrilled at the sound of the sharp intake of breath he made in response. That was the last thing she heard other than her heart's drumming as she spread her hands wide and slipped them around his smooth, hard back, finding that his skin still retained the heat of the morning's work under the sun. Atholl lowered his mouth to hers, pressing a slow kiss to her lips.

It lasted only a moment. Long enough to confirm all her intuitions that he'd be good at this. That *they'd* be good at this.

But as the warmth between them grew and the distance between them lessened, the thoughts intruded. Rich had never kissed her like this. And she'd married him. And he'd loved her. Hadn't he? Or was it never there in the first place? This kind of connection? It certainly never, *ever* felt like this.

Thought followed thought until the searing warmth faded to be replaced by other things: a little guilt, a little sadness, and as Atholl's fingertips brushed over her sides and towards her belly, a little memory of her lost baby.

He felt her withdrawing and he too pulled back. The coral cut her soles again. Funny how she hadn't felt it a moment ago.

'Let's swim,' he said, giving her arms one last warm stroke. She watched him dive.

Beatrice hadn't been able to read his neutral expression but she had understood the feelings between them; feelings of being thwarted, sabotaged from within, and a little sting of defeat.

Atholl was already resurfacing after the plunge beneath the water. Beatrice watched him swimming with powerful strokes out into the deeper water.

There was nothing for it but to take a deep breath and try to make up the distance between them.

She didn't let her head sink beneath the surface, it was way too cold for that, and she gasped at the frigidity of the waves wrapping her body in their chilly grip. The only thing that warmed her was seeing Atholl treading water, waiting for her and they swam side by side for a while. Beatrice tried to clear her mind and simply enjoy stretching out her body and letting her muscles work.

'Getting warmer?' Atholl called as he circled her.

'Much.'

'Just keep moving. Shall we swim for the horizon?' he said.

A sail boat crossed the blue skyline and both wordlessly set it as their focus. Atholl matched Beatrice's slow pace.

'Are we OK?' he asked after a long moment.

'We're OK.'

'I'm sorry if I shouldn't have done that, kissing you, I mean.'

'Didn't I tell you to stop with the sorries? ...and I wanted to kiss you.' Beatrice's breathing showed she was tiring already but swimming into the deeper water felt too good to turn around anytime soon even if she was at risk of getting out of her depth.

'*But?*' he prompted.

'But... I panicked a bit. I haven't done much kissing lately.'

Atholl waited. The water resisted their movements and the tiredness in her muscles felt delicious.

'It's been a while since me and Rich...' the words tailed off as the effort of pulling herself through the water grew harder. 'That's my husband's name. He moved out all of a sudden one day at the start of July.' Beatrice hoped Atholl would say something, anything, but he didn't, so she had no choice but to go on. 'I worry sometimes that he blamed me about the baby. He never said as much but his dad certainly did.'

'Well his dad sounds pernicious!'

Beatrice surprised herself by laughing at the word and the fierce way it rolled from Atholl's mouth.

'I suspect your man Richard was grieving, regardless of what his father had to say about it. He'd be cut up and sorry, but he cannae have blamed you.'

'What makes you think that?'

'Some men aren't good at speaking their feelings. It takes one to know one. He must have been suffering, only differently – or expressing it differently – to the way you did.'

'Well… maybe you're right.' A little lightness entered her chest at Atholl's words. How had he come by this new talent for knowing the right thing to say to relieve her pain, this man who had been so cold at first and thought himself so bad at communicating?

'He still left though. But you're right, *he* wasn't pernicious, not at all, just driven by work and he wanted things to be smooth when he got home at night, and he didn't like heavy, complicated stuff, I guess.'

She caught her breath. They really were in the deep now. She had lost all sense of the seabed beneath her and the water was growing colder as they swam.

'For a long time everything was easy, we were both enjoying our jobs, and we really only saw each other for an hour or so at night.' She was panting now with the effort. The muscles between her shoulder blades were turning numb. 'And our weekends were eaten up by work spilling over into them – I only cottoned on to the fact that he wasn't really there for me when I was struggling to cope with everything, and I was at home alone all day, getting lonelier and lonelier, and just feeling… useless and good for nothing.' She filled her lungs. 'I couldn't even trust my own body to do stuff it seemed any other woman can do. And when I tried to fix everything by getting pregnant again it just drove us further apart. I was a bit desperate and clutching at straws, if I'm honest. But I got eaten up by the sadness and eventually, it consumed our marriage, I suppose.'

'That sounds common enough to me.'

'That's not all, really. I've got used to telling myself it was work that slowly drove us apart over the years, and

244

we found we were somehow leading separate lives, and getting pregnant briefly brought us together again, but there's more… you see… I was kind of hard to live with from May right through until he left. I was charting my temperature, and monitoring my hormones and taking all these supplements and eating pineapple cores and Brazil nuts because I heard they'd help me get pregnant, and I was calling Rich at work and telling him to come home because we had to… you know, there and then. And then when we did do it, I kept crying and it was probably a bit off-putting, and I went on and on like that for weeks. So, you see, it was my fault that he left. I scared him. Are you laughing?'

'No, I'm not laughing.'

'But you're looking at me like I'm crazy?'

'Nor that.'

'And you don't… pity me?'

'Not pity, no. Admire you? Aye. Know that you've suffered and did your best to cope? Yes. Wish you were happier? Wi' my whole heart.'

Who stopped swimming first she couldn't tell, but their legs sank under the surface simultaneously and their heads came up. Beatrice glanced back to the coral beach; it was a long way off. They faced each other, circling their legs and arms slowly, stilling themselves in the water.

'I'm sorry, Atholl, I'm being a bit weird, I know it. It's just kissing you back there… really brought all that back, all the stuff with Rich I haven't really dealt with.'

The thoughts had crowded in and spilled out in a rush, running as clear as the water over her back and just as cold and biting.

'I'm sorry. That's a shame,' Atholl said, his own breath faltering.

'It *is* a shame. I never thought I'd be forty and separated, or temporarily homeless for that matter. And I always thought I'd be a mum.'

'I'd hold you if I could,' Atholl said. 'But I'd sink us both. It wasn't your fault, any of it. You should know that.'

'You'd have stayed in the same situation, would you?'

'What? If my nerves were being tested daily by someone like, say Eugene, and I was living in close quarters with them, and they were struggling to cope? Yes, I'd stay.'

'Oh.'

'You're shivering again, keep moving.'

They set off again for the horizon, the water so cold Beatrice's toes and fingers felt numb, but she could see through the crystal clear water to the white coral far beneath them as though they were in balmy tropical waters.

'It's nice of you to say that, but it really was all my fault. And it got a whole lot worse as my fortieth birthday started looming. Do you know women over forty only have a five percent chance of conceiving every month?'

'I didn't know that, but I do know my mother had my wee sister when she was forty-eight.'

She threw him a double take and blew the air from her lungs with a whistle. 'Really? Wow! Well, the fact of the matter is I'm nearly forty. I always thought I'd be a mum by now, and here I am... five hundred miles away from my husband and hiding out in the Highlands.'

'When?'

'What?'

'When's your fortieth?'

'Tenth of September.'

'So, what's that?' He lifted his eyes to the sky as they swam. 'Thirteen days?'

'Something like that.'

'When you wake up on the morra after your birthday, you'll only be forty years and one day old. That's almost the same as thirty-nine years, eleven months and... twenty-eight days as you are now. Very little will have changed between now and then.'

'But the fact remains I missed my chance. It's all irrelevant without Rich.'

'You could easily meet someone new.'

Her focus on swimming meant she didn't see his eyes flicker or the pinched line between his brows.

'And have you been on any dates recently, Atholl?' she said, trying to lighten the tone. 'Have you? The girls at the Hub used to show me their dating profiles and the men they were matched to. They were a gruesome crop of middle managers with hairy backs, halitosis and three mobile phones and ten women on the go at once. Half of them have wives!'

Breathless laughter burst from them both and they instinctively turned their backs on the wide blue horizon and the grey mountains in the far distance. They'd had enough of the deep water.

Swimming for the shore again, no words seemed necessary. Beatrice wondered why she felt so light, buoyed up by the water, yes, but unburdened too. Atholl was being quiet but he must be as tired as her, she reasoned.

That was when she realised she and Atholl had drifted apart.

In fact she was struggling to keep up with his easy pace through the water. Really struggling.

'*Atholl!*' She had called out his name before she realised she was panicking and gripped by the feeling of a hundred hands twisting around her limbs and pulling her back out to sea. In an instant she was dragged under water.

It took her rational brain a few moments to work out what was happening. She was unable to swim for some reason; pulled away from the shore by an invisible force. Was this a panic attack? No this was the water itself claiming her. She was going to drown.

Fear, animalistic and profound, overwhelmed her. Her legs thrashed ineffectually, her arms pulled for the water's surface, but she couldn't free herself from the strange grip of the cold ocean. She resurfaced somehow and gasped a deep breath, but it wasn't enough to fill her lungs.

As she was about to bob under the lapping waves again, two warm hands pulled at her wrists, her head and neck cleared the surface of the water fully and she gasped at the sweet air.

'*Rip current,*' Atholl was panting, clasping her so tightly her skin hurt before they were wrenched apart again by another pull at her body, the cold water taking her again.

No thoughts came. She could hear someone trying to shout. It was her own voice, but instead of words coming out she gulped great mouthfuls of salt water that made her gag.

When she surfaced this time, Atholl was hollering from a perplexingly long distance away, his eyes fierce. They were floating further apart with every moment that passed.

'You *must* do as I say if you want to live.'

She was alarmed to see him struggling against the pull and his chin going under the water too. Even Atholl, with all his strength, was in danger.

'Let yourself float *away* from me. Do *not* swim for the shore,' he cried.

She gasped for air, barely processing his words.

'Float *away* from me. Then, when you're free, start swimming in a great curve. That's the only way you'll escape the current. Don't swim against it! Float *with* it, back out to sea and away from me.' Atholl had turned onto his back and was floating in a starfish shape on the surface of the water all the while being pulled even further away out to sea but in an unseen current that was dragging him quickly away from her in a wide arc. 'When the current drops you again, you must *kick*, Beattie. And don't stop!'

She tried to tell him she understood but her voice was stolen by the cold water and the panic. Had he heard her? She thought she saw him turn onto his stomach and begin swimming in the opposite direction from her in a great curving arc, heading at first out to sea and then turning round towards the bay, his arms powering him in great strokes, and all the time he was shouting, 'Go with the water until it drops you.'

Her legs had no strength left and the tide still dragged her straight out to sea. Swim away from him, she thought. In spite of all her instincts to try to follow after him, fighting the tide, she overcame them.

She flattened her body on the surface of the lapping waves and let the tide pull her away from the beach, from Atholl, and out to sea, astonished at its speed. How could calm water have such ferocity just beneath the surface? After a few moment's floating, resting her exhausted limbs, she realised she was utterly alone in the water; she could no longer see Atholl and wasn't aware that he was still calling to her now he'd reached the beach, but she replayed his words over and over as she felt the current loosen its grip, 'When the current drops you again, you must *kick*, Beattie. And don't stop!'

So she kicked and she didn't stop. She kicked with all her might, and dragged her arms through the water, fighting for every breath. She felt the current's pull dissipate completely, and found she was able to turn in a wide arc. Swimming felt impossible now. Lead in her legs, her stomach empty – they hadn't unpacked their picnic, wanting to cool off with a swim before eating, her eyes and her lungs burned from the salt water. There was no hope of making it all the way back to the furthest edge of the beach, avoiding the ripcurl current. There was no strength left in her body and she felt the fight leave her.

Somehow, Beatrice wasn't sure how, Atholl was in the water again, swimming towards her, his face paler than she had ever seen and he was calling out, 'Thank God.'

Suddenly, they were swimming together. She was on her back kicking her legs and he had his arm around her body, dragging her in a one-armed breaststroke towards the shore. After what felt like a long while spent between sleep and waking, she became aware of being carried from the water, her body a dead weight. And she was against Atholl's chest, and she was alive.

The sharp shards of ancient bleached algae felt like her own plump bed at the inn as he lay her down on the coral beach. She could hear him through her exhaustion asking if she was all right and begging her to say something.

'You keep saving me, Atholl Fergusson,' she gasped out, as she brought into focus his sea blue eyes. 'I'm supposed to rescue myself.'

She saw the relief in his face before he rolled onto his back on the shore, his chest expanding with each breath, his stomach rippling with wry laughter. They both lay back under the hot sun and faced the glare of the sky.

Chapter Twenty-Two

A Blank

Beatrice was dreaming, delirious. The back of her neck was hot and there was a cool hand on her forehead. Her mum was smiling at her and she had never felt so happy to see her in her life. She knew she was crying but wasn't sure why.

'Mum, what are you doing here? Are we still at the inn?'

'She's just tired, I'm sure o' it. Best call the doctor, though.' Beatrice knew through the haze that it was Mrs Mair talking.

'She's been asleep for hours,' Kitty's voice was saying, and a man was asking if she'd swallowed any water and talking about something called secondary drowning.

She didn't hear anything else for a long time, but eventually she was aware of a voice droning on and on, never stopping. It was someone talking about babies and hospitals and anaesthetics and it sounded a lot like her own voice. 'Let me sleep,' she called out, and the voice stopped.

'Exhaustion, that's what the doctor said, and no' just from the riptide either. It's been coming on for months, he thinks.' Kitty's sweet accent rang in Beatrice's ears and she was aware the room was light but she couldn't force her eyelids open.

Someone made the mattress compress by her side and she felt a warm hip against her body and a calloused, gentle hand settling over her forehead.

'Rich?' she murmured, her brow furrowing, her eyes shut.

'Nae temperature?' a man's soothing Highland voice was saying, deep and soporific.

'No, no fever. The doctor says she has to sleep as long as she needs to. Go on, you should get away to bed too and let her sleep. Standing watching from the doorway for hours on end isn't helping her at all,' Kitty was saying softly.

She heard footsteps withdrawing and a door closing and she slipped back into a heavy, blank slumber.

Chapter Twenty-Three

Meddling

'You weren't there when I woke up.'

'Beatrice!' Atholl dropped the sack of sweet-smelling mulch at the sound of her voice and turned to face her. He straightened his spine with a throaty growl that told Beatrice he'd been hard at work all afternoon. 'I thought I'd better leave you to sleep and get your strength back.'

'You all let me sleep all of Friday night and almost all of today? For twenty-four hours?'

'Aye. And ye needed it, didn't ye?' Turning back to the compost sack, he tipped the last of its contents on top of the newly replanted lavender.

'I did, you're right. Was it Mrs Mair who came in with the soup and bread?'

'It was Kitty. Was my room all right for you? It must have been strange waking up and not knowing where you were.'

Beatrice smiled at the memory of his room which had been warm with close summer air and the curtains drawn against the sun. There had been books on the shelves and willow sculptures in various stages of completion on the desk.

Once Kitty was sure she could stand up on her own and had left her to drink the sweet tea and take a shower, Beatrice had wandered around the room, running her hands over the willow work and over his brown leather belt and the spines of his notebooks – one of which was open on the desk, filled with willow designs and technical-looking drawings explaining how to make certain knots and fastenings and strong foundational structures to support larger sculptures. She had sipped her drink and pored over his pencil marks – delicate, confident, skilled and sensitive.

She had washed with his shampoo and soap thinking of Atholl the whole time and how this was the way he lived his life. She smelled of him now that she had washed away the salt and sand.

Now she'd found him, and she wanted to tell him all this, and maybe hold him again, but he wasn't returning her smile.

'I tried to see you but Kitty said you were dead to the world and nobody was to wake you. Are you all right now?'

'I am. I don't think I've ever slept the way I did, like I really *did* drown. I think I've been tired for months, exhausted I think. I mean the *real* kind of exhausted. The ill kind. And I feel strangely altered now; wide awake and alive.' Atholl watched her raise her hands to the afternoon sky and something in the coolness of his demeanour was deadening some of this elation.

The air was chillier today, but the sun still shone weakly through watery clouds. A change was forecast, Kitty had told her, and this must be it.

'Are you OK?' she asked, concerned.

'I'm fine,' he replied, but something in the way he was looking at her unsettled her.

'You finished the lavender field then? All by yourself? They look a bit odd half submerged like that, don't they?'

Atholl turned without saying anything, walking along the rows gathering up the empty mulch sacks.

Beatrice followed after him.

'I hope it works; we could do with some rain to settle them in,' he said, seemingly to himself and looking up at the sky.

Folding the sacks into a bundle beneath his arm, he marched past Beatrice towards the open door of the But and Ben. She watched him pass, feeling hopeless.

'Atholl? Are you all right?'

No reply came as he stooped inside the low cottage door and disappeared, so she scurried after him, perplexed. What had changed while she slept? Had she dreamt their kiss? Had they not faced death together and fought to survive? Had he not carried her all the way back to the inn while she dozed against his chest? But now this? She wasn't expecting him to throw his arms around her and kiss her or anything, although that's what she'd hoped for, but now the old formality was back?

'Impossible,' she told herself in a whisper.

She watched him around the door frame, washing his hands, his back bent over the workshop's ceramic sink, and the restless, panicked feeling rose in her chest again, a feeling she thought she'd left behind her.

She only vaguely registered the sight of the gleaming copper vat with its pipes, meters and gauges newly constructed in the corner of the workshop; Lana Fergusson's lavender oil still. Atholl had obviously kept himself busy while she'd slept away her exhaustion. She couldn't know that he hadn't allowed himself to sleep for watching over her and when Kitty had at last sent him away he had toiled in the field, stopping only to nap on the hard workshop bench during the few short hours when it was too dark to work.

Before she knew what she was doing she had crossed the floor and joined Atholl by the sink, clasping his wet wrist and turning him to face her. Reluctantly, his eyes met hers.

'What's changed, Atholl? One minute we're swimming, and kissing… and drowning,' she attempted a laugh, 'the next you're barely talking to me. What happened?'

'Nothing.'

She felt the tension in his wrist as he tried to pull away from her grasp.

'This doesn't *feel* like nothing.' If she could have disguised the shock in her voice she would but it was hopeless. '"You need to learn to let other people help you." That's what you said. Well, I have, because of you, and now you're withdrawing into yourself again?'

He forced out an exasperated breath, his heavy-lidded eyes still cast down and unmistakably guilty. She'd struck a nerve.

'It's nothing, Beatrice.' Her name sounded harsh upon his lips today, so different from the affectionate way he'd called her Beattie only one long sleep ago. 'Your holiday's almost over. You've got two nights left of your stay. We've brought Kitty and Gene together, we've resurrected the lavender field, and you've given everyone their orders for the ceilidh planning. So why don't you rest and enjoy what's left of your holiday?'

'No. That's not it.' She screwed up her eyes, peering at his face. 'You can see that I'm fine. You know I love the work. No, that's not it, at all.'

'Beatrice, I don't know what you want me to say.'

She released his wrist and his hands fell to his sides as he turned to face her. Her mind flitted to the way they'd stood exactly like this in the cool clear water and she'd sunk into his kiss.

Atholl scrabbled for words, but they sounded hollow when they came and the colloquial Scots he'd slipped deeper into as they'd got to know one another, was gone. 'You've done enough to help us. It's wrong to ask for more. You're a guest here, a… holidaymaker. I was wrong to take advantage of you.'

Her chest heaved and the sting of tears burned her eyes. 'You took me to Skye. I met your family. I held your sister's baby, and I told you things I've never told anyone. You gave me the little bassinette and helped me begin to say goodbye to my baby and all that sadness, and you rocked me in your arms like you…' Her words faltered and failed. *Like you loved me*, she thought, and her eyes conveyed the words.

She watched as Atholl wet his lips, his eyes widening as he returned her gaze.

'We should get back to the inn. We've got a long day tomorrow what with the ceilidh and everything,' he said, the smallest tremor in his voice.

She watched him retreat, holding the door open for her and letting the key swing from his finger.

She joined him outside and he locked the door and hid the key beneath the shell. Nothing could prevent her from reaching out and placing a hand on his back.

'Atholl, talk to me.'

He stood frozen but didn't turn to face her. 'I had a long time to think while you were sleeping,' he said. 'You know you didn't tell me about your husband until we were in the water together, and by then we'd kissed and…'

'And? Didn't you think there'd be a husband? How do you think I made the baby?' She was forcing laughter into her voice, wanting to soothe the frustration in Atholl's tense body.

He turned slowly. 'It was only last month you were living together. He might need time out, like you did, to recover himself, then the pair of you can carry on as before.'

'What?'

'You were calling for him in your sleep, Beatrice. You miss him; you said as much yourself when we were swimming.'

'I did?'

'I don't want to be the second fiddle again, Beatrice. So, I think it's best if you just enjoy the ceilidh tomorrow and we go our separate ways on Monday.'

'Atholl!'

'You have to at least talk to him now you've worked through your feelings here, see if you want to patch things up…' He winced at the words, but let them tail off with a nod. He was resolute, she could tell. She'd heard that tone before, when Rich was set on leaving. She had recovered some of her pride since then; she wasn't going to beg again.

'I'll walk you back to the inn,' he said, indicating her way back to the path alongside the freshly planted lavender.

At that moment Eugene appeared in a hurry around the side of the cottage.

'Ah, you're here! Kitty sent me out to look for you. Your sister's been on the phone, Angela, is it? I said you'd ring her back… Hello Atholl.' He stopped to place his hands on his knees and get his breath back. 'I'll away back to the inn. You must get a phone installed up here, brother!'

'You didn't open your parcel?' Atholl had turned to Beatrice.

'My parcel? Oh, the one you gave me. No, it must be in my room. Why?'

'I got you a new phone so you don't have to use the one by the bar.'

'Oh. That was nice of you.'

'Well, if you pair are done wi' the scintillating chatter, I'll be off. Cheerio!' Gene called out before he paused, suddenly stuck to the spot, his eyes scanning the lavender field. 'What's a' this?'

'You'd better come inside, Gene.'

Atholl flashed Beatrice a cautious look as he led his incredulous brother away from the field and into the cottage.

Beatrice watched the lights flickering on inside and saw the gleam from the great copper still through the window. The low rumblings of their talk reached her but the words were indistinct.

As she approached the door, straining her ears, drops of rain touched her skin. It was cool, not at all the warm, grass-scented, dusty rain of summer. She shivered and peered inside the cottage.

'Dinner with Kitty is one thing, and even starting up the evening seafood service is all right now that I'm used to it, but *this*, Atholl? This is a step too far for my liking. Meddling with my wife's land? It was not yours to touch. It was supposed to lie still 'til she came back and...' His words ended in a gulp when he spotted the still in the corner. 'Have you built this for Lana? So she can use it on her return? Or have you built it for yourself?'

Beatrice approached the doorway and looked between the two men, panicked and guilty. 'I'm sorry, Gene, it was my idea. I wanted to help you and Atholl by setting you back on your path to...'

Eugene turned on Beatrice with tears in his eyes but determined to make his point. 'Sort your own life out before you go sticking yur nose where it's no' wanted.'

'*Eugene!*' Atholl's voice sounded a warning and a plea, but it was no use. He stalked out of the cottage and away back to the inn.

'That didn't go as well as I'd hoped.' Atholl squirmed, rubbing at the ground-in earth on his hands. 'Wait 'til he hears about the job advert I've put in the paper for a cleaner and a sous chef.'

'I'm sorry Atholl.'

'No. No more sorries eh, Beatrice? Let's just get back to the inn.'

Chapter Twenty-Four

Eugene's Escape

'So you were out at the But n' Ben last night?' Kitty said from the top of the stepladder. She'd been biding her time with small talk as they shared the task of decorating the bar room, but by now she was on tenterhooks.

'Sorry if I worried you. When I woke up I went to find Atholl.'

'Gene said as much. You know, Gene's been pretty quiet since he got back. He left Mrs Mair to do the breakfast service this morning.'

'Ah… that might be my fault… I had another one of my ideas.'

Beatrice explained the plan to resurrect the lavender field and bring both it, and Eugene, back to life again, all the while standing on the bar and helping Kitty twist long red crepe paper ribbons before securing them in cheerful strands across the ceiling. Kitty took it all in.

'I appreciate you helping him, and me, I really do, but you might just have gone too far this time. His feelings are still very tender where Lana's concerned.'

'I know that now.' Beatrice clambered off the bar to hand Kitty the end of a white crepe strip, before starting the task of twisting and pinning it into place again. 'Does, *umm*… does that bother you? That he's still so sore about

262

his wife? I mean, it's not like he'd take her back if she did come wandering in, is it? Not that it's any of my business.'

Kitty's laughter surprised Beatrice. 'Look, I know you want to help Atholl by relieving his burden here at the inn, and you want to rehabilitate Gene, but you and I will be leaving again – you far sooner than me – and then where will the Fergusson brothers be?'

'You're leaving?'

'Of course. Term starts again at the end of September. I'll stay here 'til then but I'll be lecturing at the uni again soon enough. I'll visit Gene during reading week, if he wants to see me, that is, but I think we both know he needs time to process his feelings for Lana. He's no use to me while he's still pining for her, no matter how sweet and romantic he is to me in private.'

Beatrice pulled her neck back, the surprise showing on her face, as she made a start on the canister of helium and a pile of blue and white balloons.

'*What?*' Kitty said. 'We're very fond of each other, yes. And he's soft and kind, as I imagine Atholl is to you.' At this, Kitty delivered a sly smirk at her friend. Beatrice focused on knotting a fat, squeaking balloon. 'And I like Gene more than any man I've ever met, but he's had to face up to the end of his marriage in getting closer to me and that's caused him some pain. Did you no' think it would when you set us up on our surprise date?'

Beatrice felt the sting of Kitty's gentle chastising. 'I didn't, no,' she sighed, annoyed with herself. 'Though I really should have done. I'm in the very same boat myself.' She saw Kitty cocking her head, confused, but pressed on. 'I saw an opportunity and wanted to get you two together as quickly as possible.'

'But, Beatrice, love takes time. As does healing. You can't rush these things.'

Beatrice watched Kitty's face for any sign that she might know the reasons behind her Highland dash, but saw nothing disingenuous in her expression. No, Kitty was still in the dark.

'I might have spoiled things for you and Gene before he's had a chance to heal, you mean?'

Kitty shrugged. 'If he likes me enough, he'll come around.'

'I hope he does; you two are lovely together.'

'I think so. I've been teaching him some Gaelic, and he's been teaching me how to cook. It's been a lot of fun, learning new things.' Kitty was smiling again. 'I think *you've* picked up some new things too, this holiday?' She reached for a large honeycomb paper ball decoration and climbed up her ladder again, fixing it in place at the centre of the room, her expression all innocence and wickedness at once.

'*Hmm.* I've learned a bit about willow-weaving if that's what you mean?' said Beatrice.

'That's no' exactly what I meant, no.'

Beatrice was throwing inflated balloons onto the bar room floor and they bounced and floated around her. For a second, she considered working away silently at the canister and hoping Kitty would drop the subject but she knew she'd have to tell her the whole story, and so she did. It didn't take long at all, her whole sad story compressed into a few minutes' telling, and it all culminated in kissing Atholl then getting caught in the tide.

'And so I almost drowned. And Atholl got us out of the current. If he hadn't known what to do we'd both have been dragged out to sea. You can't swim against tides like that, apparently. You have to go with it. That sounds a lot like my life recently. One minute I'm a wife and a mummy to be, next I'm alone in the Highlands, and then I'm kissing a man I only met, what, just over a week ago? The next thing, he's saving my life! When I woke up after my long sleep, I thought to myself, *that's it, that's the answer, you just have to learn to go with it.* And yesterday I went up to the But and Ben to tell him all this, and how I was ready to see how things might go here with him – offer to stay a while longer maybe, and I don't know, I kind of just wanted him to kiss me again and see how it felt this time.'

'And?'

'And he told me to go home to Rich.'

'But you like Atholl, don't you?'

'Of course I do!'

'And the kiss in the water? What was it like?'

'What was it like? That kiss! I needed that kiss. I definitely deserved it. But there was a little niggling of something not quite right, even though it was *so* right. And Atholl's absolutely correct; that thing was Rich. Up until now, hiding my head in the sand about the separation and the house sale seemed to be all I could do to get through. But I know now, after telling Atholl about him and saying his name out loud and recounting all our failings there's still so much unfinished business there and so much left unsaid. Rich was, after all, the father of my baby and we had all those years together, and you can't just throw all that away without once looking back.'

'You miss him.'

'Sometimes. Maybe not the heart-broken kind of missing him, but a simpler kind of missing. I loved him enough to marry him and I miss telling him daft things about my day, and I miss having someone who just knew me. We could talk in shorthand. We had something between us that deserved to be salvaged, at least some of it did. And it's as if the universe knows that too, because – talk about timing! – Atholl had given me a parcel and I didn't get round to opening it until last night, and it was a phone.'

'A phone? To replace the one you dropped in the sea?' Kitty said.

'And he'd charged it and swapped in my old SIM card and everything, which is so like him, I'm realising. Anyway, there were messages, *lots* of messages from Rich, going all the way back to last Sunday. They were pretty tough to read. The first ones were all about the paper-work of selling the house and dividing up our joint bank account and the life insurance, and all that stuff, and then I could tell he was getting worried, wondering where I might be and why I wasn't answering, and the last one was all concern too, but with something extra. He said he misses me, he'd "really love to talk if I can face it", and then there was a message saying he was going to ring Angela to ask her where I am. Oh God!'

'What?'

'You don't think he's trying to reach me because he wants me to sign divorce papers? I know he's been in a rush to move on but he can't be so callous as to chase a divorce already, can he? *Ugh*, my head's spinning just thinking about it all. Clarity's all well and good but, ouch, it's dizzying too. I feel like I'm stepping off a bumper car ride that's lasted two years and I have the bruises to prove it.'

'So what do you want to do?' said Kitty, gently.

'I need to do all the things I've learned to do while I've been here. I need to calm the heck down and stop fighting against life's riptides. Instead of getting carried away trying to right every wrong, I have to let life carry me along for a while. I can't fix everything, so I'm going to go home on Monday and see where life takes me after that.'

'Will you come back to the inn? See Atholl again? Port Willow's awfy bonny at Christmastime, you know?'

'I don't know what I'll be doing after tomorrow... *literally*, let alone what I'll be doing in the winter.' Beatrice's heart sank at the thought of the dark, short days to come, and remembered with a sigh which she couldn't suppress, the mortified call she'd made to her sister that morning, asking if, what with the sale of her house and everything, she could move onto their sofa for a few weeks until she could find a little place of her own.

The call had set her thinking that with the money from the sale she could afford a small place, and with a little cash in the bank and no job to tie her down she was free to look for work anywhere in the country now. She'd be at the mercy of the job markets.

Angela had read her some job ads she'd cut out of the *Guardian* for her. The pickings were slim but there was a charity fundraising job going in Barnstaple in Devon, and a community campaign manager for a hospice a bit closer to home in Coventry. Funny how she hadn't missed trawling the job pages one bit while she'd been here. Whatever was in store for her, she wasn't going to fight against it. She'd find out soon enough where she was supposed to be.

But for tonight, there was a white dress with a muted blue tartan sash hanging on the door of her wardrobe, thanks to Mrs Mair's daughter Louisa, who had long since emigrated to Cape Town, and tonight Beatrice was going to twirl in that dress under the bonny decorations at The Princess and the Pea Inn and try not to upset anyone else. And tomorrow… well, she'd think about that on her way back to England while Port Willow slept off its hangover.

'There! All done.' Kitty brushed her hands together and folded the stepladder up.

'It's perfect,' Beatrice replied, scanning the bar, now a bright confection of coloured crepe, bunting and balloons. 'That's five o'clock. The band should be here soon. Atholl's been gone for ages collecting the piper from Fort William, hasn't he? Wasn't he meant to be here an hour or two ago?'

'He'll be here soon enough. He had to collect the whisky too, remember? Have you not spoken to him today?'

'I saw him briefly at breakfast, but he had the barrels to change in the cellar and then he was busy with Gene prepping the buffet, so just a quick chat, really. I'm pretty sure he's avoiding me.'

'Be sure you speak to him before you go. Some things can only be said face to face. Just tell him everything you wanted to say to him yesterday.'

Before Beatrice could come up with a reply about how she wasn't planning on antagonising him any longer and she was going to keep her mouth firmly shut, Gene appeared from the back kitchen, taking off his apron.

Seemingly mirroring his brother's awkwardness that morning, Gene appeared to have forgotten how to act in front of Kitty too. Today was his wedding anniversary and he knew he was being observed by everyone who knew him. They were all wondering if he was going to bolt this year too.

He ran a nervous hand over the shorn hair above his right ear, barely making eye contact with the woman he'd spent almost every second of the last week with.

'I'm, *uh*… I'm away to walk Echo. And then, *uh*…'

His skin paled at the look Kitty gave him and he turned away. She wasn't going to plead with him to stay and dance with her at the ceilidh, but her face flushed and her eyes burned with hurt. The women watched him skulk out the bar and onto the seafront leaving the door swinging behind him.

'He's not coming back tonight,' Kitty said. 'He did the same thing last year, and the year before that, Atholl told me. God knows where he gets to, but he doesn't have it in him to face the ceilidh. Once he told Atholl he couldn't stand the music; it brings back images of him and Lana dancing at their wedding reception.'

Kitty sighed as Beatrice crossed the floor to put an arm around her friend and lead her to the booth to sit down.

'I was at the wedding, you know,' Kitty continued. 'And he was so happy. And Lana was so beautiful, but maybe just a wee bit *less* happy than Gene. She was young. Too young to be marrying a man she barely knew and changing her citizenship and leaving her family behind in Canada. But Gene wooed her, poured his heart and soul into their relationship, and he was so ecstatic. A dancing fool, Seth called him. Seth could see it wouldn't last, maybe we all could. I stopped coming to the village after that, so I didn't see it all breaking down, but I can see the impact it's had. I just hoped that he'd be able to face the ceilidh if I was there with him. Looks like he can't.'

'Oh, Kitty, I'm sorry. This is all my fault.' A flash of optimism lit Beatrice's face. 'But he seemed so happy when we had our planning meeting, remember?'

'That's what I thought, but he's gone now, hasn't he?'

Beatrice watched the door he'd left through moments ago. 'You never know. Maybe he really is just walking Echo.'

At the sound of his name being spoken, the dog strolled into the bar, the slow sweeping of his tail sending balloons scattering across the carpet. The two women's eyes met in a knowing, defeated glance.

'I'll pour us a drink,' Beatrice said.

Chapter Twenty-Five

The Ceilidh

The gulls squawk from their lookout on the sweet damp thatch of the But and Ben roof high above the coral beach where once in a harvest moon the tides swirl in treacherous currents beneath a calm surface.

The stubbly fields to the east are dotted with newly wrapped bales, the combines and tractors all now returned to their sheds.

The cows and their calves have been rounded up from Rother Path and are now safely enclosed for the evening in their meadow, the great red bull lowing to them over the hedge from the next field.

Every farm worker from the cottages dotted over the hills behind the village has downed tools after their long summer's work and is now taking to the country lanes in their smartest clothes, all scrubbed knees and swishing tartan.

The noisy gulls lift effortlessly onto the cool, late-August breeze which is scented with the workers' cologne, lavender, willow sap and sea salt, and they glide high in the air, their serene glassy eyes fixed on Port Willow and the last of the afternoon's tourist fishing boats now returning to the harbour with their small catch.

In the village, the streets are cleared of cars for the purposes of dancing and criss-crossed with cheerful bunting strung between every window and street lamp, and the white lightbulbs along the jetty gleam out in the dying light.

A boat, newly arrived from Skye and filled with red-haired children is mooring up at the jetty, and the older children help a white-haired, elderly woman step ashore in her ancient Highland mink and pearls.

All the villagers are leaving their houses and slowly strolling, remarking to their neighbours about how quickly the summer has passed and how the dark nights will soon be drawing in. Their chatter mingles with the drone of the piper's chanter as he works his lungs and the rest of the ceilidh band try their instruments ahead of a long night's dancing at The Princess and the Pea Inn.

This is the best and brightest night in Port Willow's ritual year. This is Harvest Home.

No one sees the woman sitting in the inn garden on the promenade, shielded from the bustling street by bushes radiant with drooping red rosehips. A tartan blanket protects her white dress from the damp bench as she clasps her steaming mug of tea and waits patiently.

–

'There you are. I've been walking the prom looking for you.'

Throwing the blanket off her shoulders, Beatrice stood and faced Atholl, smoothing down her white, full skirted dress and adjusting the tartan sash with its large bow at her shoulder. Mrs Mair had fixed it to the bodice only an hour earlier using a gleaming brown agate brooch with a small posy of white heather shoved behind its clasp, and the older woman's eyes had misted and her voice wavered as she spoke about her daughter far away who had once upon a time been the bonniest girl at the Harvest Home celebrations.

Beatrice hadn't felt so sure she could pull off Louisa Mair's Highland look this evening, thinking it old-fashioned and just far too Scottish, but Atholl's expression told a different story.

'You're beautiful,' he uttered. Instantly abashed, the colour rose in his pale cheeks. Beatrice wondered if he'd meant to say it, but her thoughts were stolen away as she looked at Atholl.

Six foot of Scottish redhead stared back, his curls dampened and swept behind his ears showing his squared jawline and fine, high cheekbones. The muscles in his jaw worked and his blue eyes shone as he let her look him over in his Highland shirt, open at the throat and with the smallest touch of creamy lace at his cuffs. One shoulder was draped over with a heavy tartan sash which hung behind him in neat folds. The silver buckle on his thick leather belt glinted in the early evening light and the mossy green kilt hung in thick pleats to his knees. She scanned his taut muscled calves, the thick Highland wool socks and gleaming brown leather boots. Distractedly, she lifted a hand to her hair which was pinned up in a bundle of curls – Cheryl and Jillian's handiwork – and tucked a soft strand behind her ear.

'What are ye doing sitting out here?' he asked.

'I wasn't sure if I was going in.'

'And are you?'

'I am now. I wasn't going to fight against a tide that wanted me to stay away.'

Atholl's brow crumpled in confusion.

'It doesn't matter,' she said quickly, dismissing her words with a wave of her hand. 'Don't you scrub up very nicely – once you've got the lavender twigs and the earth and salt out of your hair.' She smiled unrestrainedly, so glad he'd appeared before her and in far better fettle than he'd been the night before at the But and Ben.

'I'm sorry I've been away all day, and left you alone with setting up. I had a lot of things to attend to—' he said.

'That's OK,' she cut him off, not wanting to hear him explaining again how he wanted to put more distance between them. He'd come to find her, hadn't he? He wanted her at the ceilidh. That was enough. 'It doesn't matter; you're here now.'

'The band's ready to start up,' said Atholl. And as if to confirm this, a slow lament drifted out through the open inn windows.

'Is Gene back?' she asked, her brows tilting and showing all her hope.

Atholl only shook his head.

'What about Kitty, is she all right?'

'She's helping to serve the Highland punch at the bar.'

Beatrice sighed. 'We messed up there, Atholl. I'm sorry.'

'Don't apologise to me. I was the one setting up the lavender oil still and racing to finish the planting while you slept. I was the one who didn't tell Gene where I was for near on fifteen hours as I worked. I should have guessed he'd come looking for one of us. But I was consumed with wanting to work. After we got out of the rip current, after you'd opened your heart about Richard and your marriage and how you didn't know where you stood with him, I was struck with terrible guilt at having monopolised your time here when you should have been recovering, and all the while I was wantin' to see more and more of you. Selfish, I ken. So, I tried to leave you in peace and keep myself occupied. But when you woke up and ye came to me in the field in your sundress and your hair all loose, and… I knew I couldn't help myself when it came to you, Beattie. I wanted to kiss you again. It felt like a great wave washing over me, and I wanted to drown in you.'

Beatrice stepped towards him, placing a hand on his shirt sleeve. 'But you told me to talk to Rich, to see if he wanted me back. Is that what you want me to do?'

'I want you to follow your heart.'

'And it's taken you all day to think it through? Where have you been?'

'Ah, well… this morning I—'

'Evenin' young yins,' Seth called from the street. 'You'll be missing your own ceilidh at this rate, Atholl. You're needed to introduce the band.'

Atholl spun round to face Seth. Beatrice didn't see the effort it took for him to break away from her and greet his old friend. She did see the polite, if terse, nod of his head before he turned back to her to offer his crooked arm with a resigned sigh. 'Shall we go in? This is your last night in Port Willow, after all. You should dance, and taste the whiskies and be happy.'

As she passed through the little gate from the inn's garden, gripping his arm, Beatrice resolved to do as Atholl had said. He was telling her to not complicate things, and that tonight was all they had left and he wanted her to enjoy it, so she would.

They weaved through the rows of chairs lining the street. The inhabitants of Port Willow had all done as they were asked and brought out their own chairs and tables and the whole scene resembled a royal jubilee street party.

Seth, dressed in an ancient-looking kilt and tweedy jacket and still wearing his faithful green woollen beany, held the inn door open for her to pass through and Atholl released her arm as she walked in.

'Save a Gay Gordons for me, Beatrice,' Seth said with a twinkle. 'There may be more lassies here than ever before, thanks to Atholl's crafty women, but there's still too many laddies and no' enough lassies. It was ever the way at Port Willow,' he added dramatically.

'You cannae call them *my* crafty women, Seth,' Atholl warned with a droll smile. 'They're our crafting holiday patrons.'

'Well, whatever we're calling these bonny English lassies, I hope they're ready for a night's birling on the dance floor.' Seth waggled his eyebrows and headed for the bar where Kitty was ladling a bright red drink from a large cut glass bowl into cups and handing them out to a gathering crowd.

Now that Beatrice could see the whole room, her lips parted and her jaw fell. Atholl watched her expression from by her side.

She'd seen it all earlier, of course. She and Kitty had pushed the chairs to the outside of the room and hefted most of the tables out into the street in order to clear a makeshift dancefloor. The decorations she and Kitty had strung across the ceiling still looked festive and bright but now the room was swirling with dancing spotlights from the low stage the ceilidh band had rigged up earlier, and the room was packed, a patchwork of swishing tartan in every colour. Standing here and there were local women in white frocks and visitors wearing the smartest clothes in their suitcases, some looking underdressed in jeans and jumpers but everyone smiling and excited. Mrs Mair stood at the bar, her sleeves rolled up.

'No' bad, eh?' Atholl said, proudly, and Beatrice had to agree. 'Wait here,' he said, close to her ear, and he was gone, pushing through the crowd.

Over the sounds of the crowd and the chinking of glasses Beatrice heard the crackle of a microphone and Atholl's voice running smooth like water in a burn.

'Welcome, friends, to The Princess and the Pea and another Harvest Home.'

The cheer startled Beatrice. This crowd were ready to party.

'Tonight I must thank the Garleton Band who'll have you dizzy and puffin' by midnight if previous years are anything to go by.' Another cheer. The drummer raised his sticks in approval. 'I have other folk to thank, too. Two special guests. Kitty Wake, who returns to us from her university in the north. Thank you for finding your way back to us. We've all missed you.'

Beatrice had to stand on tiptoe to peer over the heads to see Kitty, ladle in hand over the punch bowl, shyly accepting the applause, looking desolate as the crowd clapped and hooted.

A quick scan around the room revealed no sign of Gene who, if he were here, would tower head and shoulders above the crowd. Beatrice felt herself shrink inwardly. She'd been responsible for hurting this kind, generous woman and she had to fix it somehow but how could she do that without meddling even more?

Her attention was called back to Atholl's voice at the sound of her own name being spoken and she found a break in the crowd where she could see his face.

'And I must thank the bonny and brave Beatrice Halliday, who came to us from far away and has found a home here, warmed our hearts and made us wonder how we ever lived without her.' He was looking straight at her and the crowd parted. She stared back.

Atholl spoke on, his lips close to the microphone and neck lowered as though he were talking only to her. 'You and Kitty are responsible for helping us host the biggest Harvest Home celebration Port Willow has seen this half century. So please join me in a toast of our gratitude to Kitty and Beatrice, thank you, and haste ye back.'

'*Haste ye back*,' the crowd called as glasses swung and whisky splashed and a hundred pairs of eyes fell upon Beatrice approvingly.

Atholl surrendered his microphone and walked through the crowd towards Beatrice who glanced around her, wondering if anyone else had the sensation that time was somehow slowing down and he was moving towards her as if through water, his kilt swishing and eyes sparkling.

She heard the slow tap of a cymbal and a broad Scottish accent declaring, 'Ladies and Gentlemen, please take your partners for a St Bernard's Waltz,' and she was in Atholl's arms and being spun to the outer edge of the dancefloor as the crowd divided into a circle of paired dancers and the whisky-supping spectators on the periphery.

She caught the eye of Cheryl at the bar. She was dressed from cleavage to knee in gold sequins and surely the most glamorous being the patrons of The Princess and the Pea Inn had ever encountered. Jillian was beside her in a glittering black dress that hugged her contours. She was accepting two glasses of punch from Kitty. Behind them in the queue stood a row of fishermen with scrubbed faces, uncomfortable in their shirt sleeves, every one of them gaping at Cheryl and Jillian and thanking their lucky stars for their arrival in the village, all of which the Bobby Dazzlers pretended not to notice, not until later in the evening anyway. Cheryl was winking at Beatrice and nodding her head towards an oblivious Atholl, making Beatrice grin back in response.

There was no point protesting. She and Atholl were the talk of The Princess and the Pea, obviously, and to be fair, it was probably for good reason. They all knew Atholl had carried her home from the coral beach on Friday afternoon and they'd both walked in late yesterday evening from the But and Ben, and they'd drawn their own conclusions. The silversmithing ladies from Sussex had seen it all too and it had fuelled a whole evening's slightly jealous gossiping.

While the Bobby Dazzlers had set about her hair and make-up earlier that afternoon Beatrice had tried to explain that Atholl thought she'd be better off with her husband and that he'd made his position perfectly clear, she was a holidaymaker here and nothing else, they had laughed and raised their perfect HD brows and told her not to be so soft. Oh well, they'd all finally see tomorrow morning when she checked out and her holiday was over. There was nothing going on between her and Atholl.

She found her voice as the musical introduction ended, 'Atholl, I don't know how to do this dance!'

'It's easy. Look me in the eyes, stay in my arms, and let me lead you,' he said, low and sure, as the circle began to move in unison.

And she found he was right. It *was* easy: easy to hold his gaze as he led her in sweeping turns around the room, the caller telling her when to click her heels on the floor. It was easy to let him push her into the middle of the floor so all the women were back to back in a smaller circle before being pulled towards him again to the outer edge of the dancefloor and swept almost off her feet in a sudden waltz of dizzying spins. All the while their bodies stayed connected as though magnetised.

When the waltzing chorus ended and the verse returned along with a repeat of the slow promenading steps she felt she'd already mastered, she said, 'This is quite a gentle dance. I thought I'd be horribly lost and thrown around.'

Atholl's eyes stayed locked on her own and his grin spread making his eyes crinkle and shine. 'Oh aye, there'll be plenty of that, this is just the beginning.'

'Well, I like it.'

'Me too.'

He danced her backwards towards the centre of the floor again.

'And I must say you look very handsome,' she added, shyly.

Atholl smiled as he expertly steered her back out to the edge of the circle. 'Thank you. I think we look braw together.'

'Braw,' Beatrice said with a smile. 'I didn't know I liked a man in a kilt, but I don't think I'll ever want to see a bloke in jeans and a t-shirt again.' Her imagination threw out an image of Atholl in blue Levis and white cotton, soft and tight in all the right places, and she found herself stumbling over Atholl's feet. 'Oops, sorry!'

He steadied her again, and they kept spinning to the music.

'*Umm*,' she fought for something sensible to say. 'What kind of tartan are you wearing?'

'Fergusson, of course. Do you like it?' He slid his arms further around her waist, pulling her closer so their hips touched before waltzing her again.

When the slower steps came around she scanned his body, loving the heavy swishing tartan folds and the leather sporran with silver buckles. 'I certainly do. And what's that?' She directed her eyes to the gleaming pewter clasp at his chest which held his sash in place over his shoulder. 'It says something on it?'

'It's the clan motto. *Dulcius Ex Asperis*.'

She enjoyed the sound of his tongue and teeth rounding out the words so much she asked him to say it again. This time he leant his face close enough for her to feel his breath on her cheek and she was sure he slowly nuzzled the few loose wisps of her hair aside with the tip of his nose, putting his lips to her ear and whispering the words, all the while guiding her in a slow spin.

She gulped and looked into his eyes just as the music culminated in a loud flourish and Atholl slowed her to a stop.

'What does it mean?'

'It means Sweeter After Difficulties. That's the literal translation. It tells us that rewards come to us after our hardships, and they're all the sweeter for it.'

The dancers froze in their circle and the men bowed simultaneously to their partners. As Atholl took his own slow bow in front of Beatrice his eyes stayed fixed on her astonished gaze and he smiled knowingly.

'A good motto, is it no'?' he said as he straightened up, taking Beatrice's hand in his own again so she could curtsey.

It felt curiously old-fashioned and her movements clumsy and yet she found herself wanting to do it well, to thank him, to show how much she appreciated his sweetness. So she bobbed down before him, crossing one leg shakily behind her other, letting her eyes fall to the ground, and when she raised them she thought how she never wanted this man to be out of her sight again.

'Stay on the floor for a Galliard,' the caller announced, and Beatrice was relieved to find Atholl adjusting his hold on her shoulders, turning her body so she was in the correct position, his strong hands shifting her waist, and everything about that feeling right and natural.

The noise in the room grew and Beatrice noticed people were spilling out onto the twilit street to drink and talk and dance but the bar room still jostled with people and Mrs Mair was doing a roaring trade in beer and drams. The singing and laughter from the street outside suggested to Beatrice that it was just as crowded along the waterfront as it was in the bar.

Beatrice was relieved to watch Seth make his way over to Kitty and take the ladle from her hands with unheard words. Kitty let him lead her onto the dancefloor with tears sparkling in her eyes. How kind he was and how gentle. He really was the all-seeing Seth, just as Kitty had said, and right now he saw nothing but a sorry young woman with a broken heart pining for a man whose affection she couldn't rely on for sure; a man who wasn't even here to see her looking so beautiful in her white dress and dancing shoes even redder than her hair.

The music struck up with a cheerful accordion and pipes and the room moved again. Even Cheryl and Jillian were joining in, having taken their pick from the handsome farm lads and rugged fishermen lining up to dance with them. There was much stumbling over the steps as the caller spoke over the music telling everyone what to do, and peals of laughter rang out.

Occasionally Atholl took over at the bar and Beatrice, being one of the few women vastly outnumbered by men, was required to dance all night.

She found herself in the tweedy arms of Seth dancing a simple waltz. The frenetic energy of the evening seemed to have calmed a little when the doors burst open and men and women poured inside from their tables out on the street all shaking great plashes of rain from their jackets.

Seth looked sagely at them, shrugging off the cold draught they'd brought in with them and said, 'There's an ill wind blowing in. We're in for a wild night.' And Beatrice had smiled and let him lead her around the floor.

The dances began to blur into one another; dances for groups of fours and for sixes, dances that required the men to take their partners in their arms and lift them off the floor, waltzes that called for heart to heart closeness, and wild spinning reels that Beatrice could barely comprehend the rules of. But she laughed and she danced and passed underneath the clasped hands held up for her, and she found that if someone offered her a hand it probably meant they intended to spin her, and everyone pointed her and the other novices in the right direction when they were lost. The entire thing felt joyful and exhilarating and hilarious.

At one point, the women, seemingly without any cue that Beatrice was aware of, called out a loud '*Hee-yeuch!*'

in unison and she found herself joining in. By the time she felt sure she'd been passed around the entire company of dancers at least fifty times, and do-si-doed, pas de basqued and curtseyed to every one of them she was dry-mouthed and hot. Mrs Mair had sold all the raffle tickets and the caller had drawn the winners to much applause and cajoling when one of the young farmworkers had won the silver ring and looked hungrily round the room for a lassie to present it to.

The clock above the bar told Beatrice it was eleven o'clock and yet the night was only just getting going; this she could tell from the determined, concerted expressions of the elderly Port Willow men waiting their turn to cut in and claim one of the few women as a dance partner.

Atholl saw that she was tired and led her to the booth table to sit down.

'Mum, you'll look after her, will you no', he said as he walked off to fetch both women a drink.

'Hello, dearie,' the white-haired woman said, her cheeks flushed and her eyes, Beatrice noticed for the first time, shockingly blue like her sons'. 'I'm glad you stayed out the whole of your holiday, I wanted to talk with you.'

Beatrice sat with the little flutter of panic that welled in her chest.

'Oh, about that day at Skye—'

Mrs Fergusson cut her off. 'Yes, about that. You like my son, do you no'?'

Beatrice looked around for him. Couldn't he come to her rescue right this second? Was the queue for drinks really so long? She was all alone and had to style out this grilling, so she resolved to be polite and smile.

'I do,' she replied.

'Well, it's him you need to tell that to, no' me. And I'm glad, but that's no why I wanted to see you. I wanted to talk to you about your baby.'

'Oh, Atholl told you about that, huh?'

'No. You did that yourself, when your heart broke in your chest holding wee Archibald. I'm no' so short-sighted as folk think I am.'

'Oh.'

'It will get easier. I promise.'

'Will it?'

'Yes. Take it from one who knows. It never stops hurtin' but the pain will stop stinging so much if you *share* your burden. But I think you might be learnin' that already?'

Beatrice followed the woman's gaze over to the bar where Atholl waited patiently and smiled back with a look that conveyed that he knew what his mother was doing but he trusted her judgement.

'I think you might be right,' Beatrice said, unable to stop herself smiling back at Atholl.

Mrs Fergusson's eyes sparkled as she revelled in the silent exchange between them.

'Have you ever seen *Brigadoon*, my dear? The musical? With Gene Kelly?'

'I haven't. Kitty mentioned it too, is it big round here, or something?'

'No, it's as old as the hills and almost as forgotten as the Harvest Home ceilidhs of the past but it's got a message I always reminded my husband of when he was heartsore for the loss of our wee Ida. It says, it is not loneliness to have loved in vain, but not to have loved at all. Even when our darlings are lost to time, we've had the blessing of loving them, and that is everything.'

Mrs Fergusson peered at Beatrice's face and took her hand in her own paper-smooth grip. 'It *will* get easier, Beatrice.'

'Eilidh, may I have this dance?' Seth was by the booth, giving off whisky vapour and a hazy smile.

'Och, Seth, I cannae see tae dance, you ken that,' Mrs Fergusson chided.

'All the easier for you to imagine you're dancing with Gene Kelly then. You can stand on my feet?'

Mrs Fergusson chuckled. 'Oh, all right. One waltz, Seth.' Mrs Fergusson pointed a bony finger. 'And no trying to dip me backwards this year!'

Chapter Twenty-Six

An Ill Wind

'Three? No four. I've lost count.' Beatrice had no idea how many of the curiously strong but easily gluggable cups of Highland punch she'd drunk. She blanched when Kitty told her the ingredients.

'Rum, ginger ale, gin, honey, oranges and lemons. The stuff's lethal, but perfect for a ceilidh. Highland folks would visit friends for a party and pour their own bottle – whatever it might be – into the shared punch bowl, so it would vary in strength and taste over the evening. There's isn't one definitive recipe. I made this one following Gene's instructions.'

Kitty and Beatrice were talking behind the bar during a lull in the music. Mrs Mair had only moments ago carried out trays of sandwiches, black bun and shortbread to the sounds of cheering and everyone had set upon the food. It was only seconds until midnight and sure enough the crowds looked as though they were refuelling for another wild bout of dancing.

Beatrice had been introduced to an army of red-headed Fergussons over the course of the evening, including Atholl's littlest sister, Kelly, but the names of the children, all now playing on the dancefloor in a noisy rabble, had escaped her.

'Things seem to be going better with Atholl, then?' Kitty whispered loudly.

'We're being friendly. It's nice.'

'Flirty, you mean?'

'Not at all.' Beatrice glanced across at Atholl behind the bar where he was trying to regain order and tidy up as people ate. He caught her looking and smiled. 'You think he's flirting?'

Kitty rolled her eyes. Their conversation was interrupted by tapping at the microphone and Seth, a little worse for wear and giggling to himself like a school boy, addressed the audience, trying not to slur.

'And now for shhum poetry.'

'Oh no,' Atholl hissed.

Seth cleared his throat, holding up his splashing whisky glass. All eyes were upon him as he began his rhyme.

> *There was a keen cyclist from Port Willow,*
> *Whose heart was aflame for his bride…'*

Atholl slapped a palm to his face, shaking his head. The same silversmithing women who'd whispered about Beatrice and Atholl over breakfast that morning were loudly wondering what was happening.

'What's he saying, Philippa? Is it a traditional Highland poem?'

'Perhaps it's Robert Burns, Georgina?'

Atholl was hastily making for the stage as Seth pressed on, thoroughly enjoying himself, while the young farmers at the bar made bawdy calls and whistles.

> *His cheeks burned bright red as she lay on the bed,*
> *And asked if he fancied a ri—'*

'Riii-ght, thank you, Seth!' Atholl snatched the microphone from him as half the room sniggered and booed at the interruption; the Scottish half.

Fixing the microphone into place on its stand, Atholl reached for the fiddle case that had lain untouched on stage all evening.

Beatrice's eyes shone as she watched him settle the instrument in the nook under his jaw, teasing out the first long, sweet note, one eyebrow lowered, surveying the audience, before jolting the bow in fast movements and starting a speedy reel. Soon everyone was clapping, even Seth, who performed a dramatic sword dance – minus the swords – in front of the stage.

'Maybe I *can* understand how Seth's wife preferred to live on the other side of the village away from him,' Beatrice joked to Kitty. But Kitty only smiled thinly.

'How are you holding up?' Beatrice asked. 'I can take over with the punch now and let you get to bed, you look tired. And this isn't your job, is it?'

'I'm fine and it's not for much longer, an hour maybe, given the state of some of these farm labourers. And I should earn my keep. I haven't a single Gaelic lesson booked in yet, thanks to Gene's computer errors.'

'You've done well tonight,' Beatrice said. 'Putting on a brave face.'

'I wish I could shake this maudlin feeling, Bea. I'm thinking of telling Atholl in the morning I can't stay. I might head home to uni.'

'Really? Oh Kitty, I'm sorry…' Beatrice began, but she was stopped mid-sentence by a growing awareness that the fiddle music had suddenly stopped and an uncanny silence had fallen over the whisky-soaked crowd.

'*Kitty Wake*,' a voice called from the doorway. 'Kitty Wake!'

Beatrice watched her friend's expression change as the voice reached her and the crowd parted, all eyes wide and wondering, as intrigued, amused faces looked between Kitty and the tall figure who'd just arrived, dressed from head to toe in Fergusson tartan and holding in his arms great long bunches of white heather.

'*Gene*,' Kitty said beneath her breath.

'Kitty Wake,' he continued in a clear, sober voice, loud enough for the whole room to hear. This was to be a public declaration, it seemed. 'I'm sorry I left you tae face the Harvest Home by yourself. I should have stayed by your side. But I'm here now, if you'll forgive me.'

Kitty was on her feet and moving towards him, her white hem brushing the knees of the gaping spectators.

Gene kept talking. 'Everyone here knows tonight was my wedding night some years ago. And everyone knows how that marriage ended. This night was special to me because I made sincere vows to a woman who couldn't quite love me enough, and I've mourned this night in my heart for years. But, I've made the decision to make a new vow, to you, if you'll listen?'

Beatrice saw Kitty's red hair bobbing over her shoulders as she made one slow nod of encouragement.

'It is customary in Port Willow to carry your beloved across a line o' white heather tae signify the beginning of a union. God knows, I've done this once before but no' with a woman as fine and bonny as you, Kitty Wake.'

Atholl had made his way to his brother's side and he placed a hand on his shoulder. The pair shared a reassuring glance before Gene stooped to arrange the heather in a long line separating him and Kitty.

Aside from the whistles and calls of the farmers too drunk to know what was happening, the room reverberated with the baited breaths and hum of nerves in every individual's chest as Gene walked around the white flowers to stand by Kitty's side. He whispered words in her ear, the crowd watched her smile grow, and Gene swept her into his arms and carried her in a long stride across the heathers.

Beatrice had never heard such a cheer, and the band struck up in a wild reel as Gene held Kitty to his chest and strode out through the open doors, held wide by Mrs Fergusson and Atholl, into the night.

Maybe it was the wild music, and the romance and the passion she'd just witnessed, and maybe the punch had something to do with it too, but as Beatrice watched Atholl scanning the crowd for her before making his way through the laughter and the toasts and the renewed dancing to where she stood, only one impulse made its way through the cacophony and into her mind. She wanted him. Even if it was just for tonight. Even if he *was* the most beautiful, talented, earnest, caring human she'd ever had the good fortune to be thrown together with. Even though they were going to part tomorrow and probably never see each other again. Even if it was going to hurt in the long run. She wanted him.

'Looks like Gene fixed everything himself in the end,' Atholl said as he reached her.

'No help needed from us,' Beatrice beamed, holding Atholl's gaze. 'Atholl?'

He reached for her hand. 'Go on.'

'When the ceilidh's over, will you spend the night with me? I'm leaving tomorrow and don't want to miss a second that I could be with you.'

She saw the blaze in his eyes at her words.

'What about your husband? I cannae be the other fella' even for one night.'

'Rich isn't my husband anymore,' she murmured, seeing Atholl looking hard into her eyes searching for the truth there, before bringing his mouth down to cover hers.

The kiss spoke of the night they'd spend together and it made her nerves thrill and shiver. The clock above the bar chimed midnight as they sank deeper into their kiss and Atholl's hands roamed over her back in slow circles. When he finally pulled away, the penetrating way he looked at her made every muscle in her body compress then soften and she found she was biting her lip.

'I'm having a word with the band,' Atholl said with sudden decision, and he walked away to speak into the caller's ear. The caller nodded and signalled to the band they were to play their last song.

Then Atholl passed behind the bar, Beatrice watching him all the time and laughing delightedly at his sudden fervour to have her alone. He switched the bright bar lights on and started closing off the beer pumps.

The ceilidh was coming to an end. The crowds were draining their drinks, reaching for coats and getting ready to step out into the rain, wishing they'd brought umbrellas. Echo chose this moment to return from his wandering and shake his coat in the middle of the room, spraying the guests with muddy water, before strolling off to bed.

As Atholl moved through the bustling crowd collecting glasses, he glanced at Beatrice, checking her whereabouts every few seconds as though he were afraid she too would leave.

Beatrice helped reunite drunken farm labourers with misplaced bowties, mobile phones and the worryingly sharp clan knives they called *sgian-dubh* as the band packed up.

At one point, the tide of the departing crowd moving lazily and heavily towards the door pulled Beatrice with them and almost out into the street, making her think of the riptide. She threw Atholl a comic smile and, seeing her struggle, he pushed through the crowd to take her hand and pull her towards him in the middle of the dancefloor, their lips meeting again in a hard kiss.

'Not long now, once the band's gone…' he whispered, not needing to finish his thoughts.

Beatrice's mind flickered to the great four-poster bed and the tower of plump mattresses upstairs and imagined how he'd follow her up the ladder and press her down hard onto the bed and she'd tell him not to be gentle and they wouldn't have to worry about disturbing the inn guests as they were all as drunk as one another, and the sounds of the storm gathering momentum outside would drown out their cries.

Her breath caught as he delivered one last kiss before breaking away, dazed and smiling, and hastening the last of the drinkers out the door. He handed over a bundle of notes from the till to the band who divvied it up amongst themselves and stuffed it into pockets before they too headed out the door with their instruments, speakers and lighting rig. They seemed to take ages to get out, Beatrice thought.

Atholl disappeared with the rest of the night's takings to lock them in the safe in the reception. In the sudden quiet of the inn, Atholl whistled a jolly Highland reel and it danced in the electric air.

'Is everyone away now, Beattie?' he called when he returned to the bar and flicked the overhead lights on, squinting at their harshness.

His heart stilled at the sight of Beatrice standing by the door face to face with a rain-soaked man he'd never seen before. He knew by instinct and the look in Beatrice's wide eyes that this must be her husband.

Atholl froze to the spot and watched them.

'*Rich?*' Beatrice breathed out the word, barely audible.

'They don't make it easy to find this place, do they?' Rich replied, standing stock still in front of her, his overnight bag dropping to the floor. 'Looks like I missed a good party. I've been driving round all the lanes in the dark. Bloody sat nav's useless round here.'

'What are you doing here?' she said, breathlessly.

Richard's stare broke away from Beatrice at the realisation that another man was watching their exchange. Awkwardly, he looked over at Atholl, then back to Beatrice. 'Umm, can we talk, in private? I've come all this way to see you.'

'The inn's full, I'm afraid, if you're planning on staying,' Atholl called across the room, his voice gruff. He had moved behind the bar where he was mechanically loading glasses into washing trays.

Beatrice spun round to look at Atholl, and she thought she saw him wince at something in her expression.

'Of course, I can make up a bed for you, if Beattie wants me to?'

'Beattie?' Rich echoed, cocking his head. When he spoke again, he addressed his wife, closer to her ear, and she watched his eyes as he spoke. '*Please*, let's talk.'

She reached for his wrist, grasping it. 'All right, come with me. I've got a room. You can get dry and I'll make you some tea but then you'll have to go.'

Echo padded back into the bar and sat upright, leaning against his master's legs. Rich eyed him warily.

'It's all right, he's a friendly soul. He'll no touch ye,' Atholl spoke with a growl.

Rich laughed. 'Hah, I'm not afraid of any sheepdog.'

Atholl's nostrils flared and he forced his eyes away from Rich, who was staring confidently at him. 'You two go on up,' Atholl said with a note of finality in his voice. 'I'll bring up a tray of tea in a minute.'

Beatrice led Richard from the bar and towards the stairs. As they passed Atholl and Echo, Rich squeezed himself against the wall cautiously, keeping his hands away from the sniffing dog.

Beatrice looked straight at Atholl, her brow furrowed and her eyes wide like a roe deer caught in headlights by the roadside: alert, tense and ready for flight. 'I'm sorry,' she whispered.

After they'd left and the stairs creaked with their footsteps, Atholl reached for the cloth he'd thrown over his shoulder only moments ago when he'd been clearing the glasses, before the shock of seeing Beatrice reunited with her husband and before his world spun off its axis. He brought the cloth down onto the bar in a hard slap, clenched his fists and took a long, deep breath with his eyes closed. When he opened them again, his gaze fell upon the sight of the trampled heather on the dancefloor. He gathered it all carefully in his arms and tossed it on the bar before making his way to the kitchen to make tea for Beatrice and her husband.

Chapter Twenty-Seven

Words at Last

'*Umm*, nice room,' Rich said, eyeing the bed with one eyebrow raised.

Beatrice chose to ignore the snarky tone in his voice. 'Richard, it's the middle of the night, what are you doing here?'

'I've been calling you and you haven't replied. In the end I asked your sister where you were and she told me.'

'She *did*?'

'Well, after she said she'd tear my bollocks off and hand them to me if I caused any trouble, but yeah.'

Beatrice's eye was drawn to the rain drops running from Rich's coat onto the rug. 'Take that off, and your boots too. You're soaked through.'

Rich was grumbling about having to park along at the train station as the street had been closed for a party. Beatrice barely heard him. All the while she was thinking of Atholl's expression moments ago. Was he about to come in here with tea for the man she'd told him had broken her heart only a few short weeks ago? What must he be thinking?

'Beatrice, I had to talk to you,' Rich was saying as he threw off his boots. Her attention snapped back to him. He was wearing a new jumper she didn't recognise and she was reminded of the long time they'd spent apart. So many things must be new in his life.

'How's your new place?' she asked, avoiding looking at the stool he'd pulled out from the dressing table for her. He perched on the chair he'd dragged over from the window.

'Fine, a bit lonely, sometimes.' He shrugged and attempted a smile. 'I called at the house this week to check it was ready for the new occupants, and to see where you were… all your stuff's still there… and *uh*, anyway, I had a man with a van coming over to get my gym equipment and with you not being there, I don't know, I started thinking.'

'OK?' Beatrice eyed him warily, still standing by the closed door, shifting from foot to foot, waiting for Atholl to come.

'I mean, really thinking, for the first time since I fucked it all up and ran off.'

She became aware that her heart was thumping uncomfortably in her chest and her face was beginning to burn. Was she about to cry? The Highland punch wasn't helping matters as it coursed through her bloodstream.

'I was horrible to you. I didn't know how to handle it all. I could have behaved better, much better.'

'It's a bit late now, isn't it, Rich? Have you come here to give me the divorce papers? Is that why you're here?'

'No, God no. I'm an arse but I'm not a total bastard. Hear me out, Beatrice. I couldn't handle you and how sad you were, and how I couldn't do anything to help you, and…'

Now she was crying, and she found herself crossing the room to grab a tissue and dropping down into the stool beside Rich's chair.

He kept talking, his words coming in an unstoppable rush. 'I didn't have it in me to fix everything. And you wanted another baby *so* much, and I...' She met his eyes. There were actual tears in them, she noticed. She had never seen him cry before. 'I just couldn't go through it all again. And I don't think you could either.'

'So you left me,' she said quietly and matter-of-fact.

'I think if you really think hard about what we were like before the baby, you might see that we weren't all that happy, not for years before—' He cut himself short and looked down at his hands. 'I feel terrible saying this to you.'

'So why say it to me now? Why come all this way in the pissing rain and the middle of the night to tell me this?'

His words had stung but deep down she had known he was right, and he wouldn't be stopped now.

'I came to apologise for the way things ended and to tell you I didn't just throw it all away – our marriage and all the memories. It wasn't working anymore, and we were actually really miserable.'

'It wasn't all that bad. If you'd managed to keep your dad in check and come home from work earlier once in a while or spent a bit less time working at the weekends when I lost my job and you knew I was at home climbing the walls, bored to distraction, maybe we'd have been able to fix it. I still think we could have fixed it, if we'd made a bit more effort.' She let her shoulders fall as the guilty thought struck her and she blew out a heavy sigh. 'Rich, it wasn't all your fault... I know that now. I'm sorry too. I was a mess. I was trying to fix things the only way I could, by getting pregnant again, and I'd clammed up, couldn't talk to you. And you couldn't talk to me either. Even if we had grown apart, which we *really* had, it's such a shame it had to end the way it did, so abruptly and with so much pain unacknowledged. We both could have handled things so much better.'

'Maybe you're right. It's too late now though, isn't it? Or are you telling me we still have a chance at something?' Rich asked, his eyes widening.

Beatrice shook her head with an exasperated huff. In spite of his tears and his sudden fit of remorse she was exhausted and ready to throw him out. She hadn't imagined their reunion being quite so fraught and she hadn't anticipated how angry and hurt she would still feel. 'Rich, what else are you wanting me to say?'

She found herself wondering if there was still time to talk to Atholl, to go to his room, apologise and try to convince him to spend the night with her, in spite of Rich's terrible timing. But when she looked back at her husband she surrendered this last bit of hope.

Rich was still talking, wringing his hands and looking up at her imploringly. 'You don't have to say anything. It's me who should have told you that I never, ever, not once, didn't want our baby.' His voice faltered. 'And I wanted to find you and tell you that. I *loved* that little baby with all my heart, and I'd have been a good dad, nothing like my father.'

'No, nothing like him. I know that.'

'And I would have tried to make it work between us, in spite of everything, but we never got the chance to find out what our family would have looked like, or how we might have been together if there were three of us.'

Beatrice's heart sank and broke all at once. She'd never known Rich could ache like this before. His pain somehow blurred his face and she couldn't quite see his features or the old Rich she used to know. The sorrow in his voice touched a deep, long forgotten part of her, the affection she'd had for him and her hopes and dreams for their future.

'Rich, we could have talked about all this months ago; you should have said something and helped me to talk about it.'

'I never got the chance. One minute we were grieving, the next we were supposedly trying again, and I was hurting so much, and so were you.' He was sobbing now. 'And somehow we were propelled apart... and, if you remember Beatrice, we were never very good at talking things through, were we?'

She wasn't sure how, but her hands were suddenly clasped together in his soft, familiar grip and they'd turned their bodies to face one another.

'I came to tell you that I loved you and I loved our baby and I'm so sorry it didn't work out for us. And I miss you. And I miss looking forward to being a daddy, and... I don't even have anything to remember our baby by—' At this, he broke down again. Tears streamed down his face.

Beatrice slipped off the chair and onto her knees, wrapping her arms around her husband, crying too, weighed down with his sadness, her hands gripping his clothes. Neither of them heard the rattle of teaspoons inside mugs outside the door and the sound of a tray being set quietly down, and footsteps retreating.

Chapter Twenty-Eight

Checking Out

The fumes from the car exhaust billowed into the reception through the open inn door. Rich swung Beatrice's suitcase into the boot and gave her an assured, gentle smile which she returned before he made his way to the driver's seat and closed the door. In his hands he held a folded bundle of soft fabric, embroidered with rainbows and clouds, his baby's blanket.

The passenger door remained open as the car idled and Beatrice, wearing Richard's jumper from the night before, turned back to the inn. Atholl watched from behind the reception desk.

'Chilly this morning,' she said as she approached him, feeling as ridiculous as she had on the day she'd first arrived at the inn. She tugged the sleeves of the jumper down over her hands and added with a shrug, 'I'd only brought summer clothes.'

Atholl smiled, conjuring all his reserve and formality into his face. She was leaving and they were going to have a decent farewell. 'Last day of August's here. September's on its way,' he said, and Beatrice scanned his face.

'I'm sorry about last night,' she said. 'I didn't know he was coming.'

Atholl waved a hand. 'He looks brighter this morning. Ten years younger, in fact.'

Beatrice paused before saying, 'He had a lot to get off his chest, I think. Anyway, there was no point in me spending nine hours on trains when he's driving back to England, is there? I'm going to…' she pointed a thumb feebly towards Rich's car without turning away from Atholl or breaking their stare. 'And I've got to clear my things out of the house now it's sold…' Her voice shook.

Atholl looked past her to Rich sitting in the car, the windows misted with condensation from the cool, dewy morning. He was nodding his head to the radio, the music escaping the car.

The whole of Port Willow was asleep; even the fishing boats were still moored by the jetty. Beatrice looked through the door into the bar room and saw that Atholl had cleared all the glasses and rearranged all the chairs and tables overnight. The ceilidh decorations were pulled down and crumpled in a black recycling sack on the floor.

'We put on a good party,' she said weakly.

'That we did.'

A long moment passed where they swallowed down words and Beatrice's hands fidgeted inside her sleeves. When they spoke, their words came out at the same time yet again and they laughed, wry and abashed.

'You first,' Atholl insisted.

'I was going to say I'd better get going. Long drive and everything.'

Atholl didn't see the little stamp of her foot and the frustrated twitch at her brow as she replayed her weak words. He was too busy lifting a small box from the reception desk drawer. Tentatively he came round to stand in front of her on the threadbare tartan rug near the door.

'I, *uh*, I have something for you.' He surrendered the box to her hands.

It took her a few moments to get it open, her hands shook so much, but when the lid released her eyes widened at the sight of the large, faceted, teardrop-shaped object and the long silver ribbon threaded through a hole at its pointed end. 'A crystal?'

'Made here in the Highlands. Crystal's another thing we crafty Scots are good at.'

Atholl reached inside the box and released the jewel, letting the heavy glass drop to the end of its ribbon where it twirled and swayed. The morning light from the inn door caught it and sent a hundred glittering, dancing rainbows across Atholl's face and chest and over the walls and ceiling behind him. Beatrice couldn't conceal the gasp she made.

'It's beautiful.'

'You said you were dreading the winter months and the dark nights. You said you weren't sure how you could face them. So I got you this. Hang it in your window, wherever ye may be, it'll catch the winter sunlight and scatter it in rainbows, lighting up even the darkest corners.'

He put the crystal into her palm, seeming to lean forward for a moment, but pulling back again.

Through tears, Beatrice stepped onto her tiptoes and brushed a soft kiss against his cheek. 'Thank you, Atholl, for this, and everything else.'

The sharp sound of Rich's car horn made them both recoil and from somewhere upstairs Echo barked. When Beatrice turned to look at Rich he was smiling placidly and still nodding along to the music.

'I'd better go.' Agitated, she pointed her thumb again to the door and this time she turned and followed its direction. She looked back once, smiled wanly, still clutching the crystal to her chest, and Atholl watched her walk through the inn door, climb into the car beside her husband and drive away.

–

Half an hour later Atholl Fergusson stalked over the headland at Rother Path and clambered down the rocks to the coral beach. He rarely walked this way now, favouring like everyone else the easy path over the meadows, but this morning he needed the distraction of scrambling down a difficult route. He passed the sleepy cows lazily chewing the long grass that lined the precarious path.

'Atholl!'

He heard his brother calling his name at the same moment he smelled the wood smoke.

Gene and Kitty had spent the night at the But and Ben and were now bundled in blankets and sitting by a camp fire on the coral, and, since there were sausages cooking, Echo had found his way to them too and was wagging his tail in an obedient posture by Kitty's side.

'Come and have some tea,' Gene shouted as Atholl stepped down onto the beach.

Kitty sprung up instantly, craning her neck for a sign of Beatrice following him down the path and understanding instantly that she really had left this morning as planned.

'Oh, Atholl,' she said when he reached them by the fire and the two lovers saw his ashen sleeplessness close up.

'Her husband came for her. They spent the night in her room and left together this morning,' Atholl filled them in with a dry monotone.

Gene pulled his younger brother to his chest and wrapped long arms around him. Kitty stepped in to the hug too and Atholl let his tears fall silently.

Chapter Twenty-Nine

Going Home to Warwickshire

The mountains hugged the twisting road and Beatrice stared out the window, watching the changing Highland landscape. The morning sun was shining through towering white clouds. Last night's storm had passed and left the cool, damp feeling of the coming autumn.

The tarns and lochs were full and still. Birds she couldn't name flitted here and there as Rich's Audi wound along the narrow road, pulling in every few minutes to allow vehicles travelling back down towards Port Willow to pass. The train tracks ran parallel to the road in the far distance and Beatrice watched a single carriage train engine trundling westward.

'Bloody caravans,' Rich was saying over the jarring sounds from the radio and between blasts from his car horn directed at the slow-moving convoy of motorhomes in front of them. Rich usually liked to drive fast. Beatrice thought how she'd grown used to a slower pace recently.

'Can we turn that off, please?' she said, screwing her eyes up. 'It's giving me a headache.'

'Too much to drink last night, eh? Were you on the whisky and Irn Bru?' Rich grinned, over pronouncing the words in a daft Scottish accent.

Beatrice thought how she *had* felt drunk last night, but it wasn't the Highland punch that had done it. It was the reel music, the dancing and being held in Atholl's arms – and her imagination playing delightful tricks on her whenever she thought of the night ahead when she'd be alone with him. All scuppered by Rich's arrival.

She turned the dial and the blaring music died away.

'I wasn't drunk. Anyway, you're the one who passed out snoring on the chaise, not me.'

'Sorry about that; it had been a long drive and I was knackered, especially after talking for so long. What time do you think we got to sleep?'

Beatrice just shrugged, thinking of how he'd talked and wept until gone three and she'd tried to comfort him by giving him their child's blanket to keep. It was only right he have something special of his own to remember their baby by. She had the pregnancy test for one, still secreted away in a drawer at home. And she had all the leaflets the midwife had given her, and the image of their tiny peanut at only a few weeks' gestation, and the letter from the hospital about the twelve-week scan appointment. And there was the yellow bunny rabbit too, and maternity jeans with the elasticated waistband, still with the tags on. All of that was back at home waiting to be packed up in boxes as she moved her belongings from the house she'd shared with Rich for ten years, the house where she'd been happy at first, back when they'd made love in every room and planned a life together, and before the disappointment, frustration and sadness had slowly crept in, chasing out all the passion and excitement without either of them really noticing or knowing that they minded. Her eyes were fixed on the blanket. He could keep it and she wouldn't miss it too much.

She thought of how, as the sun came up this morning, she'd climbed up the ladder of her towering princess bed for the last time and sat in the dawn light watching her husband sleeping, swinging between extremes of annoyance that he was there snoring loudly, seemingly unburdened and happy to have cleared the air, and gladness that they had talked and shared stories of how excited they had been at the news of her pregnancy and the devastation that had followed so soon after.

Now she was exhausted, and something else, something prickling and wistful, a tug at her heart that wasn't grief or sadness, something she was struggling to place over the mess of feelings and thoughts circulating in her chest.

Rich reached a hand to her knee and she watched as he gave it a slow squeeze before withdrawing it again.

'You know… you don't *have* to go to Angela's,' Rich was saying, casting a quick sidelong glance at his passenger sitting rigidly in her seat. 'You can stay with me in my apartment, if you'd like?'

Beatrice wished she hadn't turned off the radio.

Expectantly, he glanced at her again.

'I don't think that's a great idea, do you?' she replied. 'Not when I'd have to find my own place and move everything out again, and who knows how long it'll take me to find somewhere, and…'

'Maybe… *don't* move back out, then? Maybe… come live with me? And, *uh*… we could try again? Try being *us* again, I mean. You and me, Beatrice, we've been through too much together to throw it all away.'

She felt the softening inside her, a giving way, and she turned to look at him. 'We have been through a lot together,' she said softly.

That's when it caught her eye, a wild flash in the sky, crossing high overhead.

'What was that?' said Rich. 'An eagle?'

'No, it was an osprey.' Beatrice leaned into her seatbelt, craning to see the treetop where it had landed.

'Same thing, isn't it?'

'Do you know ospreys pair for life?'

Rich jutted his chin with a frown as if to say that was news to him.

'They leave their nests and spend the whole winter apart. But they miss each other and always return to the same mate in the same nest in the spring.'

Rich kept his eyes on the road ahead. 'Oh, come on! Will you just *pull over*!' He rammed the heel of his hand into the car horn starting a string of beeps and headlight flashes all along the slow-moving convoy. 'Holiday drivers! Sorry, Beatrice, what were you saying?'

'I was talking about true pairs, mated for life?' She shook her head. 'Never mind.' She scanned the sky again looking for the bird, but it was safely in its nest with its mate. With a flash of sudden awakening, she spoke.

'Rich, stop the car.'

Chapter Thirty

All Change at Port Willow

Atholl reached for the canopy above The Princess and the Pea bed and pulled it away from the bedposts, disturbing the faded green curtains and a decade's worth of dust. Coughing, he passed the ancient material to Gene who bundled it into boxes as Kitty opened the windows.

'Are you sure this wants doing today, Atholl? Can't we have a day of rest to recover from Harvest Home?' Gene asked.

'I want to work,' Atholl replied, making a start on stripping away the lacy duvet covers. 'We should have done this years ago. Nobody wants to sleep in a fusty old room. We need to modernise a wee bit. Make it nice for families to stay in. And I'm not fit for sitting around drumming my fingers today.'

'We're keeping the princess bed though, right?' Gene asked.

'Of course.'

Along the bay a train horn sounded and the rails rattled, heralding the arrival of a new crop of crafters to the village.

'Some of this lot could be my Gaelic students,' said Kitty, looking out the bedroom window along the water-front to the station. 'I trust you've got their bookings right this time, Gene?'

Everyone smiled grimly and thought of Beatrice's arrival ten days ago, but nobody spoke of it.

Gene shuffled out the door with the box of bed hangings saying he'd have them sent to the dry cleaners in Lochalsh and Kitty eyed Atholl from her vantage point by the window where she wiped the condensation from the glass with a cloth and made a show of dusting the ornaments on the sill.

'Will you be all right?' she said once Gene had gone.

'*Hmm*,' Atholl concentrated on stripping the silk roses and ribbons from the bed's ladder, gently pulling at the delicate old wires that hadn't been untwined since his mother had decorated the room all those years ago. 'I'll just have to be. I've little right to moan and mourn. Beatrice has a life of her own and a home to sort out… and a husband she clearly isn't free of. And she has a broken heart for her baby to heal. The grief forced them apart, I think. But now Richard's come to his senses and they're on their way back to their home town together. Maybe all she needed was a break here away from her old life to recuperate. And now she's reunited with her man, making a fresh start. Like Maggie did with her man…'

'*Pfft*, that was altogether a different kind of situation. Maggie was out for a fling, for revenge of some kind. Beatrice wasn't like that at all.'

'Either way, she was here to escape her old life for a few days, no' to throw in her lot with a bunch of strangers.'

Kitty turned back to the window, processing Atholl's words and watching Echo dashing along the pavement down below, barking at the new guests as they wheeled suitcases towards the inn.

'It's only right she should have a chance at healing with her own husband,' Atholl continued. 'Richard is, after all, the father of her bairn and they must have a long history together that I've no right interfering in.' He settled into the task of hauling the mattresses from the bed and throwing them onto the floor, his brow furrowed with the effort. 'If I keep myself busy here and at the workshop all winter, seeing through all my plans, all *Beattie's plans*, I should say, for the shop and the café and the classes, I'll survive, I'm sure.'

'She certainly shook things up around here and for the better. We'll miss her,' Kitty was saying, having taken one last look out the window before picking her way slowly towards the door on tiptoe.

Atholl barely noticed her retreating, and he certainly hadn't seen the sudden flash of light in her eyes as she stole away to greet the inn guests.

'Aye, we will miss her. *I* will. I cannae remember a time before she arrived. It's as though I was sleeping all these years, letting the inn dwindle, trying to keep Gene from dying away from his grief at losing Lana and letting my own life sit stagnant as though my own dreams meant nothing to me.' Atholl folded bedsheets against his chest and piled them on the floor, his back to the door Kitty had just crept out of. 'I never imagined somebody could come into my home and chase away all the obstructions that we'd let lie in our paths all these years, let alone someone so… alive, and so bonny. And yet, I let obstructions get in the way of me and Beattie. If I could go back to the day she arrived, I'd not have let my stubborn pride rule me and I'd have been kinder and not held back when I felt myself falling for her in spite of every rational objection I threw in our path, too afraid to tell her how I felt… *Och…*'

Atholl's words stopped in a frustrated cry as he started on the task of pulling the empty drawers from the ancient corner cabinet that had seen far better days. 'She told me she was dreading the winter, but now that's how I feel. Even with all the work ahead of me at the But n' Ben I dinnae ken how I'm supposed to get through it without seeing her, Kitty.'

Met by silence, Atholl looked around the room wondering why Kitty didn't answer. His eyes fell on the suitcase just inside the doorframe and the woman standing there holding a crystal on a long silver ribbon, the light reflecting off it as it swung in her hand, turning the daylight into rainbows scattering in dancing bands over the worn carpet.

'Atholl,' Beatrice said, through smiling lips. 'I thought we might spend the winter together, here, if you'd like?'

Atholl had crossed the floor and wrapped Beatrice in his arms before she'd finished her sentence. 'Beattie, you're here to stay?'

'Yes, please, if you'll have me.'

'What about Richard?'

'He's on his way back to his own place, I imagine. We said everything that needed to be said last night and as we were driving away I realised that I didn't have to go back to *my* old place, and I don't have to be where I don't want to be. I'm not going to let the tide drag me back there against my will. That would drown me for sure. I can make a fresh start here, with you, if that's what you want too.'

His kiss stole the last words and she found herself pulling away from him just long enough to drag her suitcase inside the room, push the door closed, turn the key in the lock and walk Atholl backwards towards the pile of mattresses and quilts now covering the floor.

–

Beatrice hadn't noticed the sounds of the tide coming in or the changing light as the sun started to fade in the hazy, watery afternoon sky, but the cool breeze over her bare skin from the open window told her it was getting late.

'We should eat something,' Atholl said in a murmur, but he didn't move, instead running his fingertips over Beatrice's side.

'*Hmmm*. Good idea. I'll get up and go any minute now.' She opened one eye dreamily but didn't move. 'Do you know you've got some mattress down in your hair?'

Reaching into the copper coils above his ear she freed the soft white feathers and Atholl took the opportunity to kiss her again, slowly and tenderly.

Beatrice shuddered at the lovely memory the kiss provoked; Atholl's curls skimming her neck and moving down over her breasts and belly as he trailed his lips over her, pressing warm, intent kisses into her flesh until her hands tangled in his hair and he delivered stroke after stroke of his tongue in languorous circles as she drew her thighs around his shoulders and forgot everything that had ever hurt her. The memory made her nerves sing and tingle.

He broke off their kiss with a smile and, looking around the room, passed her the clothes he'd cast to the floor behind him in his fervour to have her naked. 'You look half asleep, Beattie.'

Beattie. That was the name he'd called out into the still noon air when she had made him ball his hands into fists against the piled up mattresses and quilts, pushing his heels hard against them, gasping for breath like he was drowning, her hair tumbling in silky waves over his stomach.

They'd stayed hidden in their nest of feathers and sheets all afternoon, sipping whisky and kissing until Atholl had fallen asleep. Beatrice had draped an arm over his chest and watched his slow breathing until she too closed her eyes. She had known they'd be good at this. All her intuition had been correct.

Chapter Thirty-One

Return to the Coral Beach

Two pink lines streaked the watery sky as the sun began to sink into the horizon and Beatrice and Atholl picked their way across the coral beach, their arms tight around each other's waists.

'Are you sure coming here's a good idea, Atholl? We don't have a good track record on this beach, do we? I've been stampeded by cattle *and* we almost drowned. Are you sure a comet isn't about to burn through the atmosphere and put an end to us for good?'

The sound of Atholl's laughter warmed her against the chilly evening as they found their way to where Gene and Kitty had lit their fire this morning.

'You know, that was what made up my mind, in the car, with Rich. I was thinking about the few days you and I spent here and all the crazy things that happened: the cattle, the matchmaking, the trip to Skye, and meeting your family, and the riptide, rescuing the lavender field and then planning the ceilidh.'

'We certainly kept you busy.'

'Rich said to me that he and I had been through too much to throw it all away, but I couldn't help thinking that me and you have been through just as much, even in our few short days together, but I enjoyed my holiday ten times more than the entire decade I spent with Rich.'

He responded only with a satisfied kiss by the side of her mouth before tipping the pile of kindling and scrunched newspapers out onto the ashes from the earlier fire and searched in his pocket for the matches.

'Wrap up warm,' he said, as Beatrice set blankets down for them to sit on, keeping a large tartan travelling rug to wrap over their shoulders.

The fire came to life quickly with the help of only one match and Atholl's pursing lips blowing softly into the centre of the building flames.

Beatrice held out one side of the blanket and Atholl slid underneath it, smiling at the warmth and being so close to Beatrice.

They sat for a while in contented silence and Beatrice thought about the afternoon they'd spent locked away in the dismantled princess room and how Atholl had kissed her and held her as though she were a precious, tender, priceless thing, and they had made love for the first, and second, and third times.

Atholl, Beatrice noticed, was smiling to himself as he looked out at the calm water. The sunset was turning from pink to orange. Anyone passing would have been astonished at how their eyes shone in the brightness and how their skin glowed, but they were alone. Even Echo had left them to it this evening.

Atholl reached for the willow basket he'd carried with them and drew out russet apples and a curved knife. Silently, he peeled away slices for Beatrice, handing them to her one at a time, and taking crisp bites himself. Occasionally he stopped just to watch her eat or to press a kiss beneath her ear or on her cheek, and all the while they smiled contentedly.

Brushing an apple pip from the blanket, Beatrice turned to Atholl. 'You're quiet tonight. Not having second thoughts again, are you?'

'Second thoughts? *Again?* When did I have second thoughts before?'

'When you told me to go back to Rich, and the morning of the ceilidh when you disappeared all day and didn't come back till late. I sat in that garden in my fancy white frock for two hours wishing you'd come find me…'

'*Och,*' Atholl exhaled sharply. 'You thought because I disappeared all day leading up to the ceilidh that I was avoiding you? You said as much, I remember.'

'And weren't you?'

Atholl pulled Beatrice closer beneath the blanket.

'I was away most of the day yesterday because I had a lot to do. In fact, it was all your fault, setting a fire in my belly with all your talk of business plans and loans and expansion – that and Gene's words were ringing in my ears too. He told me to sort myself out before interfering in others' lives, remember?'

'Actually, I think he said that to me, but go on…'

'Well, I stayed up most of Saturday night, partly trying to stop myself bursting through your door and climbing that ladder to your bed,' Atholl's eyes passed over Beatrice's face and the wild, intense look he gave her took her back to earlier that afternoon and her nerves thrilled again at the memories. 'I told myself I couldn't come to you, and I couldn't sleep either, until I had indeed sorted out my own life. And I asked myself, what would my Beattie do?'

They both broke into broad grins and Atholl reached beneath the blanket again, pulling a piece of folded paper from his pocket. 'I made a list.'

'You did?'

'I learned from the best.'

'The best what? Interferer? Wildcard? Bull in a china shop?'

'The best healer I know. The best fixer. The best organiser.' With each short phrase he delivered a kiss upon Beatrice's cheek, the tip of her nose, then the side of her lips. 'Do you want to know what it says?'

She nodded, and turned a little to face him better. The fire had taken over as the chief source of light now that the sun was almost below the horizon. The dancing flames loved Atholl's fine features and sea blue eyes, as did Beatrice.

'OK then. Number one,' he read. 'Set interview dates for the new assistant chef and cleaners. They're coming on Tuesday, by the way. I'm leaving Gene to interview them, since he'll be their main boss and head chef.'

Beatrice smiled her approval.

'Number two. See Hector, my old tutor, the one who owns the But n' Ben. And that's what I did. I nipped in to see him on my way to pick up the bagpiper and the whisky yesterday. That's why I was away so long. I'm sorry I left you to fix everything up for the ceilidh yourself and left you wondering if I'd done a runner…'

'Never mind that, what happened!'

'Oh, once I told him my plans for a proper, year round willow workshop and a store he agreed to sign the lease over to me. In fact, he was delighted to, said he was very proud of me, in fact.'

'There you go!'

'I'd never have asked without your encouragement, Beattie.'

'And what else does your list say?'

'Oh, OK. Number three. See Davy McTavish, the builder, about doing the conversion on the But n' Ben, the one we got planning permission for years ago and I never had the resolve to actually see through. He's been there all morning measuring up for a quote. Work starts in October.'

'Good for you, that's wonderful.'

'Aye, it is. But that's no' all. Number four – and, mind, I wrote this two nights ago before I knew you'd be staying and after I'd told ye, like a fool, to run back to yer man and I was eaten up wi' the regret. I only dared to hope you would be staying then. Number four. Turn my inn rooms into somewhere suitable for Beattie to come and stay, somewhere she wouldnae want to leave. Make her a home here.'

Beatrice smiled her approval.

'And lastly, number five. Be sure to tell Beattie that you are in love with her. Actually, I've written here *hopelessly* in love with her.' He turned the page to show her and they both looked at the word and smiled. 'But in fact, I love you with nothing but hope. Hope that I can make you happy, hope that I can give you all the things you need and want from me, hope that you'll stay here forever, and hope that you'll love me back.'

'I do, I will,' Beatrice sighed. 'I'm staying here and I'm not going anywhere.'

'And will ye not mind our lives being in upheaval while we make us a home at the inn and I graft on my new business here? Won't it weary you, make you lonely?' He bobbed his head back towards the But and Ben, now in darkness on the gentle hills above them.

'No. I have a place to sleep, I'll have work to do, and a man to love – the perfect man for me. A man who likes to bring people together and help others and who now, apparently, likes to make lists.'

They leaned closer and pressed their temples together, their gentle laughter wrapping around them.

'And I've got a dog now too!' Beatrice added suddenly. 'Even if he is a bit of a wanderer.'

'Ach, Echo's always around for the important stuff.'

'That's true.'

'And I've got Kitty and Gene, too. And Seth. Even Mrs Mair. It's been a long time since I've had real friends. And I'm going to look after these ones, really treasure them. And Cheryl and Jillian have already texted me to say they're coming back next summer. Guess what they want to do?'

Atholl shrugged.

'Willow-weaving, of course! And Angela and Vic are sure to bring Clara for their holidays, try stopping them!'

'Well, I'll be glad to welcome each and every one of them. And with Kitty visiting from the university every weekend and during the holidays you'll no' miss her much either.'

'Is that what she's going to do? Good for her! And lucky Gene.'

'He's at the inn now, painting a room for them both. I'm no' the only one set on home-making.'

'I can see it all now.' Beatrice smiled into the darkening horizon. 'The Princess and the Pea Inn will be bustling with crafters and activities of all kinds.'

'With the freshest seafood.'

'And the prettiest princess room.'

'And the bonniest landlady,' Atholl smiled and pressed another kiss to her lips.

'That makes me sound a hundred years old. It's bad enough you calling me Beattie! How about, the bonniest, most amazing, co-manager?' she said, smiling into his eyes.

'Will that fit on the sign over the door?'

'It'll have to be a big sign to fit all our names on there. I'm glad Gene wants to share the task of running the inn.'

'He agreed quick enough this afternoon, did he no'? I think we'll be a good team.'

'I know it. And you'll no longer be supplying customers for every crafting business in the area except your own.'

'I'll soon have the willow workshop fully subscribed and the café thriving,' he said, his eyes gleaming. 'Not to mention the willow gift shop.'

'Quite. Bring it on, I'm ready for all of it!' Beatrice beamed. 'Think of all the lists I can make!'

'Will it be enough for you?' He looked at her meaningfully. 'Will you pine for your child? Can I be enough for you, if it is to be just us two forever?' He touched his fingertips tentatively to her hand.

Beatrice let the significance of what he'd said sink in. 'Yes. I'm at peace with it. Some people might say I'm not a mum, but I am, and I'll love my son until the day I finally meet him. But, I'm resolved now to make the most of my fresh start and to talk to you when I'm happy, or sad, or hopeful, or whatever. I feel as though the world is opening up to me again, and that's thanks to you. And… if one of the things that's opening up to me is a family with you one day, then that would be a wonderful thing, but I won't focus on that, won't fight for it. We're enough together, you and I.' She leaned her head towards his, and he let her press a soft kiss to a gently closed eyelid. 'You wanted to help me, Atholl, and I kept resisting, but in the end, it was you who knew how to start putting me back together, no matter how much I wanted to recover by myself. I won't bottle up my feelings and redirect them into panicked striving anymore. I'm just going to be contented here with my new life. How does that sound?'

'Braw. That sounds braw.' He turned his head to face her. 'But tell me one thing.'

'*Hmm?*'

'Do you really mind me calling you Beattie? I can stop if you want.'

'No, don't ever stop.'

Their lips met once more, and when they separated, Beatrice was smiling wickedly.

'Actually, Atholl… I, *umm*, I did hit upon a new idea.'

'God preserve us.'

'A dating board.'

'A whit now?'

'Well, you know how there's all these single men brooding around Port Willow with nobody to dance with at Harvest Home?'

'Go on.'

'I thought, what with all these women coming to the village for crafting holidays…'

'Ah now, that's no' quite accurate. There's a minibus load of knitters booked in for the new classes starting in December, every one of them a man.'

'Even better! The more the merrier. And there'll be all the new teachers you'll need to run the courses and the new staff working at the inn. I thought maybe I could do a spot of matchmaking with a dating board in the bar where people could fill in a profile about themselves and stick it up on the board, and we could arrange some dates and see what happens, like we did with Gene and Kitty.'

'Dating? On paper?'

'Think of an analogue version of Tinder, only with more bristly men in fishermen's jumpers and tweed. And we won't just match up the boys and girls, we'll cater for everyone, helping people find love in every shade of the rainbow.'

'Glad to hear it. Yet remember you may have had success wi' Gene and Kitty but they had known one another since we were all bairns. They weren't holiday-makers and crafters or lonely-hearted old villagers.'

'No, but they'd never have got together without a little help, would they? Same principle applies.'

'So you're going to bring love back to Port Willow, are ye? Make it the most romantic spot in the western Highlands?'

'Yes! We can do anything we want to now, Atholl Fergusson. We've got a new life ahead of us.'

'That we have.'

'Oh, and I did have another idea or two...'

'Jings, your ideas will be the death of me.'

'There's a dog rescue round here, right? I think the inn could support a couple more lonely old gents, don't you?'

'Whatever makes you happy and makes you feel at home here in Port Willow.'

'I am happy, Atholl Fergusson. I am home.'

Atholl clasped Beatrice's hand to his chest as they leaned their foreheads together once more and listened to the waves creeping slowly up the coral beach.

The summer had come to an end and two pairs of lovers had found one another. Broken hearts were gradually mending, and in the fields behind the cottage craft school, sweet stalks of lavender buried deep underground were slowly taking root and new growth was sprouting unseen, bedding in for the long winter ahead, the promise of spring not too far away.

A Letter From Kiley

The fact that you're holding my latest book *Summer at the Highland Coral Beach* in your hands right now makes me giddy with happiness and a bit nervous too because I want you to fall in love with Beatrice and Atholl, Kitty and Gene, and beautiful sunny Port Willow, just like I did as I was inventing them all.

Your interest in my writing means the world to me, as do the reviews you write and share. Reviews make a huge difference to a new author like me and help other people find my books. So I'm saying a massive thank you in advance if you're thinking of spreading the book love by writing a few words about this book. I'm hugely grateful.

As you read, some of you might recognise Port Willow as my reimagined version of Plockton in the west Highlands. It is a stunning place, packed with cafés, B&Bs, seafood restaurants and pubs, and nearby there is indeed a tricky to reach coral beach with jagged shards underfoot and calm turquoise water that makes your jaw drop. I swam at the coral beach and the water was crystal clear (and very, very cold, even in August), and I'll never forget that moment as long as I live.

But, if you're after a guide book to Plockton you'll be disappointed; they may look fairly similar but Port Willow is altogether more eccentric, magical, lost in time and in need of just the right mixture of romance and organisational zeal that Beatrice Halliday brings with her to the village. And as for the Harvest Home ceilidh, the willows, the riptide and *that* bed? Those are all my invention too.

Plockton means a lot to me because as well as having happy holiday memories of the place, it was there I received the email from Keshini at Hera Books asking for the full manuscript of what turned out to be my debut novel, *One Summer's Night* (2019). A week earlier I'd read about a brand new woman-fronted independent publisher who were open for submissions and I'd sent the opening chapters and a synopsis immediately. When I was asked for the full manuscript, sitting over my laptop by the window overlooking the bay in our Plockton cottage rental, I replied instantly, jumping at the chance to show Hera more of my writing and attaching a completely blank document because that's exactly the sort of thing I do and why wouldn't I balls up the most important email of my life?

Anyway, much like the story in this book, things worked out and I got my (publishing) Happy Ever After. That's why I'm able to bring you *Summer at The Highland Coral Beach*, my third novel for Hera Books, a love story about loss and recovery, and handsome red-headed Highlanders.

We've all survived times where we really are at the end of our tether and life feels cruel and unfair, and we've all coped in different ways. Beatrice, my hero, is just like me in that she copes by going into overdrive, trying to get the heck out of the situation she's in. She likes writing lists, doing research, planning and wrangling until things work out. This strategy works well in everyday situations, but when you're sad and grieving, as Beatrice discovers, it can lead to even greater difficulties.

As well as being a champion planner, Beatrice is also a matchmaker, just like me. Except I do all my match-making on paper. Beatrice, on the other hand, thinks love needs a helping hand sometimes and she sets to work playing Cupid on those around her. Again, great in theory, but tricky to pull off in practice, as you'll see.

I hope you enjoy accompanying Beatrice through her summer of recovery and rebuilding, matchmaking and meddling, falling in love and getting into scrapes. She deserves the love, happiness and comfort she finds, as do you all, my readers.

Just so you know, you will read references to miscar-riage in this story, but there's also hope, kindness, laughter and lots of romance too. This is a story about waiting out the storm to see the rainbows, and about sweetness after difficulties. I hope with all my heart you enjoy it.

Happy reading,

Love, Kiley x

P.S. Drop by my Twitter page and say 'hi' @KileyDunbar or follow the Kiley Dunbar Author Facebook Page for all my bookish news!

Acknowledgements

Thank you to my lovely Nic and the babies for loving me. I love you all so much.

I receive a huge amount of support from the following wonderful friends and I'd be lost without them, so thank you Michael, Stephanie, Debbie, Leanie, Sara, Laura, Kelly and Liz. I really hecking love you lot!

Thank you, Mum, Dad, John and Bron. x

Andrew R, Clare H, and Roxanne, you keep me going with your lovely messages and Facebook posts, thank you!

Nicola, Jess, Catherine, Livi, Lucy S, James and Paul at Manchester Metropolitan University and the Manchester Writing School have helped me so much in recent months as I started a new and exciting part time senior lecture-ship and then immediately fell ill with severe pneumonia. Thank you for your kindness and patience.

Thank you, Steve, for the whisky info. I know you've done painstaking research and I trust your expertise.

I also want to shine a big light on all of the book lovers and bloggers who got involved in the blog tour, organised by the incredible Rachel's Random Resources, for my second book *Christmas at Frozen Falls*. Thank you so much for being epic. And an especially big thank you goes to S.J. Lomas; Shelby at *Breakfast at Shelby's*; Stacy at *Stacy Loves Reading*; Julie at *A Little Book Problem* and Elaine at *Splashes into Books* for hosting extra wee interviews and guest posts on your blog sites.

I want to thank you, my readers, and every single person who has bought my books, sent me messages about how much they enjoyed them, or who reviewed and rated them. Your support blows my mind.

Keshini and Lindsey at Hera Books have changed my life and I'm always grateful for the fact they took a chance on me, a total newbie. I hope this book makes you proud. Thank you for everything.

Jennie Ayres and Vicki Vrint helped copy and proof edit this book so carefully and pointed out a staggering number of daft mistakes and made my prose immeasurably better, thank you. It's a pleasure working with you both.

Thank you to Jenny Crisp whose beautiful book, *Willow: A Guide to Growing and Harvesting* helped inform Atholl's romantic, heartfelt willow-weaving lesson. Jenny's book is a love song to this ancient craft and I urge you all to check it out from your local library, as I did, and pore over its wonderful descriptions of growing and weaving willow, all wonderfully illustrated in stunning photography. I may have taken a few liberties here and there with the technicalities of working willow, and that's all on me.

Last but not least, thank you and I love you to the TAM mummies. I wrote this book thinking of the heartbroken One in Four and the parents, siblings and families of babies who will be loved and missed for a lifetime.